THE
EDINBURGH
Dead

an was raising the shovel. Quire sighted along the barrel,
into the black mass of the man's chest, worrying whether
ld trust his left arm to hold the gun steady. Another half a
d of doubt, washed away by one thought: he's already killed
an tonight. He squeezed the trigger.

rasping click of the hammer falling, the flint sparking. A
, blinding light in his right eye. Smoke puffing upwards.
usket kicking his shoulder, sending out a lance of flame and
white smoke from its mouth. The crash of the shot, loud as
on out here on the ice, echoing from the trees around the
d from the great night-clad mass of Arthur's Seat.

e blinked, chasing the dancing lights out of his eye,
g through the drifting smoke. It had been a good shot,
undoubtedly; he had put the ball right into the man's chest.
Probably killed him. He was therefore astonished to find the great
dark figure bearing down on him at pace, the shovel lifted one-
handed against the sky.

By Brian Ruckley

The Godless World
Winterbirth
Bloodheir
Fall of Thanes

The Edinburgh Dead

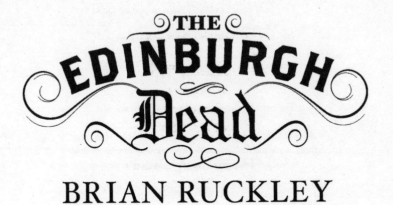

THE EDINBURGH Dead

BRIAN RUCKLEY

www.orbitbooks.net

ORBIT

First published in Great Britain in 2011 by Orbit

Copyright © 2011 by Brian Ruckley

Excerpt from *The Devil You Know* by Mike Carey
Copyright © 2006 by Mike Carey

The moral right of the author has been asserted.

A CIP catalogue record for this book
is available from the British Library.

ISBN 978-1-84149-865-2

For Daniel

Acknowledgements

This book makes liberal use of real history to tell its tale, and this time I am therefore indebted not only to the usual and indispensible support network without which no writer could function, but also to a not inconsiderable number of people who one way or another made my distorting of historical truth possible:

The staff at the National Library of Scotland and at the Edinburgh City Archives, who were unfailingly helpful and efficient.

Jim McGowan, who has never heard of me, but whose unpublished thesis on Edinburgh's police force in the first quarter of the nineteenth century was utterly fascinating and tremendously helpful.

Ewen, for the very timely provision of some audio drama recordings that really hit the spot, inspiration-wise.

Thanks, as ever, to the fine Orbit crew, as helpful a bunch of publishing folk as a writer could wish to be working with. In particular, thanks to Tim Holman for his support and assistance not just with this book – which were considerable – but all the way back to the beginning.

Thanks to Tina, my agent, for her help and support.

Thanks to my parents, for their encouragement from the first time I ever tried to write.

And to Fleur, for everything.

Contents

We have heard a great deal of late concerning "the march of the intellect" for which the present age is supposed to be distinguished; and the phrase has been rung in our ears till it has nauseated us by its repetition, and become almost a proverbial expression of derision. But we fear that, with all its pretended illumination, the present age must be characterized by some deeper and fouler blots than have attached to any that preceded it; and that if it has bright spots, it has also darker shades and more appalling obscurations. It has, in fact, nooks and corners where every thing that is evil seems to be concentrated and condensed; dens and holes to which the Genius of Iniquity has fled, and become envenomed with newer and more malignant inspirations.

Thomas Ireland Jnr, *West Port Murders*
(Edinburgh, 1829)

I

The Demonstration

Glasgow, 1818

The corpse sat in a simple, high-backed chair. A band had been tied around its stomach to keep it upright. The man – young, perhaps no more than twenty-five – had as peaceable a look to him as death might permit. A relaxed face, hands resting quite naturally, in lifelike manner, upon his knees. He was naked, but a pure white sheet had been laid across his legs and groin, for the preservation of modesty.

A few paces behind the dead man's chair, a fire burned with vigour in a metal brazier. It gave out prodigious amounts of light and heat, the latter of which in particular was hardly needed. Though the streets of Glasgow outside were awash with freezing rain and stinging winds, the air within was already close and warm and a touch stale, by virtue of the enormous audience the corpse had attracted.

They were packed in to the raked galleries of benches that occupied some three-quarters of the room's circumference. This great wooden amphitheatre had never seen quite so many beneath its domed roof. They were standing in the aisles, sitting on the steps between the blocks of benches, crowding the very highest and furthest of the doorways, craning their necks to get a view of proceedings. For all their numbers, though, and all their slightly febrile anticipation, a remarkable quiet prevailed. There was the occasional shuffling of a foot, a cough, now and again a faintly nervous laugh. But all in all the fragile, expectant silence held.

The corpse was not alone, down on the floor of the amphitheatre. Figures in long white robes moved about him, like a flock of bishops preparing a sacramental rite. The instruments of their devotion were not, however, chalice or cross or censer. Rather, a stack of metal discs, threaded on to a tall central pillar, stood on a wheeled trolley. Flat strips of copper ran from the top and bottom discs to long rods that stood upright in a glass jar. Beside this odd machinery, a man was laying out knives on a cloth. Dozens of them. And saws, and shears.

"Ladies and gentlemen," said one of the robed men, and at the first, startling sound of his voice a collective shiver of excitement thrilled its way around the whole assembly.

"Ladies and gentlemen," he said again once that tremor had passed, "you will this evening be witness to a display of true medical Prometheanism. This," he gestured towards the corpse strapped to the chair, "is Mathew Clydesdale, murderer. Executed this very day, in accordance with the sentence passed upon him by the court. And his presence here, the service he is about to perform, is also in accordance with that sentence.

"I am Professor Andrew Ure, and it is my privilege to be your guide in the first part of our explorations this evening: a demonstration of galvanic effects."

He turned and nodded to the younger men, the assistants, who had been waiting beside the gleaming and ordered array of knives. At his sign, they took up their blades. This was greeted by a swelling murmur of conversation around the theatre, and waves of shuffling and shifting as the assembled host sought a clear line of sight. But all sound, all distraction and interruption, dwindled away as the knives went to work.

A lengthwise cut was made along the inner face of the forearm, followed by two transverse incisions across the wrist and the elbow. The skin was peeled open, the two flaps of it pinned to ensure it did not slip back into place. Thus invited, the people of Glasgow looked into the meat of Mathew Clydesdale's arm, and as they did so they whispered to one another, and trembled in fascination, or horror, or wonder.

The muscles were raw, a brownish red; the bone, overlaid by them and by the straps of pale tendon, yellowish. There was little blood, for his heart had been stilled some time ago.

"Expose the cervical vertebrae, if you would," Ure murmured to his assistants, and while they tipped Clydesdale's head forward and went to work on the back of his neck, Ure bent over the exposed machinery of the arm. He probed with a short rod, and used it to elevate slightly from amongst the meat and the gristle a set of cord-like structures, somewhat grey beneath the scraps of tissue and congealed blood that adhered to them.

"Here are the nerves," he proclaimed to his rapt audience. He shifted his hand a little, letting all but one of the nerves fall back into their corporeal bed. "And this is the ulnar, the first to which we shall direct our attentions."

At Ure's instruction, the trolley that carried the tall pile of metal plates was wheeled into position beside the corpse. Ure took up one of the long metal rods attached to the apparatus and inserted it through the new opening in the back of Clydesdale's neck. Once satisfied of its position, he held it there, and raised the second rod. He looked up to the crowded benches with a grave expression.

"Now, ladies and gentlemen. Observe."

He slipped the second rod into Clydesdale's gaping arm; adjusted it, eased it into contact with the ulnar nerve.

And Clydesdale's arm spasmed. The dead hand that rested palm up on his knee twitched, the fingers clenched. There were gasps, and screams, and a shuddering of alarm. A few cheers. A few hands clapped. Ure withdrew the rod, then reinserted it. Again the fingers trembled and closed, as if trying to grasp at the life so recently extinct.

A woman near the end of one of the rows, midway up the auditorium, fainted away. She was half-carried, half-dragged from her seat and through the crowd to one of the doors, in search of reviving air.

Satisfied, Ure pushed back Clydesdale's head and turned it to one side. He nodded to his colleagues, and they set to work, cutting open the skin of the lower neck, pulling it away from the underlying structure of veins and muscles. Once they stood back, Ure delicately set the tip of a rod against a deep-buried fibrous thread.

"The phrenic nerve," he announced.

And the corpse's chest heaved. Clydesdale's whole inanimate form shifted as his ribcage rose and fell in a dreadful parody of breathing. More exclamations of amazement, and of horror. Some of those watching averted their eyes, or closed them, their morbid fascination exceeded by repulsion and unease.

"You see," Ure said calmly and clearly, "that the mechanism of breathing remains intact after death, lacking only the animating force by which it was formerly enlivened."

Though his voice was steady, his face was flushed with excitement, for he was as captivated as any by the wonders he performed.

And so the demonstration proceeded. The leg was made to straighten, jerking and kicking as if during a fit. A rod inserted into a notch cut above the orbit of Clydesdale's left eye made his face contort and convulse in a mad dance of lopsided expression. At that, another woman was overcome, and helped from the chamber. Two men departed, one after the other, each pale of visage and with a hand pressed over his mouth. One was already gagging as he made for the door.

At the conclusion of Ure's work, another white-clad figure, Professor Jeffray, took charge. He had the dead man laid out on a flat trolley, where he dissected out his every inner working, breaking open the ribcage to reveal the organs beneath, carving away until Mathew Clydesdale was rendered down to so many dissociated, exposed parts.

A state of numb shock settled across many of the observers. They shuffled out more slowly than many of them would have wished, constrained by the crowding to essay a patience few felt. Some lingered, though, after the corpse had been covered up with winding sheets, as the medical men busied themselves with tidying away the tools of their trade.

One – a tall, thin-faced and well-dressed man with a dispassionate intelligence alive in his eyes – descended from the steep slope of benches.

"Professor Ure," the man said, and Ure looked up from his rolling of the knives into their cloth parcel.

"Sir?"

"A remarkable demonstration. Fascinating."

"I am delighted you found it so. One hopes to inform and educate. Are you a medical man, sir? You have the look."

One of the attendants was damping down the brazier behind them. It hissed and crackled, spinning a few sparks up into the air.

"No, not strictly a medical man. I have some slight experience in that field, but my researches have followed a rather different course in recent years. Still, the equipment you use is most interesting."

He extended a languid arm towards the stack of discs, with all their panoply of wires and rods.

"Ah, the Voltaic pile?" Ure smiled.

"I have heard them described, of course, and seen illustrations, but this is my first opportunity to observe the thing itself. Copper and zinc plates, separated by plasterboard soaked in brine. Am I correct?"

"I believe it is charged with acid rather than brine, but in principle you are correct, yes. A quite remarkable contraption. I confess my facility with the construction and care of the things is somewhat limited. Carlyle there, on the other hand: an invaluable man. A natural and subtle talent when it comes to the machinery, whether electrical or mechanical, with which our world is becoming so crowded. He is employed here for that sole purpose, and I dare to think there is none in Scotland to match his expertise."

"Carlyle, you say?" the other man murmured, staring with acute intensity at the indicated attendant, white-clad as the others, who was examining the Voltaic pile with proprietorial concern.

"Indeed. Edward Carlyle."

"Tell me, Professor Ure – if the question is not unwelcome, of course – tell me, have you had any success in stimulating the heart?"

"No, no. Not as yet. The heart remains unresponsive. I have to say, I believe it is through stimulation of the phrenic nerve that the greatest successes will be achieved: it is my hope that it might one day even be possible to thereby restore life and its functions to the victims of drowning, suffocation. Even hanging. But we are scientists, you and I, eh? We must have a realistic view of these things. Our ignorance is reduced with every passing day – how could it be otherwise, when so many great minds are applied to the task? – but it remains prodigious.

"I rather fancy, if you will forgive me an aphorism, that we live not in the Age of Reason, as so many proclaim, but in that of Ignorance; for there is nothing reason so readily proclaims to the attentive mind as the extent of our ignorance. It transforms what were once mysteries, for ever inaccessible to human comprehension, into merely phenomena we have not yet explained, and thereby at once increases what we know and what we do not. Do you see?"

"Very astute, I am sure."

"Yes. Well. If you are interested in natural philosophy, you should consider attending some of my evening lectures. Every Tuesday and Thursday at seven o'clock. All the most recent developments are explained."

"I am an Edinburgh man. I am seldom in Glasgow, unfortunately; we came today only for your demonstration."

"Oh, I see. I am flattered. I did not catch your name, sir."

"No? Well, forgive me, I must have a word with my man Blegg over there. Do excuse me."

Blegg cut a slight figure in comparison to his master, and at that master's approach he was already sinking his head in obsequious expectation of instruction.

"Do you see the man beside the pile, Blegg? His name is Edward Carlyle. We require him, and his services, so you get yourself over there and give him my compliments. Convey my admiration of his work, and ask whether he would hear a proposal I have for him. One that could be of the utmost mutual benefit. Do you understand?"

"Yes, sir," Blegg dipped his head once more, his hands clasped as if in submissive prayer.

"And make some enquiries. We will be requiring rooms for the night. It is too late to return to Edinburgh now."

Blegg hesitated, unsure whether further commands would be forthcoming.

"Be about it, then," his employer snapped.

"Yes, sir. Yes, sir"

And Blegg scampered away to deliver the message.

II

The Dead Man

Edinburgh, 1828

The castle had colonised its craggy perch over centuries, embracing the contours of the rock with a network of angular walls, yards and barracks and gun platforms. Spilling eastwards from it, encrusting the long ridge that trailed down to the royal palace, was the Old Town of Edinburgh. There – packed inside the strict confines once set by the city's defensive wall – soaring tenements vied for space, crowding one another, making labyrinths of the narrow spaces they enclosed. It was an aged place; not designed but accreted over centuries. Thickened and tangled by the passage of years.

A multitude of gloomy and overshadowed alleyways projected, like ribs, from the great street running down the spine of the ridge. They descended into the shallow valleys to north and south, sinking away from the cleansing breezes. Through these closes and wynds the people of this ancient Edinburgh moved, and in them they lived. And died.

Down there, where one of those closes gave out on to the Cowgate, a low and grimy thoroughfare, dawn revealed a dead man curled in the doorway of a shuttered whisky shop, his blood crusted in black profusion upon his clothes and on the cobblestones around him. Looking like something forgotten, or spent and casually discarded, by the departing night.

"Who is he?" asked Adam Quire, staring down at the corpse with a faint wince of distaste.

It was not the sight of it that disturbed him, but the smell. The body stank of sour whisky and blood, and the man had soiled himself in the last moments of his life. There was a less easily identifiable dank, musty strand to the symphony, too. It all made for a noisome aura that discomfited Quire, particularly since the stale flavours of last night still lingered rather queasily in his own mouth: all the beer he had drunk and the smoke-thick air he had breathed.

"No name for him, Sergeant," said the young nightwatchman at his side. Lauder, but Quire was unsure of his forename; Gordon, perhaps.

"Who found him?"

"One of the scavengers. Grant Carstairs."

"I know him. Shake?"

"Aye. Some folk call him that. Got a bit of the palsy."

Quire kneeled at the side of the body, his knee slipping into a tiny, cold puddle couched in the crease between two cobblestones. He grimaced as the chill water soaked through his trousers.

"Nothing left of his throat," Lauder said, gesturing with the extinguished lantern still clasped in his right hand. "Look at that. What a mess."

Quire could see well enough. A ragged hole in the front of the dead man's neck exposed gristle and meat. One sleeve of his jacket was torn to shreds, as was the arm beneath. Material and flesh were barely distinguishable in the morning gloom. Furrows had been gouged in his scalp, too, the skin torn; one ear was no more than a tattered rag.

"I've not seen the like," the watchman murmured.

Quire had – and much worse – but not for a long time, and not outside the confines of a battlefield. He thought he heard as much wonder as horror in Lauder's voice. The man was young, after all; not long employed. Perhaps he had never seen at such close quarters what havoc could be wrought upon the human body. He looked a little pale, though it might be but the watery light of the winter morning making him appear so.

"He'd not have died quietly," Quire said, preoccupied now by the uncharitable fear that Lauder might empty his stomach, or faint, or otherwise complicate an already unpleasant situation.

He looked east and west along the Cowgate, then northwards up the gloomy length of Borthwick's Close. The Old Town's inhabitants were stirring from their dark tenements and gathering in silent huddles, distracted from the start of the day's business by this gruesome spectacle.

"I'll get some more men down here to help you," Quire muttered to Lauder. "Once they're here, you can start asking questions. See who heard what, and if anyone can put a name on him."

The younger man's scepticism was evident.

"Probably Irish. Cut loose once the canal was dug. Maybe he's working on that new bridge."

It was a lazy but not entirely foolish suggestion. The Old Town was full of Irish labourers bereft of labour, and Highlanders bereft of their high lands for that matter, all of them washed up here by the tides of ill fortune and poverty. More than a few had indeed found some escape from their poverty and lassitude in the building of the huge new bridge being thrown over the Cowgate, and to be named in honour of the king, George the Fourth.

But: "No," Quire said. "He's no navvy or builder."

He lifted the man's arm, turning it against the dead stiffness of the muscles to expose his palm.

"See his hand? No rougher than your own. He's not been digging earth or breaking rock. And his clothes ... might not have been a rich man, but he's no pauper either. He'll go in a pauper's grave, though, if we can't find him a name and a family. Don't want that, if we can help it. It's no way for a man to end his days."

The dead man's jacket had fallen open a little as Quire moved his arm. A flap of material there caught his eye now, and he reached gingerly in, felt the loose ends of torn stitching. He had to bend his weaker left hand at a sharp angle to do so, and felt a twinge of stiff pain in his forearm. His old wounds misliked the cold.

"Did you find anything in his pockets?" he asked.

"Nothing," Lauder grunted.

"Did you ask Shake if there was anything?"

Lauder shrugged, his cape shifting heavily. Standing watch over a corpse, on a cold dawn at the end of a long night, in the Cowgate where the city's police had no surfeit of friends ... these were not the ingredients of contentment. At the best of times, few of Quire's colleagues – the miserably paid nightwatchmen perhaps least of all – shared his notions of justice and dignity for the dead. Those things could be hard to find in the Old Town, even for the living. Easier not to try, sometimes.

"Just wait here until I get you some help," Quire said as he rose to his feet. "It'll not be long."

He began to ascend the stinking ravine of Borthwick's Close, pushing through the knot of onlookers that had gathered a short way up the alley.

"Anyone know him?" he asked as he went, but no one replied. They averted their eyes, on the whole. Only a child, holding the rough linen of his mother's skirt with one tight hand, yesterday's dirt still smudged over his cheeks, met Quire's gaze fully. The boy parted his lips in an unappealing grin, and sucked air in through the corners of his mouth. It was an idiot sort of sound.

Quire was jostled as he made his way through the crowd, but no more than he would have expected. He was a big man, wide-shouldered and wide-chested, and he knew that his angular face, framed by dense, wiry hair, suggested ill humour more often than not. Though that appearance – enhanced by his grey greatcoat, the baton at his belt and the military boots he often wore out of ancient habit – deterred most troublemakers, no assembly in the Old Town was without one or two who thought themselves above such concerns. The place had a truculent state of mind.

Quire climbed up and up the close, careful on the rough and uneven cobbles, passing dozens of small windows, only a few of them lit by oil or candle or fire. He heard someone above him, leaning out from the third or fourth storey, hawk and spit; but when he looked, there was no one to be seen, just the man-made cliff faces blocking out the sky. The close narrowed as it rose towards the High Street – if he had extended both arms, Quire could have encompassed its whole width – before burrowing through the overarching body of a tenement to disgorge him on to the Old Town's great thoroughfare.

It was akin to emerging from the Stygian depths of some mal-odorous tunnel into another world: one filled with bustle and light and all the energy and breezes that the closes did not permit within their tight confines. Scores of people moved this way and that, avoiding the little mounds of horse dung that punctuated their paths, flowing around the hawkers and stall-holders ready-ing their wares, dodging the carts and carriages that clattered up the cobble-clad road. The air shivered to a cacophony of trade and greeting and argument.

Quire advanced no more than a pace or three before a salesman sought to snare him.

"A tonic of universal efficacy, sir," the man cried, with an excess of unsolicited enthusiasm. He swept up a small, neat glass bottle from his barrow and extended it towards Quire. "No affliction of the lung or liver can withstand its beneficial application."

Quire paused, and examined the dress of the man who thus accosted him. A short stovepipe hat, a neat and clean waistcoat tightly buttoned over a paunch of some substance. The loose cuffs of an expensive shirt protruding from the jacket sleeves. Clearly the uniform of one who made a tolerable profit from the ill health and gullibility of others.

The bottle Quire was invited to examine held a pale liquid of yellowish hue.

"Looks like piss."

"Oh no, sir. Not at all," exclaimed the affronted hawker, peering with a disbelieving frown at the flask in his hand. "A miraculous elixir, rather."

Quire leaned a touch closer, gave the tonic his full attention.

"Horse's piss," he concluded, and left the man, still protesting, in his wake.

The police house was very near, on the far side of the High Street at Old Stamp Office Close. Quire cut across the currents of humanity towards it. He refused a flyer advertising a course of phrenological lectures that someone tried to thrust into his hand; narrowly avoided a crushed toe as a handcart piled high with half-finished shoes ground past.

It was all a little too much for one who had already been awake for longer than he would have wished, and he entered the abode of Edinburgh's city police with a certain relief.

The cells that packed the ground floor of the main police house were unusually quiet, even the three – the "dark" cells – reserved for the most troublesome, or troubled, guests. Perhaps the cold of the last few nights had discouraged those given to misbehaviour. The place still had its familiar stink, though: a unique medley that never seemed to change, no matter how its component parts might vary. Quire suspected it was founded on a fog of human sweat, piss and vomit that had settled into the walls. There were smaller watch-houses scattered around the city, but somehow none of them had acquired quite the depth of odour that attached itself to the Old Stamp Office Close building.

Though the place was quiet, the comparative peace had not done anything to lighten Lieutenant Baird's mood. Quire's immediate superior disliked him, and never troubled to disguise the fact. He also disliked his current duty. The three lieutenants of police each took their turn as officer in charge of the police house, a task that combined tedium and unavoidably close acquaintance with the city's least appealing inhabitants. When his turn came about, Baird's manner seldom did anything but sour. All of which led Quire to expect a gruff welcome, which he duly received.

"Took you long enough," Baird grunted, barely lifting his gaze from the ledger in which he was scratching away.

"Would you send some men to the body in the Cowgate, sir?" Quire said as politely as he felt able. "Get them asking around. There's one of our night men down there who needs to be away to his bed."

Baird put an arch of irritation into his eyebrows as if consenting, solely by dint of his own near-saintly nature, to an outrageous request.

"Is the superintendent about?" Quire asked.

"He's occupied. In the court. What is it you're wanting to trouble him with?"

Belatedly, Baird looked Quire in the eyes, and bestowed upon him a suspicious glare.

Quire shrugged.

"I was told he wanted a word with me, that's all," he lied.

Baird looked doubtful, but directed Quire with a flick of his head towards the staircase.

Two creaking flights carried Quire up to the little courtroom where justice was applied to those charged with minor crimes. There, amongst the benches, the Superintendent of Police, James Robinson, was in conference with a clutch of judicial clerks. They spoke softly, as if to protect the dignity of the chamber, with its wood-panelled walls and leaded windows and buffed floorboards.

At Quire's approach, Robinson dismissed the others with a nod and a murmur. They filed quietly out, and the superintendent rose a little stiffly from his seat and regarded Quire, his eyes narrow and inquisitive. He was a man of calm authority, with grizzled sideburns, a handsome face weathered by experience – he was a good deal older than Quire's thirty-seven years – and a deliberate manner. It imbued his gaze with a certain weight.

"You look like a man in want of sleep, Sergeant," Robinson observed. "An early start for you, I hear."

Quire nodded.

"A body, sir. In the Cowgate. Foot of Borthwick's Close."

"Ah. Is that beer I smell on you? I hope you are not testing your constitution too severely, Quire."

The superintendent's tone was almost casual, but carried a touch of circumspect concern. He knew more of Quire's history than most, and that history was not one of unblemished restraint and good judgement.

It was only the patronage of James Robinson that shielded Quire against the worst effects of Lieutenant Baird's antipathy. And, indeed, against the wider consequences he might have suffered for his occasional past infringements of law and discipline, from which that antipathy sprang. He and Robinson, bracketing Baird in the hierarchy of command, shared something the other lacked, something that inclined them towards a certain mutual regard: they had both been soldiers.

There was more to their relationship than that, though. For Quire's part, he had a vague, imprecisely formed notion that Robinson had been a saviour of sorts to him. At his first admittance to the ranks of the police, Quire had been something of a lost soul, and a drunken one at that. The years following his departure from the army had been turbulent and troubled: peace could be testing for one schooled in nothing but war. He had carried within him a certain restless anger and rebelliousness that should, by rights, have cut short his tenure as an officer of the law. That he had avoided dismissal was due solely to Robinson's patient, stern tutelage. For that, and the measure of purpose and worth his continuing employment had slowly brought him, Quire owed the man a debt of gratitude.

As Robinson regarded him now, his gaze wore a faintly paternal sheen.

"A night of indulgence, was it?" the superintendent enquired. "With that lackey of yours, I suppose ... what's his name? Dunbar?"

"Nothing excessive, sir," Quire said, smothering a wry smile at the thought of Wilson Dunbar being anybody's lackey. "I'm well enough. The drink's not been my master for a long time now."

The assertion was accepted without comment.

"So, this corpse," Robinson said. "Are you done with it for now?"

"That's the thing I wanted to ask you about. I've a mind to send him to the professor."

"Why?"

"The man was ... savaged. It was bloody work. Entirely out

of the ordinary. I'd like to know what Christison has to say about it."

"I'd not want him bothered without good reason," said Robinson. "Man's got a fair few demands upon his time, you know. I'll not have his willingness to aid us exhausted by too many requests."

"I'd have asked Baird, but he'd only tell me that: not to waste my time – or Christison's – on some nobody dead in the Old Town."

"Lieutenant Baird," Robinson corrected him. "You might make at least some pretence at observing the proprieties of rank, Quire."

"Yes, sir."

"And you're sure you're not, are you? Wasting time, I mean."

"No such thing as a nobody, sir. I've seen – we both have – enough folk of the sort Baird would call nobody die for King and Country to know that. Every man deserves a name putting to him, a bit of time spent on the explanation of his dying. The wars taught me that, and you too, I know. A man like Baird doesn't . . . "

"Don't test my patience, Quire," Robinson muttered, grimacing. "You're the best man I've got when there's rough business to be conducted, and sharper than most, so I've never regretted any allowances I've made you, but I'm not in the best of tempers. The Board of Police are trying me sorely these days, and the gout's got a hold of my leg something fierce."

"I'd never want to add to your troubles, sir," Quire said quickly. "This is the only work I've ever found myself good at, outside the army. I owe that to you, I know. It's just I can't abide the notion of one man being less worthy of our efforts than another."

"Just tell me you're sure this needs Christison's attention, that's all."

"The body's a mess, sir. Like nothing I've seen in years."

Robinson looked dubious, but there was a foundation of trust between the two of them to be drawn upon.

"I'll arrange for him to take a look then," he said. "Don't go making an issue of it with Lieutenant Baird, though."

"No, sir," Quire agreed with what he hoped was appropriately meek humility.

III

The Scavenger and the Professor

Quire found Grant Carstairs – Shake – waiting for him in the entrance hall of the police house, two days after the discovery of the corpse in the Cowgate. The scavenger sat on a three-legged wooden stool, slumped down into himself like a loose pile of clothes. When Quire appeared, Carstairs looked up with rheumy eyes that betrayed both relief and anguish.

"I've been asking after you," Quire said before the scavenger could speak.

"Aye, sir, aye. I heard as much. I've no been well." Carstairs extended a trembling hand, regarding it with a sad, piteous gaze. "The palsy's on me something dreadful, and my chest . . . "

He gave a thick, richly textured cough by way of illustration and bestowed upon Quire a mournful smile.

"Is it your body that's ailing or your conscience, Shake?"

"Oh, sir. You may have the right of it there. They say you're a sharp one, and so you are. Body and conscience, and wife too. There's the truth. D'you ken my wife at all, sir?"

"I don't."

"No, of course not. Well, have you a wife yourself, then, sir?"

"No."

"Well, my wife is a wife of a certain sort, sir. A righteous sort. A righteous woman, and not blessed with great patience for a poor sinner like myself. But for her, and for my conscience – but for the needles of the pair o' them – I'd be in my sickbed still, not come here seeking after yourself."

"Well, you've found me now."

"Aye, sir. That I have."

The scavenger rose unsteadily to his feet, one arm reaching for the wall to lever himself up, the other dancing at his side. Quire clenched his own left hand to still a sympathetic tremor; one infirmity called up by another. He grasped the old man's elbow, taking what little weight there was to take.

"Can we speak, the two of us, somewhere a wee bit more private?" Shake asked, casting nervous glances around.

There were watchmen and policemen passing to and fro, and a steady traffic of townsfolk in search of succour, or delivering accusations, or asking after relatives. And there was Lieutenant Baird, standing in the doorway. He was deep in conversation with one of the members of the day patrol, but his eyes were drawn to Quire and to Carstairs.

"I can't speak easy unless I ken it's just you that'll be hearing me, d'you see?" Shake murmured.

"Come, then," said Quire, and gently guided Carstairs into a quiet side passage.

Shake's hands began to leap and flutter with unease when he saw where he was being taken. The dark cells stood open and silent, like waiting mouths.

"Best place, if you don't want to be seen or heard," Quire said reassuringly. "That's all."

He closed the iron-banded door behind them, and the bustle of the police house was suddenly no more than a murmur. Quire could understand Shake's reluctance to take up such quarters, however briefly. It was a miserable place, redolent of the troubles of those who had inhabited it. The dark cells were only used to hold those likely to harm themselves or others, and thus contained the equipment of restraint and of punishment. The door was heavy, with just a small grille of bars to admit light. There were iron rings in the wall for the attachment of bonds. And a flogging horse – a narrow four-legged bench, with leather straps by which a man's wrists and ankles might be secured – bolted to the floor. It was there that Quire settled Carstairs to sit.

"You've a reputation as a fair man, sir," the scavenger said. "A man less given to hasty judgement or condemnation than most of his fellows, when it comes to those of lower station than yourself. I'm hoping that's true."

"Aye, well maybe I am and maybe I'm not, but we'll not know unless you tell what you came to tell, Shake."

"I'd not have come at all otherwise, if I'd not thought you'd give me a fair hearing. It's a terribly thin life, sir, the scavenger's. Needs doing, right enough, the cleaning of the streets, the carting off of the muck and the city's sheddings. But it's a thin life."

"It's hard work," Quire said. "I know it. And I know the pay's meagre."

"Aye, sir. Meagre. That's the word. So the temptation's something fierce. You find a body, and there's none but yourself about . . ."

"You go through the pockets." Quire nodded, taking care to keep his voice free of accusation, leavening it with understanding.

"Oh, you do, sir. You do if you're a poor sinner. Then, if you're a poor fool of a man, you tell what you've found to your good wife. And she'll not be having it, sir. Not at all. There'll be no rest in my house until I've put it right, and that's the truth."

"What did you find?"

A trembling hand brought forth a small object and offered it to Quire.

"Only this, sir. Only this. Inside, in a hidden pocket. Not a thing else."

A small silver snuff box. Quire took it and lifted it to one side, the better to see it in the dim light. A thing of exquisite beauty, shaped like a tiny chest with fluted edges of silver rope, and with a dedication engraved upon its flat and polished lid in a flowery hand. Quire had to narrow his eyes and hold the box still closer to the grille in the door before he could make out the words.

Presented to John Ruthven
by his colleagues in
The Society of Antiquaries of Scotland
1822

"Get yourself home, Shake," Quire said quietly. "You've done well. Done it late, but better than never, eh? Tell your wife I said so."

The Royal Infirmary was an imposing structure: two wings projecting forwards from the grand central span of the building, the whole array adorned with a strict grid of tall rectangular windows. Quire passed through the gateway, flanked by pillars upon which sculpted urns rested, but turned aside from the steps leading up to the main entrance. His path took him instead to a side door, and down secluded passageways to the place where the corpses resided.

He found Robert Christison there, and was struck by the fact that the incumbent of the University Chair in Medical Jurisprudence seemed more contentedly at home in this chamber of the dead than any man – whatever his calling – should naturally be.

The tiled walls and floor reflected and concentrated the cold smell of vinegar and soap. Cabinets were arrayed around the walls, like a mute audience for the acts performed on the four waist-high stone slabs that took up much of the room. A crude trolley stood to one side; a conveyance for the dead that now bore not a cadaver but a neat array of tools of evident craftsmanship and gruesome purpose. Long-bladed flat knives, saws, hooks and forceps and shears. The means by which the human form might be dismantled.

There was but a single corpse there, that same one that Quire had so recently attended upon in the Cowgate. Christison stood over it, absorbed in his exploration of its corporeal mysteries. He had the sort of well-proportioned good looks that spoke of a gentle and uneventful upbringing. Though only thirty years old, when he straightened and looked at Quire he did so with the confidence and instinctive authority of one in full command of his profession and surroundings.

"Sergeant Quire. I expected you rather sooner."

"There were certain enquiries I had to make this morning, sir, after some new information came into my hands." He could feel the weight of the silver box in his pocket as he spoke. "Your message did not find me at first."

"I see. Well, our subject is in no haste to be elsewhere, I suppose. I do have one or two other matters to see to, though, so we must be brief."

Christison wiped his hands on the upper part of his apron.

"Do you wish to examine the body for yourself?" he asked.

From where he stood, Quire could see more than enough. Skin parted and lifted back; pale bones couched in the meat; tubes and sacs. There was, in this considered dissection of what had not long ago been a living, breathing man, a cold calculation that Quire found disturbing despite its benign intent.

"No, sir."

Christison nodded, matter-of-fact.

"Seen all you need, no doubt, when you found him in ... where was he found?"

"Cowgate, sir. Foot of Borthwick's Close."

"Yes."

Christison made to pull the sheet that covered the dead man's legs up over his head, but paused, and glanced at Quire with raised eyebrows.

"Did you smell him, though?"

"Sir?"

Christison bent over the corpse, and gave a long sniff at the horrible wound in its neck. It was an unnerving sight and sound.

"The nose is an undervalued tool in scientific endeavour," the professor said as he laid the sheet down, shrouding that dead face. "I've found it so in my study of poisons, in any case."

"He was poisoned?" asked Quire.

"It would take a particularly confused or intemperate kind of murderer to poison a man and then decide to tear his throat out as well, don't you think? Gilding the lily somewhat. No, his end was just as it appears. But there's an odd smell about him. Faded now, but it was strong when he arrived here."

Quire's mind went back to the dawn in which he had first encountered the body, curled there in cold solitude. Stinking, he recalled.

"Yes, sir. I noticed the same thing. Some of it I could recognise. Not all."

"Quite. Excrement and whisky. But something else too. Put me in mind of wet fur. An animal aroma."

Christison took up a selection of the instruments resting on the trolley and carried them to a sink in the corner. He spoke to Quire over his shoulder as he washed them.

"There's nothing more he has to tell me. Or, more accurately, nothing further of what he might say that I have the wit to hear. Every victim of fatal misadventure has a tale to recount – so I would contend, at any rate – but it is a new and imperfect science I pursue here. If it *was* a poisoning then I might be of more assistance, but this ... a butcher could likely tell you as much as I."

Quire nodded mutely, though Christison was not looking at him. He had not truly expected any great revelation; hoped for it, perhaps, but not expected. The savagery of the man's death had seemed to call for the effort nevertheless, and for all Christison's brisk manner, he was known to be one who treated all who came under his knife, whatever their former standing, with the same disinterested, precise attention.

"There's a certain amount more we might deduce, I suppose," the professor was saying. "His hands, for example: this was a man who worked with them, but not by way of heavy labour. A craftsman, perhaps. Something along those lines."

Christison glanced at Quire, who was nodding.

"You had already arrived at a similar conclusion, I see," Christison said.

"Yes, sir."

"Very good. I am delighted that the application of logic and observation is not a habit entirely absent amongst the guardians of our safety. What else? I can tell you he was but a recent convert to the pleasures of the bottle, for all that its scent has attached itself to him. His stomach was awash with alcohol – whisky, I would say – when I opened it up, so there can be little doubt that he was intoxicated when he died, but his skin and his organs show none of the signs we might expect in an habitual drinker. Only recently fallen upon hard times, perhaps."

Christison shook the excess water from his hands, then took up a towel and rubbed them vigorously.

"As to the cause of his death, I have nothing to offer beyond the obvious. In my experience, God did not see fit to furnish we humans with the natural equipment to inflict this kind of damage, and we must therefore suspect an animal of some sort. The marks on the arm in particular are clear. There are indentations on the cervical vertebrae that I would take for the results of teeth as well. Muscles, larynx, trachea all torn or displaced. Blood vessels severed. This was brutal, brutal work. Quite horrible. Quite remarkable."

For a moment, his detachment faltered, as he cast a somewhat uneasy glance towards the covered body.

"I'd say it was the work of a wolf, if we'd not rid ourselves of such vermin two centuries gone. And they were never what you might call frequent in the streets of Edinburgh, to the best of my knowledge."

"Not a blade, then, or an axe?"

"Certainly not. This unfortunate had his flesh torn, not cut. Do we have a wild beast of some sort loose in the Old Town, Sergeant?"

"I don't know, sir. Of some sort, perhaps."

"I've never seen a dog running about the streets that looked a likely perpetrator of a crime such as this."

"No. Nor I," Quire said quietly.

The professor carried the tools of his trade with all the care of a minister of the Kirk bearing the paraphernalia of communion. He laid them out once more on the trolley, and then began to place them one by one into a polished wooden box.

"Well, I do hope you resolve this conundrum," he said. "I'd not want to be looking fearfully over my shoulder the next time I'm on the Old Town's streets after dark. Though if a beast is responsible, perhaps we must call this poor man's end misadventure rather than crime, eh? Not a matter for the police, some might say."

"Some might," shrugged Quire. "Still, he's likely got a family, wondering what's become of him. They deserve to know. And those still alive deserve protection, if it's a thing that might happen again unless prevented. Seems to me that's what the police are for."

"Laudable," Christison said. "Have you a name for him, then?"

"I'm not sure of that yet. It might be he's John Ruthven. That was the matter that kept me busy earlier: consulting the roll of electors. There's a John Ruthven at an address in the New Town."

Christison cocked a sceptical eyebrow.

"I'd not have taken him for a householder with such a distinguished abode. Not with those hands, or with the apparel in which he was found."

"No. Nor I."

"Well, let us hope the truth will out. It does on occasion."

Christison closed the box in which his implements were now once more safely nestled. It clicked solidly shut and he turned a tiny golden catch to secure it.

"Tell me, did you see a porter loitering out there in the corridor when you arrived?" he asked Quire.

"No one, sir."

Christison gave an irritated grunt.

"Would you care to walk with me, then? I must find one of my assistants to close this poor fellow up, make him fit for the grave. And a porter to take him on his way."

Quire fell into step at the professor's side. He was not sorry to leave that place.

"At least if I put a name and a family to him, he'll not find his way on to a slab in a lecture theatre," Quire said.

"My anatomical colleagues would have little use for such a damaged cadaver, in truth. But you would be surprised, I suspect, at how many families are willing to sell the deceased for that very purpose."

"Not those as have a house in the New Town, though. Takes a deal more poverty than that, I should think."

"No doubt."

Christison glanced sideways at Quire, and read something there in his face.

"You disapprove, Sergeant. Surely you would rather the schools find their supplies through such legitimate channels, rather than line the pockets of the resurrectionists?"

"It's none of it legitimate, to my way of thinking. Any man would hope for a bit more dignity in his ending," Quire muttered, and at once regretted his gruff candour.

"Ah," said Christison, pressing his box of instruments a little more firmly into the crook of his arm. "Well, we can agree upon the distastefulness of the enterprise, if not on the question of its necessity. We live in enlightened times, with the inquisitive intellect as our guide. That its discoveries come at a price is undeniable. Neither the city fathers nor my anatomical colleagues are quite so sentimental, however. To learn the secrets of the human body – and our city's fine reputation was built in part upon the excavation of such secrets, let us not forget – a man must have a body in which to delve; anatomy can be taught without a cadaver, but it cannot be taught well. If we relied solely upon the produce of the gallows, our students would have the most meagre of fare, for all the sterling efforts of you and your fellow officers."

Quire held his tongue. He liked Christison well enough and had no desire to dispute the practicalities of medical education with him. And there was, in any case, substance to what the man said: an understanding existed – never directly expressed, but present in the air like a flavour – that the police did not enquire too deeply into the means by which the dead reached Edinburgh's famed, and lucrative, medical schools.

Whatever those means, Quire reflected silently, it was never the wealthy, or the powerful, who found themselves, after departing this life, displayed and dismembered for the edification of the students. Dignity in death was, like all else, unequally shared.

IV

New Town

The New Town was another place, another world; not wholly separate from the Old, connected to it by threads both tangible and intangible, but as unlike to it as an ordered farm of cultivated fields was to the wilderness that preceded it.

The Old Town had taken centuries to form itself, a haphazard growth thickening along the High Street, knotting itself into ever tighter and more crowded patterns. The New was the product of a singular and potent vision, and had sprung up in barely fifty years. It had been laid out in stern grids and graceful curves across the slopes and open fields to the north of the Old, beyond what had once been a thin, marshy loch and was now elegant gardens that divided the two Edinburghs one from the other.

For all its grandeur there were places in the New Town, Quire knew, where life's cruder urgencies held sway, but today it presented its most gracious face to him. The broad streets were flanked by wide pavements. Some were lined with gaslights, standing to attention like an honour guard of thin, stiff soldiers. The terraces of noble houses ran on and on, most of them fronted by iron railings, all studded with great doorways. Fashionably dressed folk moved to and fro – the women in their capacious skirts, the men in their tall hats and high collars – with calm, refined purpose.

The frontage of Ruthven's house in Melville Street was not so much pleasing as stern. A few steps led up to the imposing door. A boot scraper was set into the flagstones, and Quire regarded it for a moment or two, debating whether to yield to his instinct to use the thing, merely because it was there. He sniffed and instead gave the door knocker, a heavy ring of solid brass, a few firm raps.

As he stood there waiting upon the threshold, two ladies of evident means strolled by, arm in arm. They watched him as they went, and he had the uncomfortable sense that they thought him as out of place as he felt. He smiled and nodded, and they smiled demurely back before looking away and murmuring to one another.

The great door swung open, and Quire found himself greeted not by some servant as he had expected but by a strikingly attractive woman of middle age, to whom the adjective demure could hardly have been less applicable. Her décolletage was far more revealing than had been the fashion for some time, exposing a great expanse of smooth skin, divided by the deep crevasse between the swell of her breasts. She regarded him with an expression so open, so appraising, that he found it unsettling.

"Is Mr John Ruthven at home?" Quire asked, his discomfiture putting a slight quaver into his voice.

A smile pinched at her lips, and her knowing eyes widened a little. A fragrant perfume was stealing into Quire's nostrils, all floral piquancy, much like the woman who wore it.

"He is," she said. "Have you a name I might share with him?"

She stood aside as she said it, and ushered him in with an

unfurling of her long, pale arm. He entered, catching a waft of that perfume once more as he passed by her.

"Sergeant Quire," he told her.

"How nice. I am Isabel Ruthven. Can I take your coat?" she asked him, wholly unperturbed by the appearance of a policeman on her doorstep. "You have no hat, then?"

"Ah, no. No, I don't, madam." He felt an irrational flutter of embarrassment at his lack of headgear, as if its absence constituted some grave social misdemeanour. There were few things he cared for less than the strictures of society's hierarchies, yet he could not help but be aware of them, and of the difference that lay between him and those who would live in such a house as this.

She hung his coat on an ornate stand in the hallway. He watched her neck as she did so: the line of her dress fell almost as low across her back as it did her front. He could see her shoulder blades moving beneath her white skin.

"Mrs Ruthven," he said. "It is Mrs Ruthven, is it?"

"Indeed." That smile again, which seemed at once guileless and far too suggestive.

"Could you tell your husband that I have something of his that I would like to return to him?"

"Of course. Come, he is in the drawing room. There is a seat just here you may wait on."

She escorted him down the hallway, walking fractionally closer to him than was entirely comfortable or proper, so that her voluminous skirt brushed heavily against his leg. He thought it must be deliberate, but an instant later found that notion silly and chided himself for being so foolish.

A single rug was stretched out the length of the hallway, all burgundy, blues and creams. A massive side table, its chestnut surface so thoroughly polished that it almost glowed with an inner fire, held an ornate mirror fringed with gilt curlicues. As they passed it by, Quire glimpsed himself at Mrs Ruthven's side in the glass, and noted how each of them accentuated the other by their proximity: her grace and porcelain beauty rendered his rough edges and weathering all the more acute, and his shadows made her shine all the more brightly.

A stairway folded itself up the inside of the house, light pouring down from a vast skylight four floors above. Mrs Ruthven led Quire beneath it, and beyond, to a padded bench with thick, carved legs.

"If you would just wait here a moment, I will announce you."

Obedient, he sat, and watched her approach a tall panelled door opposite. At the last moment, as she raised one hand to tap at the wood, she looked back and settled on him a thoughtful gaze. She washed it away in a moment with a smile, and turned back to the door.

Quire heard only murmured voices from within as she leaned into the room, then she was beckoning him, and closing the door behind him, and he was looking around one of the most luxuriantly furnished chambers he had ever seen. A glittering chandelier that hung from a huge moulded rose in the centre of the ceiling; paintings the size of dining tables on the walls, dulled by age; a small piano of lustrous ebony; high-backed, long-armed chairs so thickly upholstered they looked fit to smother a man should he sink carelessly into them.

And three men. Standing closest to Quire, regarding him with expectant curiosity – therefore, Quire guessed, being John Ruthven – was a tall figure with a strong, if rather thin, face and a white neckcloth tied about a high, wing-tipped collar in a bow so ebullient it could not help but draw the eye.

Beyond him, peering around his shoulder, was a man a good deal shorter and older, with a face browned and leathered by years of sun, and fronds of fine lines at the corners of mouth and eyes.

His greying hair was in the process of deserting his scalp, falling back in some disorder towards his temples.

Third and last, reclining in one of those mighty chairs with legs crossed and the elevated foot bobbing slightly, elbows resting on the arms of the chair, a man of rather wan and pinched countenance. His hands, encased in smooth black gloves, were steepled, the two index fingers just touching the tip of his aquiline nose. He regarded Quire impassively.

John Ruthven advanced and extended a hand, which Quire duly shook.

"Sergeant Quire, was it my wife said?"

"Yes, sir."

"Very good. This" – he stood aside and indicated the older man just behind him – "is Monsieur Durand. A house guest of mine."

Quire hid his surprise at finding himself in the company of a Frenchman, and they exchanged nods. Ruthven flicked a casual hand in the direction of the seated man.

"And that is Mr Blegg, my assistant. A factotum, you might call him."

Quire duly gave another nod of acknowledgement, but there was only the most miserly of responses. Blegg barely stirred, other than a slight upward tilt of his chin and a little twitching bounce of that raised foot. One less inured to the sour eccentricities of the human spirit than Quire might have taken offence at such want of common courtesy. He, though, turned his attention back to Ruthven.

"I have a snuff box of yours, sir," he said. It was not his custom to delay in reaching the nub of any conversation.

He drew the little silver casket from his pocket and held it out on the palm of his hand. Ruthven bent forward a touch, tapping his lips with an erect forefinger as if pondering some weighty puzzle. Then, quite abruptly, he took up the box and closed his large hand about it, almost entirely hiding its silvery gleam.

"Now here is a mystery," he said with a thin smile. "Quite a mystery, eh, gentlemen?"

He cast an inclusive glance towards Durand, who gave a snorting half-laugh, which made Quire think that the Frenchman was a trifle overeager to find humour in his host's words.

"How does a silver snuff box with my name upon it come to be in the possession of the police?" Ruthven said, turning back to Quire and becoming wholly, heavily serious.

"It was found in the pocket of a corpse in the Old Town, sir. A man a little older than me, perhaps, with dark hair, clean-shaven. I thought at first that that name might be the dead man's, but it is evidently not so."

"Indeed not. Did you have my address from the Antiquaries, then? They will have embroidered it with some unkind words, no doubt."

"No, sir. There was no need for that. The Town Council records were enough."

"I see. The Antiquaries and I did not part on the best of terms, but this trinket is a token of happier times. A gift in acknowledgement of some donations I made to the Society and its collections."

"And this dead man had it from you? Stole it?"

"Stole it," Ruthven said sadly. "Yes, so it appears. I confess: I did not know it was missing. But yes, certainly it was taken without my leave, as were some few other small items and coin."

"All of it gone, no doubt, save this. Most likely he thought better of offering the uncles something that would so clearly betray his guilt and the identity of his victim."

"Uncles?"

"The brokers, sir. Pawners of stolen goods. The thieves call them uncles. Like to think of it as a family affair, perhaps."

"Ah. Well, as you say, officer. As you say."

Ruthven appeared bored now. He had not looked at the snuff box since taking it from Quire. He gave no sign that being reunited with it brought him any satisfaction.

"I would be grateful for his name, sir," Quire said. "From what you say, it seems you knew him."

"Does it?" The momentary flutter of discomfiture, perhaps even irritation, did not escape Quire, though it was ruthlessly extinguished almost as soon as it was born. "Well, yes, I did know him. He was in my employ, in fact, for several years. Edward Carlyle. I was recently forced to dismiss him over some minor matters, and before departing he saw fit to help himself to certain of my possessions."

"I will need to find any family he might have had."

"I cannot help you there, Sergeant," Ruthven said, pressing his lips together in regret that Quire found not entirely convincing. "He had no family that I knew of. A solitary man, at least in all the time he worked for me. He came from Glasgow originally, though. Perhaps that would be the place to look."

There would be no effort to find any of Carlyle's relatives so far afield, Quire knew. A thief dying alone in the Cowgate would not merit it. But still: thief or not, it had been the kind of end few men deserved, and it troubled Quire. As did Ruthven's lack of curiosity as to the manner or circumstance of Carlyle's death.

"Where did he live then, sir?"

"He had a room here, until I turned him out. After, I have no idea."

"Did he leave any belongings?"

"Nothing of consequence. I believe my wife sent it all along to the charity workhouse, Sergeant. She has a most generous soul."

"Oh?" Quire raised his eyebrows in surprise. "That seems a little . . . premature, sir. To dispose of his property, I mean."

"Does it?" Ruthven frowned, and he barely troubled to

conceal his irritation this time. "I can assure you, we were in no doubt that he would not be returning. He made that abundantly clear, and had ample opportunity to clear out his room before he left."

Ruthven's ill temper was not matched by the other two men. Durand had more the retiring air of a servant than that of a welcomed house guest, though a charitable interpretation might ascribe his reticence to a limited command of English. Blegg, by contrast, was all still, passive observation. It was, Quire thought, a peculiar manner for a servant. The man's face did, though, have an unhealthy, colourless sheen to it. Perhaps the sign of some malady.

Quire's gaze drifted as he puzzled over the disjointed, odd feel of this house and its inhabitants. He found himself staring at an object unlike anything he had ever seen before: an animal's horn of some sort, as straight as a rod, almost as long as the span of his arms, tightly spiralled and coming to a sharp point. Like a lance. It rested on a wooden stand atop the mantelpiece.

"Striking, is it not?"

Quire nodded in agreement.

Ruthven carefully lifted it from its stand, holding it horizontally before him. He did not offer it to Quire.

"It is," Ruthven said gravely, "the only unicorn's horn in private possession in Edinburgh."

Quire blinked in surprise, and looked to Ruthven's eyes for some clue as to his sincerity, but the man was gazing down at the artefact with fascination, as if encountering it for the first time himself. Only slowly did he lift his eyes to meet Quire's silent enquiry. Then he laughed.

"No, Sergeant. Of course not. It is the horn of a whale from the icy northern wastes."

Quire, normally sure of his ability to read another's nature, could not tell how much of that laugh was shared mirth and how much mockery. It seemed an untrustworthy, malleable sound.

"Forgive me," Ruthven said as he returned the horn to its wooden cradle with precise care. "It is a flaw in my character to find the credulity of others a source of amusement. But I imagine one cannot be both credulous and an officer of the city police, eh?"

"Do you know of anyone who might have wished Mr Carlyle harm, sir?" Quire asked.

Ruthven gave a mildly exasperated sigh.

"Quite the dog with the bone, aren't you, Sergeant? Are all our officers of the law so persistent, or is it merely our good fortune to be visited by the most tenacious?"

"A man's dead, sir," said Quire flatly. "I'm required to understand how, and why. It's not a matter of choice."

"No. Well, I cannot be of further assistance, I'm afraid. I was not privy to Carlyle's private dealings. He was merely an employee, you understand. A low sort of man, as it turned out. Untrustworthy. Just the sort to make enemies, and come to an unfortunate end.

"Well," Ruthven said with an air of brisk finality, clasping his hands, and glancing towards the Frenchman as if to solicit agreement. "Our business is done, I suppose. We are rather busy, as it happens, Sergeant, so you will forgive me if I ask you to leave us to our deliberations. Thank you again for your diligence. I have some acquaintance with one or two members of the Town Council, and I will be sure to convey to them my appreciation of our police force's efficiency."

"No need," said Quire.

He allowed himself to be escorted out, back into the long

hallway. His business here felt unfinished, but he could summon up no plausible reason to outstay his welcome, which for all Ruthven's restored mask of geniality had very clearly expired.

"Your Mr Blegg," Quire said as Ruthven accompanied him to the door. "Is he unwell? There's a pallor to his face and demeanour, and the gloves . . ."

"Oh no, Sergeant."

Ruthven took Quire's coat down from its hook and held it open for him. Another oddity, thought Quire, as he slipped his arms into the sleeves. Where were the servants, other than Blegg? For a man with such a house to be helping his guests into their coats himself . . . Quire was no expert in the manners of New Town society, but that seemed unusual.

"I'd not expend any concern on Blegg's account, if I were you," Ruthven went on. "An illness a year or two ago left him somewhat diminished, but he is well enough in himself these days. And the gloves . . . an affectation, that is all. He has his little peculiarities, as do we all."

With the door closed behind the police officer, John Ruthven stood for a few moments in his hallway, looking down at the silver snuff box in his hand, turning it slowly over and over. He grunted, and closed his fingers so tight about the box that his knuckles whitened. Anger put an arch into his tight lips. He spun on his expensively shod heel and strode down the hall.

Quire walked slowly along Melville Street, head down, dissatisfied. He disliked being lied to, having things kept from him, particularly by those who thought themselves his better. And though he could not say precisely how, or when, he had little doubt that he had been mocked, or deceived, or in some way gulled by the performance he had just witnessed.

He was, too, unsettled by the presence of the Frenchman Durand. It had called forth memories – seldom far from the surface, often in his dreams – that made his left arm ache, and his mood darken still further. He remembered, despite all his efforts to put it from his mind, Hougoumont.

V

Hougoumont

Nr Waterloo, Belgium, 1815

A rattle of shots greeted the dawn. It had rained heavily in the night, and they wanted to be sure that their powder had not been spoiled. Doubts dispelled, each man reloaded his gun and settled in to wait for the day's bloody business to begin.

Adam Quire was twenty-five years old, and had known two things in his life: the farm in the Scottish Borders where he grew up, and war. A war that had been fought and won once already. Uncounted thousands had died on the battlefields of Europe to curb the imperial ambitions of Napoleon Bonaparte, but now the Corsican who would be emperor was returned, escaped from his imprisonment and leading his doting soldiers into battle again. So the men who had thought their task done – and Quire had spent the better part of six years fighting his way through the Iberian peninsula to earn his small claim upon that victory – were summoned once more to give of their flesh and their blood. To make another offering to the ravenous martial gods of the age.

These times, on the cusp of battle, had always seemed distinctively strange to Adam Quire. The certainty that horrors were shortly to be released should have engendered fear, but he often felt a kind of morbid eagerness. An awful storm awaited, just over the horizon of the next minute or the next hour, and until it broke there was no way to see beyond it. The sooner it broke, therefore, the better.

Today, though, there was fear as well, settled deep into Quire's bones. He was in the final year of his service in the Foot Guards, sated to the point of sickness with death. Tired, in the very depths of his spirit, of watching men die upon the whims of the great and the powerful, for reasons that seemed ever more unclear. He had thought himself done with it, but instead Napoleon had come back, and now there was no future to reach for, save this one day and its inevitable savageries.

He was not the only one possessed of dark premonitions. The red-jacketed soldier at his side was clumsily crossing himself.

"You're no papist, Jamie," Quire muttered. "Not last I heard. All that crossing'll not serve you."

"Who knows?" Jamie Boswell said indignantly. "I'll take anything I can get today. It's going to be a bad one. I can feel it in my bowels."

"If you're feeling it in there, that's fear, not foresight. Don't shit yourself, for Christ's sake. There'll be stink enough about here soon, without your adding to it."

"Craigie's at it already," Jamie observed, nodding along the wall.

One of the men had broken away from his post and was squatting in a corner of the neat garden, his trousers round his ankles.

"Aye, well," said Quire. "It takes everyone a wee bit different. You just think on keeping yourself alive, and making a few Frenchmen dead."

Jamie Boswell was young, barely a year into his uniform. Quire liked him. He was soft, untarnished and straightforward, as Quire imagined he himself must have been when so freshly come to this cruel calling, though his memories of those first months were all but buried beneath the weight of what had happened since. As was the sense of any point or purpose to all the slaughter.

Quire looked out over the wall. The woods to the south, and the orchard to the east, were quiet. Beautiful, in fact. The trees were heavy with leaves, shifting slightly in the breeze like verdant clouds tethered to the ground. Here and there beneath the canopy of the woodland, Quire could see men moving. There were Hanoverians and Nassauers out there in the plantation, which pleased him considerably. They were decent soldiers, and more importantly they were between him and the French. Whatever pose he might strike for Jamie Boswell, Quire shared all the younger man's instinctive trepidation. This day just begun had the feel of a bad one, without doubt.

As it turned out, the day meant to be a great deal worse than merely bad, but it was in no hurry to reveal the true extent of its horrors. The morning ground slowly and dully along, and nobody came to kill the men in the walled garden, or amongst the trees outside, or in the great complex of farm buildings.

It was a farm unlike anything Quire had known in Scotland: a manor – or *château* as the officers insisted upon calling it – known as Hougoumont, with barns and sheds and workers' houses all laid out around two yards. And the great walled garden in which Quire and his fellows grew increasingly restive as uneventful hour followed uneventful hour. They warmed themselves about fires, and shared meagre rations of bread, and spoke little. A pall of unreality, an inexpressible feeling of the world being adrift in a formless void between consequential moments, settled over them.

But the storm did break, in time, and it did so with fearful wrath. It began with thunder, of the cruel sort made by men and their machinery of war. The boom of cannon rolled across the fields, like waves crashing on an unseen shore. It quietened the garrison of Hougoumont, each man looking up and out by instinct, searching for the telltale pall of smoke, or the black blurs of cannonballs in flight. But they were not the target of the barrage; not yet.

The Foot Guards, Quire amongst them, had spent the evening before digging out loopholes in the walls of the garden with their bayonets, and constructing crude firing platforms behind them from whatever material they could strip from the houses and outbuildings. They stood there now, peering out through the holes punched in the wall, leaning over the top of it, listening to the dull, endless peals of cannon, and knew they would not have long to wait.

The real killing started in the woodlands to their south. They could not see it, but its signs were clear. The rattle of musket fire amongst the trees; smoke boiling up through the canopy; shouting, and screaming, and the beating of feet upon the soft earth.

"They'll hold them," Jamie breathed.

He was crouched down behind the wall, hugging his musket to him. His voice was unsteady, trembling with that fretful blend of hope and fear that Quire had heard in so many others over the years.

"Maybe," Quire muttered.

He stared out towards the trees. He could imagine what it was like in there, how foul it would be. Fighting close, seeing the eyes of the man who meant to kill you. Bayonet work. Muskets wielded as bone-breaking clubs. Too much of the fighting he had done all across Portugal and Spain had been like that: chaotic, hand-to-hand, merciless. He excelled at it, the savage business of killing, but the burden of it, the misery of it, had only grown over time. A pity, that a man should be so good at something he loathed.

The battle in the woods came closer. Men were spilling back out from the plantation, scattering towards the gates into the farm complex, or around it entirely, hurrying back towards the main lines. It went on and on.

"Oh fuck," Jamie murmured over and over. "Oh, fuck."

"Shut up," Quire said eventually, softly, "or I'll fuck you myself."

And then it was the French, streaming out from under the trees in their dark jackets, shouting, running across the narrow stretch of open ground beneath the walls. The Foot Guards spat fire and musket balls at them, flames and smoke churning along the top of the wall as volley after volley went out, laying down men like so many windblown trees. Quire fired once, twice, thrice. Jamie never rose from his crouch. The wave of the attack broke on those rocks of lead and fire.

A pause. A space between furies. Men laughed. A few dared to imagine they had already faced the worst, and would be spared now. Somewhere, someone was crying, but Quire did not look to see who it was, or why. You did not seek out such sights.

From that moment, that quiet interlude, the day raced down into the darkness. Across a great stretch of land eastward from Hougoumont, titanic battle ranged. Armies tore at one another, charged and counter-charged. War swallowed up that one piece of the world and carried it off, for a span of time, to its own place where all else was in abeyance and nothing of any consequence existed save the clash of wills and of bodies and of flesh and steel.

At Hougoumont, the French came, again and again. They flooded up to the walls and the gates, lapping at them, clawing at them. Quire fell into the calm emptiness of battle. The inner silence in which thought gave way to ritual. Fire, reload, fire. Over and over, over and over. Breathing always the smoke and grit and dust.

Musket balls and splinters of stone blasted off the wall, filling the air like hornets. Ducking down, reloading, Quire listened to them chattering above his head. Many of the others were firing blind, raising only their guns above their protective bulwark and loosing off shots wildly. That served little purpose. It needed a man to lift his head up there, into the place where the shot was whining and the stone chips flying and the smoke boiling. Some would not do it, and Quire did not begrudge them that.

He did not begrudge Jamie Boswell his fearful paralysis, either. The youth stayed hunkered down, murmuring to himself, wincing now and again. He could never have seen anything like this before, and it seemed only sense to Quire that a man caught up for the first time in such a tempest should choose not to die on behalf of distant folk in their parliaments and palaces.

Not all those present agreed, though. Sergeant Walker was striding along the line of the wall, all bile and bellows. He was a bastard of a man, in Quire's judgement, but then he had come to feel that way about almost all save the common mass of the soldiery.

"Get up, that man," Walker howled at Jamie as he went by. "Piss yourself later, boy. King doesn't pay you to hide."

"Oh, Christ," muttered Jamie, and started to rise, but Quire laid a hand on his arm and pushed him down.

Walker had passed on, turning his vitriol upon some other victim.

"You stay put, if that's what you fancy," Quire told Jamie. "Sergeant doesn't get to decide whether the King pays you enough to die for him. You do that for yourself, lad."

He surged up, got an elbow set on the parapet. He was looking out over a great mass of men, pressed up right to the base of the wall. Hundreds of them, all pushing forwards; some climbing already on the backs of their comrades, or hoisted up by the strength of their arms, scrabbling for handholds to haul themselves over into the gardens.

Quire took measured aim at the nearest of them and fired. Scraps of the man's uniform were blown off his shoulder and he fell back amongst the throng. Quire spun his musket about in his hands and used the butt to batter at another Frenchman as he tried to get astride the wall.

It was instants from then: snatched moments of consciousness, of awareness, pulled from the frenzy of carnage; offered to Quire as all that would be left of the long, bloody day by way of memory. The few minutes of ethereal quiet that came upon them now and again, unexpectedly. Wilson Dunbar running along the line of defenders, a heavy bucket full of paper cartridges packed with ball and powder in each hand, shouting: "Get your cartridges while you can, boys! Plenty for all!"

And Jamie twisting and shouting at the stocky little soldier's disappearing back: "Impervious Dunbar! Stay here, stay with us. Give us a bit of your luck."

The French coming again, more fiercely than ever. Sounds of chaos rising up from the farm buildings, so that everyone thought for a time they were fallen. But no; the struggle there receded, that around the gardens thickened. Quire stabbing a man in the face with his bayonet.

The gardens themselves, ruined, churned to bare earth and debris. The little low hedges, cut in straight lines, trampled by the soldiers running back and forth. The wounded lying there, on what had been flower beds, crying or wailing or dying silently while they waited for someone to take them to the barn where the surgeons were.

Sergeant Walker returning, standing there and screaming at Jamie Boswell, stabbing a rigid, accusing finger at him.

"You will get on your feet, boy, and kill some fucking French-men, or I'll see you flogged. You mark my words, I will."

Quire would have turned about and told Walker where to go, but a Frenchman had reached up and had hold of the barrel of his musket, trying to pull it out of his grasp. Quire struggled to twist it into line with the man's chest.

Jamie Boswell rose at his side, then, and clumsily thrust his own gun over the top of the wall. He fired, punching a ball harm-lessly into the earth at the foot of the wall. The surprise and noise of it was enough to loosen the Frenchman's grip on Quire's musket. He pulled it free, and shot the retreating figure in the back.

"Reload," he shouted at Jamie.

Then half of Jamie's head was suddenly gone, flicked away like a leaf in the wind, leaving Quire a glimpse of bone and brain. Gore splattered his face. Jamie fell in the heavy, limp way a dead man did. For a moment Quire could taste him on his lips, but he wiped his mouth and his eyes clean. He stared down at the young man's ruined visage. And vomited, heaving up a thin gruel. Something he had never done before, even when faced with worse horrors.

The insistent rhythm of the slaughter carried him numbly on. Scores of corpses piled up outside the walls, flotsam strewn along a shore after a storm. Quire drifted through it now, his mind detached from his body, which mechanically followed the habits the years had taught it. He saw both the seething mass of the French advancing once more, in futile, dogged determination, and Sergeant Walker, retracing his steps, his ire cutting through the raging cacophony.

Quire lifted his musket and set it to his shoulder, and was dis-tantly surprised to find himself hesitating, the barrel of the gun turning away from the disordered ranks of the host assailing

Hougoumont, turning towards Walker. He was puzzled by that, and wondered what he meant to do.

A ball hit his musket, close by his face, blowing it apart in his hands. He felt a punch in his left arm as the ricochet went in. A spray of hot powder, wood splinters, across his face like stinging sparks.

Quire staggered back off the firing platform, falling on the lawn. He got to his feet, grasped at the men closest to him, going from one to the next, shouting, "I need a gun, I need a gun."

They all pushed him away, caught up in their own struggles, their own dance with death, until one looked down at him and grimaced.

"Good Christ, Quire, your arm. Look at your arm!"

Quire looked, and saw the way it was limply trembling, the blood all over the sleeve of his red tunic.

"Get to the barn, Quire. Get that seen to."

The barn: an island of suffering, yet more peaceful than the storm raging outside its thick walls. The injured lying all about on pallets. The few men there to attend upon them running from one to another, fraught exhaustion and strain engraved upon their faces, the blood of others staining their shirts. Quire fell back on to a straw-leaking mattress, and stared up into the roof beams, listening to the thunder that came deep and low through the stone.

And last, later and last amongst all the frail memories left to him of that day: Quire came to his senses, not knowing for how long he had drifted. He woke to fire. Fire in the roof of the barn, racing along the struts, dropping in great gouts of embers on to the men below. Smoke, not the grey powder stuff of battle, but thick, heavy, choking black smoke, filled the place, curling down the walls and writhing over the wailing injured.

"Get them out!" someone was shouting.

Men were running about at the fringes of Quire's vision, and all the time he was lying there, staring up into the inferno above him, and feeling that it was he who floated, up above, looking down upon some terrible fire raging in the hull of a boat.

There was a sudden crashing descent: parts of the roof structure collapsing, falling down towards him in a roaring mass of flame and smoke. A huge blow struck the left side of his body, bringing searing heat that made him try to roll away. A burning roof beam pinned him, crushing his injured arm beneath its orange-hot weight. Screaming. Quire screaming, though it took him a moment or two to realise it was him.

Someone pulled at him. He did not know who. He could see nothing any more. Could feel nothing but the white, stultifying agony of his arm.

VI

Dancing with the Uncle

Edinburgh, 1828

The sky came in brutish on Edinburgh, bearing rain and sleet on its turbulent wings. Hard weather always came out of the west, breaking across the castle on its rocky promontory like waves beating at the prow of a rising ship, spilling over and around its walls and tumbling on down across the Old Town. At such times, those city folk who could not avoid venturing forth encased themselves in high-collared coats and capes and low, tight hats, leaned into the sky's blustering force and went on about their business with dogged resignation.

Dogged resignation was as good a description as any of Quire's demeanour as he trudged up the High Street. The weather, though, weighed less heavily upon him than did his own thoughts. He was preoccupied by the image of Edward Carlyle's ravaged body. That was unfinished business, and it nagged at him. Once or twice, it had even dislodged memories of Hougoumont, of Jamie Boswell and of fire from their dominion over his dreams. Visions of teeth had come to him in his sleep, and set Quire himself fleeing through an endless maze of closes with a pack of spittle-spewing wolves upon his trail.

As he strode towards the police house, head down into the wind, eyes narrowed against the flecks of sleet riding the gusts, one figure amongst the few braving the foul elemental mood caught Quire's attention. The sight drew him to a halt, and turned him about to observe: a slightly stooped man hunched up beneath a rain cape, wearing black gloves. Blegg. Ruthven's man. Hurrying along with an air of intent, so focused upon whatever his mission might be that he passed within two dozen paces of Quire without noticing him.

Quire watched the man disappear into the narrow maw of Toddrick's Wynd, a straight, steep close running down towards the Cowgate. Not a place of obvious and natural interest to the household of a man like Ruthven. He followed to the head of the wynd and peered down its gloomy length. Blegg hastened between the tenements, and met a dishevelled, rangy youth waiting in a very particular doorway. The two of them conferred briefly, and Quire shrank out of sight behind the corner as they looked about them. When he ventured to peer down the wynd once more, they were gone. Which was of great interest to Quire, given what – and who – lay behind that door.

He waited, buffeted by the ill-tempered sky, feeling slugs of melting sleet slip from his hair and inside his collar. It did not take long to tire of that. He sought refuge in Mallinder's dairy, a dingy little shop opposite the entrance to the wynd.

"You don't look like a man after milk," Mrs Mallinder observed despondently as Quire took up station just inside the threshold.

"No," Quire admitted without looking at her. "Just a bit of shelter."

She went back to folding paper around the slabs of butter on her counter.

"Well, fine," she muttered. "Don't you worry. You make whatever use you like of my roof. It's there anyway. Costs me nothing, of course, to keep a shop for the service of them as don't like a bit of rain or wind. My wee ones eat air and wear sackcloth, so it's nothing to me if I never see the King's head in my hand all day. Which I'll probably not, unless this dreich weather softens up a bit."

Quire backed up and spilled a few tiny silvery pennies on to the counter.

"There you are. Feast your eyes on good King George all you like."

Mrs Mallinder grunted.

"Fine man, no doubt, but he's no treat for the eye. Here."

She slapped a wrapped block of butter into Quire's palm before he could withdraw his hand. He glanced down at it.

"I'm not wanting butter," he said a touch plaintively.

"That's as may be, but you've bought it fair and square. I may not be running a charitable shelter here, but I'm not after the charity of others either. You take it; that way I'll not have to take offence."

Bemused, and rather disappointed with the way the exchange had turned out, Quire slipped his purchase into the pocket of his greatcoat and resumed his position at the open door.

"Could you not shut the weather out?" Mrs Mallinder enquired.

"No," Quire replied, and that was the end of that.

It was perhaps a quarter of an hour or so before Blegg reappeared, striding out of the close, turning into the teeth of the wind and making his determined way off up the High Street. Quire watched him go, and rubbed his bristly chin thoughtfully for a moment or two. He was curious about what the rest of Blegg's itinerary for the day might be, since it had had such an interesting start, but he was more curious still about what his business had been in Toddrick's Wynd, and that trail might go cold all too quickly.

He crossed the High Street smartly and ducked into the close. The door to which he went was nondescript, a little broader and more solid than most of those lining the looming tenements, but unremarkable. Inside, though, was different.

A short, cramped passageway opened out into a wide hall with a low ceiling, the beams of which had turned almost black from long exposure to smoke and other fumes. The floorboards creaked beneath Quire's feet. They were cracked and worn and scratched. There were benches around the edges of the hall. On one of them a woman of indeterminate age was asleep, bundled up in thread-bare, moth-shot blankets. On another, a creased old man was sitting, blowing out a reedy, sharp tune on a wooden whistle. His crooked fingers jerked up and down as they tapped away at the holes. Before him, eyes closed, a girl of perhaps sixteen or seventeen was dancing alone, jigging about wearily as if long spent but driven by the melody to continue. Not that her movements, so far as Quire could see, bore any relation to the old man's tune. Other than that, the Dancing School was deserted.

He had hoped to find the youth Blegg had met still here, but the thicket of tables and chairs at the far end of the hall was unoccupied, save for a scattering of empty bottles and cups, and a sheen of broken glass strewn across the floor beneath them. He picked out a path between the tables, the brittle debris crunching and crackling beneath his feet.

The door to the kitchen was of the sort a farm cottage might have, top and bottom halves separate, and individually hinged. The lower section was locked, but the upper swung easily back when he pushed on it. He leaned over and peered around.

"Only whisky," said the portly man bent over the sink without looking round. "Not a drop of ale left, if that's what you're after."

"I'm not a man for the early drinking, Donald. Glad to see you washing your own dishes, though."

The man turned about and rolled his eyes.

"Quire. Just the face I want to see at the start of a day."

Donald MacQuarrie was not the owner of the Dancing School – that distinction belonged to a clutch of men a good deal more reclusive than him – but he had run the place for as long as Quire had been in the police service, and that he had not yet found himself jailed for it was a bitter miracle built out of wit and corruption and the playing of dangerous games. Nobody – or not many, Quire might grudgingly concede if pressed – came to the school to learn to dance.

"Where's your kitchen lad, then?" Quire asked as MacQuarrie shook dishwater from his hands and dried them on the breast of his shirt.

"The Infirmary. Had an accident wi' some glass last night. Fell on it."

"Fell on it?" Quire snorted. "Come out here, Donald. I've a question or two for you."

"Get away, Quire. There's a lot of good money gets paid over so your kind'll no be coming round here asking questions."

"Aye, but it's not paid to me, so keep me in a good humour and come out here. There's none to see but these three folk, and there's not one of them looks likely to remember a thing about this morning."

The dancing girl stumbled a little as MacQuarrie reluctantly emerged to join Quire at one of the rickety tables, but the shrill song of the whistle did not falter, and caught her up again and set her turning in another unsteady reel.

Quire swept the table clear of the night's detritus with the back of his arm, and tipped a chair up to drain some of the stale beer from it before he sat down. MacQuarrie's weight set his own chair to groaning, but it stood up to the task.

"None of the other uncles about?" Quire asked innocently.

The school had three trades, once the pretence of teaching dance was discounted: the unlicensed selling of untaxed drink, whoring, and the pawning of stolen goods. Every night, a handful of the so-called uncles could be found at these very tables, waiting for their broking services to be called upon by the city's thieves. MacQuarrie himself, Quire knew but could not have proved in law, was one of those uncles.

"Don't waste my time with questions you ken fine I'll no answer, Quire. Thanks to that wee fuck of a lad getting himself cut up, I've work to be doing this morning."

"Two men just in here," Quire said. "And don't tell me you didn't see them, since there's nothing else here to look at."

MacQuarrie maintained a glowering silence. He was not one to be easily cowed by a mere officer of the police.

"One of them not much more than a boy, the other a weasel of a man in black gloves," Quire persisted.

"What of it?"

"I want to know their business."

MacQuarrie shrugged and turned his attention to the dancer and her musician. He watched with flat indifference for a moment or two and then suddenly shouted, "Can you no shut that whining up, Stevenson?"

The old man with the whistle did not pause, or miss a beat. He whined on, oblivious. MacQuarrie grunted, and spat on to the floor.

"All right," said Quire. "Give me a name, then. I know the one, but not the other. Who's the young one? Where does he stay? How does he keep himself busy?"

"Can't help you," frowned MacQuarrie. "Not with either of them."

Quire caught the whiff of the lie in the quickness of the response, and the shuffle of MacQuarrie's eyes.

"I'll not be well pleased if you've made me suffer the stink of this place for nothing, Donald. I can take a grudge for a lot less, and I'll take it all the way to the excise men if you like. Get them in to measure just how many quarts of beer your customers are pissing out in the close each night."

MacQuarrie laughed at that.

"You're a wee man, Quire. No big enough by half to put a fright into me. You're only the police, and you're surely no thinking it's the police that . . ."

Quire lunged across and pinned MacQuarrie's hand flat to the table. He whipped his baton free from his belt and held it over the splayed fingers. MacQuarrie tried to jerk free, but Quire had all the strength of his good arm pressing down.

"You'll not be washing many dishes with cracked knuckles, will you?" he said calmly.

"Do that and it'll no be you with the grudge, and I ken plenty of bigger men than you."

"Maybe, but you'll still have a broken hand. And I'm thinking you know I'm not that easy frightened."

MacQuarrie slackened, and gave a dry smile.

"By Christ, Quire. Can you no take a joke? Settle yourself down. I'll give you a wee morsel, if it'll get you out."

Quire settled back into his seat and released MacQuarrie's wrist. The big man shook his freed hand, and shook his head at the same time, as if in disappointment.

"I've only seen the younger one before," he muttered, just loud enough for Quire to pick the words out from amongst the strains of Stevenson's shrill tune. "Been in here once or twice. Likes seeing the lassies about, but no man enough to buy any more than the seeing. I've no heard his name, but I ken he stays out in Duddingston. Does labouring on the farms, I think. And digs graves."

"He's a gravedigger?"

"Aye. I think so. And maybe I caught mention of a burial when they were talking. Maybe there's a man going into the ground at Duddingston Kirk tomorrow. You tell anyone you had that from me, though, and I'll no be a happy man."

"Hah."

Quire leaned back in his chair, more than a little surprised. Whatever he had expected, however out of kilter he had thought the mood of Ruthven's house and whatever scent of wrongness he had caught there, he had never thought it might lead to this. The discovery imbued him with a sudden vigour, like a child glimpsing if not the solution, at least a hint of the solution, to some frustrating puzzle toy.

"Do you know a man called Carlyle?" he asked. "Edward Carlyle."

"I'm spent, Quire. I'll no be spilling anything more for you this morning."

"Something to spill, then." Quire grunted. "Listen, Carlyle's dead. There's no trouble you could bring down on his head that'd bother him now. You tell me something about him, it means I don't have to come back and start bothering your customers on the matter."

MacQuarrie sighed.

"You're just too dim-witted to ken when to stop aggravating folk, aren't you, Quire? Look, there was a Carlyle in here a few times, the last month or two, with Emma Slight. He made for a bad drunk, and we threw him out. Told Emma not to bother bringing him round here again. That's all."

"Emma Slight. She's one of the Widow's tenants, isn't she? In the Holy Land?"

MacQuarrie gave an ill-tempered shrug.

"You charge a penny entrance, is that right?" Quire asked as he pushed his chair back and rose to his feet.

"Aye," grunted the proprietor of the school.

Quire withdrew Mrs Mallinder's carefully wrapped slab of butter from his pocket and slapped it down on the table. Its sharp edges had just begun to lose their definition. The two men regarded it in silence for a moment, both rather surprised at the noise it had made as it flopped down, and at how strange and unexpected it seemed, lying there in all its boneless softness on a table in the Dancing School.

Quire roused himself first.

"There you are, Donald. Keep that for yourself. At least you'll have made a profit on the morning's business."

He left MacQuarrie staring at the slumping pat of butter in quizzical silence, as if he had never before encountered such a baffling object.

"No, you cannot have any men," snapped Lieutenant Baird. "There's two hundred thousand living souls in this city, Quire. Living, mark you, not already dead and beyond all earthly concerns. And we've a hundred and a half on the city police, if you include every last grubby little member of the night watch. Does that sound to you as though we've the men to spare for standing guard on a graveyard all night because you've heard some tall tale from Donald MacQuarrie? The master of the Dancing School, no less, and he's got you dancing to a silly tune right enough, hasn't he?"

Quire made to reply, but Baird was in full, acerbic flow.

"If it was one of the city yards, maybe, but Duddingston?" the lieutenant sneered. "No. Not a single officer, not chasing off after some fancy of yours just because you think one man might have been talking to another in a cesspit on Toddrick's Wynd. Not today, not any other day."

"You know fine there's only one reason for a man to be meeting a gravedigger in a place like that and asking after a burial," snapped Quire, his patience – never the most robust of his qualities – faltering. "And you know just as well that the body snatchers like to do their digging outside the city these days. Less well guarded, less closely watched."

"Fine by me," Baird grunted, settling back in his chair and crossing his arms. "Let them dig away, so long as it's not under our noses. If they think the body's worth the snatching, the Duddingston folk'll have a watch on it themselves. They know how these things go.

"What is this morbid fascination for the corpse trade you've suddenly acquired, anyway? It's not to do with that body in the Cowgate, is it?"

"Not really," Quire said.

Lying to Baird was not an unfamiliar experience for him.

"I hope not. Way I hear it, Christison's called it animals, not men, that finished that fellow off. No great loss, a drunk falling asleep in a close and getting himself gnawed on. And we've not found a single soul who's seen anything prowling about in the Old Town that might do such a thing to a man. It's nothing to trouble us overmuch."

Quire had long since lost any interest in Baird's opinion of how he should conduct himself. The lieutenant had always been at him like a baiting dog at a badger, fired up by the rumours of Quire's drinking and acquaintance with dubious women that had attended upon him in the earliest days of his employment.

Baird was a man with an eye on advancement. He cared, as best Quire could tell, hardly at all for the substance of police work, only for the opportunities of promotion it might offer him; opportunities he had concluded would not be enhanced by association with a man like Quire.

"Turning a blind eye to the theft of corpses from their graves doesn't sit right with me," Quire said stubbornly. He had tired of the exchange, knowing defeat when it arrived, but his dislike of Baird would not allow him to retire gracefully from the field. "You'd not like some brother of yours digging up and carting off to the medical schools, would you?"

"It's not something the city fathers want us bothering ourselves with too much, Quire. There's more important matters to worry us, and you might think you get to choose how you spend your time, but I know better."

Baird was pleased with himself, enjoying the exercise of his authority.

"Know your place, Quire," the lieutenant said. "That's always been your problem."

In the entrance hall of the police house, Sergeant Jack Rutherford was pinning a recalcitrant visitor to the floor with the help of a couple of others. Quire recognised the subject of their rather weary efforts: Tam Wilkinson, a thief, well-known in certain quarters, who was evidently being invited to answer for his crimes at last. Wilkinson's one free hand was scrabbling over the floor like a palsied crab, edging erratically closer to a little knife of a sort best used for peeling apples.

"Lend a hand, Quire," Rutherford suggested equably. He was fully occupied holding down Wilkinson's head and shoulders, while his two colleagues struggled to master one flailing leg apiece.

Quire advanced, and paused a moment to judge the movement of Wilkinson's hand. Then he trod on it, firmly enough to prompt a howl of protest.

"Is Robinson about, do you know?" Quire asked as he bent down to retrieve the knife. A silly little thing, he thought, looking down at it in his palm; but still, careless of them not to strip him of it before dragging him in here.

"Laid up with the gout, I heard," Rutherford grunted. He adjusted his grip, locking an arm around Wilkinson's neck preparatory to hauling the now compliant miscreant to his feet. Quire puffed his cheeks out in frustration.

"Might be he's just worn out, of course," Rutherford said. "Rumour is, he's taking a beating from the Police Board these days. Folk with no better use for their time than making other folk's lives difficult."

"Aye, there's a few like that around here." Quire nodded.

He went out on to the High Street, despondent twice over. First for the troubles befalling Robinson, a man as far as Quire could tell entirely undeserving of the wrath of his masters; second, more selfishly, for his own inability to appeal Baird's obstinacy to a higher authority. Without Robinson, it was a matter between Baird and Quire, and that was not the kind of matter that was likely to have a happy outcome. Still, some things could not be helped.

For years, Quire had marched and fought in obedience to the orders of those above him. That had eventually led him into a state he would never willingly revisit: not knowing why, beyond that mere obedience, he did what he did; not knowing, in his heart, upon which side of the divide between right and wrong his terrible deeds were placing him. The uncertainty had stayed with him, through the years of drinking and wandering and labouring after he left the army, though he had not recognised its corrosive persistence at the time. Only becoming an officer of the law had quieted it, and instilled in him a sense of convinced purpose. If he was to retain that precious, protective clarity, he had no choice but to follow where it led.

One or both of Ruthven and Blegg were involved in something they should not be, of that he had no doubt. Whether that something had played a part in Edward Carlyle's death was unclear, but Quire had no intention of letting it remain so.

It began to snow as he wandered thoughtfully down the High Street. He paused at the great crossroads where the North and South Bridges pointed their respective ways out from the Old Town and looked up at the flakes swirling in ever thickening congregation around the steeple of the Tron Church.

It had been unseasonally and bitterly cold for days now. Winter appeared stubbornly unwilling to yield its dominion.

VII

The Duddingston Ice

In the falling dusk, Adam Quire walked around the southern flank of Arthur's Seat, serenaded by jackdaws tumbling raucously beside the rock faces. There was a thin cloak of snow on the ground, and a cruel, deep cold to the air now that the clouds had cleared away, leaving a sea of emergent stars. Quire paused where the track cut through a notch in the hill and turned, looking back towards Edinburgh. The setting sun lit the western sky with a rosy wash. Sprawled between that vast, glowing canvas and the looming crags of Arthur's Seat, the city looked small, almost humble: a dark encrustation upon the land, studded with spires and a forest of chimneys. Pennants of smoke streamed from its innumerable mouths, a grey froth ascending into, and merging with, the darkening sky.

Quire had brought a lantern with him, but he did not light it yet. There was a certain peace to be had in the gloaming, which man-made illumination would dispel. Sheep were scattered along the track, and regarded him with the dull and lumpen vacancy of their kind. Arthur's Seat was the King's Royal Park, but its hereditary keeper, the Earl of Haddington, grazed his flocks over it as he saw fit. And quarried its cliffs, for that matter: if rumour was to be believed, the rock bones of the ancient hill had paved half the New Town.

The twilight was luminous enough still for Quire to avoid the little knots of sheep droppings strewn in his path, and for him to see, laid out to the south, mile upon mile of undulating farmland and copses and little settlements, and the dark, round-backed chain of the Pentland Hills dwindling away into the distance. And up ahead, as he rounded the haunch of Arthur's Seat: Duddingston village itself.

The hamlet – little more to it than kirk, manse and a few cottages – clung to the foot of the hill, looking out over the reed-fringed expanse of Duddingston Loch. The loch was a single sheet of ice; the bare trees that ringed it were crusted with snow. Quire could see tiny figures on the ice, close in by the near shore: curlers, done with the day's game, using their feet to herd their granite stones back towards the shore, exchanging boasts and commiserations.

The track descended slowly across the hill's southern face, dipping towards Duddingston. Night fell about Quire as he followed it. He entered through the village gates with the kirk on his right. It was a modest building, entirely surrounded by a small walled graveyard. At the cemetery gate hung a set of jougs: an iron collar attached by a chain to the wall. It was an old punishment for miscreants, not practised any more.

The most striking feature of the gateway, though, was the watchtower. It was a squat construction, just two storeys, but other than in height it could have been the very twin of a tower in some medieval castle; a six-sided, castellated fortress in miniature. Latticed, arched windows stood in each flat face of the tower. Half the graveyards of Edinburgh were thus fortified now, so great was the need of the dead for protection against the avaricious living. That, Quire reflected as he stood looking up at the tower's battlements in the gathering night, was a state of affairs fit to amaze and dismay any who spared it some thought. Any, at least, not so bedazzled by the city's glorious reputation as a centre of learning as to be blind to the dark foundations of that glory. He allowed himself only a moment of bemused, rather mournful, reflection.

Quire unhooked his baton from his belt – its presence there in the first place being open to question, since it was in all ways that mattered his badge of police office and, as Baird had made entirely clear, this was not a matter for the police – and rapped upon the door.

A tremulous voice arose from within, barely seeping out through the wooden planking on to the night air.

"Who's there?"

"Edinburgh police," Quire said, putting a decorative flourish upon his wilful disregard of Baird's instructions. There were any number of things that kept Quire from sleep of a night; disobeying Lieutenant Baird was not one of them.

"Oh no," the inhabitant of the watchtower said, and then fell silent. To Quire's surprise, the door showed no sign of opening. He looked up and down the road. It was empty, and the village quiet. He took hold of the iron handle on the door and pushed, but some lock or bar stymied him.

"Would you let me in?" he called with studied calm.

"Oh, I couldn't do that, sir."

Again a silence ensued, instead of the further explanation Quire would have appreciated.

"Why is that?" he asked heavily.

"Not without my father's say-so, sir. He's an elder of the church. In charge of the watch."

"Where is your father?" Quire asked, his spirits sinking rapidly.

"In the Sheep Heid."

"Oh, aye? And what's his name?"

"Mr Munro, sir. Duncan Munro. The elder. By which I don't mean a church elder – I said that already – but Duncan the elder. I'm the younger."

"Of course you are," said Quire.

The Sheep Heid was an inn of some repute. On another night, Quire might have found its seductive advances wholly irresistible. As he stepped across the threshold, he was taken in a warm and welcoming embrace of fire-heat and tobacco fumes, neighbourly talk and laughter.

Mounted on the wall above the bar was the head for which the tavern was named: that of a four-horned ram, observing the comings and goings with what struck Quire as a somewhat judge-mental eye. It was quite a beast, one set of horns re-curved around its ears and back towards its cheeks, the others erect and sharp as knives. For all the smoke and chatter bubbling about it, it had an air of detachment, as if come from another time and place to gravely preside over this assemblage of men.

"I'm after Duncan Munro," Quire said to the nearest of the drinkers, and was directed to a corner table currently occupied by a boisterous party exhibiting good cheer and ruddy cheeks. Curlers most of them, Quire reckoned, cheeks and humour alike enlivened by their return from the ice to this cosy lair.

The man he sought was no recent arrival, though. He was sett-led in his chair with a loose ease only lengthy occupation could bestow, and the colour in his face was all too clearly the product of drink and the heat of the inn's fire.

"I was looking for you in the watchtower," Quire said by way of blunt introduction.

The conversation faltered. Every eye turned to him, Munro's a little more sluggishly and blinkingly than most.

"Me?" the church elder asked.

"I'm a sergeant of police, over from the city, and wanting a word with those watching the graveyard tonight."

"That would be me, right enough," Munro confirmed.

"What are you doing here, then?"

"Preparing for the long night ahead," Munro replied with an explanatory shake of his tankard, and an appreciative chuckle from his companions.

"Well, the night's not waited for your preparations to be completed," Quire observed, pointing to the little thick-paned window behind Munro. "It's gone and started itself."

"Surely not."

Munro twisted in his seat, those closest at hand shrinking away from his dangerously rocking mug. He took in the darkened scene beyond the glass at some length, and then gave out a considered, thoughtful grunt.

"The nights do come in fast this time of year," he observed.

Quire walked close at Munro's side as they covered the short distance from the Sheep Heid to the gates of the kirk. Before leaving the inn, he had set a light to his lantern, and now angled its shutters to lay out a guiding beam before them. He was concerned for the other man's safety, since the roadway was snowbound and Munro's stride a touch unsteady. His concern proved unfounded, though. The man was sure-footed, perhaps aided by the ballast of a girth that placed considerable demands upon the belt and waistcoat tasked with its containment.

A feast of stars was strewn above them, food for the eye, and the crescent moon like a knife of polished ivory.

"Quire, eh?" Munro said as they drew near to the watchtower. His good humour had survived his removal from the inn thoroughly intact. "That's a name with a fine religious tone to it. A churchgoing family, perhaps?"

"No," Quire said, glad that he had not shared his forename as well. "A farming family. Until I left the land, at least."

"Ah. Ah."

Munro sounded a little disappointed, but shrugged it off easily enough.

"Well, a believer in the sanctity of life, at least, and that of the righteous dead, or you'd not be troubling yourself with our business tonight. Am I right?"

"More or less."

Munro pounded on the door of the tower.

"Open up, lad. We've an officer of the law come calling, to share our heavy duty."

Duncan the younger gave them admittance to a cramped little chamber which a crackling fire had packed with so much heat that Quire felt dizzy. The son eyed his father cautiously as the older man sank into a low wooden chair with a contented sigh, while Quire's attention was taken by the gun resting across pegs above the hearth.

It was properly known as a Land Pattern flintlock musket, but Quire, and everyone else with any soldiering in them, knew it as the Brown Bess; a soft, almost companionable name, he always thought, for something that had spat such storms of smoke and fire and lead and spilled such torrents of blood the world over these last hundred years. This lady had been midwife and nursemaid in the savage birth and nurturing of Britain's empire.

"What is it you're here for?" the youth asked him.

"He thinks there's those who mean to rob our grave tonight," his father said before Quire could answer.

The older man's eyes were already closed, and his clasped hands rested comfortably upon his stomach.

"I've explained that we've had no trouble like that here in years, and not likely to have when there're lights in the windows of this tower, and smoke from our chimney."

He opened one eye and cast an investigate glance towards the window that looked out over the graveyard.

"Lights in the windows," he said again, pointedly. "Man can talk as much sense as he likes, and profit by it not at all if nobody's listening."

His son hastened to find a candle in the drawer of a long table that stood against one wall. He lit it with a taper from the fire and set it on the window ledge, its fluttering flame a precautionary beacon against whatever men of ill will might lurk in the outer darkness.

"Ground's frozen, anyway," Munro said. "Who'd be so set upon transgression that they'd try to dig through that?"

"They'd need to be determined upon their course, right enough," Quire agreed.

"Or most fiercely in thrall to greed. They say the anatomists pay ten pounds for a body."

It was a good deal more than Quire could earn in a month.

"How long do you keep watch after a burial?" he asked.

"A week or so," grunted Munro, closing his eye once more and sniffing. "They come early, if they're going to come at all. After that, the corruption of the body . . . well, nobody would want it then. And only when the one we've buried was taken in the prime of life, and sound in wind and limb. As this lad was."

A sorrowful weight settled over his words.

"Drowned in a ditch. The worse for the drink, they say, but I don't know. Anyway, the Resurrection Men don't much want the old ones, or the sick ones. So people say, in any case."

"It's true," Quire acknowledged.

"Is it true they put cages about the graves in the city yards?" the younger Munro asked hesitantly, perhaps embarrassed by his morbid curiosity.

"Sometimes," Quire said, seating himself far enough from the fire to avoid its fiercest heat. "If the family can afford it. Mort safes, they call them. Great iron things."

Munro grunted, in a heavy, languid way that suggested sleep could not be long delayed.

"Hellish times we live in, that the dead should be disturbed in their sleep by pagans and atheists. Pagans and atheists, the lot of them: the diggers and these so-called medical men alike. Lapdogs of Satan. No grave should be opened, unless it's at the end of days."

And with that judgement issued, the elder of the church lapsed into lugubrious slumber. He snored, softly and gently, and it was a soothing sound. Rather like the contemplative rumbling of waves upon a pebble beach.

The sleeper's son perched himself on the window ledge, beside the trembling candle, and began to read a bible so old and well-used that its leather binding had softened to the flimsiness of cloth. His lips moved as he read, though Quire was not sure whether it was unconscious habit or deliberate recitation.

"You spend a lot of nights in this little castle, lad?" he asked the boy quietly.

The young Duncan, sitting there with the holy book open on his lap, lifted a stiff finger to his lips, pointed at his torpid father, and returned to his study of the text. Quire could not help but smile at the impertinence, loyalty and faintly submissive obedience that were all bundled up together in the scene.

The heat, and the lullaby of Munro's snoring, worked their soporific magics upon Quire, and he found his thoughts drifting aimlessly. His gaze rested upon the gun lodged above the fire, and he wandered into a remembrance of past times that was as much dream as memory.

He had carried a Brown Bess of his own all across Portugal and Spain, and into France. She had done as much as – more than, perhaps – any other woman to make him who he was. Taught him, certainly, more memorable lessons than the few teachers he had known in his brief schooling.

What sound it was that interrupted his hazy reverie, and how much time had passed, Quire could not say. But there was something; some dissonant shard of the outside world that jarred in his ear and was gone before he was wakeful enough to take hold of it.

He jerked upright in his chair, scraping its feet on the flagstone floor. The fire was still crackling, though it had sunk a little lower in the hearth; Munro still snored, though it was a feeble, whistling kind of snore now. But the son, perched upon the ledge of the dark window, was the embodiment of tension, staring out into the night. The soft bible in his hands was forgotten, on the verge of slipping from his grasp.

"What is it?" Quire asked.

"I don't know," the youth said uneasily. "Something."

And then it came again: a scrape of metal on stone, so faint as to be barely distinguishable from nervous imagination. But distinguishable – and real – it was. Quire surged to his feet.

"Get away from the window," he snapped. "You'll not be able to see anything anyway. Snuff that candle."

As Munro the younger did as he was told, Quire kicked his father's outstretched foot. Even that was only enough to bring the man haltingly and blearily back to wakefulness.

"What's happening?" he asked, rubbing at his eye.

"That's what we're going to find out. Do either of you know how to load that gun?"

"What?"

Father directed a fearsome enquiring glare towards son, who shrank beneath its force and said, apologetically: "There's someone out there."

"Is there?" The doubt was evident in Munro's voice, but so was a fragment of alarm. "It'll be nothing. No need for the gun."

"And if it's not nothing?" Quire demanded. "There's many kinds of resurrectionists, Munro. Not all of them are students, not all of them are gentle. Arm yourself. It might put some handy fear into them, if nothing else."

It was evident at once that the man had not handled a gun in a long time, if ever. He fumbled even as he was digging a cartridge out from a pouch. He held the musket too low, and it swayed and rocked in his grasp. He was afraid of the gun, Quire knew, for he had seen it in others before. Afraid of the gun and of what it signified.

Quire took it out of Munro's hands and, for the first time in many years, found himself loading a Brown Bess. Tearing at the paper cartridge with his teeth, catching the smell of the powder and thinking it a touch stale. Spit out the scraps, prime the pan. Stand the gun on its heel and pour the rest of the powder down the barrel. Turn the cartridge, feeling the weight of the ball in his hand; press it into the barrel with a fingertip. Tight enough. Slip the ramrod out from its seat under the barrel, punch down with it, pack ball and paper wadding and powder down firm. Replace the ramrod.

Quire looked up. Both Munros were regarding him with unease.

"There's a man who knows his way about a musket," the elder said quietly. Sadly.

But Quire knew he had been slow and imprecise. At his best, at Waterloo, he had been amongst the fastest in the company. Four shots in a minute. Not any more. Not nearly. It was not a skill he wished to rediscover, any more than was the killing of men. He offered the gun to Munro, who regarded it with distaste.

"I'll take it," said the man's son.

Quire heard a hint of enthusiasm in the proposal that he did not entirely trust, but the older Munro nodded.

"He's used one before, true enough." But he fixed his son with a beady glare as Quire handed the weapon over. "Don't you go firing that thing off, though, lad. Just for show."

"Where's the body?" Quire asked. "The fresh burial?"

"Far side of the kirk," Munro told him. "The loch side."

They went out into the graveyard, a still and strange place on a night such as this, with an icy tang to the air, rumpled snow blanketing the graves. The beam of Quire's lantern flung the stark shadows of headstones across that white canvas and up on to the walls of the little church. There was a silence, of a depth only winter could provide, and the crunch of their footsteps fell into it like stones into a deep pond.

They went around the south side of the church. A gnarled apple tree, leafless and fruitless and sleeping, leaned over the cemetery wall. The lantern light bounced and tumbled through its branches. Quire meant to lead the way, but Munro – perhaps from protective fatherly concern, or just in the belief that the authority and responsibility here were his – moved quickly past him, striding over the snow without regard to caution or concealment. It occurred to Quire, belatedly, that the role of the men who watched over the graveyards of Edinburgh was not to capture body snatchers, but to deter them. To frighten them off. His own desires and expectations might not entirely jibe with those of his companions.

He glanced back, to where young Duncan was tramping along behind them, bringing the lantern round to light the boy up with its yellow glare.

"Get your finger off the trigger," Quire hissed.

Duncan came to an ungainly halt and blinked at Quire uncomprehendingly. Quire pointed at the Brown Bess.

"Don't walk with your finger on the trigger," he muttered, "not on ground like this. You'll blow someone's head off if you stumble."

"You there," Quire heard the boy's father suddenly saying, and he spun back to see what was happening.

The lantern's light swept up and around, washing over the church, picking out for a moment the rough surface of the stone blocks, flashing from icicles hanging from the edge of the roof, rushing on and down. It fell across Munro's shoulders and spilled around him, conjuring up out of the darkness ahead a strange tableau.

One man was already partway out over the graveyard wall. He dropped down out of sight even as Quire drew breath to shout, leaving only the image – a mere fragment of a moment, glimpsed at the light's edge, and then gone – of a black-gloved hand clinging to the top of the wall.

That left one bulky figure inside the graveyard's bounds, turning back towards them even as Munro drew near. There was a shovel hanging slack in one of the man's big hands.

"Wait," shouted Quire, trying to rush forwards but hampered by the snow that gave and slipped beneath his boots.

He glimpsed the disturbed grave: the sod slightly lifted, some black soil exposed. The body snatchers had hardly begun their work before being interrupted.

"Have you no shame, man?" Munro was shouting, entirely overcome by outrage.

"Wait," Quire cried again.

He was staring at the grave robber's face, though he could not see it well, for Munro's head kept casting it into shadow or blocking his view as the church elder continued his querulous advance. But what little he could see worried him. The object of Munro's ire was impassive, looking at them with a blank indifference entirely unsuited to the moment. His unblinking eyes seemed to encompass the whole dark scene without comprehension, as if he were unable, or disinclined, to distinguish living man from inanimate stone and snow.

"You're desecrating . . . " Munro began.

The grave robber took one long stride forward, his leading foot stamping down into the snow. His arm came up smooth and fast, sweeping the shovel through the night air as if it were weightless. Its metal blade hit Munro's head edge on, crunching in just above the crest of his cheekbone.

The terrible blow turned Munro about. He spun, and toppled, falling face first. He did not raise his arms to break the fall.

Everything after that happened quickly. Munro's attacker made for the wall. Quire dropped the lantern and went to his knees beside Munro. The fallen man's son slumped down as well, taking his father's hand in his own.

"Father, Father," he said, over and over again.

Quire tried gently to turn Munro on to his back. He knew, at once. He could tell, in the leaden weight of the shoulder at which he tugged; the utter motionless of the form. The side of Munro's face was smashed in, bone visible in the crevice the shovel had opened up. His left eye was displaced. Shallow, flighty breaths rushed in and out of him, but Quire knew they would soon cease. It would be only minutes. The man was dead; his body just had not yet conceded the fact.

Quire looked over his shoulder. The second grave robber – the murderer – was atop the wall, swinging his lagging leg over. Not hurrying, not looking back. The bloodied shovel scraped against the stone.

"Father," Duncan Munro whimpered.

"Stay with him," Quire said. "Give me the gun."

He made that last demand with reluctance – loading the thing had been reminder enough for one night of times past – but he was not about to test his skill with the baton against a shovel. The young man did not hear him. He was entirely possessed by the awful sight of his father, whose last breaths were pluming out between already pale lips, frail nets of steam cast into the winter night.

Carefully, Quire reached for the Brown Bess, dropped and forgotten in the snow. His heart ached; he had some sense of the inexpressible, appalling holes being torn in the younger Duncan Munro at this moment.

The fallen lantern lay on its side, flame still fluttering, throwing unsteady sheets of illumination across the graves. Quire left it where it was. Duncan might need it, and Quire surely did not. It would rob him of his night eyes, and you could not shoot into darkness without eyes accustomed to it. He had learned that quickly enough in Spain.

The wall was a head higher than Quire. He threw himself at it, got both elbows hooked over, and dragged himself up.

Rough ground sloped away from the foot of the wall. Humps and hollows, their underlying nature disguised by the snow, made an undulating descent towards the banks of Duddingston Loch. Two figures were fleeing across that narrow expanse. The first was already disappearing into the dense, obscuring vegetation at the edge of the ice; the second, bigger, slower, shovel still held loosely in one hand, was closer.

A fatter, brighter moon would have helped a good deal, for the world was indistinct. Imprecise. All shapes and shadows and shades of grey. But Quire knew – everybody knew – that the Resurrection Men did not come on the nights of a full moon. They liked the dark. So be it.

He dropped down from the wall far more carefully than his surging anger would have wished. He did not want a turned or broken ankle ending his hunt before it was properly begun. The snow cushioned his landing, and he sprang forward. Down across the field he ran, leaping from high point to high point, snow making clouds about his pounding feet. He carried the musket in one hand, hip-high, barrel to the fore, pointing the way ahead.

The first of the grave robbers – Blegg, a silent voice insisted over and over again within him; Blegg – was out of sight, vanished into the willow trees and reed beds, swallowed up by the enveloping darkness. But the second, Quire knew he could catch. The man had a long stride, but he ran with a strange lack of urgency. He was only now crashing noisily through the tangled bushes that marked the transition from land to water. Land to ice.

The slope levelled out beneath Quire's feet. He found himself, surreally, running through a thick stand of tall reeds and bulrushes. Running on ice. He slowed, and that very caution, the change in his stride, sent his leading foot skidding out from under him. He fell heavily on his side, trapping the musket beneath his body and grinding the knuckles of the hand that held it into the ice. For one moment he was looking up through the forest of reeds, seeing them swaying above him, and beyond them the starry sky, black as ink.

Then he rolled on to his hands and knees, pushed himself up, and ran out on to the ice. A flat, open field of snow, stretching almost to the limits of his vision, though he knew that by day this did not seem a great body of water. Ghostly, almost, in its featureless perfection. Not silent. Quire could hear three things: his own increasingly heavy, increasingly strained breathing; the hollow, crunching thud of his feet beating on the hard skin of the loch; and another set of feet, out of time with his own, up ahead.

He saw his quarry lope to a gradual halt, and turn about and stand there, almost at the very centre of the loch. The grave robber waited. Quire's blood was running hot and hard, but not sufficiently so as to render him witless. He slowed too, and approached the man at a slow walk, hefting the Bess in two hands now. Hoping that it would still discharge, if called upon; it had been so long since he had had to think of such things that he had failed to check it after climbing over the wall, or falling on the ice. Perhaps his blood was indeed running too hot for his own good.

"Put that shovel down, would you?" he called as he closed to within twenty paces.

He was startled by how loud and clear his voice sounded on the still, frigid air with the ice to set it ringing out in all directions. He stopped, and stood with his finger resting lightly on the trigger.

The man to whom he had spoken gave no response. Gave no sign at all, in fact, that he had heard Quire, or noticed his approach. Quire frowned. It was difficult to be certain, for he could see not much more of the man than his outline, but he did not seem to be breathing hard, as his exertions should surely have required.

"If you make me ask again, I'll not be so polite," Quire said.

The man came forward without haste; one, two long strides closing almost half the gap to Quire.

"For God's sake, man," Quire shouted, alarmed by the sudden arrival of a moment from which there would likely be no good outcome.

He hesitated, just for the space of one breath, hampered by an acquired restraint that never would have troubled him in his younger days. He had unlearned just enough to make him pause, make him think where once there would have been no thought.

He set the Brown Bess to his shoulder, shouting as he did so: "Stop."

The man was raising the shovel. Quire sighted along the barrel, staring into the black mass of the man's chest, worrying whether he could trust his left arm to hold the gun steady. Another half a second of doubt, washed away by one thought: he's already killed one man tonight. He squeezed the trigger.

The rasping click of the hammer falling, the flint sparking. A flaring, blinding light in his right eye. Smoke puffing upwards. The musket kicking his shoulder, sending out a lance of flame and more white smoke from its mouth. The crash of the shot, loud as a cannon out here on the ice, echoing from the trees around the loch and from the great night-clad mass of Arthur's Seat.

Quire blinked, chasing the dancing lights out of his eye, squinting through the drifting smoke. It had been a good shot, undoubtedly; he had put the ball right into the man's chest. Probably killed him. He was therefore astonished to find the great dark figure bearing down on him at pace, the shovel lifted one-handed against the sky. That great spade was about as long as Quire's own arm, and looked to be solidly made; how this man was wielding it like a little axe for chopping kindling was beyond him. His bewilderment did not slow him down.

Ears still ringing with the sound of the shot, he slithered to one side, finding the ice so treacherous that he had to go down on his haunches and up again to keep his balance. He lurched sideways, to avoid the blade of the shovel as it came scything down and bit into the ice, sending up a spray of chips.

Quire set both hands on the barrel of the gun. It was hot, but not unbearably so. He swung it without taking too much trouble about the aim. Just connect with the dark form assailing him; just knock the man down. He did land the blow, but it was inconclusive, the butt of the musket skidding off shoulder and forehead. The gun's weight carried Quire round, his heels sliding helplessly over the ice.

He fell backwards, banging his skull against the rock-hard skin of the loch. It saved him, for the shovel came lashing back on a flat arc that would have struck him had he not fallen. Quire rolled. Heard another blow crunching down where he had been. Heard too a splintering, creaking groan run through the ice upon which he lay; felt a tremor. Fear coursed through him, then. They were far from the shore. Far from the thickest, firmest stretches of ice where it was anchored to the land. Too late to discover caution, though.

"Bastard," he hissed, scrabbling, rolling.

A ferocious kick caught him in his stomach, just under the ribs, and lifted him, sent him sliding. It drove the wind from his lungs too, and his chest cramped down upon its own emptiness. The musket fell from his hands. He looked for it, and reached for it.

And he saw his assailant, poised for that one brief shard of time on one foot, go down through the ice. It gave with a brittle crackle of defeat, whole plates of it fracturing, and the big man slipped silently and instantly into the black water beneath. The ice beneath Quire's legs gave too, and his feet dipped into the chill loch. He gasped and clawed himself forwards. He could hear the whisper of cracks running beneath him. His hips broke more ice. His flooded boots were like chill fists about his ankles, pulling at him. He hauled and strained, panic putting a desperate strength into his raking fingers and his shoulders, and he dragged himself just far enough to be able to swing his legs up and out of the water.

Quire lay on his back, sucking in the frosted air, blowing out grateful fogs of breath. The stars above glimmered. Moment by moment his breathing slowed, and he mastered the shock of fear. He got on to his hands and knees, every movement tentative, measured, and reclaimed the gun.

He looked back into the dark maw opened up in the ice. Little tremulous waves in the water's surface caught tiny glints of moonlight. There were no hands reaching for the jagged edges of the hole. No sign at all of the grave robber.

Quire did not get to his feet. He did not trust the ice. Instead he crawled like a child, testing each placement of hand and knee before allowing his weight to fall through the limb, dragging the musket along as he went. His feet were numb and heavy.

Only when he had put a slow twenty yards between him and the broken ice did he rise cautiously, holding the Brown Bess out horizontally as he did so in the hope it might wedge itself across any gap should the ice break. He was starting to shiver.

He stood and looked out over the dark plain of the loch. All was still and quiet, as if nothing had happened, as if there were only the ice and the water beneath it and the world was just as it had always been. Quire blew into his left hand, the hot breath stinging his gelid skin.

Then there was a crunching thud from far across the loch. Quire squinted into the night, and saw nothing. It came again, a strangely muffled, dull sound. Like someone beating at a distant door. At the dimmest, furthest extent of his vision, he saw a patch of ice burst up, close to the southern shore. Numb – his body from the cold, his mind from disbelief – he watched the surface of the loch break apart from beneath and a dark form rise from it and force its way towards the land. He could hear quite clearly the ice splintering and shattering as the figure made its lurching retreat into the darkness.

After a moment or two the sound died away, and Quire could see nothing more. He stared out into the night for a little while longer, then turned back towards Duddingston village and began to walk, shaking.

VIII

Calder's

"Of course I'm blamed for it. I was there."

Quire was bent over his tankard, clutching it with both hands, elbows resting on the table. He peered down into the brown, foamy liquid as if hoping the mere sight of it might ease his troubles. But he knew that only the drinking of it would do that, and only for a few hours. Much as he craved that stultifying release, he had learned – belatedly, but better so than never – how illusory such respite was.

Wilson Dunbar had already drunk enough to liven up his opinions of anyone's troubles.

"Well maybe if there'd been more than just you," Quire's stocky companion exclaimed, "if they'd listened to you in the first place, it'd all have fallen out differently. Maybe the man'd still be sucking air if . . . ach, but it's never the officers pay the price, is it?"

"I'm an officer now," Quire muttered. "Sergeant, anyway."

"Aye, true enough. The damnedest thing, for those of us as've known you a while, but not to my point. It's a matter of blame: those it sticks to, those it don't. Your Lieutenant Baird –

he's one it don't. Me and you, we're ones it does. Nothing fair about it."

"It's fair," grunted Quire. "The man was happy in his beer until I dragged him out of the Sheep Heid. To get his own head stoved in. First time I've seen a man killed like that, in front of me, since . . . since a long time."

Dunbar snorted. He had always been a disputatious sort, even when in uniform. Long retirement from the soldier's life had not changed that, and nothing brought it more nimbly to the surface than drink. Not that it needed bringing far.

"You know fine death doesn't need your help or anyone else's when it's set its eye on someone," Dunbar said, flourishing his own near-empty tankard. "Comes when it likes."

"Maybe it does. That bastard on the ice thought to visit it upon me, as well, and that makes it personal to my way of thinking. I'll have him. I'll have all of them."

Calder's tavern was crowded, as it most often was of an evening. It did not take many bodies to make it so, for it had a low ceiling of plaster and beams, and a long-striding man might spring across its breadth in a half-dozen paces. Even so, it packed in a rare variety of customer. Quire might be the only policeman there – and that was a part of its appeal to him – but there were soldiers and brewers, glass-blowers and grocers, clerks and lamp-lighters. Sometimes footmen and stable hands from the nearby palace itself, though they kept to themselves as often as not, per-haps fearful of leaking secrets the Keeper of Holyroodhouse would rather stayed behind its grand walls.

Tonight, the mood – save in the corner Quire had made his own – was boisterous. A soldier was rattling out a hectic beat on a table with drumsticks. A little group of women who sold can-dles on the Canongate were engaged in good-natured argument over who had done the most business, and should therefore be buying the drinks. A solitary old man was complaining to no one but himself about the bad tobacco that would not hold a light in his pipe.

"And those fine gents buying the dead off the bastard body snatchers," Dunbar cried. "There's more could shoulder a bit of that blame you're cuddling. How many times is it the corpse of a rich man that ends on the cutting slab, eh? If it's a matter of such importance, did you ever see one o' them teachers themselves give over their carcass to the knife once they were dead and gone? Or their dead father or mother or brother? You did not. Explain me that.

"No, don't waste your time, I'll do it for you: it's the poor and the nameless get opened up for those precious little students to leer at, just like it's the poor and the nameless get to bleed when there's a battle to be fought. The French had it right, for a while at least: give us nameless folk a few guillotines and a wee revolution, see what a difference that'd make. Let others do the bleeding for a bit."

None of which Quire would dispute, but tonight he could not share in Dunbar's fervour. He watched Mrs Calder pushing her way through the throng of customers. She was not only proprietor of his preferred drinking den, but his landlady, and a solicitous one at that. She and her serving girls saw to the cleaning of his rooms a few floors above, the washing of his clothes, and now and again to his feeding. He had earned her kind regard, along with a handsome reduction in his rent, some time ago, when he dissuaded – forcefully – some disreputable fellows from taking her husband's debts out of his hide. Mr Calder had been carried off by a fever not long after, but his widow's affection for Quire persisted, undimmed.

"You never bled yourself, as I recall," Quire muttered to Dunbar. "Impervious Dunbar, come through all the wars with nary a scratch."

"Thank Christ. Though I doubt he was watching."

"I shot the man who killed him," mused Quire. "Put a ball in his chest from no more than twenty paces." He tapped hard at his own sternum for emphasis. "Didn't much bother him. How does that happen? When did you ever see a man take a shot from a Bess in the chest and not blink at it?"

"Well, not ever," conceded Dunbar. "But I've seen men lose their arm to a cannon shot and not know it was gone till I told them. And there was that Spaniard you gutted at Talavera . . . "

Quire winced.

"Aye, but that was then. It's a different life I'm supposed to be living now. I'm a different man."

"Trying to be a different man, maybe, but you've always had a rare talent for the violence, and it a rare longing for you. The two of you've never been long parted."

Quire cracked his mug down on the table, splashing a little of the beer out over the rim. He licked it from the back of his hand as he glared at Dunbar.

"Do you not think a friend might try to offer some comfort?" he growled. "And if you say that's what you're doing, I'll say you don't know comfort from your arse."

"Truth's a better remedy for any ill than comfort," Dunbar said with a flutter of pomposity.

"That's a whole stream of piss, wherever you heard it."

"Aye, I suppose it is right enough. But this different man you're trying to be still keeps guns and a sword under his bed, doesn't he? You've no more left the past than it's left you."

"Are you saying you've no loot from Spain hidden away somewhere? They're worth a fair few shillings, those guns. And that sword's a good one. Might need the money one day."

"Aye, right. Listen, a man needs ballast in his life, Adam, if he's to hold a true course. Not trophies from old battles; not beer even, though it pains me to say it. Ballast. Bit of weight in the hold to keep from turning over, and that you'll only get from others, not yourself. Family, friends, children. God knows, there's nothing like children when it comes to ballast, take it from me. Children and a wife."

"Christ, Dunbar," Quire muttered.

"Aye," Dunbar said, suddenly quiet. Suddenly knowing he had strayed into territory where truth walked hand in hand with hurt. "Aye, well."

They lapsed into silence, each communing with his own thoughts. Quire's spiralled in tight, beer-guided circles, seeming to be revelatory from moment to moment, yet somehow yielding nothing by way of lasting insight or conclusion.

At length, Dunbar pushed back his chair and took hold of Quire's mug as well as his own. Quire had not emptied it, but he raised no protest.

"I'll buy you some more comfort, then," Dunbar said. "That I can do."

He sank into the crowd, and Quire was left to ponder the mysteries of the tabletop. And to pick away at the knot of his problems. Baird had kept him well away from the aftermath of the events at Duddingston. Well away, and well aware of where Baird thought responsibility for the disaster lay. Quire could have done with the protective arm of James Robinson about his shoulders, but the superintendent was still sick, confined to his quarters atop the police house with none but wife and the gout for company.

Quire had told them to go after the gravedigger – Davey Muir, it turned out his name was – but the youth was, as yet, nowhere to be found. He had told them Blegg's name, too, and where to find him, but that had proved equally fruitless. The men dispatched to Melville Street had been sent on their way in no

uncertain terms by John Ruthven, who swore upon God's judgement that he could vouch for Blegg's whereabouts on the night in
question. And a man such as Ruthven was not to be gainsaid by
a mere sergeant of police, not without the weight of some evidence or incontrovertible testimony behind him; such testimony
could only come from Davey Muir, in all likelihood, and Quire
doubted the boy would be seen in these parts again.

But Quire did not feel in need of more evidence, or testimony,
to render his own judgement. He had no name for the ponder-
ous hulk of a man he had shot, nor an explanation for the failure
of musket ball and icy loch alike to kill him; but he was as sure
as he could be, allowing for the darkness of the night and the
rapidity of events, that it had been Blegg disappearing over the
kirkyard wall in Duddingston, and away into the night. If he was
right in that, Ruthven had lied. And that made him, at the very
least, accomplice to grave robbing and murder.

"I saw Catherine Heron in the street the other day," Dunbar
said, setting a pair of brimming tankards down on the table.

"Did you?"

Quire was taken aback by the unexpected turn in the conversation.

"She's a good lass, for what she is," Dunbar observed as he sat
himself down.

"She is," Quire agreed. "Have you a point beyond the flattery
of someone who's not here to listen?"

"Ballast, that's my point. For a while, I thought the two of you
might be going to set each other on an even keel."

"And I thought you'd decided to keep quiet on the subject of
ballast for tonight. You know fine well why that broke off. I'd not
have my work now if I'd kept on down that path."

Dunbar shrugged, and made a show of looking around the
smoky tavern.

"Just a thought," he said lightly. "Never you mind it. How about this, then: I'll educate you in the fine art of making kites. I've been fashioning a pair for my boys, and you'd not credit the time it takes to do the thing right."

Quire listened patiently to Dunbar's disquisition on the subject. He noted – not for the first time – the miraculous transformation that marriage and fatherhood and the passage of years had worked upon his friend, turning as capable and willing a soldier as Quire had ever known into a model of domestic affection. For all his truculent instincts, Dunbar carried within him a kernel of peace that Quire could only envy. He had nothing in his own life to which he could hold quite so firm, save perhaps his work, and his doing of it.

The night subsided into gentle sloth as Dunbar's company worked its gradual charm. Inconsequential talk and the steady flow of beer put just enough of a distance between Quire and his worries to soften them, and blur their outline.

The two men were the last to depart from the tavern. Mrs Calder permitted Quire a latitude few other of her customers could hope for, so they finished their last tankards at leisurely pace, with empty tables about them. In the close outside, the two of them paused, looking up at the cloud-flattened sky.

"I could see you home, if you like," Quire said, the words rumpled by drink.

"You're hardly fit to find your own home, for all that it's just up the stair," Dunbar snorted.

"Fair enough."

"Get yourself some sleep, that's my advice."

Quire swayed only a little as he climbed the narrow stair into the body of the tenement. He steadied himself with a hand against the wall. The darkness was absolute, and the steps uneven, but he needed no light for such a familiar journey.

The nebulous contentment that had settled over him did not long outlast his arrival at the door to his rooms. It took him a puzzled moment or two to realise that something was amiss. The door stood fractionally ajar, and as he fumbled at the handle, his fingers encountered splintered wood. It had been broken in.

That realisation sharpened his senses and cleared his mind. He reached instinctively for his baton, but he had left it inside. He pushed the door gingerly, and it scraped open.

He waited on the threshold, squinting into the gloomy apartment, straining to catch the slightest sound. There was none. That someone had been there, though, was undoubted. Quire had few possessions, but they still made an impressive mess, strewn about in disorder as they were now. He advanced cautiously, stepping around and over the clothes scattered across the floor, the shards of broken wash bowl and jug, the toppled chair.

He went to the bed, and knelt beside it. He reached underneath and felt about with splayed fingers. They quickly found what he sought: a hard, smooth box. He withdrew it, set it on the bedding and lifted the heavy lid. Within, two fine pistols were safely nestled in their proper place. He had taken them from the baggage of a French captain, after he had killed the man at a farm in the wilds of Spain. Killed him while he slept, in fact, for it had been that kind of war and Quire had fought it as seemed necessary at the time.

Satisfied, he gently closed the box and returned it to its hiding place. A moment or two more of searching under the bed found the only other item of even modest value he owned. It was a sabre of the type carried by thousands of French soldiers in the late wars – a *briquet* – and that, Quire had acquired from an anonymous dead musketman on ... he no longer even remembered which battlefield.

Puzzled, he rose to his feet and surveyed the shambles. Thieves who left behind the only things that might have repaid their efforts were not a species he had encountered before. It did not take him long to restore at least a semblance of order, and in doing so he discovered his one loss. A shirt was gone. Only that. A humble, old shirt. All else was accounted for.

It was only at the very end, as he dragged a chair across the room, meaning to wedge it against the door to discourage – or at least give him some warning of – any returning visitors, that he noticed the strangest thing of all. Hanging on the inner face of the door was a crudely fashioned star of twigs. They were bound together with thin strips of bark and decorated, at each point of the star, with black feathers.

He stared at that mysterious token with sudden and deep unease. A dark substance encrusted some of the twigs, and though he could not be certain, he guessed that it was blood. Seized by an urgency he could not entirely explain, he tore the star down. As soon as his fingers touched it, a shiver ran through him, rushing up his arms, over his shoulders and crackling down his spine. He made to crush the foul thing in his hands. Some instinct restrained him, and he set it on the table, but turned away quickly and did not look at it again.

Drink usually made Quire sleep deep and sound, but his slumber that night was neither.

Davey Muir had been an occasional digger of graves at Duddingston Kirk for only a few months. It was a way to get a little coin over the winter, just like the digging of ditches and the dry-stone walling he did on the Marquis of Abercorn's estate east of the village when the work was there to be had. In summer and autumn he worked the harvests on the farms further south. Come spring he would be sowing and maybe helping with the lambing. He turned his hand to whatever there was that would keep him from the poorhouse.

Gravedigging was far from the worst of it – that would be the walling, he reckoned, since he was clumsy and always ended up with bruised, sometimes bloodied, hands – and it paid better than most. He was too young and carefree to concern himself with the gloomy nature of the task: the dead needed burying, to his way of thinking, and it never had bothered him much to be around corpses. Spend any time around farms and you saw plenty of dead animals. Dead people troubled him little more than those.

Now, though, everything had gone very wrong. Now, he was thinking that taking the job at the kirk had been the most foolish thing he had done in all his short life. He had never once regretted leaving his turbulent family behind in Prestonpans, out along the east coast, when he was fifteen, but this might be the time to head back that way, and try to make amends with his brute of a father and slattern of a mother. Just to get a safe roof over his head for a while, in a place where no one would know where he had been, or what he had done.

It had seemed so easy. A man offering better than a month's wage just for a few words. News of a burial, that was all. A day or two's notice of any man headed for a grave without broken bones or the taint of sickness upon his corpse. Davey knew what that was about, of course. Everyone knew how the Resurrection Men went about their work. But what harm was there in it? The boy was dead and gone, with no need for what he'd left behind. And none to know, if the grave robbers did their work right: close up the coffin and re-lay the sod once they had lifted out the body. Leave it all neat and tidy.

But there was nothing neat or tidy about the business. Duncan Munro's head was broken in. Davey had known the man a little;

never had anything but kind words from him. Even so, it was not guilt so much as fear of consequence that grievously afflicted him now. Murder was a different thing to the mere theft of the dead. A thing to put a rare vigour into the police, and though they had not caught up with Davey yet, he knew they likely would. He had spent two days and the night between without a roof over his head, mostly up on Arthur's Seat, shivering, bemoaning his misfortune; sheltering beneath a leaning crag from the drizzle floating in on the westerly breeze, watching the thin covering of snow melting away. He could bear it no longer. He had seen, from his elevated vantage point, the police who had been going from door to door in Duddingston village depart as dusk fell, trudging off back towards the city. So now, in the misty darkness, he crept back down to his lodgings.

He had a single room, cramped and a touch damp, attached as something of an afterthought to a short row of cottages. He lingered behind a concealing hedgerow for a minute or two – which was all his stunted patience and miserable condition would allow him – to make sure there was no one waiting for him. All was quiet. The thin mist and the encroaching twilight seemed to offer shelter enough for what he needed: just time to get stouter footwear, a cape, a few of those apples he'd lifted from the provisioner's shop near the kirk. It was a long walk to Prestonpans.

Davey slipped inside as quickly as he could, lifting the rusty latch on the door with unaccustomed care, lest its creaking should betray his presence. Once within, he did not light a candle, but relied upon memory and the faint, faint light from the window to find his way about. The oiled cape first, pulled out from under his low bed; apples off the shelf and into a small sack; a candle or two, on impulse, though how he might light them he was not sure.

In reaching for those, his fingers encountered something unexpected, lying atop the box in which he kept the candles. Something small and strangely shaped. He took it up, and frowned at it, squinting. He could barely make out anything of it, but it seemed to be a figure of some sort; a little carved man, just two or three inches long. Davey shook his head in puzzled alarm and turned towards the window, the better to make it out.

"I'm grateful to you for taking it into your hand of your own free will."

Davey yelped, dropped figurine and sack and cape alike, and stumbled back a couple of paces until his legs jarred up against the edge of a table.

The door was open, and standing there, framed against the very last watery light of the day, was a man Davey recognised with a lurching, dizzying dismay. It was not the face that told him who had come for him, but the horribly soft black gloves the man was already pulling from his lean hands.

"That will help a little, later," Blegg said, stepping inside.

He used his heel to push the door closed behind him, never taking his eyes from Davey. The youth folded his arms across his chest, clutching his shoulders as if in pathetic defence of his vitals.

"Good Christ, you frightened me," he gasped.

"Hush now. You'd not want the good folk of Duddingston hearing that you're back amongst them, would you?"

"No, no. I'm away, this very night."

"That you are. That you are, Davey Muir."

IX

The Holy Land

Superintendent James Robinson was propped up in a chair with a high, curved back of solid oak. Cushions and pillows were packed in behind him, and under his arms. He looked a touch wan, a touch red around the eyes, and as tired as Quire had seen him in a long time. His wife was an intermittent, solicitous presence, drifting in and out of the room and each time casting a surreptitious glance of concern her husband's way. Quire suspected that she did not entirely approve of his presence in their apartment atop the police house, but it had been Robinson who had asked to see him.

"The gout still afflicting you?" Quire asked.

"That, and a fair herd of other things," Robinson replied. "Most of them nothing to do with the failings of this carcass of mine. The board find some new petty fault to charge me with every week, it seems. The Provost has never much liked me, truth be told, nor I him. He relishes every chance to prick me. Including that offered by dead kirk elders in Duddingston. And now there's this complaint."

"Complaint?" said Quire, and then, realisation dawning: "Against me?"

Robinson gave a curt nod of his head.

"It's a serious charge. Not one I believe a word of, and I've made that clear, but it'll take a bit of tidying away. A Mr John Ruthven has reported that you tried to sell back to him some stolen property of his that you recovered. A silver box. Says when he refused to pay, you let him have it only after lengthy dispute, and that you've now accused his man of involvement in body snatching by way of revenge."

Quire snorted in contemptuous disbelief.

"That's a lie."

"Of course it is. You've your fair share of faults, Quire, but stupidity and venality are not amongst them. But still: when you were drinking and keeping the wrong kind of company, those charges I could quiet easy enough; this is a different sort of thing."

Quire sprang to his feet and began to pace up and down on the thick rug. These rooms were in sharp contrast to the police house at the summit of which they perched. All carpets and cushions and homely understatement. Soft. The place felt comfortably inhabited, in a way no abode of Quire's had ever achieved. It was all entirely out of tune with the mood now taking hold of him.

"That bloody bastard," he growled.

"Sit down, man," Robinson muttered with a placatory wave of his hand. "It'll go no further, if I have my way. But you need to keep your wits about you. Ruthven's not the kind of man you're used to dealing with. I gather he went straight to the Sheriff Depute with this, favoured him with a lengthy discourse on the shortcomings of the city police. The Sheriff was not best pleased.

"It's a cosy little fellowship that occupies the heights of our city's society. They are a collegiate body of men, few of them inclined to think themselves fit subjects for police enquiry. I'm not sure you have ever entirely understood that, but you would do well to give it some thought. Goad one, and that one can make sure plenty of others feel it."

"I've done nothing but what seemed right," Quire said, still standing.

"I know that. And I know you: you've a rare affection for justice – or what you decide is justice, at least – and the stubbornness of an ill-tempered mule. Laudable attributes in many ways, and neither of them as common beneath this roof as they should be; which might be, in part, why you've not made yourself quite as many friends and allies here as you could do with now. But if you mean to hold your course on this, you will need to learn discretion."

"Will you take some tea?" the superintendent's wife asked from the doorway. "There's no better poultice for the nerves."

It was a genteel but pointed suggestion. Quire understood her desire to swaddle her recuperating husband in calm. He shook his head, and forced himself to fold his tense limbs down into a chair.

"No, thank you. No."

She nodded and retired once more.

"I'm curious, though." Robinson sniffed, pulling a blanket from the arm of his chair and settling it across his knees. "You must have shaken something loose, to drive Ruthven into making false accusations. This started with that man dead in the Cowgate, did it?"

"Edward Carlyle. Yes. He was in Ruthven's employ, so there's been one of his men torn to pieces in the Old Town, and another digging up graves in Duddingston. Whatever's happening, Ruthven's at the heart of it."

"You're sure of that, are you? That it was this fellow Blegg in the graveyard?"

"As sure as I can be. It was dark, and I only had a glimpse of him. It's nothing I can prove, though."

Robinson sniffed again.

"Makes no sense. There's not enough coin in the corpse trade to interest a man like Ruthven. Still, he'd hardly be trying to pull you down if there was nothing to it."

"I've had someone break into my home, too," Quire muttered bitterly. "Might not be part of it, but it was like no housebreaking I've seen. Nothing taken but a shirt."

That put a frown on Robinson's brow. He leaned forward a little.

"You be careful, Adam. Could be that you've made yourself some bad enemies here. They've already killed at least one man, and that's not the sort of folk you want knowing where you live."

"I've had the same thought. Bad enough someone trying to kill me out on the ice at Duddingston, without them digging around in my home. And spreading lies about my conduct. I don't take well to being the hunted."

"Yet that's what you are, it would seem."

"If so, they've made themselves a worse enemy in me than they could ever be, and I know fine where Ruthven lives. If he wants to make it a personal matter between him and me, that's a game I can play."

"Steady, steady," Robinson muttered. "This isn't some street brawl or army grudge you're mixed up in now. Needs a bit of discretion, as I said. I recommend the cultivation of it to you, one old soldier to another. You need to keep yourself clean and quiet for a bit, or the Police Board'll have you, no matter what I might say."

Quire ground his fingers into his temples, staring blankly into the middle distance. There was a rare ire burning in him, unlike anything he had felt for years. It had taken him a long time to get his life on to some sort of steady path, and his eyes clear enough to see it. He despised Ruthven for threatening that, and for making him angry enough that he might even threaten it himself.

"What do you mean to do?" Robinson asked quietly.

"Baird wants me to leave the Duddingston thing to others."

"That's good sense, for now at least. I don't suppose he's saying it for your good, but it'll do you no harm to keep out of sight on that matter."

"Ruthven told me he'd had some falling-out with the Society of Antiquaries. Might be they know something of his habits. And there's still Edward Carlyle. I'm not ready to believe there's nothing more to that."

"Dogs, I hear."

Quire gave an unguarded, derisive snort.

"When did dogs ever kill folk in the Old Town? The man breaks with Ruthven and he's dead inside a few weeks. It's not coincidence that stinks of. I've got the name of the woman he was passing time with before he died. She might be worth the talking to." He glanced apologetically at the superintendent. "I'll need to pay a visit to the Holy Land."

Robinson rolled his eyes.

"Did I not just explain the merits of discretion to you, Quire? Of keeping yourself clean? You and the Holy Land don't mix well. Was almost losing your job once before not enough for you?"

"I'm not about to start digging myself back into old holes," Quire said quickly, anxious to reassure his patron. "I'll be quiet about it. Quiet's often better in the Holy Land, anyway."

"Quiet's always better, Adam," Robinson grunted. "I'm glad you know as much, though the knowing and the doing seem the most distant of cousins in your case."

The Holy Land stood shoulder to shoulder with the Happy Land and the Just Land in Leith Wynd, a narrow roadway running

north from the High Street. Of the three ill-reputed tenements –
each of them named with the dour irony that was the natural
tenor of the city's self-regard – it was the Holy Land that bore the
foulest stains upon its character. Before ascending the common
stair, Quire spared a moment to check that his baton still hung
securely from his belt.

He climbed the spiral stairway, every step of which was bowed
by the wear of decades. Even now, with the daylight seeping in
from a few infrequent windows, he had to watch his footing. To
describe the little square openings as windows was to glorify their
ruined state, in truth. The glass was long gone, as were the
wooden frames, all stripped out for sale or use elsewhere. Now
they were nothing more than holes in the skin of the building, by
which weather and a miserly ration of light were given admittance.

The first landing was deserted, which did not surprise Quire.
The rest of the city might be about the day's labours, but those
who called the Holy Land home kept a different routine. Most of
them would not be found out and about before midday; some
were owlish creatures, rarely stirring from their lairs until the day
neared its end.

From above, drifting down the gloomy stairwell, came the faint
and indistinct sound of someone singing. A woman, with a sweet
voice. She was drunk, of course, but still: sweet. Quire paused,
just for a moment, and listened. The passing thought that here
was some intoxicated, and apparently quite happy, siren calling
him on to whatever rocks lay above put a wry smile on his face.
Then the song collapsed into fading coughs, and the stair was
silent again.

He ascended, and found two figures waiting in the shadows of
the next landing. They stirred themselves and straightened as he
arrived, and held their arms loose and ready. Though it was

difficult to be certain in the muddy light, Quire did not think he knew either of them by sight or name. Their demeanour, however, told him all he needed to know.

"I'm not after any trouble," he said promptly. "Just visiting a friend."

"Is that so?" one of the men – the nearer of the two – grunted. He had big hands, and an accent fresh from the heather. Men from the north, then. A bit desperate, like as not, and thinking the sort of customers frequenting the Holy Land stair of a morning would be easy pickings.

"The thing is this," Quire smiled, "it's police business I'm on, and you, I would guess, might be new in the town. Now maybe you don't know that the Widow won't take kindly to strangers disturbing her house, and you certainly don't know that I'm having the sort of day as'd put a saint in a foul temper, so let's just say you go along, and we'll not be troubling one another further."

It was never likely to work, not with men who had encountered neither him nor his reputation before, so Quire was unsurprised when the man moved. Those big hands came up, and reached. It was slow and obvious by the measures Quire put on such things. He kicked the man, hard, in the crotch and, as he squealed and folded down, broke his nose with a rising knee.

"Don't be stupid," Quire told the second of them, and that was all it took to put an end to it.

"Pick him up and get him downstairs. I don't suppose you've the sense for it, but I'll tell you anyway: there's not much room in this town for newcomers to squeeze themselves in to the sort of business you've chosen. Find yourselves a less perilous occupation."

The fallen man spluttered bloodily and moaned as his comrade hauled him to his feet and helped him hobble off down the stairs. Quire stood patiently listening to their unsteady descent, just to be sure that there would be no sudden resurgence of courage or vigour. He felt sorry for them: Highland men, probably evicted from their lands, destitute, short on options. He, or his colleagues in the police house, would likely be coming across them again.

Quire turned to the nearest door. It was battered and split, clinging to its hinges with no more firm a grip than a swaying drunkard in the street might apply to some convenient railings. Disrepair was the permanent condition of most doors in the Holy Land; there was no point in mending that which the police, or the inhabitants themselves, would soon unmend. He pushed gently, advanced across the threshold and was greeted by smiles.

Emma Slight was bent over a low table, pouring whisky from an unmarked bottle into a china teacup. She was wearing only a loose, long nightgown of thin white material that did nothing to hide the weight and contour of her breasts. Catherine Heron – who was a great deal better known to Quire than was Emma – sat upright on a rickety bed, light from the narrow window above giving her limp auburn hair a hint of life. She was clearly naked, though she concealed that nakedness beneath blankets that she had drawn up almost to her chin. Her presence, entirely unexpected, discomfited Quire, and he felt a hot blush rising in his cheeks.

Cath was the younger of the two women, her features not yet dulled or slackened by the years of hard living that had taken their toll on Emma. But she followed the same path, towards the same end: the disordered mounding of the bedclothes did little to mask the presence of another in her bed.

"Sounded like you had a wee bit trouble on the stair," Emma said placidly.

"Nothing to worry about," Quire said.

It was a struggle to shake off the unsettling effect that the discovery of Cath here had had upon him. And to dispel the confusing, confused tremble of past and present desire it engendered.

"Will you take the morning dram with us, Sergeant?" Emma asked, extending the teacup, a healthy measure of amber liquid within it. The cup was finely painted with flowers and briars. It was chipped and cracked, but once no doubt graced the table of a grander house than this, before being liberated by some light-fingered visitor.

"No, thank you," Quire said. "I'll take a look at whatever that is Cath's got hiding under her bedclothes, though."

"Ach," said Catherine with a pained expression, "you've not forgotten what it is I've got down there, surely?"

"Hush. I've no time for games, Cath. I'd not thought to find you here this morning – it's Emma I was after a word with – and though I'm not minding you listening in, your shy friend there's not welcome."

"No games?" Catherine gave a disappointed pout. She was allowing the blankets to slip a little lower, revealing more pale skin. "Well, you're not the man you used to be. Anyway, my friend's only a wee bairn. He'd be of no interest to you."

"Show yourself, man," Quire snapped.

A crestfallen face shrugged its way out from beneath the bedding. Smooth and fair skin, tousled hair youthfully thick. Eyes bright with trepidation.

Quire arched his eyebrows.

"Let me guess. One of our university's finest?"

The young man bit his lip dumbly, but Quire did not need to have his question answered to know the truth of it. He growled in irritation. The student sat up straight beside Catherine, averting his eyes, distractedly toying with a little amber bead strung on a thong about his neck.

"I see Cath's gulled you into buying one of the Widow's

charms," said Quire. "Comforting, to know the nation's future rests in the hands of those who find their pleasures in the Holy Land, and think some magic trinket'll keep them safe from the consequences."

He took some unworthy satisfaction from the embarrassment – perhaps even shame – that put a rosy tint in the man's cheeks. The feeling did not linger, though. He was hardly entitled to much in the way of self-righteousness on the subject of Catherine Heron's company.

"Speaking of the Widow, does she ken you're here?" Emma asked pleasantly. "She does like to know what's happening before it happens."

"You can have the pleasure of telling her yourself, Emma, after I'm done with you. It's only a few questions I've got in mind."

"Can't help you, Mr Quire," the older woman said as she lifted the cup to her cracked lips.

"You might at least let me ask before brushing me away," Quire said, and returned his attention to the bewildered youth in Catherine's bed. "Are you a student of the sciences, or of medicine perhaps?"

He received a hesitant, faintly alarmed nod of the head in response.

"You should know better than to think that bead's got the magic to keep you free of the pox, then."

"He's safe enough with me," Cath Heron muttered, affronted.

"Oh, I know that, Cath," Quire said quickly. "I didn't mean ..."

He took Cath's dark frown as a warning, and abandoned the topic.

"You get yourself off, back to your books or however it is you're supposed to be spending your time," he snapped at the student.

Quire, Cath and Emma watched in silence as the young man

hurriedly, clumsily dressed himself. Humiliation enough, perhaps, to keep him away from the Holy Land for a while.

Once he was gone, Quire turned back to Emma, who had settled on to a chair and was sipping with incongruous delicacy from her cup of whisky.

"Edward Carlyle," Quire said.

Emma scratched the side of her nose and pretended intense interest in whatever residue her fingernail collected.

"I'm told he was keeping your company of late," Quire persisted. "Did you know he was dead?"

She did not trouble to conceal her surprise at that, but still said nothing. Cath was less circumspect.

"Oh, that's a shame. He seemed decent enough. Did he not say, though, that he feared for his life?"

Emma greeted the question with a scolding grimace of displeasure, but Cath was unperturbed, and shrugged her bare shoulders.

"Well, he did say it."

"You knew him as well?" Quire asked, his heart sinking.

Finding Cath here had been dismaying enough; if she became a more central part of all this, he would find himself having to navigate treacherous waters, both personally and professionally.

To his relief, she shook her head.

"Not in the way you're thinking." She said it with a hint of rebuke that Quire supposed he probably deserved, for he had indeed been reaching for the easy conclusion. "Just to speak to, when he was visiting. Once the drink was in him, he always ended up fretting about what might happen to him."

"All right, all right," Emma interrupted. "You'll only tell it wrong. Truth is, he talked all manner of silliness when he was in his cups, and I can't see you making any more sense of it than I did, Mr Quire."

"I've nothing more profitable to do with my time," Quire replied, to Emma's evident disappointment.

"It's your time to be wasting, I suppose," she sniffed. "He was always on about how he'd got himself tangled up with bad folk. Evil, he called them. Never said who or why, before you ask. But he was frightened, right enough. Frightened of them, frightened of what they were doing and where it would all end, with him along for the ride."

"Said it was the Devil's work," Cath observed from the bed.

"Maybe he did," Emma continued. "Didn't do much for his humour once he got out of it, though. Turned up here drunk as a lord, saying he was done with it all, never going back. You'd think that'd settle him some, but he was weeping like a bairn. Said they'd never let him go. He was scared as any man I've seen, right enough."

"He never gave away any names?" asked Quire.

The mention of Devil's work put him at once in mind of that strange symbol left hanging upon the door of his rooms by his uninvited visitor. The mere thought of it, and of the intrusion that it had accompanied, made him uneasy.

Emma shook her head.

"Never a name, not that I heard. Are you sure you'll not take a dram?"

She carefully refilled her own cup as she asked the question. The death of one of her customers was not a matter to disturb the rhythms of her day.

"Let me have some of that, would you?" Cath asked, and Emma brought another teacup down from the sagging shelf upon which it rested.

Quire watched the two women sharing their whisky out into fine china. A strange, distorted mimicry of refinement. A habit that put a shape into their day just as the civil, sober ritual of tea drinking did for the kind of people who must have first owned those cups. Quire found that a melancholy thought, but it was a tangled kind of melancholy, for not so very long ago it had been him sharing the whisky with Cath, just as he had shared her bed.

"Have you not got your own rooms any more then, Cath?" Quire asked quietly.

"Roof's leaking," she said with a faint smile. "Emma here had a bed to spare."

Quire nodded, and held her gaze for just a moment or two. Cath had been chief amongst those matters that had almost ended his career in the police before it was properly begun, for consorting with such as her carried the penalty of instant dismissal. Superintendent Robinson had saved him from that consequence, and Quire was glad of it, but had never freed himself of regret at the loss of her companionship. His affection for her – if that was all it could be called – had proved a stubborn thing. He had thought the passage of time might diminish it. Standing there, watching her, he learned anew just how resilient it was.

X

The Resurrection Men

"We're wasting our time," Quire observed.

Sergeant Jack Rutherford appeared entirely unperturbed by Quire's doubts. He appeared, in fact, in thoroughly equable mood.

"He'll turn up sooner or later. I've got it on good authority."

"I mean we're wasting our time chasing the man in the first place."

"The city fathers put coin in my pocket every week for the very purpose of buying my time," Rutherford said, peering into the bowl of his little pipe. "I've sold the stuff already, so I'm not bothered how they decide I should occupy it. Pay's the same."

"I'd want paying better, myself, if I was selling my time just for the wasting. I'd rather be doing what needs doing."

"That's where you go wrong you see, Adam," Rutherford said with a wry smile. "The thing is to be doing what you're *told* to do, not what *needs* doing. That way lies a peaceful life, and a decent pension."

He tapped his pipe gently against the stonework of the bridge. Spent tobacco spilled out and fell in a scattering cloud about their feet. The two of them were leaning on the parapet of a low, single-span viaduct across the Leith Water. The river rushed along beneath them, in eager haste to reach the sea. Or in haste, perhaps, to escape the clutches of the mills and distilleries clustered along its banks, a great congregation of brick and stone behemoths gathered to drink deep of its sustaining flow. So close and steeply did some of the buildings press that they made a dark and sheer-sided ravine for the river.

From their vantage point midway across the bridge, Quire and Rutherford could see into the yard of one of the smaller distilleries, a rather gloomy little square bounded by featureless brick walls. There were any number of empty barrels stacked up down there, and now and again booted and aproned workmen emerged from the enormous doors – like those of a huge barn – that stood ajar, but in the main nothing was happening, as it had been for close to an hour.

"You're the one made the Resurrection Men so popular in the first place, so why you're complaining now, I don't know," Rutherford said. "We're not to let a single one of them rest easy till the Duddingston murderer's found, that's the word from on high."

"Aye, except I've already told them where to look. Merry Andrew's nothing to do with it. I was there, and it wasn't him waving a shovel around at Duddingston."

"The way I heard it, looking where you told them didn't get them anywhere. So every other body-snatching crew gets the benefit of our attention, and no doubt we'll be turning up stones and prodding the worms beneath until the end of our days. Or until someone more important than us loses interest."

"It wasn't normal, what happened that night. When did any body snatcher kill a man, before Duddingston? Half of them are students, for God's sake. They'd piss themselves at a harsh word."

"Maybe," Rutherford nodded, "but there's nothing soft about Andrew Merrilees and his lads. There're students and then there's them that make a business of the trade. That's two whole different kettles of fish, as you well know."

"Aye. I'm not saying he's not deserving of a bit of our attention. Just that he's not the man I'm after."

"The man we're all after, Quire. That'll be what you mean?"

"Aye. Aye."

"Nights are drawing out," Rutherford said companionably. "Merrilees and his like should've hung up the tools of their trade for the summer by now. Too much by way of light. Word is he's short of coin, though. Needing to do the work out of season."

Quire stared down at the racing current below. The Water of Leith was nowhere very deep, not until it got down almost to its mouth on the Firth of Forth, and he could see the rocks of its bed quite clearly. There were a few traces of green weed streaming out from them like storm-stretched pennants. A pair of ducks were paddling furiously, making no progress upriver but holding station against the current. There must be some reason, Quire assumed, for their determined exertions, but he could not divine it.

The futility of his own assignment gnawed away at him. It was punishment, of a sort. He knew that well enough. Lieutenant Baird meant to grind his nose into the fact that it was not for him to choose who was pursued.

It galled Quire all the more that he was standing here on a bridge no more than a few minutes' walk from Ruthven's house. The New Town had spread so far in recent years that its north-western boundaries ran right down to the Leith Water. The banks of the river itself, though, remained a noisy, cantankerous bastion of industry; the workers laboured there while the owners enjoyed their luxurious new accommodations within earshot and eyesight.

To think of Ruthven and Blegg somewhere up there, savour-
ing the comforts of their graceful home, left Quire thoroughly
sour. There was unfinished business between them. To judge by
the events at Duddingston, and what Emma Slight had told him
of Carlyle's last weeks, it might be brutal work.

"That's him there," Rutherford said in a calm and conversa-
tional tone. "Merry Andrew."

The two of them, in almost perfect synchrony, lifted their
elbows from the bridge's parapet and stood straight.

"Which one?" Quire asked.

"The one on the wagon. Walks like a puppet on sticks. You'll
see when he gets down."

The cart had turned into the yard from the lane that ran along
the landward side of the chain of warehouses and workshops. The
man sitting atop it, tugging at the reins of a big dray horse, was
tall and thin and angular. Like a scarecrow. He even had unruly
little clumps of hair sticking out from under his soft cloth hat, like
so much brown straw. And when he dismounted, and led the
horse over to a water trough, he did indeed walk like a puppet on
sticks. He was all stiffness and jerks, as if his limbs had a life of
their own.

"Huh," Quire grunted in amusement.

"Aye, he's a funny-looking fellow," Rutherford agreed, "but he's
a mean and vicious bastard too, so watch yourself."

"Shall we go down and introduce ourselves, then?"

"Give it a minute. We'll get two of them if we employ a wee bit
patience."

Quire suppressed his frustration. To be moving, in whatever
cause, would be better than all this waiting. But this was
Rutherford's hunt, not his.

"There you are," Rutherford murmured soon enough. "Spune."

A man in a tight leather cap, a much less remarkable figure

than Merry Andrew, had come out from the dark maw of the distillery. He had a close-cropped beard and a red sheen to his features.

"That's who Merry Andrew's come to fetch," Rutherford said. "Never lifts a spade or digs a grave without Spune on his right hand. Shall we meet them on their way out, then?"

Quire fell in behind as Rutherford led the way off the bridge. He spared a last glance towards the yard. Spune walked lazily up to Merrilees, and they exchanged some casual greeting in the manner of men long and well acquainted. A little of Quire's slumbering enthusiasm bestirred itself. It might not advance his own particular concerns, but there was no harm in giving some of Edinburgh's more notorious Resurrection Men a fright. And those engaged in the odious trade were a tight-knit community; it might just be that Merrilees would know something about Duddingston, if it could be prised out of him.

From the bridge, the narrow lane bent back sharply to parallel the Water of Leith's curving course, itself overshadowed by looming brick cathedrals of industry just as the river was. As it turned out, Merry Andrew and Spune had spent little time on pleasantries, for the big black horse pulled the cart out from the distillery gateway just as Quire and Rutherford drew near. The horse was a dull-looking beast, but Merry Andrew was a good deal more alert to his surroundings. He looked up and down the lane as they bumped out on to the cobbled roadway, and then glanced sharply back to stare directly at Sergeant Rutherford.

"He knows me!" Rutherford called to Quire, and broke into a run.

Quire sprinted forward himself, and was amazed and not a little annoyed to see Merrilees flailing away at the horse's rump, goading it into life. The animal, it transpired, had a better turn of pace than its appearance might have suggested, for it leaped away and swept the wagon off, thumping and banging over the uneven cobblestones.

There were plenty of folk in the lane – millworkers, barrow-men pushing along handcarts piled with bloated sacks and rolls of cloth – but the spectacle and cacophony of a big horse hauling a cart at such speed cleared a path quickly enough. People pressed themselves against the walls as the wagon thundered past with Quire and Rutherford in furious pursuit.

Merry Andrew was all elbows and wild gesture as he beat at the horse, twisting now and again to look back over his shoulder. He and Spune were bouncing violently on their seat, and Spune at least seemed less than happy with the situation, for he clung with both hands to the bench and hunched down.

The lane sloped gently up, and the river bent away in a sharp loop, a cluster of grim-looking manufactories crowding the tri-angle of land thus enclosed. There was another bridge up ahead, Quire knew, and beyond that only countryside and the long, straight road out to Queensferry on the distant shore of the Forth estuary. Whatever Rutherford's thoughts on the matter, he reck-oned he was not paid nearly enough to be chasing a cart on foot all the way out of the city, and he redoubled his efforts, racing over the cobblestones with a certain sense of exhilaration.

Jack Rutherford evidently shared the sentiment, for he put in a burst of speed and got himself up to the back end of the cart, seizing hold of the rocking frame.

"Merrilees, you daft beggar ... " Quire heard his fellow sergeant shouting, and then Rutherford fell and Quire was leaping over him.

He glanced back – Rutherford was sitting on his backside, rub-bing his arm but wearing a look that said that his pride had taken the worse injury – and then threw himself onward.

The bridge was up ahead, much higher and broader than the one

Quire and Rutherford had kept watch from. The cart was heaving up and down and from side to side as it approached. Coming to a quick calculation of where his best interest lay, Spune suddenly jumped from his seat and rolled inelegantly to a halt in a heap up against the low wall bounding the lane. Quire ran past him, interested only in the chief of this particular gang. If Baird would not let him pursue Ruthven and Blegg, and wanted him chasing Merry Andrew instead, that was what he would get, and let him try to complain about Quire's inability to take instruction then.

The clatter of the cart's wheels took on a deeper, heavier sound as it rattled out on to the bridge. The wind, much brisker up on this exposed viaduct, snapped the hat from Merry Andrew's head and sent it tumbling out over the parapet and spinning down towards the river far below.

It took Quire several paces to catch the wagon, and get a grip he could trust on its bucking bed. His weaker left arm ached at the exertion. Man and cart, the one clutching the other with fierce determination, flashed by a couple of washerwomen, who stopped and stared at the unlikely coupling.

Quire jumped up, and flung himself on to the back of the cart. It bounced and smacked him hard in the face and chest as he came down, which did nothing to improve his humour. He looked up from his prone position. Merry Andrew seemed oblivious to his arrival, and was lashing at the horse with ever more wild abandon. A long roll of white cloth, tied with coarse rope and containing something heavy to judge by the way it thumped up and down, lay close to Quire.

He got carefully on to one knee, swaying from side to side, and edged himself further up the cart's length, all the while clinging to the side.

"I think you're done now," he shouted to Merry Andrew.

Who looked round, at first startled and then fiercely resolved.

Twisting on his seat, he raised the switch with which he had been belabouring the horse.

"Don't be ..." Quire began, but was too busy ducking to finish the suggestion, as Merrilees tried to whip him about the head.

"Right," growled Quire, fumbling for his baton.

Something in his tone, rasping out over the cart's creaking protests, or perhaps the way the horse slowed now that it was no longer subjected to the whip's encouragement, drained the resistance out of Merrilees. He slumped slightly, in so far as anyone of his elongate construction could be said to slump, and lowered the switch. Horse and cart came to a groaning halt.

Quire stood up and surveyed their surroundings. Open fields on one side, the grounds of a small and austere orphans' hospital on the other. He looked back, over the narrow valley of the Leith Water, and could see clear across the receding terraces of the New Town to the castle on its high rock.

"Turn us around and get us back," he instructed, and sat down heavily. His legs were tired, now that the immediacy of the chase was gone.

"You're a lucky man I'm not in the mood to lay a beating on you for your stupidity," he added for good measure.

"Who are you, anyway?" Merry Andrew asked as he pulled on the reins to bring the horse about.

His voice had an eccentric, spiky shape to it, of a piece with his appearance. He did not seem overly concerned at his capture, for all the sincerity of his efforts to evade it.

"Sergeant Quire."

"Oh, aye? I've heard of you."

"I'm honoured."

"Speak well of you, some folk do. Say you're a fair man. Fair as any bastard police can be, at any rate."

Quire regarded the cloth-wrapped parcel beside which he sat.

He tugged at one of the ropes securing it, and finding it loose, opened up the whole thing. Within, all tied up with their own cord, were a lantern, a spade, a crowbar and a pair of large canvas sacks.

"Would you look at that," Quire said.

Merrilees glanced round, and sniffed in mock indifference.

"Got a job doing some fencing out west," he said.

"Is that right? Fencing with a spade and a crowbar? At night?"

"Fencing. Aye. Early start tomorrow morning."

The flat assurance of Merry Andrew's voice said he cared not at all whether Quire believed him.

"Are you armed?" Quire asked, reminding himself, perhaps belatedly, that this was not a man to be taken lightly.

"Not tonight. Not for fencing," Merrilees said, and smiled maliciously at him.

They trundled back towards the bridge. Quire settled himself against the side of the cart, his legs stretched out over the grave robber's tools.

"We were only wanting to talk to you, you know," he told Merrilees. "It's not you we're after. There's another lot of men about, doing work at night. Might be you've come across them?"

Merry Andrew said nothing, but he laid a sharp blow across the horse's hindquarters that gave it a start.

"Killed a man at Duddingston," Quire went on. "You heard about that?"

"Might've done."

"Might you have heard about who did it, then?"

Again, Merrilees fell abruptly dumb. A flight of seagulls went squalling raucously overhead, following the course of the Leith Water towards the ocean. Merrilees glanced up, and watched them go, and then turned his eyes back to the road. The horse went sluggishly out on to the bridge.

"We've got our orders," Quire said. "No peace for you and your kind. You'll not be able to lift a finger, nor take a piss, without there's one of our boys watching you. Annoying you. Stealing a body or two, that's one thing, you see, but killing a man, that's another altogether. That's the kind of thing that can make life miserable for everybody."

"Aye, it is," grunted Merry Andrew, his demeanour now entirely out of kilter with his name.

Quire looked ahead. Rutherford was standing in the middle of the lane. Spune sat cross-legged at his feet, despondency incarnate. Merrilees could see them too, but he abruptly pulled the horse to a halt, and turned about on his seat; an ungainly manoeuvre.

"See a lot of things when you're doing your work at night," he said levelly to Quire, who nodded and raised his eyebrows in expectation of more. Merrilees sniffed.

"This last winter, there were some bad folk out and about. Evil. New folk who don't follow the rules. Might be I met them one night, round about Greyfriars Kirk. Might be they did one of my lads a good deal of hurt, breaking bones. Near enough killed the boy."

"You see, that's the very kind of folk I'm wanting to hear about."

"Well, if you mean to hang them, I'm all for it. Good riddance. I'd give a lot to meet them again myself, but only if I'd a bit of an army at my back. These are men who don't say a word, not a word. Don't bleed – not any kind of blood I recognise, at least – nor feel no pain even if they're cut. They're not right, not right at all. Not natural."

His voice had taken on a distant, low quality. He stared out over the lip of the bridge and across the roofs of the manufactories.

"Got dead eyes. Stronger than this horse here. Something of

the Devil in them, I'll tell you that. You go chasing after them, police, I'd take a lot of folk along if I was you. That, or a priest."

With that, he turned away once more. He nudged the horse onwards.

"Do you know who's buying their wares?" Quire asked.

"Couldn't say."

"Come on, there's a only a few it could be. The anatomists at the university; one of the private tutors. The law's no use against these bastards unless someone talks. Might be I could get someone at the buying end of things to tell me what I need."

"Couldn't say," Merrilees insisted irritably. "You do your work, and leave me to do mine. If you lay hands on these folk you're after, I'll be wishing you well, with all my heart I will, but I don't fancy your chances much, police. I'm telling you, they're not like you and me. They're something else. You've no idea."

"I've an idea," Quire said darkly. "I was at Duddingston myself. I saw things there that don't make a lot of sense."

Merry Andrew grunted at that, but would say not another word, for all the prodding and the pestering Rutherford and Quire belaboured him with.

XI

The Antiquaries

The great hollow of land – once marshy, now neatly gardened – between the long rising ridge of the Old Town and the sweeping grace of the New was crossed by a construction of inglorious name but remarkable scale: the Mound. A huge descending ramp, it carried much of the constant traffic between the two Edinburghs.

From its summit, an observer might look out northwards across the geometric splendour of the New Town, and beyond its spires and chimney stacks glimpse the white-capped waters of the Firth of Forth, with the rolling farmlands of Fife as distant backdrop. That same observer, descending the Mound, might look back and be amazed by the chaotic drama of the Old Town: the gargantuan angular mass of the castle atop its rock and the dark crags of the tenements trailing away to the east of it, like a host of giants petrified in the act of clambering one over the other as they reached for the cloud-heavy sky.

Just there, at the foot of the Mound, stood the Royal Institution. A low slab of a building, with a veritable thicket of massive columns forming a huge portico and a panoply of cornices and carving and stone flourishes all around the edges of its roof. It squatted upon the land in splendid isolation, with Princes Street, the expansive boulevard that marked the beginning of the New Town, running along before it.

As Quire approached the steps that led up amongst those serried ranks of pillars, the wind was rumbling its way down the full exposed length of Princes Street, and his long coat snapped about his legs like a heavy flag caught up on a fence. The hessian sack he carried loosely in one hand bucked against his grip. There were few pedestrians about. Those who had to move were doing so on wheels: hackneys and broughams and plain old wagons rattled and trundled along Princes Street.

Quire pushed through the massive, solid oak doors and entered the Institution. Instantly, the rough and raucous weather was only a memory. A restful quiet prevailed within, almost churchly in its stillness. In the lobby, a soberly dressed and mannered doorman directed Quire towards the cloakroom, and seemed decidedly perturbed when he declined.

A broad spiral staircase of polished stone took Quire up to the offices rented by the Society of Antiquaries. Papers were piled upon tables, with little evident order to them. Shelves of leatherbound books ran around the walls, many so worn and frayed that they looked as though they might fall apart in whatever hand lifted them. The place had a smell that Quire was unaccustomed to: that of parchment and dust and learning. He did not find it unpleasant.

A small, bespectacled man sat behind a desk so laden with documents and books that its surface could hardly be seen. He pulled his eyeglasses a little further down his nose with one finger, and peered at Quire over the top of them. Satisfied, he returned them to their former position.

"Can I be of some assistance?" he asked, scribbling a few last notes in the margin of a heavy tome open before him.

"I'm hoping so, if you know anything of the Society's members and its past. I'm a sergeant of police. Quire."

"William Anderson, secretary to the Society," the man said, rising and extending his hand.

Quire shook it. The secretary's hand felt small in his.

"John Ruthven," Quire said. "That's who I'm interested in."

"I know the name, but his involvement with the Society ceased some time before my appointment, I'm afraid. I am not long in post, you know."

"I understand. Nevertheless, he told me that he left in unfortunate circumstances. Ill humour on all sides, as he had it. Might be the sort of thing that's remembered? Talked about?"

Anderson pursed his lips.

"I regret it is not something I would be able to assist you with, Sergeant. I pay little heed to gossip and hearsay, when it comes to matters that pre-date my responsibilities."

"An admirable trait, I suppose," said Quire. Improbably incurious, he might have added. "Perhaps you could suggest someone more talkative for me to go and pester?"

Anderson looked doubtful, and gave the bridge of his nose a thoughtful pinch, bobbing his glasses up and down.

"Mr Macdonald is here," he said with an air of reluctance. "Alexander Macdonald, assistant curator for the collection. He is in the store rooms, cataloguing. There is always cataloguing to be done."

"Let's hope he lacks your scruples when it comes to loose tongues."

Quire found Alexander Macdonald in a long, gloomy chamber filled with rows of free-standing shelves, upon which resided a chaotic host of boxes and crates and grimy glass cases. Even as he advanced between the tight-packed stacks, Quire could feel his nose tingling and tickling beneath the assault of dust.

The assistant curator was standing on a low stool, reaching perilously upwards to feel about in a crate that rested on the uppermost shelf. Flakes and strands of straw packing drifted down as his apparently fruitless search grew more vigorous. He glanced down at the sound of Quire's cautious approach. Quire was moving with a good deal more care than was his habit, for fear of dislodging some priceless artefact from its place. The shelving had evidently not been arranged with men of his size in mind.

"Ah, a visitor," Macdonald exclaimed; redundant, but at least a touch more enthusiastic than Quire's reception by Anderson.

Before Quire could explain himself, the curator gave a grunt of satisfaction and produced a short, flat length of enormously corroded metal from the crate. It was pitted and fractured, in places as thin as paper, and quite black.

"*Gladius*," Macdonald said, as if that explained everything. "A Roman sword. So we think, at least. A precious token of our deep history. There was some concern that the thing might have gone missing, but I suspected ... well, never mind. Is there something I can do for you?"

He slipped the rotted blade back into the crate and stepped down from the stool.

"Sergeant Adam Quire. I've one or two questions in want of an answer."

"Oh?" Macdonald's raised eyebrows suggested a lively interest. "A criminal enquiry, is it? How exciting."

"A few years back, there was some trouble between your Society and John Ruthven. Your secretary told me you'd be the one to shed some light on the matter for me."

"Oh," Macdonald said again, a little deflated this time. "Yes, I suppose Mr Anderson would not wish to involve himself in such matters. He's most protective of the Society's reputation, you know. Wouldn't want it to come out that he'd reported matters that put the Society in an unflattering light."

"You needn't worry about that. It's just that I'm wanting to know more of Ruthven. Something of his nature, his activities. You follow me?"

"Would you care to sit down, Sergeant?"

Macdonald led Quire to the far end of the storage rooms, where, in a cramped corner, two rickety-looking chairs flanked a little round table. Quire had to move a box of papers bound up with ribbons before he could occupy the one to which he was directed. He carefully laid the hessian sack down flat on the table before him.

"It was a small unpleasantness in our history, the Ruthven business," Macdonald said with an air of world-weary regret as he took his own seat. "Nothing more than that by all accounts. You must understand, many of our members are men of considerable reputation, and intellect, and ... let us say they are men of robust character and strong opinion, often on the most arcane and obscure of topics. There is always some dispute grumbling away to enliven our proceedings."

"Must have been of some consequence, if Ruthven resigned from the Society over it."

"Resigned ... well, in a manner of speaking." Macdonald fluttered a hand in the musty air. "Difficult to be precise about meanings. You might say, though, that Mr Ruthven chose to leave our ranks rather than face the ignominy of expulsion. He had fallen out with a number of the other senior members over some considerable period of time. You've met him, you say?"

Quire nodded, but chose not to expand upon that simple confirmation.

"You'll have formed your own opinion, no doubt," Macdonald went on, recovering some of his initial animation. "He has – or had then, at least – some rather eccentric views on various historical and philosophical subjects, and a somewhat rough manner with those who did not share them. Matters came to a head ... well, I believe some questions were raised over a number of items that went missing from the Society's collections."

"He stole them?"

Macdonald was alarmed. He raised a splayed hand to fend off the very words.

"I did not say that, Sergeant. I very purposely did not say that. Questions were raised and no satisfactory answers could be agreed upon, so he and the Society parted ways. That is all."

"What items went missing?" Quire asked.

"Oh, nothing of especial significance or value, either monetary or historical, as far as I know. Some pieces from Major Weir's house, a lock of hair reputed to have been cut from the head of a witch before she burned. A set of keys once owned by Deacon Brodie. That sort of thing. Minor relics of the darkest corners of Edinburgh's past, if you like. Interesting to a local historian of macabre bent, but not central to our collections."

Quire could not keep the look of disappointment from his face. A few inconsequential trinkets gone missing years ago were no kind of lever with which to prise open Ruthven's – or Blegg's – secrets. That disappointment went entirely unnoticed by Macdonald, who was carried along by his own more recondite lines of thought.

"All of a piece, really, with his interests and descent," the curator mused. "You may not know, Sergeant, but Mr Ruthven is distantly descended from a notable family of dabblers in the arcane. So he liked to imply, in any case. Men who, in less enlightened times than our own, were drawn to alchemy, and much darker arts. Delusional mystics, would be the current judgement, fortunate to have avoided the stake and the fires of witch-hunters.

"There was a namesake of his, a John Ruthven of the sixteenth century, who habitually carried about his person a bag filled with magical wards inscribed upon plaques of wood in Latin and Hebrew. To guard against evil spirits, or some such. He was executed as a conspirator against the Crown, so you may judge for yourself the merit of such precautions."

There was a twinkle of amusement in Macdonald's eye.

"And that John's brother – a certain Patrick, Lord Ruthven no less – was reputedly an even more active dabbler in the black arts. Curses and charms, that sort of thing."

"Ruthven lives in some comfort," Quire observed. "He must come from money of some sort."

"If you say so. I've not had the privilege of calling on him at home, and I am certainly not privy to his financial dealings. He did display some generosity towards the Society in happier times, mind, so he undoubtedly had funds at his disposal. I have a vague recollection that he has some modest landholdings. Farms or some such. Perhaps there are rents . . . "

The suggestion faded away with a rising, questioning tone and another flutter of his hand.

Quire regarded the shelves of boxes and crates glumly. This talk of the black arts put a sour twist into his gut. His fingers, of their own accord, tapped at the sack laid on the table. He turned his head, and looked down at them, as if they belonged to someone else entirely.

"I did wonder . . . " he murmured. "Another matter I thought someone here might be . . . "

He was hesitant, straying into areas that he neither understood nor gave any credence to. Ever since he had been called to look upon Carlyle's body, though, he had felt himself moving slowly but surely on to unfamiliar ground of one sort or another. It was too late to turn about now.

He pushed the sack across the table. Macdonald regarded it with surprise.

"Perhaps you could take a look at that, sir?" Quire asked. "Tell me what you make of it."

Macdonald reached in, his brow alive with curiosity. He withdrew the fragile, crude star of twigs that had been left affixed to Quire's door. The curator held it on his spread hands and frowned at it. With the delicate precision appropriate to his vocation, he turned it over. The little black feathers brushed softly over the twigs. Tiny fragments of bark came loose.

"I thought it might be old, at first, but it's not, is it?" Macdonald said.

He sounded neither alarmed, nor overly interested. That went some small way towards easing the tension that had crept into Quire's arms. He thought himself foolish, to be so unnerved by a silly decoration some child might have put together, but it was one thing too many amongst several he could not quite explain. And he had, when he first held it, felt something strange. Still, Macdonald evidently felt nothing untoward.

"If it had some age to it, it might have been interesting. From an antiquarian point of view, I mean. It does bear a passing resemblance to one or two illustrations I have seen. In books relating to witchcraft, I believe. Not something one would think to see in our times, now that our path is illuminated by the power of rational intellect, eh? Might I ask how you came by it?"

"Not important," grunted Quire. "You've no thought on its purpose, then?"

"I really could not speak to its significance or intent. Not my field, you know: the intricacies of these particular extinct beliefs. I'm afraid there are no practising witches in these parts nowadays, to the best of my knowledge, otherwise I might have referred you to an expert."

Macdonald said that last with a twinkle of humour, in which Quire could not share.

"Does look a little ill-omened, though, wouldn't you say?" the curator observed. "Even to the untrained eye. One suspects that it might be a warning, or threat, or curse, or fell invocation. Back when people took such things seriously, of course."

"Of course. You keep it, sir. I've no further need for the thing." Macdonald frowned down at the object.

"Not something we would particularly wish to add to our collections, I think."

"Dispose of it, then," Quire said, a little too sharply.

He wanted to be rid of it now. He was not a superstitious man, but he hated and mistrusted the way his eyes were drawn to that frail construction of sticks and feathers, and the way it made him feel. It was not fear precisely that pinched at him; sharp unease, perhaps. Or trepidation. Its presence seemed even to lend the long store room in which he sat an oppressive, dark atmosphere.

"Ruthven seems to make a habit of parting with folk on poor terms," Quire muttered as he folded away the sacking and pushed it into the pocket of his long coat. "An assistant of his – Carlyle – fell out with him recently. I don't suppose you know the man?"

Macdonald shrugged apologetically, and then shook his head for good measure.

"What about Blegg? Do you know that name?"

"Blegg, Blegg." Macdonald frowned and gazed up towards the ceiling, in pursuit of an errant memory. "Yes, I think he's been attached to Mr Ruthven for a considerable number of years. I have some vague recollection of him. Quite the shy fellow. Obsequious, to be honest."

"That's not entirely my experience of him."

"No? Well, I don't know the man, of course. Only ever saw him fawning at Ruthven's elbow, but it has been a good few years.

Perhaps he has changed. Many of us do, with the passage of time."

Quire grunted. Men changed less often than most thought, in his experience, and seldom in the deeper fibre of their character.

"A Frenchman by the name of Durand?" he asked without great expectation, and was surprised to see Macdonald's expression brighten considerably.

"Oh, yes indeed." The curator nodded. "Him, I have met. A fascinating man. Do you know him, then?"

"We were introduced, that's all. Nothing more. I had the impression he was not much given to conversation. Not in English, at least."

"Oh, he is exceptionally fluent in our language, Sergeant. A fellow of the Institute of Sciences in Paris, with – so it seemed to me, in any case – a quite profound knowledge of the antiquities of the Levant, and Egypt. He was a member of that expedition which accompanied Napoleon's invasion of Egypt, you know. A dreadful business, no doubt, but they obtained a remarkable amount of ..."

"He's lodging with Ruthven," Quire interrupted. He had no desire for an education in Napoleon's achievements in the East.

Macdonald blinked, whether in surprise at the information or at Quire's curtness it was difficult to say.

"Is he? I did not know that. I met him perhaps eighteen months ago, when he was only recently arrived here. I had the pleasure of showing him around some parts of the collection."

"What's his business here? In Edinburgh, I mean?" Quire asked.

"I took him to be a simple traveller with a thirst for knowledge, seeking out those of like mind. And I envied him that, I must admit. The freedom to wander at will amongst the world's great centres of learning ..."

Quire watched the curator drift into a reverie of itinerant scholarship. Then he sneezed, which returned Macdonald to more immediate concerns.

"If you want to renew your acquaintance with Durand, you would likely have the chance tomorrow," the curator suggested. "There's to be an exhibition. You must have seen the preparations for it downstairs. No? An American artist showing his wares. Ruthven invariably attends such events, I believe, and the exhibition is entirely unconnected to the Society, so he will undoubtedly have received an invitation. I'm attending myself, as it happens. Most exciting. I should imagine Durand would accompany Ruthven, if he is indeed his house guest. The French are great ones for painting, you know."

XII

Mr Audubon's Exhibition

A fog embraced the city the next day. It had the sharp scent of industry and smoke buried within it, but the salt tang of the sea, too; the work of both Man and Nature.

Amidst it, the gaslights along Princes Street burned: diffuse globes of pale fire suspended eerily in mid-air. They receded, each in the chain a little fainter than the last, into the grey oblivion that shrouded everything.

From that murk, the carriages emerged one by one, the clattering of their wheels muted by the dank air. They came to the Royal Institution and disgorged on to its steps Edinburgh's moneyed, propertied elite. Men of the law and of science and of letters; landowners, merchants and clerics. They came in their finest clothes, with wives and daughters upon their arms, walking canes in their hands – though they were not much given to walking on a night such as this – and tall, stiff hats crowning their heads.

On a finer night, they would have lingered on the plaza outside the Institution; taken the air, greeted one another, measured the mood and appearance of their fellows. Beneath the damp weight of the fog, they were not so inclined. Each time the heavy doors were opened to admit a newly arrived party, there was a spill of light and of chatter out into the mist.

Quire stood amongst the columns, watching them arrive. He recognised a goodly number of faces; doubted whether any more than one or two of them could have put a name to him in their turn, for it was in the nature of the influential to be known by those they did not themselves know. He kept to the shadows, in any case, withdrawn behind one of the fluted stone pillars.

He had taken up his station later than he intended. There had been some slight disorder at the police house – a band of drunken apprentices disputing their detention, after putting in the windows of several houses – and it had delayed him. As a result, watching the carriages come and go in slowly decreasing number, growing ever colder and ever less comfortable, he began to suspect that he had missed his quarry. If Ruthven was attending, he was likely already inside.

Quire knew he should be in his rooms by now, warming his bones by the fire or his guts around one of Mrs Calder's stews. Such had been his intent, until almost the very end of the day, but a restless, nagging urge had hold of him. An anger, born in part of frustration at his inability to close the net he longed to set about Ruthven and his cohorts. It was Quire himself who felt ensnared, rather than his quarry. The Police Board were demanding his suspension now, and threatening an enquiry. Superintendent Robinson was fighting a rearguard action in his defence, but whether and for how long that would succeed he had been unable to say. Matters seemed clear to Quire: he was in a race, and its finish would see either him or his enemies brought low.

The accumulation of obstacles on that path only served to raise up to the surface his worst qualities: the stubbornness and the anger and the instinct for confrontation. Worst qualities now, perhaps, yet they had been his best once, when there had been battles to be fought.

So he meant to make Ruthven feel a little of the heat. See if that would make the man betray himself, through error or arrogance. Not a course Robinson would approve, but Quire could not stand to allow others to fight all his battles for him. That thought was enough to carry him over the threshold and into the Royal Institution.

Where as elegant an event as any he had seen was resolutely under way. Edinburgh's finest drifted to and fro in small groups; or rather, its pre-eminent members occupied their chosen stations and the rest moved from one to another like roving bands of supplicants paying their respects at a succession of shrines. All was smart waistcoats and billowing skirts, immaculately pressed shirts adorned with flamboyant neckcloths; tiaras and brooches, and servants gliding about with silver trays bearing veritable thickets of champagne glasses.

As backdrop to all this, countless luminous paintings of exotic birds filled the walls of the small galleries through which the crowds ebbed and flowed. Every imaginable hue and form of bird was represented, all of them depicted with such startling precision and realism that Quire stood for a moment quite still, staring vacantly at the nearest of the images, wondering how a man might produce such a thing.

A tall, stiff waiter broke the spell with a rather pointed clearing of his throat. He extended his oval tray, but Quire could see in his eyes that he was not certain he was offering the champagne to quite the right man; it was an act of habitual duty rather than conviction. Quire glared at him until he moved off in search of a warmer welcome elsewhere.

Quire realised that Sir Walter Scott – near-destitute now, he had heard, but still the most lionised of all Edinburgh's great men – was standing no more than a dozen yards away from him, surrounded by an appreciative gaggle of admirers.

"He is somewhat reclusive these days. A friend of the artist, apparently, so he makes an exception tonight."

Quire looked round to find Alexander Macdonald at his elbow, the curator's eyes gleaming with barely restrained delight as he watched the renowned writer hold forth.

"Very fortunate for you," Quire murmured. Even he, to whom such things hardly mattered, was not wholly unimpressed by the presence of this most famous of all Scots, but his feelings hardly approached Macdonald's devotional awe. He was not a great reader of historical romances.

"Fortunate indeed," Macdonald said. "Quite the gathering altogether, don't you think? Did you see Mr Audubon? The American Woodsman, they call him. Extraordinary paintings, quite extraordinary."

"They're very fine," Quire agreed.

Already his attention was elsewhere. He could see, beyond the intervening shrubbery of heads, John Ruthven.

"Excuse me," he said to Macdonald, and moved away, weaving through the throng, letting the hum of genteel conversation wash over and around him.

He drew a number of curious, sometimes disapproving, stares as he went. That did not surprise or concern him. He was hardly dressed or prettified appropriately for the occasion, after all. A mongrel intruding upon a pedigree herd.

Ruthven stood with a glass folded into the crook of his elbow, and a snuff box in his hand. Between thumb and forefinger he pinched up some of the brown, dusty powder and raised it to his nose, the other three fingers delicately fanned. He sucked it into the nostril with a single sharp sniff. The snuff box was not, Quire noted, the silver one Shake Carstairs had liberated from Carlyle's corpse.

Durand stood at Ruthven's side, his air that of a man craving anonymity. Nothing like the robust, insistent presence of Isabel Ruthven, who was drinking deeply from her own glass and scouring the room at the same time with a lively gaze. She wore a red gown with a great cascading bustle at its back like a crimson waterfall sculpted in cloth. Her hair was coiled up atop her head, and pinned there with an ivory comb.

She was the first to see Quire as he approached, and she lowered her glass slowly from lips already easing into an anticipatory smile. Ruthven followed her gaze, and his response was of an entirely different sort.

"Can I be free of this irritant nowhere?"

"Do try not to cause a scene, dear," his wife murmured before Quire could reply. "I am sure the sergeant has no wish to spoil the evening for everybody."

Her voice had the liquid ease and looseness of one who had already greatly enjoyed the Institution's hospitality.

"And I am equally sure he is not here to speak with you, my dear," Ruthven said. "I would not have thought you a patron of the arts, Mr Quire."

"Sergeant," Quire corrected. "And you're right. I'm not here for the paintings."

"No, indeed," smiled Ruthven. "Your dress evidences that rather clearly. Come, your face is thunderous, man, but surely you should be in good humour? I'd have thought you in the mood for celebration, as a former foot soldier in the Duke's army, now that he's risen to the highest office in the land."

Quire looked away. The Duke of Wellington, victor of the Peninsular War and of Waterloo, had become prime minister just a week or two before, but whether that should count as advancement, or cause for celebration, was not obvious to him. He did not have the highest opinion of politics, or its practitioners, since it seemed an underhanded art to him. Still, it interested him that Ruthven knew of his army past; the man had evidently been making enquiries.

"Your Mr Blegg is not with you tonight?" Quire asked.

"Of course he is not. This is hardly the sort of occasion . . . "

"No. Perhaps he has other business to be about once night has fallen?"

"I'm not sure I follow your . . . "

"Other matters to attend to," Quire said. "Did he mention that he and I met the other night? He must have done, I suppose. We didn't have the chance to exchange as many pleasantries as I'd have liked."

"You are a slow learner, Mr Quire. One lesson in the costs of making baseless accusations not enough for you?"

"Oh, when it comes to threats and the like, I'm the slowest of learners. But if I was after a schooling in slander, you can be sure you're the very man I'd come to. Would you rather discuss Edward Carlyle? I've learned one or two things about his concerns, and his employment with you, since last we spoke. No? Perhaps I could speak with Mr Durand, then, if you're not feeling talkative?" Quire suggested, switching his gaze to the Frenchman, in whose eyes he saw quite plainly the alarm the very notion awoke.

"Leave my guest out of this," snarled Ruthven.

Quire drew considerable satisfaction from the fury boiling up through Ruthven's veneer of restraint. He would goad the man to the point of eruption, if he could. If that was what it took to let a little light in on the secrets Quire could smell hidden away in there.

"Do keep your voice down," Isabel Ruthven said, never losing her grip upon the elegant smile she wore like paint.

"If I need advice on comportment, I will find it elsewhere, beloved," Ruthven hissed at her.

But he did take a couple of breaths to compose himself, and smooth the anger away from his features. Quire was more interested for now in Durand, who was, with the utmost discretion, edging behind and away from Ruthven. Removing himself from the fray.

"You should be aware, Quire, that I will take it as the most grave personal insult if you persist in your harassment," Ruthven said.

"Well, that's what it would be, right enough," Quire said, watching Durand sink into the throng. He knew a man desperate to escape a trap when he saw one.

"Ah, there's the Sheriff Depute," Ruthven said, suddenly bright and loud. "Do you know him? Shall I introduce you? He might be glad to discuss the proper conduct of police affairs with you."

That, Quire recognised very clearly as the cue for withdrawal. His sense of caution was not so entirely withered as to blind him to the dangers of sparring with those whose reach he could not match.

"Not leaving already, are you?" Mrs Ruthven said, evidently reading some preparatory shift in his posture. He was at a loss to know how she layered such simple words with so many flavours: regret, protestation, suggestion. Appeal, perhaps.

"There'll be another occasion, I'm sure," he told her, and took one sharp step closer to Ruthven, dropping his voice to a rasping whisper.

"You've picked the wrong man for a fight, Ruthven. I thought you should know that. If you think you can tangle me up in enough knots to keep me away, you've misjudged me, much to your disadvantage."

Ruthven gave him a chill smile, and his eyes carried an animosity that Quire found surprisingly steady and calm.

"I promise you, Mr Quire, that the error in selection of opponent lies entirely with you. I have a great deal more weapons in my armoury than you would imagine, and after tonight's performance, I think I can promise you an education in the matter of disadvantage that you will not soon forget. Now go. I do not think we will meet again, and for that I am entirely glad."

XIII

The Hounds of the Old Town

Quire did not know whether or not he should regret his actions at the exhibition of the American Woodsman's paintings. He knew what Robinson's judgement on the matter would be, if news of the encounter between Quire and Ruthven at the Royal Institution found its way back to him, but that could not be helped. What was done was done, whether it was ill done or not. He spent the better part of two days expecting repercussions. There were none. Perhaps on this occasion that anger he had brought home from the wars, and which it had taken him so long to set reins upon, had not done his cause too much harm.

He sought to lose himself, for a few hours, in more normal and less contentious duties. It seemed wise to avoid the main police house, so he went round half a dozen watch-houses – the generally grubby, rather gloomy little posts the men of the day and night watches used for shelter and sustenance and storage – checking that there was nothing needing his attention.

He chased a lad who stole a loaf of bread from a baker's window right before his eyes; chased him all the way from the well at the east end of the Grassmarket, up Candlemaker Row and

through the works for the new George IV Bridge over the
Cowgate. And then gave up, for his legs were sore and the boy
looked like he needed a good feed in any case.

He spent the better part of an hour trying to persuade a drunk
youth to come down from halfway up the cliffs beneath the castle
walls, fighting to get himself heard above the cheerful throng
gathered to see what happened. Eventually, the boy fell asleep up
there, sitting on a narrow ledge, bathed in sunlight. It looked,
Quire conceded, a rather pleasant perch, but he sent some men
to bring the sleeper down in any case.

A day spent in such a way seemed almost restful to Quire, in
comparison to his recent experiences. It left him, if not exactly
contented, certainly restored to a kind of calm.

He stopped, on his way down towards the Canongate, to buy
an apple from a stall. As he walked on, crunching through the
hard, sour flesh, he watched the evening sun light up the roofs of
the tenements on either side. The High Street was in shadow, but
up there every chimney, every roof tile, was washed with a sheen
of gold, as if each dour building had been crowned.

He stopped in at Calder's before climbing the stair to his apartment. A pint of ale and a thick slab of bread were enough to carry
him through to the fall of night. He found a not unpleasant
weariness settling over him, a gentle weight in his limbs and a stillness into his thoughts.

As he sat on his bed, pulling his stiff boots from his feet and
setting them side by side on the floor, his mind, of its own accord,
settled upon the notion that he would have done better to leave
Ruthven to enjoy the paintings in peace, but that if no harm came
of it, he need not condemn himself too harshly.

The South Bridge carried, on its vaulting arches, the city's life and
traffic over the shadows of the Cowgate. The huge new bridge

being built on a parallel course a little to the west would do the same, but for now it was barely begun. Its gigantic stone legs were sprouting from amongst the teeming tenements that they would in time merge with, or bury, or accommodate.

In the deepest part of the night, down there in the darkness of the lower city, a stillness reigned. There were no gas lamps here, as had sprouted on the streets of the New Town, nothing to blunt the severity of night's grip. The last of the drinkers and the indigents had found shelter, and left the shuttered shops and dark doorways to the explorations of rats. The wynds were empty of sound, save some occasional cry or cough or curse emanating from within the towering tenements.

But the city had stiller, and darker, places yet. Up and ever up the buildings had soared, built one atop the other. Layers of rooms, of cellars, and of tunnels had been all but entombed. Dank and silent corners, nestled into the deep fabric of the city like ossified voids, had been consigned to the past by a populace that no longer needed them, and chose to forget them. Some could yet find a use for them, though.

In that deserted night, a lone figure came softly beneath an archway and into a tight, grimy quadrangle enclosed by tenements. The man turned to an old and scarred door that had been little enough used to allow dirt and straw and the droppings of rats to accumulate at its foot.

There was no handle or lock apparent on the door. The man pushed at it gently. It creaked back to give admittance to the bowels of the city.

The air within was fetid and heavy, hardly disturbed for years and grown old just as the crumbling walls that enclosed it had done. There was no light, not the slightest sliver. The man closed the door behind him, and advanced into the gloom.

Only the sound of his feet on dirt and stone dust gave some

hint of the smallness of the passageway, and even those feeble echoes were dulled by the sodden air. He went carefully but without hesitation, unhindered by the utter darkness.

After a few paces he turned aside and ducked his head, avoiding the invisible lintel of an aperture that opened into a side chamber. And there, a new sound arose in response to his arrival. A shifting, a movement, a rustling. He stood quite still, and bodies brushed against his legs, pressing close. With unhurried precision he loosened each finger of the glove on his right hand and pulled it free. He reached down.

Matted hair greeted his touch. Coarse fibres crusted with grime and worse things. He ran his hand down the line of the backbone, then lifted it and stretched his arm further into the dark. A cold, dry tongue drew its rough surface over the palm of his hand, and he dipped his fingers to let it curl over the back of them. There was a crust of dried blood upon the harsh lips that couched that tongue.

"Be still, little brothers," the man said, his voice gentle. "Be soft. I've something here for you."

From an inner pocket of his coat came a scrap of material. A sleeve, torn from a shirt. He squatted down, holding the rag stretched between his hands, extending his arms so that the beasts could gather round it, and press their noses to it, and taste it.

"Do you have it?" the man whispered. "Do you have what you need?"

He balled the sleeve up and pushed it into each of the three mouths that opened, one after another, to greet it. He pressed its fabric against teeth.

Dim and distant sounds reached in, the creak of muffled wheels on cobbles, the tread of hoofs sheathed in cloth. The man rose to his feet, and folded the shirt sleeve away into a pocket once more.

"Your carriage is here."

The shapes that shared that dark hiding place with him grew more urgent in their movements. Claws scraped on the floor.

"Hush," he hissed, nothing gentle to his words now, nothing but the crack of the whip. "Not a sound, or it's to the fires with you. The flames and oblivion for any who betray us."

And they were still at that, cowed.

The man retraced his steps and opened the door to peer out into the night. A cart was drawn up on the street beyond the low archway, its driver already pulling back heavy canvas sheets to reveal the cages it carried.

The man turned back and spoke into the blackness of the under-city, where his beasts waited.

"Come, then. There's work to be done tonight. It's not far. Not far at all."

Quire was torn from sleep by a pounding at his door. His waking was so abrupt and violent that for an instant he was bewildered, wondering what the noise was. Then the door shook again, beneath repeated blows, and he was scrambling to haul himself up out of the bed.

"Who's there?" he called, but there was no answer.

He snatched his trousers up from where he had dropped them on the floor and clambered into them, almost toppling over as he hopped briefly on one foot. He pulled on his boots. The cold leather was not pleasant against his bare feet. He heard a heavy tread on the stair outside.

It was not quite fear that was in him, but it was something close kin to it. He shrugged his long coat on over his naked shoulders, and took hold of the door handle. Before he lifted the latch, he thought better of such incaution.

He unhooked his police baton from the belt draped over the back of a chair. He held it ready as he carefully lifted the latch and let the door come open just enough to give him a view of the stairway. Nothing but darkness there, a faint shaft of moonlight falling from a tiny window. But he heard those footsteps again; down below this time, retreating hurriedly.

"Who's there?" he shouted again angrily, and began to descend the stairs.

He went cautiously, concerned to ensure that no ambush awaited him in the gloom. That was answered soon enough by ear, rather than eye: the slap of shoes on cobblestones told him his visitor was out of the stairwell and into the close.

Quire followed, but still did not rush. He saw a figure, difficult to make out clearly, making off towards the South Back of Canongate, the lane that ran along between a row of workshops and the small, walled fields that marked the edge of the King's Park. He had suspected this might be some youth, drunk as likely as not, thinking it clever to play a prank on the sergeant who lived above Calder's. Watching that figure vanish around the corner on to the South Back, he thought not. It was a full-grown man, clad in heavy coat and soft, formless hat.

Quire fastened a couple of the buttons on his own coat, closing it up. It was by no means cruelly cold, but nor was it the kind of night to be running around bare-chested. There was an eerie silence settled over the Canongate, he noted as he jogged down towards the South Back. That alone was enough to tell him that it must be the very dead of night, for it was only then that no one was to be found abroad.

He glanced up, found the moon high on its course, shining dimly through a sheet of thin cloud. Almost enough light to go chasing after whatever miscreant this was, but perhaps not quite. The last time he had done something similar, he had ended on the ice of Duddingston Loch. That was not the sort of experience he longed to repeat.

He peered down the South Back. On one side of the lane, the high walls and locked gates of workshops and yards and small breweries; on the other, a much lower dry-stone wall, beyond which lay only a narrow field and then the great black natural fortress of Salisbury Crags. From where Quire now stood, those ramparts obscured a great swathe of the eastern sky, and hid their approaches in impenetrable night.

He could see a little further along the line of the South Back. There, just about to disappear from view, the man who had been beating at Quire's door was moving steadily away. He was trotting down the centre of the lane. Not looking back, not running. Apparently not greatly concerned at the possibility of pursuit.

Quire advanced a little further. These circumstances were too strange for him to trust them entirely. He walked along South Back, drifting closer to the wall bounding the fields on his right, so that he could look over it and sweep his gaze across the open grass. Nothing. He looked back towards the man, and in that very moment the night closed about that retreating figure and hid him from view.

Quire stopped, and stood there staring. The cold was starting to get in and lay its fingers across his chest. He shivered. He would not sleep again now, he knew. Not with the memory of that sudden assault on his door so fresh. He would be relieved, though, if all this mysterious encounter cost him was the loss of half a night's sleep.

Then he heard, faint, out there in the darkness that had swallowed the man, a soft cry. Not frightened, but pained. There was a muffled, indistinct thump, as of something falling to the ground. Quire took a few more steps in the direction of the sound, wishing the clouds would be kind to him and permit – even if only for a moment – the moon to throw its full light over this small portion of the city.

A part of him wanted to call out, but the greater part was too uneasy to accede. One more stride, and he could just make out, slumped in the middle of the lane, a prone form. He looked behind him. Still he was entirely alone. He frowned at the fallen man. Could it be, he thought, that this was nothing more than a fool, hopelessly drunk, beating at random doors in the Canongate and now overcome by his own excesses? That would be annoying, but at least he might get himself another hour or two of slumber, if there was no need to fret about what might happen as soon as he closed his eyes.

The man was not moving at all. Quire wondered whether he should go down there and give him a good kick; see what that revealed. In the next instant, all thought of drunks, and of sleep, was utterly gone.

Out of the darkness beyond the prostrate man, stepping over and around him, came hounds. Three of them. Huge, rangy beasts, perhaps wolfhounds. Quire's breath caught in his throat. The beasts arrayed themselves in a line across the South Back. Quire could not be certain, but they looked to be unkempt, their coats scrawny. They stood there, staring at him. He stared back, thoughts of Edward Carlyle's torn corpse flickering through his mind. Behind the hounds, the man who had been lying on the ground rose, entirely unhurt, entirely sober. He kept his back to Quire and walked away into the dark, as casual as anyone heading out for a lazy stroll on Arthur's Seat. The dogs never once took their eyes off Quire.

He turned and ran. He heard their claws scrabbling on the cobblestones as they sprang after him. They would be far too fast for him. He put everything into the sprint, but he knew they would have him. His arms pumped. He expected at any moment to hear the hounds give voice, but there was nothing; not a sound from them but that of claw upon stone.

Quire stretched his mouth open, slapped his baton in there crossways and clenched his teeth tight on it. He veered sharply towards the high wooden gate of some manufactory yard. They were nearly on him now. He could feel them there, at his back.

He threw his arms up and leaped for the top of the gate. It had looked good and solid, but it swayed and groaned as he hit it and grabbed hold. He smacked his face against the wooden planking, and almost spat out his baton.

He scrambled with his feet, hauled with his arms, and managed to get an elbow hooked over the top. Then there was a hard blow to his left boot, and he looked down to see one of the dogs biting on it, shaking its head from side to side. He felt no pain, so could only guess that its teeth had sunk into the low heel.

The other two hounds were rushing up, and within that one quick glance, he registered the wrongness of them. Matted hair, caked with all manner of noisome dirt; jaws agape, but entirely dry, no sheen of spit even on their pale and limp tongues; lifeless eyes. Silent, as surely no dogs would be at such a moment.

Choking back what might easily become blind terror, Quire struggled to drag himself up and over the gate, but the weight of the creature pulling at his leg was too much. Another of them sank down and began tearing at the foot of the gate with teeth and paws alike. The third jumped at him. Somehow he managed to sway his body just enough to avoid its teeth. It fell back, lost its footing and rolled.

Quire straightened his left ankle, pointing his naked foot. It slid free from the boot and the dog dropped back to the ground, trophy firmly grasped in its jaws. In an ungainly windmill of legs and arms, Quire pulled himself up and toppled over the gate. He hit the paved yard on the far side hard enough to knock the wind from his lungs and set his head spinning. He let the baton fall from his mouth and lay on his back, groaning.

A furious attack was now launched upon the gate. There was a gap of perhaps half an inch between it and the ground. It was a chaos of snapping teeth and scraping claws. All three dogs were breaking away fragments of wood, sending cracks running up through the planks. They were sure to do themselves harm with such ferocious brutality, but Quire was almost certain that that would be of no great consequence or concern to them. These were surely beasts of the same kind as the man he had fought on the ice. The gate would yield before they did.

Quire rolled carefully on to his hands and knees. His fall had done him no lasting damage, but it felt as though most parts of him were aching. He looked about, trying and failing to ignore the ever more ominous sounds of wood breaking apart. It was a cooper's shop and yard. The walls were higher than the gate, though there were several barrels standing about that might give him enough of a start to get out and over without doing himself worse injury than he had already suffered.

He got to his feet, cursing as his bare foot inevitably found a tack or sharp pebble the night had hidden. One of the dogs had got its paws and a good part of its head through a ragged hole in the bottom of the gate. Some of the planks were splitting away from one another and starting to lift as the beast thrust itself forward again and again. Quire stopped and picked up his baton. It was heavy, but he was not sure it would crack open a dog's skull quickly enough. The doors of the workshop itself were shut, and had a light chain and lock across them. He went to the window to look inside, but could make nothing out. The gate creaked and cracked ominously behind him.

Quire kicked at the workshop doors once, twice. Thrice, and the lock gave, the chain fell slack and he was in. It seemed to him that running was not likely to improve his position greatly, and if the dogs were set on coming in under the gate, that would give him as good a target to aim at as he was ever likely to get. He had seen coopers using some vicious-looking tools to work wood in the past; he could only hope that this one was no different. Any craftsman in his right mind would have his best tools away home with him, but the old ones, the no longer used ones, they might still be here.

Within moments he re-emerged into the yard clutching a broadaxe. It was short-handled, wide-headed. Not of the sharpest sort, as best a quick run of his thumb along the blade could tell, but a great deal better than a baton.

He had to move more quickly than he had anticipated, for the first of the dogs was almost in. Its mouth a mass of broken teeth and wood splinters, it was dragging itself through on its belly. It snapped at him as he drew near, and lunged, but the gate was strong enough – just – to keep it pinned for a moment longer.

That was all Quire needed. He hacked down at the dog's neck. That first blow did not go deep, but it parted the skin, and it taught Quire the weight and balance of the weapon. His second opened a yawning wound, exposing meat and bone and gristle. The third widened it, and the fourth went through and separated head from shuddering body.

The jaw still worked, as that head rolled free. It snapped shut, and slowly opened. The headless torso still scraped feebly at the ground. There was no blood. Just a spreading slick of some stinking liquid of imprecise, pallid shade. A stench of decay and rot burst from the stump of the neck.

The other two dogs were still ripping the gate to pieces, bit by bit. If they came both at once, Quire suspected he might have a problem.

Someone was shouting. Quire looked round and up. At one of the windows high on the Canongate tenements, a woman was leaning out, a lantern in her hand.

"Watch! Watch!" she was screeching, and a fairer sound Quire had never heard. "Thieves in the yards! Thieves on the South Back!"

Another window was lifted, another voice – a man's this time – added to the hue and cry. Through it, Quire heard a single long, thin whistle, coming from somewhere out on the South Back. At once, the two remaining dogs broke off from their attack, and Quire heard the soft tap-tap of their brisk walk away.

He waited for the span of several deep, restorative breaths, revelling in the continued accusatory yells coming from that blessed woman. He doubted she could even see him, especially waving a lantern around in her own face, but he blew her a kiss anyway.

Then he dropped the broadaxe, sat down heavily on his backside and stared at the dog's head lying at his feet.

XIV

Surgeon's Square

Quire did not bother to knock at the door of the Royal Infirmary's autopsy room. He pushed it open and walked straight in, for he did not mean to be refused an invitation.

Robert Christison and a pair of assistants were gathered about a corpse on one of the slabs, all clad in soiled aprons, all leaning over the open body with expressions of rapt interest. Quire's abrupt appearance brought them erect, and interest was replaced upon their faces by alarm at the dishevelled apparition manifested before them.

"Sergeant Quire?" Christison said in surprise.

He held some strange sort of tongs or pincers in his hand, and tapped at the air with them, in Quire's general direction.

"You are looking rather the worse for wear, Sergeant," he said.

"Yes, I'm sorry about that, sir."

Quire could hardly dispute it. He was unshaven, his chin and cheeks darkened by grizzled stubble. His eyes must, he knew, betray the sleepless night he had just passed, and the heavy sack he had cradled in his arms was filthy. He presented more the appearance of an indigent than a sergeant of police, no doubt.

"I don't believe I was expecting a visit from you," Christison observed. "Even the police are not encouraged to wander too freely into rooms such as this, you know, Sergeant."

"I'm just hoping for a few minutes of your time, sir. I think you'll find them well spent."

Christison spread his hands above the partially dissected corpse. Though Quire was trying not to look too directly at the gruesome spectacle, he could not help but see that it was a woman, perhaps fifty or so years old.

"I am, as you can see, engaged in rather important business at the moment. Extremely important, I would say. This woman's death was taken for an unhappy accident – an excess of laudanum – until certain aspects of the case drew my notice. Certain bruising about her person, to be precise, suggestive of forced administration of the drug.

"The body will not take a bruise after death. Were you aware of that, Sergeant? Or, to be more precise, the bruising that occurs after death is distinctive and does not result from force or blows, as might be the case in life. I am, I believe, the first in the country to have demonstrated and documented this with what might be called the proper rigour of the scientific method."

Quire shifted uncomfortably. The sack he carried was heavy, and his weaker arm was aching.

"Just a few minutes, sir," he said. "I swear to you I would not have come here if I didn't think it important."

Christison sighed, and rubbed his chin.

"Very well. Very well. Give me a minute or two with Sergeant Quire, would you, gentlemen? Go and smoke a pipe, or take the air, or whatever pleases you."

The two assistants – current or recent students of Christison's, Quire guessed by their youthful looks – went reluctantly out, bestowing upon Quire glares of grave disapproval. It almost made him laugh, seeing those rosy-cheeked innocents so affronted by so trivially unexpected a turn of events. How ordered and polite they must imagine the world outside their cosy little bastions of learning to be.

"What is it, then?" Christison demanded.

"You're the only man I know can read the tale of a corpse," Quire said, advancing towards a vacant slab. "I'm in sore need of that today."

"Well, I do like to think . . . " Christison began.

Quire unceremoniously emptied out the contents of the sack on to the slab. The dog's decapitated corpse flopped down with a wet thud. The head tumbled after it, hitting the slab with a bonier crack, and rolled almost to the edge before coming to rest and fixing Quire with its lifeless gaze. The tongue protruded stiffly from between the yellowed teeth.

"Good God, man," Christison exclaimed. "Have you lost your mind?"

"Not entirely, sir. Not yet."

"I could have you thrown out for bringing such a thing in here. I could probably have you arrested, for God's sake, and how would that look?"

"Please, sir. All I'm asking is that you look at it. Unless I've misunderstood what it is you do here, you'll surely see something of interest. And if you don't, I'll leave the moment you tell me."

Christison glared at him. Quire was testing their relationship to its very limits, he knew; quite probably beyond them, for it had never been more than a formal acquaintance as a result of their joint endeavours. But if he was any judge of men at all, Christison was the sort to give him the benefit of the doubt, and to succumb to his own innate curiosity.

Christison took a step closer to the dog's body and leaned to examine its raggedly severed neck.

"I see no blood. There should be rather obvious evidence of catastrophic bleeding, internally, externally – everywhere, really – in a case of decapitation. There does seem to be some other fluid here, though."

He looked quizzically at Quire, who simply nodded. Christison took hold of the hound's stiff legs and turned it over. He ran his fingers through its noisome fur, using them to push it apart here and there, seeing down to the skin. He grunted and muttered to himself quietly. Shook his head.

He moved round to the end of the slab, set one hand on each corner of it, and leaned down to peer into the stump of the dog's neck. He remained in that pose for some time; far longer, certainly, than Quire could ever have spent upon such an unappealing sight.

For Quire's part, he waited patiently and in silence. He watched Christison, and thought it a good thing that he had come here. He disliked the room, the way it reduced death and the dead to mere matters of so much bone, so much muscle. Like carcasses in the Flesh Market. It was all too unemotional and calculating for Quire's liking; but unemotional and calculating were the very things he now needed.

Christison took hold of a small clump of the dog's hair between his forefinger and thumb and gave it a sharp tug. It came easily away, a little solid mat of it. He grimaced and wiped it off his hand on the edge of the slab.

"Someone is having a little fun at my expense, are they?" he said at length to Quire, looking anything but amused. "It's an ill-timed jest, if that's what it is."

"No jest, sir," Quire said earnestly. "I'll swear to that any way you like."

"Clearly a contrivance of some sort, nevertheless," Christison said. "This animal was dead before it was decapitated. There are incisions that were made in its chest wall and in its neck, and then sewn up again. Also after it was dead, as best I can tell. Why, precisely, would anyone wish to cut holes in a dead dog and then stitch them up again? Have you taken to the study of canine anatomy, Sergeant Quire? Or embalming?"

"No, sir. I'm a student of much cruder sciences. It was me cut the head off this dog, and I promise you it was moving about just fine until I did it. In fact, it kept moving a wee bit after I'd done it too, but it stopped eventually."

"Not possible," Christison said emphatically. "That it was alive when its head was separated, I mean. I think I can tell the difference between ante and post mortem as well in a dog as I can in a human. And I assure you, I can tell the difference very well indeed in a human."

His brow suddenly crunched into a frown, and his eyes narrowed as he looked from Quire to the dog and back again.

"Now just a moment," he said, pointing a finger at Quire and then shaking it as if to free up his nascent insight. "Is this about that body you brought through here ... what was the man's name?"

"Edward Carlyle. This is one of the beasts that killed him, I think. This one or one much like it."

"Really?"

And there was that vein of lively interest threading itself into Christison's voice that Quire had hoped for. The stirring of his curiosity.

"You said it was a dog that did it," Quire observed, "and here's the proof that you were right. There were two more like this, but they escaped me. Or I them, to be honest."

"Well, your persistence with such an unpromising case is admirable," the professor said, bending to prod at the stump of the neck with his tongs. "Still, there is clearly some confusion at work here. What *is* this fluid? If I didn't know better, I'd say it is from the beast's blood vessels. Hand me that blade, would you, and the bone shears beside it."

Quire lifted the implements, surprised at the weight of them. They still bore the residue left by their application to the woman lying on the other slab. He gave them to Christison.

"Let us just take a quick look, shall we?" the professor murmured.

He cut open the dog's chest. The long, flat knife slid through the animal's hide smoothly, as easily as Quire had ever seen any blade cut. Christison cut along three sides of a rectangle, and pulled the large flap of skin roughly back, revealing the dog's ribcage.

A foul stink burst from the carcass, potent enough to set Quire – and even Christison – grimacing. The rotten stench of putrefaction. Quire clasped a hand over his nose and mouth.

"That smell, Sergeant, is decay," Christison said pointedly. "This animal has been dead a good deal longer than you seem to think."

He took the shears to the dog's ribs. They crunched through the bones as if they were twigs. Then he cut away at the animal's innards. He did it roughly, quickly.

"Not taking my usual care, of course," he said.

The heart came free, the size of a pear. Blotched, discoloured and feeble-looking. Pale liquid dripped from it. Christison frowned. He set the organ down beside the corpse, neatly sliced it with a single sweep of the knife, and spread it. It opened like a butterfly of flesh.

"Look at that," he exclaimed as that same pale liquid flowed out from the exposed chambers. "Whatever this beast had in its veins, it was not blood. This is most puzzling."

He glanced at Quire with narrowed eyes.

"You're certain this is not some prank, Sergeant?"

"I am. I've come across a good deal that is puzzling of late, sir. Things I can't rightly explain, and I don't know that anyone can except by means I can't bring myself to believe in."

Christison raised a sharp eyebrow.

"And what do you mean by that, precisely?"

"I've had one or two folk mentioning the Devil to me lately," Quire grunted.

"Ha! Come now ... ah, I see you are serious. Look, Sergeant, you strike me – and sound, I must say – like a man under a good deal of strain. Perhaps some rest and recuperation ... "

"I'd agree with you, were it not for the fact that some folk seem set on killing me. Not the moment for a nap, I think. There's something I need to ask you, sir, in confidence. I need to find a man can testify to the involvement of certain ... gentlemen ... in the business of body snatching. Without a witness, my hands are tied. Can you tell me ... "

Quire hesitated. He was asking a great deal of the professor now, he knew. Challenging his loyalty to his calling, and his colleagues.

"Can you tell me who has been buying corpses from the Resurrection Men of late? Who is most likely to be taking delivery?"

Christison scowled at him, and Quire's heart sank. He had overstepped the mark.

"Sergeant Quire," the professor said, "if you seriously expect any respected anatomist to publicly testify to his receipt of cadavers from disreputable sources, your sense has truly deserted you. It matters not that the trade is common knowledge. It is unspoken knowledge, and should it cease to be so, the damage to the reputation of all those concerned – to the whole business of the teaching of medicine in this city – would likely be irreparable."

"Yet there have been murders committed," Quire said bluntly. "There's those as are wishing I was numbered amongst the victims. I have to tell you, at this moment I care little for the protection of reputations, sir."

"Well said, I suppose," Christison grunted, though he did not sound convinced. "But really, Sergeant, you don't need me to tell you where to look, surely? I thought you a perceptive man. One capable of deductive reasoning easily sufficient to this task."

"I don't follow you."

"It is in the nature of any trade that goods flow as the demand for them dictates, is it not? I think it was one of the recent great minds of this very city, Adam Smith, who shed light on such matters, but I suppose you find little time for recreational reading. Let me tell you this, then, and this alone: there is one dissection table in particular that is never short of a cadaver.

"Dr Knox has five hundred students subscribed this year. More than all the other private tutors combined, I believe. No teacher of anatomy has ever drawn so many, and it is the steady procession of the dead passing through his school that brings them. Even our own students buy their way into his theatre, since the university cannot match his certainty of supply."

"Robert Knox," Quire murmured.

"You know him?"

"No. Only in ... no, not really. I know the name, and something of the reputation."

Not the whole truth, but as much of it as Quire wished to share.

"Well, I'd not put too much weight on reputations, Sergeant. They're flimsy things that conceal more than they reveal. But remember: you did not have his name from me."

"No, sir," Quire said distractedly.

Knox's name was one that had not been in his thoughts for a

long time, and it came with an unsettling cargo of memory and connection.

"I'll be away," he said to Christison. "Let you get on with your proper work. Do you want me to take this?"

He indicated the dog's torso and head.

"No, don't trouble yourself," Christison said. "I'll have it burned."

Quire nodded, rolled up the empty sack into a loose ball and threw it on to the slab beside the dog. He pulled open the door.

"We really don't live in a world in which dead dogs kill people, you know, Sergeant Quire," Christison said behind him.

"You might not, sir, but it seems I do," Quire said quietly without looking round.

Surgeon's Square was a sedate and graceful enclave, nestled into the south-east corner of the old city wall, no more than a minute or two's walk from the Infirmary. Grand frontages clustered about a small garden, rather austere, but neat and well ordered. The square was an interloper, like a fragmentary forerunner of the New Town nestled into a hidden corner of the Old. Here, many of the men who had built Edinburgh's mighty reputation in the medical sciences had for years plied their trade; and a lucrative trade it had been, as the buildings so clearly evidenced.

The Royal Medical Society stood on one side; the old hall of the College of Surgeons on another. Quire's destination was nestled between them, and though not quite so grand, it still presented a distinguished façade. Number Ten, Surgeon's Square. The teaching rooms of Dr Robert Knox.

Quire paused on the doorstep. He could not bring himself to reach out and make his presence known. Robert Knox. He had not seen the face that went with that name in more than ten years, and in truth remembered its features imperfectly. He remembered the circumstance of their meeting all too well, though. Better than he would have liked.

Coming here had been an instinctive reaction to Christison's mentioning of the name. To hear it so unexpectedly, after so much time, had caught Quire off his guard. Now, as the vigour of the impulse faded, he mistrusted it. But still: it seemed he was caught up in a struggle to the death, and one he felt in imminent danger of losing. An approach to Knox might well be fruitless, but the most unpromising of handholds would look attractive to a drowning man.

The soft, deliberate clearing of a throat disturbed his line of thought. He turned to find a slight man with decidedly sharp and hawk-like features standing there, already dipping his head in submissive greeting. The little bowl of a hat he wore bobbed.

"Can I be of assistance, sir?" the man asked.

"I don't know," Quire said, letting loose a little of the irritation at his own indecision. "Who are you?"

"Paterson, sir. Doorkeeper." He held up a little package, brittle paper tied with string. "Been to get some ink for Dr Knox, or I'd've been here to greet you. If it's greeting you wanted."

"I wanted a word with Dr Knox."

"Who should I say is calling?" Paterson asked, moving smoothly past Quire and reaching for the door.

Quire held aside his coat to show the baton hanging at his belt.

"Sergeant Quire," he said.

"So, you've taken it upon yourself to lecture me, have you?" Robert Knox cried. "I won't have it. I won't!"

It was a fearsome display. The doctor's fury seemed entirely uncontrived, a wholly natural thing welling up from inside him. It put a beetroot blush into his cheeks and a wild gleam into his one good eye; the left socket was unnervingly empty. He had less hair than Quire remembered – a balding pate ringed by slightly greying fringes and sideburns, though he was no older than Quire – but what there was of it trembled now with his anger.

Quire stuck stubbornly, if with rapidly faltering enthusiasm, to his course.

"I mean only to say, sir, that these grave robbers have . . . "

"And you presume some connection between them and me?"

The strength of his indignation appeared to exhaust Knox. He slumped back in his chair, away from the great desk, and regarded Quire with something approaching disbelief.

It was an uncomfortable attention to be subjected to, but Quire's discomfort went a good deal deeper than that. The room in which the two men sat – that prodigious desk between them like the polished bole of some huge fallen tree – was in part study, but only in part. It also served as a storehouse of what were, to Quire's eye, grotesqueries.

Two short skeletons stood in glass-fronted cases, an honour guard flanking Knox. Their empty eye sockets seemed to Quire to be watching him with as much disdain as their owner. Atop a cabinet was a collection of disarticulated bones, each of them mounted on a wooden stand, the better to display their deformities. Every one of them was bent or twisted or gnarled with bulbous outgrowths. Beneath a dusty glass dome was a human hand, bleached of all colour, its fingers splayed, its skin peeled back to expose the intricate web of bone and tendons and muscles beneath it. There were gas fittings on the walls, small brackets like candle-holders. They were not burning now, but Quire could imagine how starkly eerie the place must seem when their light threw shadows from Knox's strange collection.

The human body was here reduced to a parade of oddities and afflictions, its constituent parts exhibited in a menagerie of disease. Quire could guess at the educational justification of it all, but he could not look upon it without being put in mind of those whose remains had found their way into the collection. He could not help but wonder about their lives, their suffering. He somehow doubted that such thoughts greatly troubled Dr Knox.

"Are you a religious man?" Knox asked at length, his tone much moderated.

"No, sir. I am not."

"Very well. You should then, being rational, be aware that the light of reason has shone brightly in this city these last fifty years. Great men have walked these streets, and their learning, their insight, in every field of thought from the arts to science to philosophy has illuminated all the land and driven superstition into exile. The flame is less bright now, perhaps, but still there are some men of exceptional talents, with the will to feed it. You do your city, and your nation, no service if you seek to traduce the reputation of those who strive to keep it lit."

"That is not my intent, sir," Quire said blandly. "I know only that we cannot have murder going unanswered, and that I am required, by duty and inclination alike, to find those responsible."

"Again, you presume some knowledge upon my part that does not exist."

"They are resurrectionists, sir. Lifters of corpses. It's a matter of common sense to make enquiry of those through whose hands a great many corpses pass."

"A very common kind of sense, indeed," snorted Knox. "I smell the prejudice of the mob in it. The irrationalities and misguided sensitivities that would set shackles upon scientific endeavour. Let me make it clear, Sergeant: corpses do not pass through my hands, as you so casually put it. They receive the attention of my knife, and such skills as I possess, for the education of hundreds – many hundreds – of young men who set a not inconsiderable value upon it.

"Paterson, my doorkeeper, manages the supply of cadavers, and I can assure you they are acquired by means that need be of no concern to you and your ilk. Now, if you will excuse me, I have matters requiring my attention. Be so good as to give me some peace, would you?"

Knox rose at that, and came briskly out from behind the desk, extending an open hand. It was, Quire supposed, the politest dismissal he could have hoped for in the circumstances. He stood, and shook the proffered hand. Knox's grip was firm, almost excessively so. It was the grip of a man unfamiliar with the inhibitions of self-doubt; or inured to them by force of will.

"You do not recall me, sir, I suppose?" Quire said.

"Recall you?" Knox frowned as he released Quire's hand from its imprisonment. "Why, have we met before?"

"You saved my life; or my arm, at the least."

"Did I? In what circumstances?"

"Brussels. Thirteen years ago now."

"Ah." Knox nodded slowly. "Waterloo. Yes, there was a good deal of work for me there. You should have introduced yourself as a fellow veteran of those struggles in the first place, man. Why did you not tell me sooner?"

"It was not to the point of my visit, sir. And I did not expect you to remember."

"Your arm, you say. Let me see, then."

Taken aback, Quire found himself quite motionless, and with no words offering themselves to his tongue.

"Come, man," Knox said with a rather cold smile. "Allow the craftsman to inspect his former works. You say I saved the limb. Let me see it, then."

Quire tried to pull back the sleeve of his jacket, but the material was too thick and tight.

"Take it off, take it off," Knox muttered.

Quire did so, and draped the jacket over the back of a chair. He rolled up his shirt sleeve to expose his left forearm, and turned it – with an uneasy tightening of embarrassment in his chest – so that Knox could examine the scars on its inner face.

"Burns," the doctor murmured as he took hold of Quire's wrist and ungently lifted the limb closer to his eye.

The skin was thick and messy and hairless, with an unnatural shine to it like wax that had hardened and smoothed in mid-flow. Ridges and furrows knotted themselves over the surface. In the midst of that wound, another, more distinct, resided: ugly and slightly raised, like a corrupted boil.

"And this?" Knox asked.

"You extracted a ball fragment, sir."

"Ah. Well, you were fortunate, then. To work amidst burns, digging around in there – nine times in ten I'd think to lose the limb. Or the entire patient."

"They told me afterwards that you prevented them from amputating it. You thought it might be saved. Removed not just the bullet but several pieces of my uniform from the wound."

"Yes, yes. Often overlooked. It is rarely the lead itself that carries rot into the flesh, but what it takes with it. Very well. Cover yourself up."

Quire pulled down his sleeve with relief, his left hand making a fist of its own volition, tensing against shivers of pain in his arm.

"Not my best or neatest work," Knox said, handing Quire his jacket. "But that is to be expected: I was learning my trade then, on the army's coin, and there were a great many demands on my time over those few days. That Corsican dwarf made sure of that, eh?"

"He did."

"Well, luck was with you. And an astute surgeon, dare I say? Or one filled with the hubris of untrammelled youth, in any case."

Knox's manner was greatly mellowed, perhaps by self-importance, perhaps by fond reminiscence. Quire shared neither, and had no memory of any luck worthy of the name attending upon him in those days. Quite the reverse, in fact.

"Come, then," said Knox, opening the great panelled door and ushering Quire out to the head of the stairway. That his teaching practice was successful, as Christison had intimated, was beyond doubt. The oak staircase, the paintings upon the walls, the wide entrance hall below, all put Quire in mind of the house of some noble family; and this was not even Knox's residence, merely his place of teaching.

"Paterson!" Knox shouted, leaning over the banister and peering down.

There was no response from his doorkeeper.

"Ach, that man," muttered Knox. "Unreliable staff are a blight upon every enterprise, Sergeant, you mark my words."

"I will make my own way out, Dr Knox," Quire said.

He glanced back as he descended the wide stairs, but Knox was already gone, retired to his desk and his gallery of silent specimens.

XV

Robinson's Last Day

Adam Quire's dreams, when he remembered them at all, had once been of fire, darkness and little else. Never, in other words, conducive to a restful slumber. Now, they were fiercer still. Teeth and shadows and horrors unnamed. He would come roughly out of sleep, trembling or sometimes rigid with morbid fear, to find himself entangled in his sheets and blankets.

Quire awoke, unrested, in just such a state of disorientation. Only the intrusion of the mundane upon his senses finally shook him free of the nightmare's grasp. He heard the haberdasher's wife on the floor above berating her husband – the disappointed tune to which their whole marriage was sung, as far as he could tell. He smelled, with the unique clarity of early morning, before familiarity blunted the pungency of their fumes, the breweries.

By such small, insistent statements, the world demanded his attention. The hallucinations of his sleeping mind retreated. In their wake they left only a dull fretwork of pain deep in his left forearm: a stubborn memento of his thrashing about. He dispelled it by making a fist, then flexing his fingers, grinding the thumb of his stronger right hand into the palm of his left.

Still wrapped in a thick, heavy woollen blanket, he sat on the edge of the bed and hooked out the pisspot from beneath it with his foot. While he urinated, his gaze drifted over the loaded French pistol he now kept at the side of his bed, and to the heavy bar he had fixed rather crudely across the door to his apartment. A man who felt in need of such fortifications in his own home could hardly be expected to sleep well, he supposed.

He listened to the clatter of the foundries rousing themselves from their own slumber. Down here in the Canongate, where once the wealthy had congregated, industry now colonised every space. Most of the rich and the titled had emigrated to the New Town, leaving their former haunts to men of a meaner sort. Amongst whose number Quire was quite content to count himself.

The sky and the city, and the light that served as go-between, carrying intimate and subtle messages to and fro, were in constant discourse. That morning, the heavens spoke in sharp and bright phrases, flinging gusts of wind down from amongst the scudding clouds to bluster over the roofs of the tenements and bundle their way down the length of the High Street. It was the kind of day Quire liked: sunlight illuminating the eastern face of every building, making even the ramshackle seem crisp, and wind enough to keep the Canongate from gathering an industrial fug over itself. A clean day.

He began the long ascent from the threshold of Holyrood Palace up towards the High Street and the distant castle. He had Mrs Calder's hot, heavy porridge in his stomach like a cannonball, which was both fortification and slight handicap. He could only be grateful for it, though: without his landlady's solicitous attention, he would likely leave his rooms each morning unfed.

At the foot of the Canongate, wagons and horses bearing goods to and from the manufactories were already getting themselves tangled up in great logjams outside the very walls of the palace. As Quire left that maelstrom behind, he glanced back over his shoulder and saw the vast rumpled mass of Arthur's Seat rising behind the palace, its folds and furrows and hummocks as familiar to him and every Edinburgh resident as was the patina of their own face seen in a mirror. Most striking of all its features was the long rising curve of Salisbury Crags, a battlement of cliffs standing atop a steep rampart of scree and short grass, sweeping around that part of the hill closest to the city like a defensive bulwark against human encroachment upon the wild, high ground. Quire was fond of that view; or had been, for now sight of the hill put him in mind of Duddingston, hidden behind its great bulk, and of what had happened there.

The further up into the Old Town Quire walked, the higher the buildings rose, the more crowded became the herds of chimneys atop them, the more tumultuous the ebb and flow of rude humanity that moved in their shadows. At the head of Leith Wynd, where Canongate became High Street, Quire encountered one member of that crowd he had not expected to see.

Catherine Heron was emerging from a whisky shop, clutching a wrapped bottle to her breast. The ragged hem of her wide skirts brushed the ground. She looked dishevelled, a little bleary-eyed, but there was a blushing tint to her cheeks – a token of resistant health.

Quire met her eyes, and an acknowledging half-smile escaped him before he could restrain it. He would have left things there, but Catherine hastened to fall into step beside him as he marched on.

"I was glad of your visit. It was good to see you again, Adam."

"You thought so?" he said, a touch more briskly than was needful.

"I did think so. Been a long time."

"I didn't know you were sharing rooms with Emma now. It was her that brought me there."

"Aye, you said."

Out here, amidst the bustle, her manner had none of the brazen confidence she carried within the fortress of the Holy Land. She spoke softly and held her arms close, as if to pass unnoticed.

"I wasn't sorry to see you," Quire admitted, softening.

He could not sustain the pretence of indifference. He was tired, and aching, and as beset by threat and animosity as he had ever been. Cath brought good memories, and the warmth of old but unforgotten affections; a seductive comfort in hard times.

"We were short of the means to start the day," Catherine said, giving the whisky bottle a little jiggle by way of explanation.

"I thought it was early for you. I can't tarry, Cath."

Quire stretched his stride a fraction to make the point blunt. However that affection might cling to him, he knew it could be a trap of sorts. He had troubles enough without courting afresh those he thought had been laid to rest some time ago. It cost him more pain than he would have guessed to set that cold armour about his heart, though.

"Such haste," Cath said, gentle reproach leaking into her tone.

"I'm sorry. You know I can't be seen consorting with you. You know that."

"My sort, you mean," she said, already falling behind him, letting him go.

"I'm sorry," Quire repeated sincerely. "If it had been my choice, I'd never have broken off with you, Cath. But there are rules, and I'd not keep my . . . "

But she had stopped, and stood in the middle of the street watching him as he strode on.

"You were glad enough to break them before," he heard her say with sad resignation, and he came to a halt, arrested by guilt and sympathy. But the traffic of bodies and barrows was already closing between them, and Catherine had turned away. He might have called after her, and wanted to. The certainty that picking away at a wound was the surest way to keep it from healing held him back. He caught a last fleeting glimpse of her turning down into Leith Wynd, and was left in the company of only his own failings and indecision.

The encounter put him in a black humour, and he advanced upon the police house with head down and brow furrowed. He paid little heed to those about him, who now included sternly dressed advocates on their way to offices or court, men of the cloth making for the austere bulk of St Giles' Cathedral, rich merchants in grave discussion as they headed for the coffee houses. There was wealth aplenty still in the Old Town, and it mingled intimately, indifferently, with poverty and sloth just as it had always done.

Quire's absorption in his own inner world meant that he was taken unawares by the sudden appearance of Jack Rutherford at his side. His fellow sergeant had a buoyant gleam in his eye, in sharp contrast to Quire's mood.

"Is it true what I'm hearing about dogs?" Rutherford asked, full of excited, disbelieving curiosity.

"Aye," said Quire.

The man could not know what it had been like, Quire supposed, but a little more concern and less enthusiasm might not have been out of place.

"By Christ, Quire, what is it you've got yourself mixed up in? It must take some doing to get yourself bitten by a dog in the Canongate of a night."

"I didn't get bitten," Quire grunted. "And there were three of them."

Rutherford shook his head in amazement.

"So what do you mean to do about it?" he asked as the two of them drew near to the police house at Old Stamp Office Close.

"Kill them," Quire said quietly, and even he did not know precisely to whom – dogs or men – he was referring.

"I am dismissed, Adam," Superintendent Robinson said, with a calm and quiet that at first disguised the meaning of the words from Quire.

"Sir?" he said blankly.

"The Lord Provost has seen fit to dispense with my services, forthwith."

Quire slumped down on to the bench that ran the length of the cloakroom. Robinson had found him here, trying to clean flecks of vomit from the breast of his waistcoat. A woman of considerable size had been found, unconscious from drink, in one of the wynds close by. When the watchmen brought her in to sleep it off in a cell, Quire had chanced to be there and volunteered to help carry her to her new domicile. An act of charity he regretted when she stirred from her beery slumber just enough to empty her stomach.

"It'll be the gossip on every lip soon enough," Robinson said, "but I wanted you to hear it from me first."

"On what grounds?"

"Oh, enough to give them an excuse. Truth is, there's just a few too many on the Police Board don't like my way of doing things. I've grown weary of fighting them, in any case, and the gout is plaguing me dreadfully these days. But I'm afraid you might soon feel the consequence of it. I refused to suspend you from your duties yesterday. There was a . . . lively, you might say, debate on the matter."

Quire hung his head.

"If they've turned you out on my account . . ."

"Don't flatter yourself overmuch," Robinson gently chided him. "You're a brick in this particular wall, right enough, but only the one. It's not helped, though, that you apparently caused some small disturbance at the Royal Institution. At an exhibition of paintings, of all things. Birds, was it?"

"Anyone calling it a disturbance has never seen the real thing," Quire said.

But he had not the heart to be argumentative, or truculent. He felt only sorrow at Robinson's fall, and shame that he might have been, in however small a part, a cause of it. Robinson was a better man than the people who had seen fit to dispense with him. A man who had served his country in war, and his city in peace. But past service counted for little these days. The world, and those who governed it, moved too quickly to be carrying such burdens as memory and gratitude. So it seemed to Quire at that moment, at least.

"Listen, Adam," said Robinson, leaning a little closer. "You're in deep water. They'll be coming for you, like as not, now that I'm gone. I know something of what this work means to you; what it'd cost you to lose it. Go carefully."

"It's too late for that. Ruthven's tried to kill me. If he had not gone so far . . . I don't know, maybe I could have let him be. But they came to my house and tried to kill me. That's not a thing can go unanswered."

"This business with the dogs?"

"The dogs, aye. Whatever's at the root of this, it's foul as a cesspit. There's a darkness to it. Not just the killings. Something unnatural . . . maybe evil. I don't know. Would you walk away from it, if you were me?"

"Probably not." Robinson gave a rather sad shrug of his

shoulders. "We all do things that are not in our own best interests sometimes. Just don't do them blindly, or without thought. You'll have little enough help to call upon inside these walls, I fear. It will be some while before my successor is appointed; in the meantime, Lieutenant Baird is to be acting superintendent."

Quire groaned.

"Indeed," sniffed Robinson. "Not by my recommendation, of course, but my influence is spent. If I can be of any assistance to you, come to me. But I fear the most I can do now is wish you luck."

Message boys were a vanishing breed in Edinburgh. At the height of the city's intellectual ferment late in the last century, half the inns in the Old Town had a couple of lads loitering about outside, happy to wait there for hours on the chance that a customer would have a message he wanted running to someone elsewhere. Those boys working the better establishments would have a split stick in which a written note would be carried, and a simple lantern of some sort for navigating the wynds after dark. Most, though, had relied solely upon hand and eye and quick feet.

With the growth of the New Town, and Edinburgh's slow sprawl to all points of the compass, the sight of boys racing along the streets, wax-sealed notes in hand, had become a rare one. But not entirely unknown. Most of the lads who did the work now did it only when other trades they practised – thievery or scavenging or chimney-sweeping – were going slow; they were but part-time practitioners of the art of message-running.

One such found Quire at the police house that afternoon. A dishevelled-looking little fellow, skinny like a coursing dog. Well pleased with himself, though, for having landed such a simple assignment.

"There's no note?" Quire repeated, looking down at the boy.

"No." The boy held out his hands, palm up.

"And you've just come from the Royal Exchange? Not a hundred yards?"

"Aye." A big smile.

"And you were paid for this, were you?"

"Only a penny." The smile snapped out of existence, replaced by an expression of courageous stoicism in the face of life's small injustices.

"Not so bad, is it, a penny?" Quire said. "Not for taking a wee stroll like that, with not even a letter to carry."

The boy shrugged.

"Let's be having the message, then," Quire said.

"Misher Durand would like to speak with you. He is in the Royal Exchange coffee house and will be there for the next hour."

It was clearly not the first time the boy had recited the message. Quire could imagine him, standing there before his client, made to parrot it until he had it right.

"Misher Durand?" said Quire, hope stirring to life in him. "*Monsieur* Durand. Is that it?"

"Aye. I said, didn't I?"

"Good lad."

Quire pressed a silver tuppenny bit into the boy's hand.

"Don't drink it, mind," he called as the boy darted off in a state of delight. "Buy yourself some proper food or something."

But the boy was already out the door and away across the High Street, and Quire's advice fell only upon his unresponsive heels.

XVI

Coffee

Quire was not a frequent visitor to any of the coffee shops scattered through the centre of Edinburgh. He had never acquired a particular taste for the thick, dark brew, and found that its expense considerably outstripped any pleasure it might offer. Others heartily disagreed. Every vendor did a thriving trade; none more so than the Royal Exchange coffee house.

The Royal Exchange was a mighty building, enclosing on three sides a cobbled quadrangle, archways on the fourth opening out on to the bustling High Street. The higher floors were given over to offices of various sorts, but the ground floor was dedicated almost entirely to commerce. Colonnaded walkways ran around the courtyard, each full of shops.

The coffee house was entered by a flight of steps that sank down into the ground on the left side of the courtyard. A curved sign formed an arch at the top of the stairs, with a lantern hanging from it. Passing beneath this, the visitor was greeted by a pair of dark doors with small glass windows set in them. It was a modest portal for a place that was, on the inside, a hotbed of greed and debate. More business was transacted about its crowded tables than in half the shops and offices in the city. Entire shiploads of goods landed at Leith were auctioned off there; contracts were entered into for this or that service, this or that exchange of land and property. Philosophies were discussed, literary endeavours planned or decried.

Few crimes were committed, however – not those recognised by the law, in any case – and Quire's duties had thus brought him through the door no more often than his pleasure had. The smell within was nevertheless instantly familiar, rich and bitter and warm: coffee and tobacco smoke.

He saw Durand at once. The dapper Frenchman was sitting alone at a small round table of polished mahogany, sipping dark coffee from a china cup. A silver coffee pot stood beside him. An ivory-topped walking cane rested against his knee.

As he had been on their first encounter, Quire was struck by the sun-browned tone of Durand's skin. It was not, to say the least, a common appearance amongst Quire's fellow Scots. Durand must be approaching sixty years of age, and a good portion of them had surely been spent beneath clear, hot skies.

Durand looked up almost as soon as Quire entered. An intelligent gaze, a touch nervous, but not nearly so veiled as on their previous meetings. He beckoned Quire over, and gestured towards an empty chair.

"Coffee?" he asked as Quire sat down.

"No, thank you. Not my drink."

"I find it as much food as drink, myself. One of the few pleasures of true luxury your city offers."

The man's voice was flowing; heavily accented, but in the controlled way of one entirely comfortable with a second language.

"If you say so," Quire said. "What was it you wanted to talk to me about, Monsieur Durand?"

"Ah, you treat my language with a little more gentleness than most of your compatriots."

"And your English is excellent."

"Thank you. I have a certain facility in languages, it is true. And I have had the time to master yours: I became an exile from my homeland many years ago. London was my refuge. And latterly here, of course. A beautiful city you have, Sergeant Quire."

"I'm sure it's very happy that you like it. Is there something you're wanting to tell me, sir?"

"Not so gentle when it comes to pleasantries, I see. I have found that to be a common trait of your countrymen. Not that I complain. Not that I complain."

Durand took a sip from his cup. He held it delicately. An increasingly loud argument – or perhaps it was a negotiation; it could be hard to tell the difference in these avaricious times – at the next table distracted Quire, and he shot an irritated glare at its occupiers. The two men concerned were sucking away at cigars in between their expostulations, blowing out jets of blue-grey smoke. That was a sight and smell that Quire always considered a little odd, not because he found it unpleasant – he rather liked that deep scent, in fact – but because it spoke to him of Spain. There had been hardly a cigar to be found in Britain until its officers and men came back from the Peninsular War, having learned the habit from the Spanish. The long struggle against Napoleon had all but bankrupted the country, and delivered only strange little trophies.

Quire turned back to Durand.

"Do you know what happened to Edward Carlyle? Can you testify to what occurred at Duddingston Kirk?"

"So hasty," Durand said quietly, setting down his coffee. "No, I regret I will testify to nothing. Not in a court of law. Not unless I am assured of my safety, and that, I fear, will be a great deal harder to secure than you imagine."

"What use are you to me, then?" muttered Quire in frustration.

"I confess, I am more interested in the question of what use you might be to me. Are you familiar with the Shelley book?"

"I'm not much of a man for poetry."

"No, the wife. *Frankenstein. The Modern Prometheus.*"

"Not much of a man for reading in its entirety, to be truthful."

"Not a requirement of your profession, I suppose. Never mind. Tell me: you have the manner, and are of the right age ... you fought against my countrymen, perhaps?"

The change in the course of the conversation did not greatly surprise Quire. For all his poise, Durand was a man quite evidently ill at ease with his situation, and with his company. His hand betrayed it, tapping nervously at the boss atop his cane. His eyes betrayed it, flicking from the thick, steaming black coffee to Quire's face, to the door over his shoulder. The man needed a little indulgence, Quire judged, and he bit back his impatience.

"Seven years in the army, near enough. I was at Waterloo; Spain and Portugal before that."

"Ah. Do you think me your enemy, then?"

"No, sir. That business is over and done with. If there are current matters fit to make you my enemy, of course, that's different. But I'm hoping still that you're here to make yourself a friend."

"Indeed. I met Napoleon, you know." A brief loss of focus to those nervous eyes, a glance towards memory. "It was a long time ago, before I fell out of favour with his regime. In Egypt. I was a member of the scientific expedition that accompanied him in his conquest of those lands."

"I know."

Durand's surprise was obvious. Quire had no intention of

providing an explanation for his knowledge, though. Let the man ponder the fact that he was not the only one with secrets.

"He was very small, I heard," Quire said.

"Napoleon? *Oui.* A giant spirit, contained in modest accommodation. Not a good man, you understand. I do not claim that. But a great one."

"Caused misery and havoc enough, if that's what you mean by greatness."

"True, monsieur. Quite true. Greatness is no guarantor of wisdom, or of a peaceable nature. Believe me, I have cause to know that better than most. Are you sure you will not take some coffee? Or something else, perhaps?"

"I don't need anything."

The door behind Quire banged open, and Durand's eyes went to it instantly, bright alarm in them for a moment. Quire's arms tensed in response, but he saw the Frenchman's features relax, and he almost smiled at how easily one man's unease might attach itself to another.

"John Ruthven might have been a great man once," Durand said.

Quire leaned in, his interest on the hook now. He said nothing, for fear of diverting the Frenchman from his course.

"But great men can go . . . astray, that would be the word, no?" Durand said. "More easily than lesser men, perhaps. He has a rare mind, Ruthven, a gift to see further and deeper than most of us. He has done things . . . ah, they would amaze you. But his is not a kind gift, for what he sees has clouded him, drawn him down paths better ignored."

"Maybe I can do some correction of that."

"Maybe. I am not innocent in this, no more than John Ruthven. Not one of us in that house can lay claim upon innocence. You know Mr Blegg?"

"Not as well as I'd like."

Durand smiled at that, and sank back in his chair. It was a sad smile, almost one of pity.

"He is not a man you would wish to know better, Sergeant. I assure you of that. And he is not so easily understood as you might think. Blegg is not his only name. I have heard Mr Ruthven call him Weir, and other names. Darker names. Such is the company I keep, at the gravest peril to my immortal soul."

The regret in Durand's voice was all but palpable, and Quire could hear in it a vast acreage of mourning. Mourning, perhaps, for a life gone wrong.

"What's Ruthven doing in the body-snatching business?" he asked. "Can you tell me that? He can't need the money."

Durand gave a twitching snort.

"You think that is what this is about? Selling the dead? Nothing so harmless. But in any case, you misjudge Ruthven. He is no longer a rich man, Sergeant. Not by any means."

"I've seen his house. I know what rich looks like."

"You have seen one room, no? The public façade. It is a large house, and contains many surprises. Much emptiness. But as for the digging of graves ... I do not think you need concern yourself with that. I have the impression that certain recent events may have convinced those involved to stay away from your cemeteries for a time."

"Tell me what I need to know," Quire pressed, tiring of Durand's coyness. "I'll fix what's needing fixing."

Or break it, he thought.

"I do not doubt that you will try, Sergeant. You have already proved yourself a most ... troublesome sort. That is why I am here. But be certain of this: you would be dead by now, were you not a member of the police. You are not the sort of man who can simply disappear, not without hard questions being asked.

Especially as you have not been precisely quiet about your suspicions of John Ruthven. They have been circumspect. Had you been but an ordinary man . . . well."

The Frenchman spread his hands, inviting Quire towards the obvious conclusion.

"I'd not call setting their damned hounds on me circumspect."

"The dogs? I did not know that. I am not as trusted as I once was. I am no longer fully in their confidence. It does not bode well. But still: a man killed by dogs is accident, not murder, is it not? Circumspect, as I say."

"What are they, anyway? Those dogs?"

"An early venture on Ruthven's part into dark territory. A failed experiment, you might say. But he has learned, since then; with my assistance, to my utmost regret. Make no mistake, I come to you in desperation. I am surely doomed, if the charnel house they have built cannot be destroyed, to its very foundations, and them along with it. I hope you might be the man to do it, but it is a slender hope only. An illusion, most likely."

Durand shook his head. He looked around the coffee shop, though Quire did not think he was truly seeing that which his gaze fell upon.

"I am a man in need of salvation," Durand said softly. "If not in the life yet to come – that might be a lost cause – at least in this one. I cannot stay in that house, in that company, for fear of losing my mind. Yet I cannot leave, for fear of worse. Monsieur Carlyle taught me that. As he was perhaps intended to."

He sighed, and hung his head, and then seemed to come to some abrupt resolution. He straightened his back, looked Quire in the eye.

"Do you understand that this is not a matter of investigation, of mere crime? That there is a battle to be fought here, against forces far darker than you would think possible? There is knowledge in the world much older than the new wisdoms of science and thought that so preoccupy men now. It is potent. You can be of no help to me, Sergeant, nor I to you, unless you know that. Unless you prove as fierce, as savage, as I think you might be. You must match that which you oppose, if you and I are not to be dragged down. Damned."

"When men set dogs on me – dogs that don't breathe, don't bleed – and a man tries to kill me with a shovel, and won't fall down when I put a ball in his chest ... I know this is not mere crime, Durand. And I know there'll be folk dying at the end of it all, one way or the other."

"Good. You do not sound so much like an officer of police now."

"I'm not like other police," Quire said.

The truth of it saddened him. He was becoming once more the man he had thought behind him: the man of war, the man of violence, possessed by cold anger. But it was what he needed. There would be folk dying at the end, right enough, by hangman's noose or otherwise. One of them might be him, if he could not summon up all that old ferocity.

"I will show you, then," said Durand. "That is your trade. You can only know what you see, what you can touch. Then perhaps you will understand what needs to be done, or be ready to hear it from me, at least. Mr Ruthven has a farm."

"I had heard as much." Quire nodded. "Some landholdings, I think I was told. But I don't see what ... "

"You will see. Cold Burn Farm. It is on the western side of your Pentland Hills. Not far. Go there, but go in numbers and well armed."

Durand tossed his head back and emptied the last thick dregs of the coffee down his throat.

"Go to the farm, that is all. You will find your answers there, and there will be no turning back. There. I have done it. I have cast the dice. Let the matter fall out as it may."

The Frenchman rose, and scattered a few coins on the table.

"Goodbye, Sergeant. Perhaps we will have the opportunity, and the cause, to speak again. Please do not come looking for me, though. You will only betray us both if you do that."

Quire followed Durand out of the coffee house only a little later. He walked thoughtfully up the steps and into the quadrangle of the Exchange.

Men were cleaning the cobblestones of the yard. One stood by a barrel on a handcart, banging a long handle up and down with vigorous determination. A second held the canvas hose that emerged from the pump and played the rather intermittent jet of water it produced over the ground. A third swept with a wide brush.

Quire paused to watch them briefly, shuffling aside when the splashing water came too close to his boots. It seemed somehow unreal, this scene of mundane labour, when set beside his conversation with Durand. A misleading token of normality in a world descending into chaos.

He could not entirely trust Durand, for all that he believed the sincerity of the man's fear and unease. But if the Frenchman could not, or would not, directly implicate Ruthven or Blegg, Quire could see little option but to follow where he directed him.

It was annoying, though. It would take a mail coach to get him out to the Pentlands, and he hated travelling in those rickety, noisy, cold old things.

XVII

Cold Burn Farm

Quire came in towards the farm buildings along hedgerows. He felt foolish, creeping under cover as if he was back in the Peninsula, fearful of an ambush, rather than scrambling across wet fields on the edge of the Pentland Hills; but his every instinct had told him this was the way to do it. Perhaps if Durand's despondent fear had not been so apparent, Quire might have marched straight up the main farm track and hammered on the door of the farmhouse. But he had seen just how frightened the Frenchman was, and he had apprehension enough of his own as to what might await him here. So he came at the farm along hedgerows, and waited for dusk to fall before going down amongst the buildings.

It was a long wait, for the Carlisle mail had put him out at the side of the road not long after noon, and though it was a fair walk from there to Cold Burn Farm, it did not take Quire much time to get on to a rise of ground from where he could look down into the main yard. The Pentland Hills were at his back, a chain of rounded heather-cloaked mounds rolling away into the south. The moon came up; a vast yellowish orb hanging over the shoulder of those gentle peaks.

What Quire saw caused him some puzzlement. He knew a working farm, and a well-kept one, when he saw it, and this looked like neither to him. There was a thin trail of smoke drifting up from the farmhouse chimney, so the place was clearly occupied. But there were slates missing from the roof of the biggest barn. There was a broken-down cart, missing a wheel, collapsed on to its axle and lying there in a corner of the yard like a skeleton. At the edge of a field where it backed on to a long, low cowshed, there was a wide black stain, a circular scab of ash and soot and burned grass. Even the hedgerow beneath which Quire sheltered had a look of neglect; its thorns had grown leggy and gnarled and gappy. Too long since they had been laid or cut. He could neither see nor hear any animals, not in the fields, not in the yard. So why did Ruthven keep a farm at all, if it was not being worked?

Night came on, and Quire tired of his vigil. He eased himself up, flexing his legs to break out the stiffness in his knees, and trotted down towards the buildings. He kept in the lee of the hedge, and ducked his head down to ensure he did not break the skyline, or frame himself against the lambent moon.

A soft light was in one window of the farmhouse now; the kitchen, he would guess. He made that his first target. If there was a whole gang of brawny farm lads waiting to spill out and kick him around, he wanted to know about it. Durand's insistence that Quire should not come to this place alone had been easily, if regrettably, dismissed: the Frenchman could not be expected to know that the Edinburgh police had no authority out here beyond the city bounds, nor that Baird, the current master of the police house, would sooner gnaw off his own thumb than pay heed to any suggestion, on any topic, emanating from Quire. In fact, Quire had taken it as his life's calling to stay beneath Baird's notice, as far as that was possible.

It was easy enough to reach the corner of the big barn unseen. There was no smell of animals on the still night air. None of the straw or hay he would have expected to see scattered about. He watched the lighted window of the house across the yard for a little while. It was blurred by condensation, so he could not be certain, but there was no obvious sign of movement within. Only the faintly inconstant light of candles; and that thread of smoke, still just visible ascending from the chimney into the moonlit sky.

Quire knew better than to run, even though the beating of his heart told him his body wanted it. Instead he went slowly and silently across the yard, bent low, hands almost brushing the ground. He balled himself up against the wall beneath the window, straining his ears for any human sound leaking out. Nothing. No voice, no movement. He breathed deeply. And ventured a quick look.

He put his head above the sill of the window, and squinted in. The steam beaded on the glass made everything vague, but he could see enough to know it was indeed the kitchen. An empty one, as best he could tell with the moment's examination he permitted himself. He settled back down on to his haunches.

Then, footsteps, and a rattling of the handle on the farmhouse door just a few yards from where he squatted. A tingling excitation of fear ran through the skin of his hands and arms. The door jerked open with some violence, and a lurching figure emerged in a flood of light.

A big man, but all his strength was in his chest and arms, for his hips were narrow and his legs spindly. Not someone Quire recognised. He staggered a little as he came out from the farmhouse, taking a few steps in and out of the pool of light falling from the open door. He laughed to himself as he did it, amused by his own incoherent feet. First belch, then fart escaped his swaying form. At which he laughed again.

Quire shrank back into whatever meagre shadows there might be beneath the window; he willed himself to fade, become thin and faint, and berated himself for not waiting for some cloud to veil that vast moon. He pressed his shoulders to the wall, narrowed his eyes to slits lest the whites of them should give him away. He held his breath.

Peering out between his touching eyelashes, he watched as the man set one wide hand against the wall of the farmhouse, leaned heavily on it and with the other unbuckled his trousers. A heavy ring of keys clattered on his belt as he did so. A strong stream of piss played over the stones. The man was humming to himself as he urinated. The flow faltered, and dwindled in fits and starts to nothing.

The man hauled his trousers up once more and fumbled clumsily with his belt. Still Quire did not breathe. He could feel a crushing tightness building in his chest and throat, but he kept his jaw clamped shut, and wished with all his might for this drunken fool of a farmhand to remember how to buckle his own belt.

A fox barked, some little way off in the fields behind Quire. The man straightened and looked that way, hands still at his waist. He blinked stupidly and frowned into the darkness. Quire counted his own heartbeats; fought with his desperate need to suck in some air. And the big man's gaze dropped, fell upon Quire's face, slipped drunkenly away from it. But then the eyes sharpened a touch. The gaze returned to Quire. The man opened his mouth.

Quire surged up, emptying his burning lungs and filling them again in the space of one long pace. He put his shoulder into the man's midriff and lifted him bodily from the ground. It was not easy, to turn in mid-stride with that much weight across him, but he did it, and punched the man back against the farmhouse wall.

He heard the bony crack of the man's skull against stone, but had brawled with enough drunks to know that beer was a mighty shield against blows that would take any sober man down. He put a pair of hard, quick strikes in under the ribcage with his right fist; pushed up with his left hand under the chin to smack head against wall again. Then he could feel the strength go from the man's legs, could feel his weight sinking him.

Quire lowered him to the ground and knelt beside him. His knee was in the pool of urine, and he could feel the last vestiges of its quickly fading warmth through his trousers, but he ignored that. He listened. Nothing. No cries of alarm, no pounding feet. The farmhouse door still stood open, its light and warmth flooding into the night, but no one emerged.

Quire put a hand under each armpit and dragged the insensible man across the farmyard. Hard boot heels scraped on the cobbles, but that seemed unlikely to rouse any pursuit if it had not already been sparked. He could smell the drink coming thickly off his captive. Hopefully any companions he had left behind in the farmhouse were similarly befuddled. All Quire wanted now was a bit of time. He knew better than to taunt the gods of luck. Discovered once was more than enough.

The closest of the farm's many buildings was the long, low, rather decrepit cowshed at one end of the yard. The moonlight was falling full upon its face, and Quire could see a heavy bar across its door, secured by chain and padlock. He unceremoniously pulled the ring of keys from the man's belt and examined them. One looked a likely fit for the lock.

He clamped the key crossways between his teeth and, one step at a time, hauled his captive towards the shed. Any unconscious man – or a dead one, for that matter – had a terrible weight to him, and Quire knew that. He had not expected, though, quite how quickly his damaged left arm would weary of the task. He could feel it slipping out from under the man's shoulder, moment by moment.

Had the shed been a few yards further, he might have lost his grip. As it was, he reached the door with his left arm trembling and cramping. He took the key with that hand, bearing the man's full weight on his right arm and hip. He was relieved at the ease and quiet with which the padlock clicked open. The chain made a little more noise as it came free, and the key fell from the lock and rang softly on the ground before skittering into shadows. Quire glanced back towards the house. There was still no further sign of life. It might be that fortune had belatedly chosen to smile upon him, and there was no one else around to trouble him.

He lifted the bar and eased the door open; not much, just enough to let him enter. The silence and darkness that awaited within were welcome. A few last, painful heaves and he and the farmhand were inside, and the door closed behind them.

Quire sat for a moment on the hard floor, sucking in a few deep breaths. He reached blindly in the darkness, found the man's arms and folded them across his chest. He let his hand rest there, feeling the rise and fall of the ribcage. Satisfied that no lasting harm had been done, he ground a thumb into his left palm, trying to ease some of the taut discomfort in the muscles. As he did so, his surroundings slowly, subtly impressed themselves upon his senses.

The place smelled like no cowshed he had ever encountered. It had a dry, almost herbal scent to it. And the distinctive stink of goat. As his eyes adapted themselves to the traces of moonlight seeping in through the ill-fitting door, he picked out a strange complexity of shapes. There were no byres, no stalls, as best he could tell; none of what was needed to handle cattle. Only some odd constellation of objects – he could not tell what in the gloom – hanging from the rafters above him. Jars or other storage vessels along the walls. Down at the far end, at the very limit of what his eyes could detect, perhaps tables or desks.

And sound. So faint, so tenuous, that he had to hold his breath to track it. In the most distant corner, where the darkness was complete and impenetrable. Cloth brushing against flagstones. Something – fingernails? – scratching on wood.

Quire tugged his pistol out from the deep pocket inside his coat. Its weight in his hand was a comfort of sorts, but he sincerely hoped it would not be needed. The noise would dispel any last hope of concealment, and he had brought only enough powder and balls for three shots. He had come meaning only to look, not to fight.

He peered into the furthest corner of the shed. There was something there, something moving. Something or someone. But he could not see anything, only hear the telltale frictional scrapings.

Quire's legs wanted to run, carry him out into the fields and away from this strangely desolate and dark farm. The unconscious man at his feet might wake at any moment; some other curious guard might emerge from the farmhouse. But he had not yet seen anything to explain Durand's fear, or the importance of this place.

Though there was a hollow foreboding taking root in his guts, Quire set himself on his haunches and whispered: "Who's there?"

The response was immediate. A thrashing about in the darkness. Limbs battering against walls or furniture. Not a word, though. Nothing to say if it was man or beast that lurked there. Quire could hear objects falling to the ground, breaking.

He tightened his grip on his pistol and cursed his misfortune. Or ill judgement, perhaps. It hardly mattered now which it was. He turned his back on the tumult in the shadows, his spine tingling with apprehension at the act, and peered out between the doors of the shed, angling his head to get a narrow view of the door to the farmhouse. Still open, still spilling light.

He heard wood cracking, splintering in the darkness behind him. His heart hammered. He looked back, blindly, into the depths of the cowshed. The frenzied thrashing grew louder still.

He slipped out of the shed and settled the bar down across its pegs on the door. He reached for the chain, at his feet, and found it tangled. He spent a precious moment or two trying to get it back in its place, but heard something overturned, a terrible crashing, from within; no longer in that far corner of the shed, he thought, but closer to the door. Time, he judged, was against him.

He let the chain fall and went on his toes – quickly, but quiet – to the corner of the shed and around into the deeper moon shadows. There was a crude outhouse of some sort leaning against the stone wall, with a sloping roof like a chicken coop. Quire brushed against it as he passed, and there was an eruption of excitement within. He recoiled from it, stifling a cry of alarm in his throat. This noise he could decipher more easily than the chaotic racket that still emanated from the main shed; this time, he could hear blunt claws scrabbling against the wooden planks. His nostrils caught the sharp, rotten stink of dog. Fear took hold of him. Simple, deep fear.

He ran, no longer caring about concealment. He pounded across the yard, the tail of his long coat flapping behind him, pistol still clutched in one hand. The light falling from the open farmhouse door bathed him, then he was beyond it and into the moon-softened darkness again.

Behind him he heard the doors of the cowshed shaking and groaning beneath sudden assault. He did not look back, not even when he heard the beam that held them shut fracture, the deep, booming breaking of its back unmistakable.

He ran straight down the curving rough track. No time now for retracing the steps of his more cautious approach across the fields. The surface was a hopeless mess of humps and hollows, ruts and stones, that set him stumbling and made his flight ever wilder. The path fell in amongst trees, and the lantern of the moon's face was taken from him. His eyes failed him. He almost fell, but staggered instead to lean against the trunk of a birch. He was panting, as much out of the anxious urgency of the moment as his exertions.

He looked back the way he had come. The steading was a black and menacing outline against the moon now, the line of smoke from the chimney laying a crack across that pale orb. More troubling was the heavy sound of footsteps. They were drawing near. Quire peered into the gloom.

It was a lone man, and not a large one at that, coming steadily down the track. He ran with his arms hanging loosely down at his sides. Trailing from one of them was a cord or rope of some sort, and still bouncing along at its end the iron ring by which it must have been secured to the wall. Quire could not see his face.

"Hold up, there," he shouted, stepping into the centre of the track. "Are you a prisoner? I'm with the police."

The approaching figure made no reply, just came jogging on, into the darkness cast by the trees crowding in on either side.

"Can you not talk?" Quire demanded uneasily, lifting his pistol.

Without breaking stride, the lean, rangy man swept up one arm and brought the iron ring roped to it lashing round in a wide curve towards Quire's head.

"Jesus Christ," Quire exclaimed.

He ducked, and the ring went hissing over his head. He leaped to one side as his assailant rushed at him, but his ankle turned on the lip of a rut in the track, and he fell to one knee. Before he could rise, there was a hand on the lapel of his coat, and another scrabbling at his belt.

Quire discharged the pistol into the man's stomach. The flame and noise and smoke erupted between them, blinding him, burning up into his nose. The shot had no effect upon its target.

The man got a hold on his belt, and in the space of a single heartbeat Quire was off the ground. He was taller and broader than his opponent by some way, yet he was lifted bodily into the air. He tried to club the man in the side of the head, but could not land a sure enough strike. And then the man threw him.

Branches slashed at Quire's face. He hit a tree trunk with his hip. It spun him round and he fell head first amongst bushes. The pistol slipped from his grasp. Dazed, he rolled on to all fours and began scrambling through the undergrowth. He could see almost nothing in the deep shadow beneath the canopy, in the thick scrub. But he struggled forward, stems and thorns scraping his face and arms, driven on by the sound of crashing pursuit behind him.

He forced himself up on to his feet and blundered ahead, beating away saplings in his path. As he went, he took his baton from his belt; used it to flail at the vegetation before him. There was that emptiness in him now which he had not felt with such clarity for years; the dread simplicity of being in the presence of imminent death. As it had always done, it lent strength to his limbs.

He burst out from the copse and into the moonlight once more. His feet went from under him and he fell on his side into a ditch running along the edge of the field. It was clogged up with dead wood and fallen branches, but there was a foot or more of water in it too, and he sucked some of that into his lungs before he could get his head up.

The moon was abruptly obscured, and a great weight landed on Quire's back, punching him down into the bottom of the ditch. He rolled over, spitting filthy water, flailing for a hold to pull himself up. Brittle wood broke beneath his grasp. Hands pressed down on his chest, forcing his head underwater. He blinked as he went under, caught a glimpse of a face above him, one side of it gilded by the moon. It was Davey Muir, the gravedigger he had seen with Blegg at the Dancing School.

Muir got a hold of Quire's throat, and the fingers were like steel bands. Spots of colour flared inside Quire's eyelids. Water was in his nose. He clubbed with his baton at the arms holding him down, but it made no impression. The boy had an impossible strength. It was as if he was made of stone.

Quire's body was howling for air. He let his baton fall, and instead took hold of Davey's left hand; broke the third and fourth fingers backwards. It did not seem to bother Davey, but it did weaken his grip a fraction. Just enough. Quire managed to force that crippled hand away from his throat. He got his feet into Davey's stomach and kicked out with all the desperate strength he could summon. It tore Davey free, and Quire burst up out of the water, roaring in fear and fury. And pain, for those fingers ripping away from his neck had felt as if they were taking his windpipe with them.

Quire got to his feet. His coat was as heavy as lead, soaked through. Water poured from it. He spat and sputtered. Davey was rising in front of him, the iron ring on its rope still hanging from his wrist like a manacle.

Quire fumbled about at his feet and dragged up a length of knotted branch. He swung it at Davey's head. The gravedigger got an arm up, and the branch broke in two across his elbow, leaving Quire with just the stub of it.

Davey surged forward, piling up the filthy ditchwater in front of his pumping legs. Quire threw himself to one side, sprawling on the bank amidst a fringe of rushes and rotting logs. He tried to push himself, backwards, up and out into the field beyond, but the soft earth gave beneath his hands and heels and sucked him back down. Davey loomed over him, the light of the moon spilling over his shoulders, and flailed at him with the rope-tethered ring. It thudded into the ground by Quire's head, spattering his cheek with wet mud.

Quire rose, sheer terror for once giving his left arm the strength to do what was needful. He threw himself inside the reach of the descending circlet of iron, and stabbed Davey in the eye with the broken stump of wood, leaving it planted there in the socket.

There should have been a scream. Writhing; panic; something. Davey simply faltered for a moment, and pawed rather ineffectually at the shaft of wood lodged in his skull. Quire hooked a leg behind Davey's knee and barged him over. The youth toppled back, half in and half out of the water. The moonlight fell full on his face then, and Quire could see the ruin he had wrought. No blood, though.

He saw, too, the remaining eye staring up at him, and that filled him with resurgent terror, for it was an empty, animal eye, devoid of human intelligence, or sentiment, or awareness. He felt no kinship of any kind with whatever lay behind it.

Already Davey was trying to rise, hampered only by the slippery mud and unstable banks of the ditch, not by his broken bones or destroyed eye.

"God damn you," Quire cried, shaking.

He did not know why he shook, whether it was from fear or anger. He did not care; he only cared that Davey should stay down, that this should end. For the first time, he could see the youth's hands clearly, and they were a mass of little dark scrawlings, far too small for Quire to make them out in the darkness. It was as if some fine-handed scribe had taken a quill to the boy's skin. Not tattoos, as best he could tell, but what else they might be he had no idea.

As Davey rolled on to his front, the better to push himself to his feet, Quire put a foot into the back of his right knee and took hold of his ankle. He might have baulked at what came next, had he thought about it. But there was no time, no thought; there was only life and death, and the cold, old Quire who knew precisely what it took to stay on the right side of the divide.

He stamped down with his foot, twisted with his arms, spun himself and put his whole body weight into the task of breaking out Davey's knee joint. He felt it go, heard it crackle and tear, but he didn't release Davey's leg. He lay across it, and kept pushing, kept trying to turn the ankle further, until he was certain that limb could not bear the gravedigger's weight. And never would again, most likely.

Even that, even the destruction of his knee, brought no wail of protest from Davey. Even though his foot projected at an absurd angle, his lower leg limp and twisted and loose, even with all that, he simply tried to rise, tried to reach Quire.

"God damn you," gasped Quire. "God damn you."

He had to lean back against the far bank of the ditch then, for he was trembling so violently that he thought he might fall. As it was, he only vomited, heaving his guts up into the dark water at his feet, while Davey slipped slowly down the opposite bank, still staring at him with that single, unblinking eye.

Quire turned away and pulled himself laboriously up into the field. He got unsteadily to his feet and staggered away, quite numb. He did not know if anyone – or anything – else would come after him. If they did, he had nothing left with which to oppose them. All he knew was that he needed to put as much ground as he could between himself and the gravedigger, still stirring feebly in the drainage ditch. Get himself away from this foul farm and out from under the light of this leering moon.

Beneath the powerful mid-morning sun, Davey Muir's hand clawed weakly at the soft earth. His fingers dug in, gouging out little ruts, piling up the grass between them. He had left a scrabbled trail of mud through the field, where he had hauled himself from the ditch, dragged his broken body another few dozen yards.

Blegg stood looking down at him. The lower half of Davey's left leg was rotated a good quarter-circle further than it should have been, the knee joint ruptured. A stick protruded a few inches from the ruined socket of his right eye. He made no sound. Just reached, and took a feeble handful of soil and grass, pulled it towards him. Reached, and held, and pulled.

"Go back to the farm," Blegg said without looking round to the man standing disconsolately behind him. "Get a fire started."

The man did not move at once. He stared in dumb horror at the crippled form on the ground.

"Wallace, did you get deaf as well as drunk and stupid last night?" Blegg snapped.

"No. No."

"Then go back to the farm and get a fire started. Same place as we did the one got shot at Duddingston. I'll bring this."

Wallace turned and began to trudge away, sluggish. Blood still crusted his hair where his head had been cracked against the farmhouse wall. As he walked, he favoured his left side, protective of the aching bruises put there by a couple of good punches.

"When we're done, you'll need to start loading the wagon up," Blegg called after him. "Everything. This place isn't safe any more. Not after this. Ruthven's equipment'll be needing another home."

Blegg bent down over Davey and pulled the stick from his eye.

Fragments of skin and eyeball adhered to it. Blegg threw it casually away. He regarded the sluggishly moving figure for a moment or two, then turned to shout at Wallace's receding back.

"Have you a knife?"

Wallace paused and looked back.

"Not on me."

"Get one from the kitchen, then. I may have a use for a part of this thing yet."

Blegg picked Davey up, slung him without difficulty over his shoulder and began to walk after Wallace.

"Quire," he murmured, with a strange mixture of loathing and relish.

XVIII

Quire's Last Day

Dr Robert Knox paused, his blade poised above the cadaver, and looked up. A whole gallery of attentive faces gazed down upon him from the seats of his teaching theatre. Two hundred or more young men waited for the incision and what it would reveal. The fractious whine of the gas lights was the only sound, as if every breath in the great chamber was held.

Knox slowly set down the scalpel and clasped his hands.

"You are privileged, gentlemen," he said, taking a pace to interpose himself between the corpse and its audience. "Privileged to have been born into an age of comprehension. A transformative age. By your presence here, you accept an invitation to join a brotherhood of sorts."

He looked up, and addressed himself to the highest corner, where wall met ceiling. His voice swelled with passion the better to fill the space. And though this was not what his students had expected, they listened with rapt concentration.

"It is a brotherhood that holds reason, and its fearless application, to be the holiest of sacraments. It is a fraternity built upon the achievements of men who laboured long and hard to uncover secrets, and render unto all of humanity the fruits of their labours.

"Yet I was reminded, not so long ago, that there are those who would set obstacles in the path of reason. Those who would forbid us to follow where it leads, because they find our discoveries, or our conclusions, or our methods – particularly our methods – distasteful. They care nothing for the benefits mankind may derive from the rational, clear-headed pursuit of knowledge. They are prisoners of their superstitions, and their fear, and would have us be the same."

Knox returned to the side of the dissecting slab at his theatre's heart. He looked down at the naked form lying there: a middle-aged woman. Blotched skin, shorn hair. Nameless and empty.

"A great enterprise is under way," he called out, so sharply as to set a few of the assembled students jumping on their hard benches. "A noble enterprise, and you are all a part of it, though it was begun before a single man of you was born. It will change our world entirely. It is the substitution, gentlemen, of superstition and mysticism with a spirit of rational enquiry that promises to make possible wonders of every kind."

He pointed with a thick, long finger at one of the gas jets burning so brightly on the wall.

"It is by the light of just such a wonder that you see me at this moment. There have been boats out upon the Forth this very day driven not by the wind or the strength of men but by engines. We shall, undoubtedly, have the railway in Edinburgh before this decade is out, and then we all shall make our journeys not by stagecoach but by steam carriage. Wonders, gentlemen!"

Knox carefully reached down and took hold of the scalpel once more. It was small in his big hand, but its blade took a gas-fired gleam from the air and sparkled.

"It is our joint responsibility, we members of this rational brotherhood, to stand firm against the assaults of those who would hobble our investigations. We pursue higher ambitions than they conceive, and cannot be bound by the petty concerns of mob, or church, or polite society. It is both our burden and our honour to stand above such considerations."

He surveyed the attentive faces, as if to determine their worth.

"In one more way are you privileged, gentlemen," he proclaimed with a dramatic flourish of his scalpel, much as the conductor of an orchestra might wield his baton. "It is this: you have found your way into my charge. I tell you frankly that you are most fortunate, or wise, to have arrived at such a destination."

A ripple of amusement tumbled down the steeply raked gallery of seating. His students knew the shape of this theme. They had heard it often enough before, and it was one that seldom proved less than entertaining.

"You have escaped, some of you all too briefly, from under the dead hand of the university. These men they call lecturers and professors" – Knox gestured at the wall with his blade, sending their imaginations out beyond the Royal Infirmary, over the tenement roofs, to where the great college of the university lay – "they rest upon laurels earned by those now dead. They rely upon the notes of men who gave the same lectures, word for word, thirty years ago. There is no movement. And thus they allow the torch that they inherited to falter, its flame to dim."

He lowered his voice at last, surveying his assembled acolytes with one final sweep of his distinguished head.

"Not here, gentlemen. Here we still pursue the mysteries. Here we still stride forward, admitting of no restraint that lesser mortals might seek to set upon our advancement of human knowledge. So. Let us see what discoveries await us this evening, shall we?"

He bent over the dead woman and set his scalpel to her throat. A pause. An expectant hush. Then, with a single firm and unerring movement, he cut her open from neck to stomach.

"I've a sworn statement that you were seen in the company of whores, Quire."

There was a lascivious looseness to the way Acting Superintendent Baird said the words. He savoured their feel in his mouth far too much. Quire stared back at the man, not bothering to conceal his distaste.

Baird occupied like a thief the seat in which James Robinson had so recently sat, Quire thought. A usurper, entirely too enamoured of the authority he had stolen. Delighting too much in its exercise, as men so often did when they were not truly deserving of the power they wielded. The less they had done to earn it, the more it pleased them to display it.

"Who's done the swearing?" Quire asked.

The dead weight of his voice should have been a warning to anyone alert to such things, but Baird was not one such.

"Not your concern. The truth of it, that's what you should be pondering."

"Have I no right to know my accuser, then?"

"This isn't a court of law," Baird scoffed. "It's a matter of discipline. You've breached the regulations of your employment, and for that I'm your judge and the Police Board your jury."

Quire knew then that he was caught. A fish in a net, and all his thrashing would do nothing but wind him more tightly in the mesh. He had sensed trouble, without knowing its shape, as soon he got back to the police house, to be greeted by the message that Baird required his immediate presence.

Until then, the day had been quieter than most of his recent experience. He had woken, still aching and stiff from his exertions at Cold Burn Farm, after sleeping fitfully through the best part of a full day and night. He had half expected to be roused by the sound of men, or hounds, at his door, come to put an end to him. Instead, it had been the cries of a gypsy woman out on the Canongate, proclaiming the luck-giving properties of the sprigs of heather she had for sale.

He spared only a few moments to take the edge from his bleary-eyed, dishevelled state. A splash of cold water across his face; a passing glance in the cracked mirror he used for shaving, revealing the tracery of scratches laid across his cheeks; a comb tugged painfully through his grimy hair.

He had not gone directly to the police house. Instead, he had walked almost the whole length of the city, to Melville Street. He wanted to see if his visit to Cold Burn Farm had brought some change, or commotion, to the place. And, if he was honest, to try to clear his mind of the numb bewilderment that threatened to engulf it. He did not know how to oppose that which Davey Muir had become, nor hounds that knew neither death nor life. But a man, living a life like all his neighbours in the New Town; that he could oppose.

It had been fruitless, though. The mute façade of that grand house had stared back at him, lifeless and impenetrable as the obdurate wall of a castle. He could not, it seemed, reach those sequestered within; could not draw them out to meet them upon his own territory. He would find a way, though. He knew that if he worked away at the mortar hard enough, he could break out the stones in that wall and see what lay beyond.

So he had thought, in any case, until this moment. This ambuscade.

"If there's been some spy dogging my footsteps, I'd like to know of it," he said tightly to Baird.

Who snorted in dismissive contempt.

"Never mind your bruised feelings. Do you deny it? That's the question, Quire. Are you going to tell me you were not in the company of a whore on the High Street, plain as day, on the very morning of Superintendent Robinson's dismissal?"

That left Quire mute for a moment or two. The denial, if he was to offer it, had to come at once to his lips. He needed to snap it out unhesitatingly, with all the force he could muster. But he did not. The breath he needed to utter it faltered in his throat, snared for that instant in the thought of Catherine, and his sudden reluctance to so casually repudiate her. Not in a cause that he knew was already lost. He would not give Baird the satisfaction.

"No, you don't." Baird smiled. "Of course you don't. No point to it. And it's not even the first time, is it? The very same woman who so nearly put an end to your career once already. Robinson might've saved you from the consequences of your indiscretions before, Quire, but I will not. You can be assured of that."

"I'd never have doubted it."

"You know that any man of the city police who consorts with such folk is at risk of dismissal. You know that fine well, and if you thought it an empty threat, you'll be learning otherwise, I think."

Quire said nothing. There was an emptiness hollowing itself out in him, the impotent feeling of being atop a cliff, swaying at the very precipice, unable to turn away.

"Too many marks against your name, Quire. I've another complaint to hand already. A Dr Knox. Claims you have harassed him with groundless accusations."

Quire rolled his eyes.

"Questions, not accusations, and hardly groundless. He seemed content enough when we parted company. Shook my hand."

"Did he? Must have reconsidered his judgement of the matter

once no longer exposed to your charms, then. He'd hardly be the first, would he?

"You're a fool, to think you can go around laying charges at the door of Ruthven and Knox without consequence. You think you're some lone wolf, do you, unconstrained by the proprieties, the proper conduct to which the rest of must adhere?"

There was real bitterness in Baird's voice now. A personal animosity. It called up Quire's anger, for all his efforts to control himself.

"I've never thought myself anything more than a man trying to do what was needful, and right. It's not something you would understand, given that you're a piss-poor excuse for a police officer. If you were anything more than that, you'd be wondering why these folk want me gone. You'd be worth telling what it was I saw out on a Pentland farm, and how it was I got these scratches."

"A Pentland farm," snapped Baird. "There's the very thing, isn't it? What in God's name are you doing out on a Pentland farm, Quire? You've no authority there. Have you taken to trespass as a way of passing the time now, is that it?"

Quire held his tongue. He clamped his hands together, squeezing hard, to keep his anger and frustration locked away within. It was not only that he refused to let Baird see the extent of his dismay; it was that he feared what his hands might do to the man if he let them free.

"It'll all need to go to the board," Baird was saying, sinking back in the chair, cuddling his satisfaction about him. "That means you're relieved of your duties, on half-pay, until the decision's made. Barred from the police house, barred from speaking with your fellow officers. Do you understand?"

Still, Quire did not respond.

"I'll need your baton, too," Baird said.

"I lost it," Quire told him.

"Lost it?" Baird was incredulous. "What are you talking about, man?"

"I lost it while I was trying to keep myself from getting drowned in a ditch on Ruthven's farm. Do you want to hear the tale? I'll tell it if you do. Give you a chance to remember what it is we're supposed to do here."

"Ruthven, Ruthven," muttered Baird. "Have you learned nothing? There's no evidence against the man, Quire."

"There's my testimony. And if you sent a dozen men out to Cold Burn Farm, like as not you'd find something might count as evidence. The dogs that killed Carlyle, and almost killed me. And worse, much worse. If you'd seen the things I have ..."

"I can't charge a dog with murder, attempted or otherwise, Quire," Baird said wearily. "And henceforth, I think you'll agree, any court might find your testimony more than a little tainted. Get out. You'll be told of the outcome of the board's deliberations, but I'd not be holding your breath if I was you. I'd not be expecting a happy result, either. I'll be recommending they dismiss you, and making sure they know of your past infringements. I imagine they'll be only too happy to start cleaning away the mess Robinson left behind him."

Quire went leaden-footed down the stairs, hearing nothing of the banter and chatter of the police house, seeing nothing. He passed out into the High Street, and the bustle of it caught him up and swept him away down towards the Canongate, helpless flotsam on the current.

Wilson Dunbar sang to his children that night in their little house at Abbey Hill. He sang them songs he had heard in Spain, twenty years ago. Sang them the tunes, at least; he did not remember most of the words, and those he did were not fit for the ears of children, so he made up nonsense ditties to ride along on the melodies. Silly things, childish things, which were to him the sweetest things of all.

Ellen, his wife, sat quietly in the corner with her embroidery, a constant smile upon her face as she passed the needle back and forth through cloth stretched over a round wooden frame. A hundred times this scene had been repeated, since Angus – the older of the boys – had been a mewling babe in his cot. Dunbar sang then because the sound of it soothed and softened the child; he sang now because it was what he did, part of the pact between him and his boys. They expected it of him, and he obliged them gladly. It was as much a part of the fabric of their home as the stones in the wall, the slates in the roof.

And when he was done, and those Spanish tunes were spent, and the boys were asleep, he sat with his wife by the sinking fire. They did not talk much, and did not need to, for they shared in a single, swaddling contentment that required no expression beyond their presence there, together, and the sound of their children, shifting lethargically in their sleep. All was right with the world, within the walls of that house, and in that company.

XIX

Old Acquaintance

There was no older tavern in Edinburgh than the White Hart on the Grassmarket. Lined by inns and low houses and shops purveying every kind of provision, dominated by the castle and the craggy cliffs atop which it stood just to the north, the Grassmarket had been a place of commerce and execution, revelry and riot for centuries. Through a great many of those years, the White Hart had stood there and been witness to countless dramas played out before its windows. For generations, every scandal and oddity and delight of the Old Town had been chewed over by its patrons. The idle talk of choice now was diverse, little of it distinguishing between the real and the imagined: tales of plague skeletons uncovered in the course of the works for the new bridge over the Cowgate; the bakery boy attacked by a wild mob of rats at the West Port one dawn; the girl at the tannery along the way growing fat with child, and her all unmarried but a friend to half the soldiers in the castle barracks.

Amidst this hubbub of speculation, one man sat alone and quiet, nursing a mug of ale that he never drank from. His eyes did not stray from the foamy head of his beer, and his hands – still in their black gloves though the little room was warm – remained clasped around it. If the great crowd of drinkers packed into the White Hart found his solitary, silent presence odd, they gave no sign of it. None paid him any more heed than a brief glance.

Two men entered, though, whose roving eyes picked him out at once, and they shuffled and elbowed their way to the little table he occupied.

"Is it Blegg?" the taller one asked curtly, his voice rich with the tones of his Irish homeland, and at that Blegg did lift his gaze, and fix it upon these newcomers with still clarity.

"Sit," he said, and they ferreted out stools from amongst the forest of legs and bodies.

"Are you buying us drinks?" one asked as he slapped his back-side down.

"You pay your own way until we've taken the measure of one another, don't you think?"

The two Irishmen looked at each other, in silent consultation, until one grunted and rose with evident annoyance.

"I'll get them in, then," he grumbled, and began to push his way unceremoniously towards the bar.

Blegg watched him sink into the crowd, and then turned slowly back to the other.

"So. You've my name. What should I call you?"

"Oh, I like to keep my name close, like a sweetheart, until I know a man a little better."

"You've a pretty turn of phrase, for an Irishman."

"Is that so? You've a cocky tongue, for a Scotsman."

"Hah." It was an entirely cold and humourless little laugh. "Nice. And what's your trade?"

"What's it to you? I could mend your shoes if you've a need for a cobbler, but that's not what we came to talk about, is it? I'm not looking for employment."

"I like to know what manner of men I'm dealing with. And maybe you are looking for employment, of a sort. That's what I heard, in any case."

"Did you."

It was a curt, sharp utterance. The Irishman glared at Blegg, the look thick with the spontaneous animosity that might easily arise when two men scented difference of temperament or type between them. Blegg was unmoved, and stared passively back, contemptuous amusement tugging at the corners of his lips. It was the other who looked away, watching his countryman barge his way back towards them, bearing his precious cargo.

"I've lost my thirst," the seated man muttered as he was passed a cup.

"Why's that?"

"Don't like his manner." He flicked his chin at Blegg. "Thinks he's clever, this one. Cleverer than us, anyway."

"I'm not caring who's clever and who's not. Clever's fine, if it comes with money. Knox's doorkeep said it'd be worth our while meeting with you, that's all. Fifteen pounds' worth, he said."

"Ah, now you're a forward kind of man," Blegg said approvingly. "Not like your fellow here. What's your name, friend?"

"The two of us share one name – William – and part thereafter: he is Burke, I am Hare."

"Now what did you go and tell him that for?" Burke snapped. Hare shrugged.

"There's half a dozen folk in here know my name, and yours as well. If he wants to know, he can find it easy enough."

Burke was unappeased.

"This cocky bastard wants to know who he's dealing with; I say we do too. I've no more than a name for him, and I'd want more."

"Would you?" Blegg murmured. "It'd not profit you to have it.

Look at Mr Hare, here. He's not caring what more there might be. Just the price, eh? And it's fifteen pounds, right enough."

Burke drained his mug in a single long series of gulps, and smacked it down on to the table with a touch more force than was needed.

"Don't care if it's a hundred pound." He leaned closer to Hare. "I'll not bargain on things such as this with a man I don't trust. And I don't trust this bastard. Nor like him."

Blegg looked away, evincing disinterest.

"Come away," Burke urged his companion. "We're not needing him. We've got all the arrangement we need with others."

Hare looked doubtful, and Blegg abruptly turned back, and stared at him. When he spoke, it was to Burke, though his eyes remained fixed upon Hare.

"You'd best be away, right enough. I'm not needing *you*, that's sure. But your friend here I'll buy as much drink as he likes."

"I'll stay a bit," Hare said softly.

"On your head be it, then," Burke growled, angry. "He's the stink of trouble, and I'll not be sharing it with you."

He pushed himself up from the table so firmly that the little stool toppled over backwards. He kicked it aside as he made for the door. Blegg looked after him with a sour expression.

"Have you cold hands or something, then?" Hare asked, eyeing the black gloves with which Blegg held his still full mug of flattening beer.

"Something," Blegg grunted. "Listen, our mutual acquaintance, Mr Paterson in Surgeon's Square, tells me you're the very man I need to talk to on the matter of . . . well, shall we call them certain goods that are not easily obtained? I pay him well enough to put some faith in his advice. Is he right?"

"Maybe so, maybe not."

"Come, don't be coy. I've no wish to intrude upon whatever

trade you're plying with Knox. My needs are modest, and you'll
be well recompensed if you can meet them."

Hare eyed his new drinking companion, a touch reserved.

"Is it an anatomist you're working for, then?" he asked.
"Something like that?"

"Something like that. Something like that."

Hare wrinkled his nose.

"It's courting ill luck," he said, "to be talking of such things in
the very place they've hanged men for less."

"Oh, they've not had gallows in the Grassmarket for a time
now, William." Blegg smiled. "They build them elsewhere these
days. And it's more fitting a place than you might think. Do you
not know the meaning of the sign under which we meet?"

"The White Hart?"

"Herne the Hunter," said Blegg. "The white hart is his beast.
His totem. It was a white hart that wounded him, when he was
a mortal man, wounded him unto death. But he was returned to
life by a maker of magics, who bound the hart's antlers to his
head. Thus was he restored."

"I've no interest in your folk tales," Hare grunted.

"No? As you like. Let us talk of more practical matters, shall
we?"

Quire still ached. His body was taking its time in forgetting his
misadventure at Cold Burn Farm. It did not seem too great a
burden, though, for he was warm, and well rested, and for now
at least content.

He rolled and draped an arm across Cath Heron's naked shoulder. The bedding was rough, and the mattress lumpy, but her skin
was soft and her hair where it lay across the pillow between them
put the scent of her in his nose. She stirred at his touch, almost
awake, but not quite.

It was unaccustomedly quiet. Too early for the inhabitants of the Holy Land to be up and about, certainly, but too early as well for the rest of the Old Town to have come but a little way out of the night. The scavengers would be finishing their rounds, wheeling their barrows full of Edinburgh's scraps off the streets. The forges and breweries down in the Canongate would be beginning to wake, but they were far enough distant that he could not hear the flexing of their iron and coal muscles. Seagulls, he could hear; always seagulls, called up from the coast by the riches of the city.

It had been many years since Quire had been easily able to sleep late. Wakefulness came, whether he wanted it or not. This night, at least, had been dreamless, the horrors of his past and present banished, for once, from his sleeping mind. His slumber had been deep, and sated, and restorative. The drink had helped, no doubt, but so had Cath. So had his yielding to desires long denied.

He blew gently upon her cheek, and her eyes trembled. A thin hand came sluggishly to fend him off. He wanted to share these still, quiet moments. There were few enough such in his life these days, and in Cath's, he imagined; they seemed a gift, not to be lightly squandered.

She blinked at him, rolled towards him just enough to fold herself into his arms.

"Sergeant Quire," she said, pressing her face into the crook of his neck. "I thought you might be gone when I woke."

"Not yet," he murmured.

They were alone in the rooms. Cath had sent Emma on her way as soon as they came in, a little unsteady on their feet, and the older woman had gone willingly enough, favouring Quire with a knowing smile as she went. A woman in want of a bed would have no trouble finding one in the Holy Land at night.

Quire ran his hand down Cath's flank beneath the bedding, slipping it over her buttock and on to her thigh. There was comfort even in that simple motion, and the memory it carried of their congress. It called up once more the cleansing, emptying heat of their union; its capacity to banish, for a time, all thought and all self, and free Quire of his troubles and his fears. Fears. That was right enough, and having let the notion of it into his head, he lost hold of his tranquillity. He withdrew his hand, and swung his legs out to sit on the edge of the bed.

"God, it's early," Cath moaned, reading by long experience the soft fall of light through the window. "Can we not sleep a bit longer?"

She ran a fingernail down his spine. That made shivers race through the skin of his back. He stood, naked, and stretched his arms. He had never been troubled to hide the scars on his arm from Cath. From the first time she had seen them, her ease at the sight of them had made itself his own. Today, it was his other marks that drew her attention. A great bruise as many-hued as a summer thundercloud was just beginning to fade, spread over his hip and flank where Davey Muir had thrown him into a tree.

Cath reached out to touch it, tracing its yellow-black shape.

"Look at you, Adam. Look at you."

Her voice was laden with sympathy, with sorrow. That had been, in part, what he had needed last night, Quire supposed: the simple comfort of caring company. He had been drunk, so it was not easy to recall exactly how his mind had been working, but he knew it had been a whole web of longings. All his old affection for her, only sharpened by his long resistance to its call; his selfish need to be taken out of himself for a time, to have another set aside his dark thoughts for him, since he could not seem to do it himself.

There had been no restraining sense of consequence, for he was already accused, and half-convicted, of that which he now did. It had felt the most natural thing in all the world to turn for comfort and companionship to Cath. And she had been welcoming, forgiving. As if he had never wronged her.

Her hand was easing itself around his thigh, straying towards his crotch, and he felt his desire stirring in anticipation of her touch. But he slipped beyond her reach, and began to collect his clothes from the floor.

"Already?" she asked.

"I'm sorry," he said, and meant it. "I'll be back, Cath. I promise you that."

As he pulled his trousers on, his gaze fell upon an open box sitting by the window. Curled up in it were the amber bead amulets that the Widow's girls sold as protective charms to their customers. That put a sour twist to the moment, reminding Quire of how many others had shared Cath's bed, but more immediate preoccupations chased the thought away quickly enough.

"So do you think these things work, then?" he asked, holding up one of the trinkets.

It was not a question he would once have asked, but if he had learned nothing else of late, it was that there were mysteries to the working of the world he had never imagined.

"The folk who buy them do, that's what matters," Cath grunted, rolling away from the sight, shrugging the sheets back up over her shoulders.

She did not like to be reminded, any more than Quire did, of her trade. Not in this moment. Quire realised then, in his sluggish way, that he was not the only one who had tried to make a kind of release and escape for themselves last night. He was ashamed to have so crudely drained the morning of its gentleness. But still he held the charm, and squinted at it.

"Where do they come from?" he asked. "Does the Widow make them herself, or are there folk still doing little magics like these?"

"Aye, there's folk like that," Cath said into the bedding. "There's always been folk like that. You've just got to ken where to look."

Later, as afternoon turned to evening, tired but still lighter of heart than his situation and his fears warranted, Quire met Wilson Dunbar outside St Giles' Cathedral on the High Street. It was a long-standing and regular arrangement, that had made more sense when Quire had actually been employed at the police house, just over the street.

The cathedral – a great crouching mass surmounted by a grandiose stone crown – always put Quire in mind of a titanic black beetle squatted down and bearing carbuncles on its back. He found Dunbar waiting for him on its steps, and together they walked down through the crowds towards Calder's.

Dunbar was working as a builder these days. Some kind of combination of quartermaster, labourer and gang master, as far as Quire could tell, happily engaged in the construction of the grand new High School on Calton Hill. He smelled of stone dust and mortar. He examined Quire with critical eyes as they wove through the evening crowds.

"You look in a better mood than I've seen you of late," he opined.

"Do I?"

"Aye, you do. It's unsettling, I'll tell you. Like the sun coming out at midnight."

"Might be I spent some time with Cath last night," Quire said.

"Ha!" Dunbar clapped his hands together loudly enough to startle a boy carrying a basket of oysters past. "First smart thing you've done in a wee while. Last I heard, you had a fair few reasons you couldn't be doing that. What happened to them?"

"The Police Board happened to them. I've already been suspended from duty. They're working themselves up to turning me out on the street."

Dunbar stopped in the midst of the street, his mood abruptly overturned. Quire walked on a few paces, then stopped and turned back.

"What happened?" Dunbar asked.

"Got myself on the wrong side of the wrong folk. Come on, don't stand there like a fool. Calder's is waiting on us."

He led the way on down towards the Canongate.

"They're the fools, to be thinking they're not needing your services," muttered Dunbar darkly.

"Maybe. World's full of fools. Might be I'm one of them. I had my chances to leave things be."

"And why didn't you?"

"Because there were dead men needing answers. One of them got his head broken in with a spade in front of his son. Because I can't abide anyone thinking they can be party to that and never have to pay the price. Because they came after me. Thought they could frighten me off; or kill me. Because I'm a stubborn bastard. Take your choice of those."

"Reasons enough," Dunbar said.

"There's more. The men who've got the blood on their hands . . . there's strange things happening. Not like anything I've seen before. Not like anything you'd give credence to, without seeing it yourself. It's dark as it gets, at the heart of this, I reckon."

Quire was pleased, and not a little surprised, to find his mood surviving even this gloomy talk. He could feel the sinking sun still warm on his back. They passed the head of Leith Wynd, and he smiled to himself at the memory of Cath.

"Can you not let someone else do the stopping?" Dunbar asked despondently, his tone betraying his foreknowledge of the answer.

"I'd be a long time waiting for that to happen. Best I can tell, I've got fewer friends in the police house, and certainly on the board, than the bloody murderers themselves. If I thought he was smart enough for it, I'd even wonder if Baird – Superintendent Baird – wasn't in their pay, the way he's gone after me."

"Or maybe he just doesn't like you," Dunbar suggested. "He'd not be the first."

"True enough. But anyway, would you be sitting by your fire twiddling your thumbs, if your work and your livelihood were taken from you, and you had folk coming to your house at night to try to kill you?"

Dunbar grunted.

"Ah," said Quire, slapping his friend on the arm. "I'm not wanting to talk of it tonight. It's a bit of drink and forgetting I'm looking for. I thought you'd be the very man for that task. Was I wrong?"

"Not wrong, no," Dunbar said.

There was renewed levity in his voice. Quire thought it a touch forced, but perhaps not entirely so.

They arrived at Calder's to find their hopes and expectations abruptly curtailed. Workmen were milling about within, setting up a great clattering and banging. Lengths of coppery pipes were being passed in through the open door from a wheeled trolley parked up in the close.

"That's a blow," Dunbar said despondently.

Quire was inclined to agree. The two of them stood, peering in through the windows, at a loss how to proceed now that their den of choice was denied them.

Mrs Calder herself appeared on the threshold. She smiled apologetically in answer to their silent appeals for guidance.

"There's to be gas laid up the close," she said, "so we're getting all the fittings. Lamps and such like."

"Gas?" moaned Dunbar. "Place'll never be the same."

"No," Mrs Calder agreed, "it'll be better. You should get used to change, young Wilson, since it'll come whether you like it or not. Do you boys want some feeding, then? I've a beef stew with tatties."

"Aye, all right," said Dunbar, brightening considerably, though Quire knew the invitation was mainly meant for him.

They passed a fine evening in the Calder kitchen, devouring the hot thick stew and slabs of hard bread, and Mrs Calder found a mug or two of beer for them to wash it down with. They talked, in the easy, lazy way of old friends, for a long time: about Dunbar's family; about Cath, and whether or not Quire was good enough for her; about whether there would be money enough to finish that school Dunbar was so proud to be building.

When the plates were empty, and Mrs Calder chased them out with all the good humour of one satisfied by her evening's work, Dunbar went contentedly on his way, humming to himself as he disappeared off down the Canongate. Quire climbed the stairs to his rooms in similar buoyant temper. He smiled still, his lips shaping themselves thus without his bidding.

It had been a good day, for all his bodily aches, and for all the intransigence of the problems confronting him. A day of renewed affections, and of hearty eating. Better than most he had known, in his former life, upon the eve of battle.

XX

The Widow

A closed black carriage processed slowly along the road skirting the southern edge of Hope Park. Most folk called it by the simpler title of the Meadows now, this long stretch of open grass, edged and crossed by stately paths that ran between avenues of trees, but Hope Park suited its grace a little better.

It pleased a certain type of Edinburgh resident to promenade there, when the weather was compliant. Many strolled, at a pace fit for contemplation and for the certainty of being observed, along the tree-lined walkways. Couples arm in arm, soft with love; groups of ladies, parasols bobbing like clumps of flowers; men of business or of learning, deep in conversation as often as not. Others took to their carriages and rolled along behind horses groomed to their highest state of beauty.

Most of these carriages went with hoods folded down, their occupants sitting tall, displaying themselves. Not so the black one easing its way round the Meadows. It went along like a great dark molluscan shell mounted on wheels, heavy curtains drawn, secrecy preserved. A more suitable home for it would have been in the midst of a funeral cortège, but there it nevertheless was, in all its brazen sobriety, taking its place amongst the jaunty barouches and fancy phaetons that paraded their equally gaudy passengers for all to see. Even the horses hauling this austere interloper were funereal: black and sedate.

Quire was waiting at the foot of a lime tree, one in a tremendous line of them stretching the whole length of the Meadows and laying their shadows out across the grass like the sketches of fallen pillars. Or, he supposed, the bars of a cell. He leaned against the tree, idly chewing on a long, twitching stem of grass he had plucked from its base. The sap that bled out between his teeth was watery but very faintly sweet.

He watched the to and fro of promenaders with an uninflected detachment. A disconnection had settled upon him since he had embarked upon his present course, a shard of distance put between him and the city and its people. He observed them, and felt that some flaw had entered into his understanding of them and of the lives they led. The change was not in the place, or its inhabitants, but in him.

He was, in many ways, now the Quire of old. Of Hougoumont. He had settled himself back into that former self, like a man pulling on a long-neglected coat. It still fitted him. He felt, as he had so often all those years ago, a strange kind of yearning for the struggle to commence. There would be no more manoeuvring, no more bluff or restraint. Only resolution. He felt coldly calm at the prospect. Intent.

The black carriage pulled up in front of him. The driver, perched on a high seat like that of a mail coach, looked down meaningfully at Quire, who returned the gaze impassively. Even that driver was a part of the display. He wore a tall, stiff black hat, and dark suit and waistcoat. He looked a sour man, Quire thought, and that too seemed fitting.

The two of them regarded one another in silence as the prettier folk passed by. Eventually, the near door of the carriage swung open.

"Don't be a tiresome arse, Quire," a light, feminine voice called out. "Get in."

"I was just waiting for the invitation," Quire grunted as he climbed aboard.

The door closed behind him, sealing him into a warm, humid softness of worked leather and quilted cushions, and those pendulous curtains shutting out much of the sunlight. Everything was coloured from the same sombre palette: black and dark browns, muted burgundy. Even the woman who sat opposite Quire, watching him with sharply intelligent eyes.

She wore a black skirt and bodice, both of them trimmed with black lace, and had her hair tied up in a bun with a black silk ribbon. She possessed a certain rather dry and studied beauty, Quire had always thought, but there was little about her that could be called warm. She gently tapped the shell of the carriage behind her head with a knuckle, and they jerked forwards before settling back into the slow and steady pace of before.

"Could we not let a little light in?" Quire wondered, toying with the edge of the nearest curtain.

"No, we could not."

"You're not in the best of moods this morning, then."

"And you've been drinking," she said, with a faint and entirely inappropriate hint of accusation in her voice.

"Not this morning," Quire said, affronted.

"No, but last night. I can smell it on you."

"Well if you'd just open the curtains, maybe we could let a wee bit of air in along with the light."

"Leave them be. I am in mourning."

"I know you are, Mary. I know you are."

Mary Coulter. The Widow. Landlady and unchallenged ruler

of the Holy Land; part-owner, it was said, of the Just and Happy Lands too. Queen, in other words, of the worst nests of vipers and vice the city had to offer. So she had been ever since her husband, the king of that same territory, died eight years ago. And ever since, she had been in perpetual mourning.

In truth, Quire would have welcomed a little of the air a tweaking of the curtain might admit. It was stuffy in that sealed box, with the full weight of the sun beating down on its black skin. He did not particularly want this interview to be a long-drawn-out affair.

"So," the Widow said, perhaps sharing the sentiment, "Cath told me you wanted to see me, but not the why of it."

"Aye. I wanted to tell you that myself."

"I heard you were fallen upon hard times. By the smell of you, you've not taken well to it."

"If this matter of my smell is causing such offence, I've already told you . . ."

"You're quite a capable man, Adam," the Widow interrupted him firmly. "A man, perhaps, in need of gainful employment. In need of pay?"

"I'm not entirely dismissed yet," Quire protested. "Still on a half-wage."

"And what's half a sergeant's wage? Five shillings a week? I can do a little better than that for you."

She could be quite charming when she wished. Quire had witnessed that on occasion. But anyone who spent any time poking around in Edinburgh's shadows would discover, sooner or later, that she had her darker attributes too. No one could run the Holy Land on charm. Quire was yet to decide whether Mary had come today equipped only with that charm, or with rather sharper weapons. So far as he knew, she had a certain grudging respect, perhaps even affection, for him, but it was nothing he would care to rely too heavily upon.

The carriage slowed and swayed and gave a couple of shy little creaks. Quire could feel it turning about. They had evidently reached the end of the avenue and were to retrace their path.

"I'm not after the kind of work you'd offer," he said, trying – not too hard – to keep it from sounding like an insult. "And like I say: I'm not dismissed yet."

"Oh, but you will be, Adam. You know that, don't you? There are folk of consequence in this world, and there are those of none. You are about to become one of the latter, unless you take hold of a helping hand when it's offered. And you know better than most what becomes of men of no consequence."

That annoyed Quire. Not just the philosophy, but the flawless confidence with which she expounded it. As if she was herself untouchable, unimpeachable and inarguably correct. Which she might well be, of course; but still, it annoyed him.

"I've seen a lot of people killed in my time," he said, allowing himself to sink back into a corner, resting his arm on the padded windowsill. "Most of them what you'd call inconsequential men, I suppose, slaughtering one another at the behest of those who think themselves better. I never thought them dying was a matter of no consequence. Never."

"I know that. It's why you have – had – a good name in the Old Town, even when you were locking up a fair number of its folk." Her tone had softened somewhat; she was essaying a companionable warmth. "Doesn't make you right, but it might make you useful. You can put that good name to use with me. You're not daft enough to think it's only the police who keep order in the city."

"I'm not going to be policing the Holy Land and its people for you, Mary, so please don't ask again."

"A pity."

Quire lifted the curtain to look out. The light was sharp,

making him wince. The noble trees that lined the road went by, one after the other, with their black, furrowed bark and bright green leaves. Quire wondered idly whether they would have to go when the gaslights came, as they surely would one day, to stake their claim to that same stretch of roadside along the Meadows. It would be a shame, he thought, to lose the trees. They looked to him as though they must have been there for a long time.

"A peppermint?" the Widow asked him.

She was leaning over, holding out a little tin box, its lid open to reveal a score or more of dusty white lozenges. He shook his head, and she returned the box to a purse at her waist.

"I was hoping you might arrange a meeting for me," Quire said.

She smiled, and for once achieved a more or less natural, relaxed appearance that brought her face to life.

"Well, I do like it when folk owe me favours, so I daresay I'll help if I can. What – or who – was it you were after?"

"Your witch."

"What?"

"Cath says you get your charms from an old witch woman. I want to talk to her. Only if it's not all some game you play, mark you. I don't care about those silly wee beads – I daresay they're no use for anything but taking pennies off the gullible – but I need to talk to someone who knows about . . . whatever it is such folk know about. Darker matters. Can you oblige me?"

There was an element of suspicion in the gaze to which the Widow subjected him. An appraisal, too; trying to reach a judgement, perhaps, on whether or not he was serious.

"You're a man full of surprises," she said at length. "It's an appealing trait, in moderation. I'll see what I can do for you, but I make no promises. The woman concerned makes her own decisions."

"Fair enough. There's one more matter. I've a feeling I'll be needing somewhere to stay. My own rooms have been attracting some unwelcome attention of late, and I need to be a wee bit harder to find, just for a time. I was thinking Cath might . . ."

The Widow laughed, a rich and strangely generous sound to Quire's ear.

"Why, Adam. You must be in the direst of straits if you think the Holy Land a safer bolt-hole than your own roof. There's one or two in there who'd not count themselves your friend."

"You put it about I'm under your protection, I'll be safe enough. It'll not be for long."

"And you think Catherine will have you, do you?"

"I think so."

"You might be right, at that."

XXI

The Witch of Leith

The harbour at Leith was not large, but it seethed with activity. Boats of every kind were tied up along the curving quay that lined the Water of Leith's mouth. A naval cutter big and brash amongst a little flotilla of fishing smacks; a coastal barge discharging a cargo of baled cloth beside a snub-nosed ferry waiting for its passengers. The masts and rigging made a thin forest stretching along the sea's edge, all swaying and rocking in time with the chop of the water. Crew and dock hands clambered about and over the boats like so many busy, noisy ants.

The quayside itself was no less lively. The last few boxes and trays of fish from the morning's haul were still being sold, drawing a busy crowd of those late from their beds, or hoping for scraps disregarded by richer, earlier buyers. This was Edinburgh's port, separate but bound to the city by the long, straight run of Leith Walk, and all manner of city folk came here to buy the sea's produce and the cargoes it bore upon its back.

Quire sat a short way from that crowd, balanced somewhat precariously upon an iron bollard. He had been told to wait there, and did so with more than his usual degree of patience.

It was no great chore, with the Forth's bright air blowing in and ruffling his hair, and wheeling, screeching seagulls swirling above him.

The rhythmic creaking of the ships lining the quay had a comforting solidity to it, as if it knew what an ancient, unchanging sound it was and through how many scenes just like this it had threaded itself over the centuries. There were a handful of steamships in these waters now, Quire knew, but today the harbour was all rigging and furled sails and festoons of rope.

Quire was absorbed in his ruminations, and thus did not notice the woman approach him until she was right in front of him, blocking off his view of the fishermen and their customers.

She was old enough to be a little creased, a little worn, but not so old as to be diminished or hampered by the years on her back. Beyond forty, not yet fifty, Quire guessed. Her face had the faintly sallow, pinched look a hard-working life bestowed, but there was nothing frail about her. She was holding a swaddled baby in the crook of her arm. The infant was blinking and mewing softly to itself, apparently content.

"My granddaughter," the woman said. "Mother's gone work-hunting down the shore, hasn't she, beautiful?"

She tapped with a crooked finger at the baby's lips, and the tiny girl duly tried to suck at it.

"You're Quire?" the woman asked, still looking down with affection at the infant, still tickling at it with her finger.

"I am. And you're Agnes McLaine?"

"Who else would I be? Do you get that many women coming up to you with your name on the Leith harbour that you can't keep them straight in your head?"

"No."

"Come away with me, then. We'll get ourselves into a wee bit of privacy."

She led him away from the docks, into the back streets. While the alleyways of Edinburgh's Old Town had order of a sort to them, most cutting straight away from the High Street, those of Leith had tangled themselves up in an impenetrable intestinal knot over the years. For all that it was a small place, it was a crowded maze of a place too. The narrow streets and closes coiled and crossed and folded upon one another in a density bewildering to one unfamiliar with their pattern. Quire was one such, and followed after Agnes like the novice he was, trying and failing to memorise their course.

The whole warren smelled of fish and ale and waste. Washing hung from the tenement windows. Every open door seemed to have a fishwife or a child or a sullen seaman loitering in it. There were dogs, too, little mangy things on the whole, sniffing through piles of rubbish industriously. The raucous seagulls mingled their cries with those of the equally raucous inhabitants. The sun sent the birds' shadows racing across the upper reaches of the tenements.

"The Widow said you might be able to help me," Quire said as they walked. "Mary Coulter."

"I ken who the Widow is, son. Have done for half her life or more. And her husband too, miserable bloody bastard of a man that he was."

"Can't have been that bad, since she's mourning him still," Quire observed, stepping carefully over a pile of oily rags in the midst of the alley.

"Shows how much you ken," Agnes said with a gleam of amusement in her eye. "Not so keen on him when he was breathing, Mary wasn't. Not so keen at all. Better a widow than a beaten wife, eh?"

She broke off to nod a greeting to a much older, tiny woman who sat on a stool in the doorway of a tobacco shop. Somewhere inside, a child was bawling. The sound of it put a little frown of consternation on the face of Agnes' granddaughter.

"That's saying enough of that, though, I reckon," Agnes said briskly as they moved on. "Widow'd not like us trading gossip about her name."

"If she's not in mourning, though, why . . . "

"Hush, man. Are you daft or something? Did I not just say that was enough of that? You'll make me wish I'd left you there at the dock if you're not careful."

She turned aside without warning and led him up a stair into the body of a tenement. It was dark, and smelled dank. Agnes had her home on the first floor, and it was a good deal less grim than its approaches would suggest. A thin blanket hung across the window to shield a broken pane of glass, that was true, but as for its contents, Quire had seen far less salubrious quarters countless times in Edinburgh's Old Town, Cath's rooms amongst them. The low bed had neat sheets and a thick woollen rug laid across it. Three candles in pewter holders stood on a shelf. The hearth at the back of the room held a low heap of glowing embers. It had plentiful kindling and coal in a bucket beside it, a good iron poker hanging from a hook and clean copper cooking pots piled up, nested one into the next.

There was a long, narrow basket sitting on a table, and Agnes settled the baby into that with a few murmurs of comfort.

"Will you have a drink?" she asked as she tidied the girl's swaddling clothes. "I've nothing strong, mind. Just tea, or I think I've a bottle or two of ale somewhere. Won't have liquor in the house. It's the Devil's nectar, that stuff. In a manner of speaking, of course."

She said that last with a quick, knowing smile. Quire was not entirely sure how amusing he should find it.

"I don't need anything to drink," he said. "Thank you."

"Sit yourself down, then. On the bed, if you like."

Agnes pulled a stool out from under the table while Quire settled himself.

"I trust Mary's sense in most things," Agnes said. "Not always in the judging of men, mind, but I'll give you a hearing. Though what a sergeant of the city police has got to say to me, I've no idea."

"I'm not sure I'm still a sergeant of police. And it's not strictly their business I'm here on, either. Not to hear them tell it."

"Oh." Agnes, oddly, looked a touch disappointed, as if deprived of some small piece of her expected entertainment. "Well, might be you've still something interesting to say. Stranger things have happened."

"I'm needing help in understanding things I've seen," Quire said. "That I'm still alive now is more luck than judgement, I'm inclined to think. I don't know what it is I'm fighting, not really, nor how to fight it."

Agnes raised her eyebrows at that, and scratched her chin.

"Might need a pipe for this," she muttered, and went to a chest on the window ledge. From it, she dug out a long-stemmed clay pipe and a leather pouch of tobacco. The baby began to whimper and splutter. Agnes glanced at Quire as she packed the brown, pungent fibres into the bowl of the pipe.

"Give her a finger to suck on. That'll quiet her for a bit."

"Me?" Quire asked stupidly.

"Aye, you. Who else?"

Quire rose and went to lean over the unsettled infant, looking down into her pink face. This was not an area in which he possessed any great expertise. He closed his fingers into a soft fist and extended a thumb towards the babe's mouth.

"Your wee finger, man," Agnes grunted, "not a thumb. You wanting to choke the poor wee thing? Give her something she can get her lips around. She'll not bite it off. Anyone'd think you'd never seen a baby before."

"I've never nursed one with a finger, if that's what you mean," Quire said, bristling just a touch at the accusation of inadequacy. Not that he could dispute it.

Agnes squatted down by the hearth, and lit a taper from the ashy, gleaming coals there. She puffed away at the pipe to get it going, watching Quire out of the corner of her eye. The baby had set her delicate lips about the tip of his finger, and was once more content.

"That'll do, that'll do," Agnes told him as she returned to her stool.

Wisps of smoke coiled up from her pipe. Quire went back to his place on the bed, relieved to have successfully discharged at least that one small responsibility.

"Let's have it, then," Agnes said.

"I've seen things lately I can't explain. Not easily. The kind of things . . . I don't know, but maybe the kind of things you would know about."

"Is that right? What manner of things are we talking about?"

"I've met men who feel no pain, and don't mind broken bones nor a musket ball in their chest, and can go down under ice and come up through it again. They don't utter a word, and you don't see much of anything when you look in their eyes. And with strange writing, like tattoos or something, all over their hands. Dogs, just the same."

He said it all at once, in a rush, as if by doing so he might make it sound less implausible to his own ears. What Agnes might make of it, he had no idea, whether he spoke it quick or slow. She said nothing, chewing thoughtfully at the stem of her pipe. Quire shifted uneasily on the bed.

"I'm no great believer in anything but flesh and blood," he said with a shrug, "but there's something here. God knows, I need help from somewhere. What these men are doing ... there's grave robbing a part of it, and murder a part of it, and I'm sure as I can be there's something unnatural a part of it, too.

"And because I know all that, they'll come for me now. As soon as I'm cut loose from the police. It's what I'd do. They can't leave someone who's seen what I have wandering about free."

"Aye," Agnes said around her pipe, "you've the look of a man who thinks he needs help, right enough. And it's not much odds whether you're a believer or not. There's more things in the world that are old and deep than these men of philosophy and science we're infested with these days can admit of. Forgotten, maybe, by most; not the same as being gone."

She exhaled a great cloud of bluish smoke.

"Not sure what you think I can do for you, though," she said. "I'm more in the way of gentle wee charms these days, son. Easing a hard birth, softening a laddie's heart for a lass who's after him. Ridding a bairn of a fever. That sort of thing."

"I've had a feathered star of twigs nailed to my door," Quire said. "Is that some sort of gentle wee charm?"

"Oh, that's interesting. What sort of feathers?"

"Black. A crow, maybe. Does it matter?"

"Might do. Might not. Who are these folk you think are doing such things?"

"John Ruthven, for one."

"Aye, I ken him," she said, much to Quire's surprise. "Never did meet him, though." She gave a pleased little laugh. "He came down this way, a few years back, wanting to talk to me. Ask me some questions. How he heard of me, I've no idea, but there he was, waiting on the quayside, poking around in his fancy trousers and his pretty wee necktie. I watched him for a while, but I didn't like the look of him, so he never did lay eyes on me."

The baby was softly smacking her lips in her sleep, as if to savour the spicy scent of her grandmother's pipe smoke.

"Do you know what he was wanting from you?" Quire asked quietly, careful not to disturb the babe's slumber.

"No. Can guess, if you like. Ruthven's an old name. Lots of history in it. Plenty of folk as have worn it down the years thought themselves seekers of lost arts. Most of them just dabblers, playing around with things they'd not understand. That's the worst sort, the most dangerous sort: them as want to make themselves important and clever. I'm guessing he thought I could tell him something or other would help in whatever dabbling of his own he had in mind."

"There's another man, called Blegg. Or Weir, perhaps, or something else. His name's not a fixed thing, I've been told. Works for Ruthven."

"Never heard of a Blegg. Weir, I ken. So do you."

"Weir?"

"Major Weir. Do you not ken your history, son?"

Quire frowned. A connection he had not made before, struggling to be born in his mind: Macdonald, the antiquary, had said that Ruthven had taken items found in Major Weir's house from their collections.

"Well? You're sitting there like a glaikit sheep," Agnes prompted.

"The name's familiar, aye. Major Weir. Burned at the stake. Might be Ruthven's interested in him too, from what I hear."

Quire was remembering old stories. Silly little tales, told around drinking tables, or to frighten children; tales he had not thought of for so long that they had lain buried, all but forgotten, in his mind.

"Hundred and fifty years ago," Agnes mused. "Weir was strangled and burned at the stake at the Gallowlee. They're building their fine houses over it, on the road between here and their nice New Town. That's the way of things now, isn't it? They build over the past, think that makes it gone.

"His sister hanged in the Grassmarket. There was hundreds burned, and hardly a one of them deserving the fate, but Weir maybe did. There was something fierce in him, no doubting it. Something dark."

She rose slowly from her stool, and crouched by the fire, taking one piece of coal at a time in her hand and tossing each on to the dwindling embers. The place was hardly needing more warmth, Quire thought, but her movements had the absent-minded sloth of habit, a soothing exercise to keep the thoughts moving in her mind.

"These are old names you're tossing about," she mused. "They've got a long reach, back to before all this gas and steam and bright new world folk are making. Back to different times. Inscriptions upon a man's skin, that might be binding work, or a protective endowment.

"A feathered cross nailed to your door: now that might be just a thing meant to frighten, but it's the shape of old workings. Divination, or curse, or both. Bring down misfortune on a man's head, that could, if done right. Mark him for death."

"I've not been overburdened with good fortune, the last month or two," Quire grunted. "I'm of a mind to share around some of the misery now."

"Is that right?" Agnes was distracted, hardly listening to him. "Weir. Not a good name to be talking about, not if there's dark business being done. I'll be damned if it's not an ill omen. His house is still there, you know. Empty, for a century and a half."

"I didn't know that."

"Been a long time since those who think themselves sensible worried about such things. But it's still there. I'd thought it'd been forgotten, and good riddance to the memory, but if there's folk using his name, thinking on him ... maybe not."

She tapped the bowl of her pipe gently against the edge of the table, spilling a tiny drift of spent ash.

"Can you show me?" Quire asked her.

"Might be I could. Might be worth a wee look, now you've brung up the old times. I'd a mind to come up to the big town anyway, get myself some cloth for the making of a skirt. Are you paying, though, son?"

"I could put a shilling or two your way," Quire said.

And Agnes nodded at that, and took a hard enough suck through her pipe to set the tobacco glowing in the bowl.

XXII

The House of Major Weir

"It's a grim-looking place," Quire observed.

The courtyard he and Agnes McLaine peered into was narrow, gloomy. Desolate. A low-browed, vaulted passageway had brought them in beneath the soaring tenements of the West Bow to this hidden square, buried like an abscess in the very heart of the Old Town. They could hear the thud and grind of the building works on the new bridge; they could hear, less clearly, the rattle of carts over the West Bow's cobbles and the cries of hawkers in the Grassmarket. But all of that was as the sound of another world, for the courtyard felt abandoned and lifeless.

There was a crust of grime on the ground, and heaps of debris scattered around: rotting pieces of wood, piles of cloth or clothes so filthy it was impossible to say what colour they might once have been. The dusty smell of mould was in the air. A rat ran along the foot of one of the walls, its head bobbing up and down. When it realised it was no longer alone in its foraging, it vanished into a narrow crevice in the stonework.

Yet the place was not abandoned; there were clearly some folk calling it home. There were doors around the yard, and dark stairways leading up into the surrounding tenements like burrows cut by maggots. Some of the higher windows, Quire saw as he cast his gaze upwards towards the distant square of sky, were open. A white sheet hung from one of them, though there was no breeze to dry it in this tight little space.

"A few in here who'll not be happy to have a sergeant of the police poking about, I'd guess," Agnes mused.

"I'm not with the police," Quire said. "Not any more."

And that was true. He was cut loose from the foundations he had tried to set under his life in the last few years, his name struck from the books of the Edinburgh police.

It had been unceremonious, abrupt. No opportunity to defend himself, or to face his accusers. Just a courier at his door, presenting letters signed by Baird himself, in ostentatious style, that informed Quire he was dismissed, on grounds of misconduct. No pension would be paid, no appeal heard.

Reading those formal, impersonal lines of text, Quire could imagine quite clearly the satisfaction with which Baird must have signed his name beneath them. Seldom would a man have been so pleased to be the conveyor of bad tidings.

"That's where we're bound," Agnes said, nodding towards a door at the far end of the courtyard.

She had come with her head and shoulders wrapped in a woollen shawl, though the weather was clement enough.

They crossed the square side by side, Quire going cautiously and with a certain trepidation, Agnes advancing in her heavy leather shoes with an almost eager tread. The door they approached was black with rot, its wood drilled through by worms and decay. There were gaps between it and its frame. When Quire put his eye to one, he felt a cool touch on his skin, the dank apartments beyond breathing out over him.

"It's dark in there. Should have brought a lantern."

"There'll be light enough," Agnes said.

Dismissal should have dismayed Quire more than it did, perhaps, but he was numb, and unsurprised. He had already resigned himself to this outcome. His life was being shaken apart, like a fox cub clasped in the jaws of a hunting dog, and he had come to expect little better. His mind had set itself to other purposes, though, and was too bent upon them to admit of mourning for his losses. He meant to do some shaking of his own now, of Ruthven and the rest. He needed only to find the right grip upon them.

Agnes gave the door an exploratory rattle, curling her fingers around its edge where rot had eaten back the wood. Little flakes and splinters fell from it, even beneath such slight assault.

"Should open up all right," she said, but instead of testing that assumption, she took a step back and groped around in a pouch looped over the waistband of her heavy skirt. She brought forth a finger length of brown wood, unworked and unpolished. Just a section cut from a thin branch, with a hole in one end through which cord was threaded. She fastened that cord about her left arm so that the little piece of wood hung there, a pendant at her wrist.

"Rowan, cut at Samhain," she told Quire. "A ward against spirits, against evil."

Quire regarded the crude bracelet with a faint sense of puzzlement. He could still hear the shouts of the workers struggling to raise that huge new bridge over the Cowgate. He was standing in the midst of a city famed throughout Europe for its fostering of rational, secular thought; a city, it was said, that had lately held more learned men in each square foot than any other the country had ever seen. Yet he was looking at a witch's charm, something out of a folk tale, and believing it might work; a wise precaution, perhaps.

"Have you got another one of them?" he asked Agnes, and she smiled.

"Course I have." She dropped the second pendant into his outstretched hand. "Can we call you a believer yet, then?"

"Call me what you like," Quire sniffed. "I stopped knowing what to believe a while back. I'm playing the game by the rules my enemies have set for the next wee while, that's all."

He held up his arm, rolling his wrist to set the rowan charm swinging.

Agnes pushed at the door. It shivered, and caught on the uneven ground, came free and scraped open. Cold air flowed gently over them as they stared into a short, dingy passageway with a low roof and undulating, unpaved floor.

For an instant, at the touch of that air, a terrible, lurching dread ran through Quire. His hands trembled suddenly, and he was seized by the urge to flee. He steadied himself.

"You feel something?" Agnes asked.

"Aye."

"Not without its protections, this place," she said, but offered no further explanation.

She made to step across the threshold, but Quire barred her way with an outstretched arm.

"I'll go first," he said.

"Oh? Well, if it'll make you happy."

She sounded faintly amused. Quire found her lack of a caution a little discomfiting. He had not told her of the pistol he had tucked inside his jacket, and did not mean to. Most places he went now, he went armed.

It was colder in there than he had expected, like a cave. That shawl draped around Agnes' head suddenly did not seem so redundant. The walls, when his fingertips brushed them, were damp to the touch. Hundreds of small webs were tucked into the edges of the ceiling. The floor had a disquieting hint of softness to it, the layers of dirt giving beneath his feet. Not a cave, not quite; a tomb. Quire felt himself to be disturbing a place that had been asleep for a long time.

He advanced a few paces, accompanied in every step by that awful dread; that moaning fear within him, pleading with him to turn about and run. He could feel sweat upon his brow.

Agnes lingered, just inside the doorway. He turned towards her, wondering for a moment whether she was overcome by the same gnawing unease that assailed him.

"See?" she asked, gesturing at the crumbling wall of the passage.

He looked where she pointed. Just barely, he could make out a thin line of some brownish, earthy material, running directly up the wall.

"All the way round," Agnes said, swinging her arm up and over.

Now that Quire's eye was tuned to it, he could see clear enough that the line did indeed traverse the ceiling, descend the opposite wall of the passage and run back across the floor to join with its own tail.

"What is it?" he asked.

"A warding. Grave soil, I'd guess. It's why you're feeling set to piss yourself, and why you can't stop thinking what a fine idea it'd be to get yourself out of here and never come back. Like as not, if it wasn't for that wee twig at your wrist, you'd have run off already."

"Visitors aren't welcome, then," Quire murmured.

"So it seems."

Quire pushed his way into a side room, through another stiff and resistant door. There were floorboards, almost lost beneath the drifts of soggy dust. They grumbled beneath him, yielding with murmurs of exhaustion. Dark smears were all over the walls, where water had come through to discolour the plaster and spread stains of mould. Patches of that plaster had fallen away, from walls and ceiling alike, littering the floor like plates of bark shed from a tree.

Quire's breath sounded loud to him. He stifled it, making himself calm. The air he drew carefully in tasted sour and stale, as if nothing had stirred it for years. There was a fire grate, rusted away and almost collapsed in on itself; a dull red and black skeleton of gnawed bones. Piles of crumbling wood that might once have been furniture, but it was impossible to say of what kind in the gloom.

"I heard there was an old soldier rented it, a long while back," Agnes said behind him, and her voice was so sudden that Quire started and gasped, and then put his hand to his brow to compose himself. He felt the subtle weight of the rowan charm against his sleeve.

"So beat down he could find nowhere else for him and his wife to end their days," Agnes went on. "First one to dare the place in a hundred years, and the last. Didn't get past the first night, way the tale's told."

"What happened?" Quire whispered.

"Woke in their bed to a visitation. There's different things I've heard. Some said they saw a calf, or a cat; familiars of the Devil, come seeking their dead master. Some said they saw Weir himself, standing right there watching them while they slept." She sniffed. "Don't much credit it myself."

Another room. Another musty silence. Quire shifted some of the detritus about with the toe of his boot. Each time he disturbed it, he smelled putrefaction, and the piss and dung of rats. In this chamber, there were roof beams stretched across the ceiling. They sagged. The vast weight of the tenement above, the lives being lived in it, bore down upon that small dark place.

"What did he do?" Quire asked. "Weir, I mean. To get himself burned."

"I'd not think anyone could tell you that," Agnes replied. "I ken what he was accused of: unnatural and perverse congress, with his sister and with beasts of the field. The corruption of those about him. The invocation of Satanic powers."

"Did he have children?"

"Not that I ever heard."

"Blegg can't be a descendant of his, then."

Muted light was seeping through another doorway. Quire went towards it, and looked through into a last room. There was a small window, caked with filth, in the far wall, but a door had been propped against it, blocking out most of the light. He eased it aside and scraped some of the dirt from the glass. The window let out into some boxed-in little square of flagstones, to which no doors, no passageways, gave access; a forgotten fragment of ground, engulfed by the city.

Quire straightened, looked at the grime now clinging to his fingertips. He rubbed them thoughtfully on the leg of his trousers.

"Someone's been here," Agnes said.

Quire turned to look at her.

"There's footprints."

Now that there was more light reaching in, he could see them. Not a legible trail, but the rough impression of boots here and there on the grubby floor.

"Place reeks of darkness," Agnes said. "Evil spends long enough in one spot, it can never be right again."

She was only now starting to sound as uneasy as Quire had felt all along. He put his hand to his side, just tracing the shape of the pistol through his jacket. It was no great comfort. The oppressive atmosphere of Weir's old house was not something that could be dispelled by a gun. Nor was the overwhelming sense of being an intruder, undesired and uninvited.

There were sudden footfalls, muffled but distinct, above their heads. Quire tensed, and found himself reaching for the pistol despite himself. He froze, and Agnes did too, both of them standing there with their heads back, staring at the ceiling. The footsteps moved from one side of the room to the other, dwindling as they went, slipping away into silence.

Quire puffed his cheeks out and let his hands hang loose.

"Place'll never be clean," Agnes murmured. "Not unless it's torn down. Burned."

"Who would come here?" said Quire, shaking his head.

He found it difficult to imagine anyone voluntarily lingering for more than a few moments in a place so unsettling, so polluted. Even the most destitute, the most desperate, could find better hovels than this to doss down in.

"No one," Agnes agreed with his unspoken thoughts. "No one but the one who set that ward upon the door, eh? One who didn't find it quite as foul a place as us ordinary folk do. One who liked it, even. Might be, if you've got the art to use it, there's strength to be had here. It'd take a heart as black as the place itself for that, though."

Quire walked slowly around the room, running a hand along the wall, prodding the corpse of a rat with his foot. There was a small pile of rags and rubble, with the broken spars of a shattered chair projecting from it. As he turned, his trouser leg caught upon the jagged end of one of those fragments of wood.

Irritated, he bent down to unhitch the material. As it came free, he saw, still caught there on the splintered stub of wood, something that made him kneel, and lean close. He did not want to touch it, for the fear and trepidation still ran strong in him, but he did not need to.

"Dog hairs," he said quietly.

"Dog hairs?" Agnes repeated.

"There's been dogs in here, and not so very long ago, most likely. One of them snagged themselves here, just as I did. It's Ruthven, then. Maybe this is his idea of a kennel, for keeping his hounds when they're not out on the farm. When they've got work to do in town, like Carlyle. Or me."

"Carlyle?"

"Doesn't matter. Let's get ourselves out of here. This place is too much for me, rowan charm or no."

"You'll not be getting an argument from me," Agnes said, and led the way back, moving carefully through the short chain of rooms towards the passageway.

As Quire followed her, he was distracted by a dull, frayed cloth tacked up to one of the walls. It hung there like a limp tapestry, its dismal form of a piece with the decrepitude of the house. An oddity. A purposeless elaboration. He tugged gently at it and it came away easily, bits of the wall itself crumbling out as the little nails slipped free.

And Quire found himself staring into a face. The skin of a human face, nailed to the wall; hanging there, soft and horrible, without the structure of bone or muscle to give it shape. Eyelids, nose, cheeks, lips all sagging, a glove puppet taken from the hand it once covered and hung there like a gruesome trophy. For a moment, just a moment, he thought it a piece of worked calf hide, or vellum, formed by some craft he could not imagine into the mockery of a human visage; but he knew it was not. He knew it was precisely what it appeared to be. A man's face, peeled from his skull.

Quire felt cold horror locking his limbs. He opened his mouth to speak, and no words came. He could not take his gaze from the baggy, ragged pouches of the eye holes. Scraps of the ears clung to the edges of the dreadful mask, a few stray strands of dark hair where it had been torn – or roughly cut – from the scalp.

"Look," he managed to murmur.

There were little downy feathers tied to its edges with threads. There was a vile, slack weight to the way it hung from the nails.

Quire heard a hiss from Agnes.

"Get out," she rasped.

But it was too late. The face moved. A slight, convulsive tremor as if some unseen muscles pulled at it. A curl put into those lifeless lips, a tightening of the skin around the voids where the eyes should have been. The fringing feathers shivered. Quire could not breathe. He was pinned by the empty stare, could feel its cold caress upon him. It was, he thought for a fleeting instant, Davey Muir, staring into him from that void; but that sense was at once lost. Someone – something – else regarded him through the flesh.

"Get out, get out," Agnes cried, pushing past him, reaching for that foul semblance of a man.

Quire took a faltering step or two backwards, his legs weak, almost buckling. Agnes tore the face from the wall, and inside Quire's head, deep within his ears and his mind he thought he heard a rasping wail of loathing.

The face sloughed through Agnes' fingers, its skin liquefying into a stinking dark discharge. Melting and falling from her grasp to the floor in gobbets of corrupted matter. She shook her hand, spilling drops of softened skin. With her other hand, she pushed Quire firmly in the centre of his chest.

"Get out, son," she said more quietly than before, but still fraught. "We're seen."

They went quickly, stumbling over the rubble of the years, cracking shoulders against the door frames in their haste, blundering in the now suffocating gloom of the place. Pursued, Quire felt, by something terrible at his back, wanting him, reaching for him.

Out into the passageway, rushing for the dismal light of the doorway and the courtyard beyond it, that had seemed so grimly miserable at first but now looked like salvation and sanctuary. Staggering as he veered, Agnes on his heels, into the vaulted tunnel beneath the brooding mass of the tenements, and running through it, footsteps echoing, and into the West Bow.

Bright light burst upon them as they emerged on to the street, dizzy with relief. The sun was dazzling, disorienting. Quire breathed deep, a man starved of air, coming up from dark waters. It tasted sweet, after the stale must of Weir's house; it tasted of life, not death. Only then did his morbid terror begin to recede.

A squall of children went past, chasing a rolling hoop down the street, laughing and shrieking. A woman bargaining with a street vendor turned to look after them and smiled. Shopkeepers gathering water in pails from the wellhead down at the foot of the West Bow, where it opened out on to the Grassmarket, paused to watch the happy gang spill past them. Quire trembled. He felt himself suspended between two worlds – the radiant bustle of the city, and the black pit of decay behind him – and did not know which was real.

"What was that?" he asked Agnes.

The witch of Leith had her hands on her knees. She was bent over, panting, looking for a moment as if she might empty her stomach out on to the cobblestones. But she mastered herself, and stood straight once more. She wiped her hands on her skirts.

"That was the foulest of magics. The blackest. A sentry."

"A sentry," Quire echoed numbly.

He clenched his fists, opened them and clenched again, forcing down the fear. Gathering himself.

"Whoever set it there saw us." Agnes grunted. "Looked through it, and saw us. You've someone in this nice city of yours practising the most bloody, evil business. I'd do whatever I could

XXIII

Durand

Mathieu Durand looked out through the tall window on the uppermost landing of Ruthven's house. He stood far enough back from the glass that he was confident he could not be seen from the street. There was no light burning up here at the top of the house, and the night outside was dark enough to hide him from any curious eye.

But there were no answers out there to the doubts and fears that assailed him.

He withdrew, backing away from that wall of glass. He walked towards the top of the long, many-flighted stairs. His feet were loud on the bare boards. The upper floors of Ruthven's house in Melville Street were, in the main, places of echoes, and of dusty voids. There were no rugs or coverings on the floors; the walls of even the grandest rooms were bare of paintings or hangings or any decoration. Uninhabited spaces, from which the household had withdrawn, one by one, closed the doors and shut the silence away.

Durand had his bedchamber up here, at the top of the house. There was nothing in it save a simple bed, a washstand with its bowl, a crude wardrobe for his clothes. Those things, and the boxes that held some of the objects by which he had been first entranced and now brought low: fragmentary relics of the Orient upon which he made some pretence of study, and sought, by that pretence, to preserve his life for a while longer.

He had told Ruthven that he had not yet found the key to unlocking all the secrets held by those dozens of inscribed clay tablets, but he lied. He had read them all, for he had mastered the secret languages of their authors. They were nothing; they added nothing to the catalogue of his previous discoveries. The few precious alchemical tracts had been amongst the first he decoded, and their wisdom he had already shared with Ruthven. Everything he had read since then was useless. Lists of produce harvested by the temple workers of Ur. Religious tracts extolling Anu, Enki, Enlil, the dead gods of a dead civilisation. There was nothing in them that could aid Ruthven or Blegg in their mad quest, but so long as they believed there might be, Durand could hope they would suffer him to live. So he clung to his pretence, and bore it like a shield.

The whole house was one grand pretence. A *trompe l'oeil* of consummate craftsmanship. Ruthven hosted dinners, attended his share of grand events and soirées, and generally portrayed himself as a man of means and standing, but he did it all by sleight of hand. The rooms any guest might see – and the guests were invariably the greatest worthies of the city, advocates and bailies, guild masters and councillors – those rooms were elaborate fictions, grandly furnished, immaculately maintained. But the rest of the house was stripped down to its rude fabric. Everything had been sold, piece by piece, save that which was indispensable, or worthless. All the servants had been dismissed long ago; when cooks or serving staff were needed, for the preservation of illusion, they were brought in for a few days only.

Ruthven was descending into penury, month by month, his fortune whittled away by his pursuit of secret knowledge, and by his purchase of influence, the better to conceal the ghoulish horrors into which that pursuit had descended. They all, every member of this blighted household, must know it could not last, yet they were trapped in the lunatic dance, unable to break away from the spiral of lies.

Now, standing at the head of the stairs, Durand could hear Isabel Ruthven playing the pianoforte, far below. Glittering arpeggios spilled out from the drawing room, fluttering their way through the house, up the great stairwell, coiling about the banisters. It was not a melody Durand knew, but it was pleasing to the ear. She played it well.

Durand descended, one hand resting lightly on the banister. He was hungry, and there was no one to bring him food, or prepare it for him. Nor could he any longer venture out at will to find sustenance. His movements were circumscribed now, and watched. Mistrust hung thick in the air of the house, along with all the lies. He was like a rat, living by scavenging and foraging in a half-empty palace, imprisoned by fear of the terrible retribution awaiting him should he stray.

In the gaps between the notes cascading from Isabel's fingers, he could hear raindrops pattering on the great skylight far above his head. There was something of the waterfall in Isabel's music, and the accompaniment of rain did not seem out of place.

He was glad to hear her playing, not for the quality of the music, but because it would likely mean that Blegg was in there with her. Durand devoted much effort to avoiding Blegg, and that was a great deal easier when he knew where he was.

The kitchens were at the back, on the ground floor of the house where a humble lane ran along the rear of the noble terrace, for the use of servants and delivery men so that they would not sully the smart frontage by their presence. Little use was made of it for its intended purpose in the case of Ruthven's house, and Durand was thus startled, and dismayed, to find a transaction in progress.

Blegg stood with another, heavier man, a huge sack lying on the floor between them, tied shut with rope. Its contents were irregularly shaped, stretching it in one part, leaving it slack in another.

"Ah, Durand," Blegg said. "You've not met William Hare, I don't think?"

The other man grimaced and bared his teeth. There was an animalish ferocity to it.

"Don't give him my name," Hare growled.

He had an accent Durand could not quite place. Not Scottish, assuredly. There was nothing of the affected refinement of Edinburgh in his words.

Blegg dismissed Hare's concerns with a flick of his gloved hand.

"You don't need to worry," he smirked. "Durand here's no trouble to anyone, are you, Durand?"

"Just give me the money, and I'll be gone," said Hare.

Durand stared down at the great sack on the cold stone floor. He had no doubt of what it contained. The shape and bulk of it told an unmistakable tale. He shook his head, wondering at the brazen madness of it all. They took delivery of a corpse, here at Ruthven's very house, as if it were no more than provisions for the parlour.

"So keen to be about your business," Blegg said approvingly to Hare. "But no more for a time, if you can bear to wait. You've met my needs for now, and these are not the easiest goods to store."

Hare scowled and held out a stiff, open hand. Blegg pressed folded banknotes into it. With a last, ferocious glare at Durand, laden with contempt and baseless loathing, Hare turned on his heel and went out, banging the back door on its hinges and slamming it closed behind him.

"A man who's found his calling, that one," Blegg said with harsh amusement. "Why don't you carry this down to the cellar, now that you're here, Durand?"

"No. I'll not set foot there."

"Oh? Finally decided you can't bear any more dirt on your precious little hands, have you? Too late, old man. Much, much too late."

With that, Durand could heartily agree. Far too late to save his hands, or his soul, from the stain of complicity. Far too late to save himself from the ruin that could not be long delayed now. There was a reckless, wanton air taking hold, as if all the sins of the past could only be concealed and justified by piling fresh sins atop them. The fragile edifice behind which all their exploits were concealed grew ever more impossible to sustain.

Enough, Durand thought dismally. Though it would mean his death, and his damnation, he could bear the waiting no longer. Better to bring those things down upon himself than endure this tortured, haunted existence any longer. He had no life worth the living now, so what purpose could there be in prolonging the fever dream in which he was ensnared? If the edifice was to fall in any case, he would tear out its foundations himself.

XXIV

Masquerade

The harlequin stared back at Quire. It was a full-face mask of lacquered papier mâché, its lower half pale, almost like ivory, the upper gleaming with black and red diamonds laid out over the brow and cheeks. Two eyes stared out through neatly cut holes. There was a slit for a mouth, too, but the harlequin was not saying anything. He wore the traditional suit: luridly matching jacket and pantaloons, both a patchwork of coloured diamonds, all seamed and trimmed with gold thread; a three-horned hat of black felt, with a tiny bell jiggling at the tip of each horn.

"Well, what do you say, man?" Quire demanded, raising his voice above the music spilling through the open doors of the ball-room. "It'll not be for long. Easiest shilling you'll ever earn."

"If anyone found out ... " the harlequin whimpered.

He was a big man, beneath that garish costume – that was why Quire had chosen him – but not beyond intimidation once a bit of bluster and bluff was applied.

"Nobody'll know," Quire insisted. "It's just for a prank on a friend of mine. No harm can come of it. Damn it, make it two shillings, then. How much are you getting paid for your night's work? I must be doubling or trebling it at least."

"And using my money to do it," Wilson Dunbar observed.

Quire shot him a sharp sideways glance to discourage further interruptions, but Dunbar had always been resistant to discouragement.

"What? It's true enough, isn't it?" he said with an innocent shrug.

He leaned closer to the harlequin and spoke loudly into his ear.

"I'd take the money, if I was you. This one's stubborn as all hell when he gets an idea in his head."

The harlequin nodded. He did it hesitantly, so that the bells on his hat barely tinkled, but he did it. And that was enough for Quire to take hold of his arm and guide him firmly towards the cloakroom.

The attendant watched in faintly perturbed confusion as Quire, Dunbar and the harlequin pushed in amongst the racks of coats and cloaks, hats and canes. They got themselves to the cloakroom's furthest corner, out of sight of the trickle of guests still flowing through the wide lobby of the Assembly Rooms. Hidden away there, amidst the garb and accessories of wealth, Quire began to strip off his jacket and trousers.

"Come along," Dunbar said jovially to the harlequin, prodding the man in the arm. "Sooner it's done, sooner it's done with."

Stiffly, no doubt burdened by second thoughts, the harlequin reached up to take the mask from his face.

Cath had come to find Quire with the message. He was lingering – had been lingering for a long time – around the stalls on the High Street.

For all his gratitude at Cath's willingness – eagerness, in fact –

to take him in, and put a roof over his head, he found the Holy Land a hard place to be. She was wont to lie late in her bed, and though he could share in that ease for a little while, he tired of it sooner than she, and would take himself off on whatever errand he could think of.

He had told her almost nothing of the reasons for his abandonment of his own lodgings, and she asked few questions. That was the training of her trade, and her life, he supposed; but also, perhaps, that she was simply glad of his arrival, and cared not what had brought it about.

"How long does it take to buy a bit of bread, then?" she asked him now.

Her hair was tousled, still disordered by sleep, and she clasped her arms about herself as if not yet ready to embrace the day. It made Quire want to hold her to him, but he merely smiled.

"A while, it seems."

"There was a boy come looking for you at the Land. Had a message for you, and I thought you might be wanting to hear it sooner than later."

It was telling of the narrow, insecure path Quire walked that his first thought was not of the content of the message, but of its mere arrival.

"How did he know where to look for me?" he asked, frowning.

Cath shrugged.

"Said he went to the police house first. Must not have known you're not much seen round those parts any more. Someone there told him where to find you."

"I'd not really wanted them to know where I was, either."

"The Holy Land leaks secrets like a sieve, Adam. You'd maybe have better thought on that before. Anyway, are you wanting this message or not? It's not warm enough for me to be up and out this early."

She gave a little demonstrative shudder of her shoulders. That made Quire smile.

"Aye, all right."

"Durand says he'll be at the ball, and if you can get him safely out from there, he'll come away with you. Whatever that means. The wee lad thought it was all a grand adventure; said this funny-talking man whispered it in his ear, and put a coin in his hand, all in a moment or two, outside some New Town shop. Then walked off with a couple who came out, acting like nothing had happened."

"He'd not want to be seen sending messages off, right enough," Quire murmured, distracted. "What ball's he talking about, though?"

"Oh, do you not know anything, Adam?" Cath scoffed. "The Fancy Ball, at the Assembly Rooms. Best of the season, they say. They'll all be there, with their noses in the air and their snouts in the trough."

So Quire found himself pulling on the camouflage of a harlequin's clothes in a cloakroom, while the sounds of exuberant merriment roared out from the ballroom.

The Assembly Rooms were the heart of the New Town, in as much as it could be said to possess such a thing. Placed midway along its most noble boulevard, George Street, they were the hub about which the pleasant life of the inhabitants turned. Coming in through the busy lobby, Quire had seen posters advertising a host of diversions for those with the time and money to spare: a performance of *The Tempest*, down at the East End Theatre; a phrenological lecture here at the Assembly Rooms; and this very Fancy Ball, from which none who thought themselves members of elevated society would dare to be absent.

There was only one of that society Quire had any interest in tonight. If Durand was indeed here, he was leaving with Quire. That was the plan, in any case. Whether the rudimentary scheme Quire had thrown together in such haste truly merited the title of plan was debatable, but he had done what he could in the time available.

His guilt at dragging Wilson Dunbar into this was heavy, but he had not been sure he could manage it on his own. Dunbar, to his credit, had been all too willing to lend a hand. That, of course, might be because Quire had not told him everything. Had not troubled him with the details of Cold Burn Farm, or of Major Weir's house.

Nor had he told James Robinson why he needed two tickets for the Fancy Ball. He knew no one other than the former superintendent who might be able to provide such things, and as it turned out, Robinson had no need of those he and his wife already possessed.

They were settled in a modest house on the south side of the Old Town, which seemed comfortable enough, but Quire was saddened to see how reduced Robinson already appeared, after so short a time. His eyes had lost a little of their life, his voice had softened. Perhaps, Quire hoped, it was just the burden of the gout, a visitation of which was the cause of their lack of interest in the Fancy Ball.

Robinson had asked not a single question, beyond his first: "You're not going to do anything foolish, are you?"

"I hope not," was the best Quire had been able to do by way of answer.

The harlequin: that was improvisation. Seeing all the serving staff hurrying to and fro, every one of them clad in this same festive disguise, Quire had been suddenly taken by the wisdom of donning a mask. It had required a degree of patience, waiting for one of the waiters going in and out of the ballroom to display a build to match Quire's bulky frame, and now that he was dressed in the pantomime outfit, Quire was not so sure of the idea.

He could already feel sweat forming over his face. The mask was unpleasantly confining and close-fitting. The harlequin costume itself was a little looser, but heavier than it had looked. It would not be long, though. He told himself that and hoped it was true. If this did not happen quickly, it would likely not happen at all.

"Right, you wait here and I'll check the lie of the land," he said to Dunbar, who held his hand to his ear with an exaggerated flourish.

"Speak up, man, you've something covering your mouth there."

"Wait here, and I'll have a look inside," Quire growled.

Dunbar swapped the heavy cape he carried folded over his right arm to his left, so that he could flick a mock salute at Quire.

"You look like a fool," he said, "but then so did most of the folk I've taken orders off, so I'll not hold it against you."

Quire grunted, and made his way down the lobby of the Assembly Rooms. Wide wooden staircases rose on either side, towards the many meeting rooms and exhibition spaces on the upper floor, but there was only one place to be this evening, and that was the grand ballroom at the far end of the hall. Its doors stood open, held back on brass hooks, and through that portal, Quire saw a tumultuous sea of colour.

The cream of Edinburgh society swirled about the dance floor, or thronged its edges, in a great, flamboyant crowd. There were pirates and princesses, soldiers and highwaymen; tartans and silks and jewels and feathers. A fanciful world of ebullient dreams.

A small orchestra played on a dais at the back of the hall, and the dancers spun about in graceful circles, a hundred bright eddies in a many-hued pool. Masked harlequins worked their way through the lively throng, distributing drinks and candies and sweetmeats. It was a bewildering maelstrom, for a man in search of a singular and particular quarry.

Quire looked up, not to the glittering chandelier with its dozen gas-jet pinpricks of white light, but to the wide balconies that ran around the hall. They were filled with seating, for the ballroom served as lecture hall too. He found his way up there easily, and it seemed a safe enough vantage point. He could look down upon the whole delirious scene, and saw not a single face, masked or otherwise, lifted up towards him; the entire population of the ballroom was entirely absorbed in the festival they had fashioned for themselves.

It took him a little while to find them. The cacophony of sight and sound down there on the floor was distracting, making it difficult to pick out the details he needed. But there they were: Ruthven and Isabel, his wife, dancing with the rest, close to the musicians. He a turbaned corsair, complete with a great sabre at his belt that Quire could tell even from this distance was a fabrication; she an Ottoman princess, or harem girl perhaps, radiant in pink silks, flowing skirt bedecked with glimmering glass beads.

Durand stood alone, right back against the wall near the doors. Exactly what character he was meant to portray, Quire was unsure, for the Frenchman looked little different from his usual dapper style, save for the addition of a powdered wig of the most old-fashioned sort. He was sipping from a tall fluted glass, but did not give the impression of a man greatly enjoying the experience.

Quire went quickly down and slipped out once more to find Dunbar, who was leaning on the counter of the cloakroom, keeping a discreet watch to ensure that the servant Quire had deprived of his costume did not change his mind and raise a hue and cry.

Quire pushed the suffocating mask up on to the top of his head, and savoured the release from its confinement.

"You look like a bit of roast meat," Dunbar observed.

"Never mind that," Quire said, wiping the sweat from his face with his chaotically coloured sleeve. "I've seen the man I need. I'll send him out to you. You'll know him when you see him: small man, about fifty or so, wearing a stupid little wig."

"What about you?" Dunbar asked.

"I'll hang back, just for a minute, to make sure we're not followed. We need to spirit him away, if we can, and leave them not knowing we've got him, let alone where we've taken him. You just get rid of the silly wig he's wearing off his head, and wrap him up in the cape. If you can sneak a hat out of the cloakroom, maybe put that on him, too. I'd have brought one if I'd thought of it. Anything that'll make him harder to spot or recognise. I don't need anyone even remembering the sight of him, so they can't say where he's gone if they're asked."

"Aye, and I don't want to know myself. Whatever it is you're up to, I'm about at my limit for getting involved."

"Quite right. Don't worry about that."

Quire hurried back to the door of the ballroom, eager to ensure the dance did not finish, and the Ruthvens abandon the dance floor, before he had done what he came to do. Everything was, thus far, playing out more easily than he could have hoped, and he did not mean to mock his good fortune by pushing it any further than it wanted to go.

He plunged into the gorgeous assembly, and made his way directly towards Durand. He went through the crowd a little more roughly and urgently than was fitting for a servant, but that seemed a risk worth the taking. A jester he bumped against turned sharply and made some complaint, but Quire was already beyond him, closing on Durand. He was no judge of the sort of music to which these grand folk danced, but there seemed to be a rising, speeding vigour to the orchestra's playing that suggested the end might be drawing near. Time was short.

He knocked Durand's glass firmly against his chest, spilling its contents down the front of the Frenchman's waistcoat.

Durand stared down at the spreading stain in surprise.

"Listen," Quire said as clearly as he could. "You need to clean yourself up. Go out into the lobby as if that's what you mean to do. There's a man waiting there, by the cloakroom. He has clothes to make you a bit less obvious."

Durand stared in disbelief into the variegated mask confronting him.

"Sergeant Quire?" he said.

"Yes, of course. Get out there, man. You're coming away from here with me tonight."

"I think it unlikely." Durand shook his head dolefully, a little of the excessive powder that had been applied to his wig drifting on to his shoulders. "They are suspicious of me, and ..."

Quire seized him roughly by the arm, squeezing the flesh of it above the elbow. He put every fierce sentiment he had cultivated over the last weeks into his voice.

"I need to know everything you know, Durand. Everything, not hints and games. So you're coming away with me now, or so help me I'll add you to the list of folk I've got a quarrel with."

The Frenchman stared into Quire's eyes.

"You misunderstand me. I am not unwilling, but I fear perhaps they are forewarned. Blegg accompanied us tonight, a thing he never does. He is outside somewhere, on the street."

Quire ground his teeth in exasperation. But he steeled himself.

"You'll not likely have another chance, Durand. You've got two men here, tonight, willing to do all we can to help you. We'll not be coming again."

Durand hesitated. Then he nodded, just once, curtly.

"Go," Quire snapped through the mask. "Tell the man waiting in the lobby I'll need the pair of you to wait for me. We'll all go out together."

The music died behind him even as he watched Durand working his way rapidly towards the doors. A ripple of applause rolled around the room. Quire made his own way through the crowd, going carefully, making himself as anonymous as a big man in a harlequin costume could; it should be possible here, tonight, if nowhere else.

He was stymied, though, by a stiff arm thrust out to block his path. An angry jester brandished a belled and beribboned stick at him.

"Was it you, just barged into me?" the jester demanded. "Not so much as an apology, not so much as an excuse me?"

Quire shook his head mutely, and made to move away.

The jester tapped him on the chest with that ringing stick.

"Disgraceful, sir! Quite disgraceful. I will be making a complaint to your employer."

"Aye, go ahead," Quire said and moved decisively away, striding quickly enough to leave his assailant in his wake.

He got himself into the doorway, and turned back to cast his eyes over the bobbing hats and wigs and tiara-laden heads. He looked for Ruthven's turban, or for anything that might be suggestive of pursuit, and saw nothing. The musicians were tuning their instruments, putting violins back under their chins. There would be another dance in moments.

He spun on his heel.

"Mr Quire," he heard behind him. "Mr Quire, that is you, isn't it?"

He could have kept going, perhaps, but he feared Ruthven might raise a commotion, even have him detained. That would leave Durand and Dunbar alone.

He stopped, and turned about, and faced Ruthven, who must have come up to the door along one of the walls, out of Quire's line of sight, and must have done it quickly. He was taking the absurd turban off his head, and ran a long-fingered hand back through his hair to straighten it.

"I thought I recognised the set of those shoulders. Do take that ridiculous mask off, man."

Quire did so, and glared at Ruthven.

Another harlequin, carrying two empty trays in his hands, came out of the ballroom. Ruthven moved out of his way, to one side of the doors.

"I really thought we had done with you, Mr Quire," he said, picking at the cloth of his headgear. "I really did. Blegg predicted I would learn otherwise, and so it transpires. I am very sorry to find I was mistaken. Sorry for you, as much as anything."

"Oh, don't you worry about me."

The music started up, snaking out from the dais, through the open doors, rolling around Ruthven and Quire. A waltz, Quire thought.

"No," Ruthven was saying. "I don't intend to worry about you, I can assure you of that. I'll be leaving the question of what to do with you entirely to others now."

"That wouldn't be your Mr Blegg you're talking about, would it?" Quire smiled. "I've formed the impression he maybe does a fair bit of your dirty work for you."

"Believe me, you have no idea. None at all."

"Well, I'll look forward to my education, then."

"I doubt that. Blegg tells me you have been sneaking about on my farm, and at a certain hovel in the Old Town."

Quire said nothing, but he felt the tremor of confession in his own face.

"I see it's true. How enterprising of you. Evidently I have misjudged you from the very beginning of our unfortunate acquaintance."

Still Quire said nothing, hoping that Dunbar would have the sense to keep Durand out of sight. Ruthven pursed his lips.

"Look at you," he said. "Not even on police pay any more, and still you're nipping at my heels. Why don't you just go home, Mr Quire? Alone."

"The difficulty I have with that is I'm thinking I'll not be long above ground, now you know I'm still paying you some attention. Am I right?"

Ruthven smiled thinly.

"Do you know," he said, "I think you might be. There, now: we all know where we stand. What have you done with Durand, by the way? I don't see him."

Ruthven peered over Quire's shoulder, eyes narrow and questioning.

"I've not seen him, so I couldn't say," Quire said.

"Oh. I really did think I was paying sufficient attention to his whereabouts, but once again you have managed to surprise me. What a pity the police decided to dispense with the services of such a resourceful fellow."

Ruthven sniffed in dry amusement at his own barbed humour. He glanced around, taking in the traffic of gaudily dressed celebrants, like a parade of exotic birds.

"There's been about two things in my life I was any good at," Quire said levelly. "Soldiering and policing. Maybe I can't help but be one or the other of those, paid or not. I'm ready to try the policing line, if you are. Are you going to come along to a judge with me and tell him all that you've done?"

Ruthven smiled, almost pityingly.

"No, Mr Quire, I am not."

"No. You're not. Then maybe it's the soldiering line for me after all."

"I see. I see. You know, I think you have the advantage over me, for there is only really one thing I have ever been good at. I have attempted a number of roles in my life, but the truth is I found no great success in any of them: farmer, merchant, investor. Husband. I was not suited to any of them.

"But, do you know, I have done things in the last few years that men will one day wonder at. I have tapped into the well at the very root of life, and made the vital forces flow at my command."

"And how many deaths have been caused by your miracle-working?"

"I do not suppose you could be expected to understand," Ruthven said, almost sadly. "There is a price to be paid for reve-lation, Mr Quire. For revolution. Knowledge is not always paid for solely by the sweat of the brow. A hundred years from now, the knowledge, the wonders will persist. The price paid for them will be forgotten. Forgiven."

"You buy it with blood, I say it's not worth the having."

"You're wrong. I can say nothing more than that. Well, I must return to my wife. There will be talk, you know, if I seem to be neglecting her."

He slipped the turban back on to his head, and with a last lin-gering look down the length of the lobby towards the doors out on to the street, he turned back and sank into the costumed host of his kind.

Quire blew out a long breath and went slowly towards the cloakroom, casting many a backward glance to ensure Ruthven did not reappear. He found Dunbar and Durand in a secluded corner, just inside the main entrance, and dropped his now useless mask to the floor there. Durand had been stripped of his distinctive wig and enclosed in the overly capacious cape. A plain and rather shapeless soft hat was pulled down over his head.

"Can we go now?" Dunbar asked with a rather plaintive hint to his voice.

"We can, and the sooner the better," Quire said. "I'm not sure how this is going to go, mind. There might be a problem or two."

Dunbar rolled his eyes.

"Do you know where Blegg is?" Quire demanded of Durand.

"No," the Frenchman said. "Outside somewhere. Beyond that, I cannot say."

"I was going to get us straight into a hackney cab outside, but it'd be too easy to follow us. We'll get down on to Princes Street. There'll be plenty of hackneys down there, and it'll make Blegg show himself if he's about. We either shake him off, or deal with him a bit more roughly."

Durand looked downcast.

"You are a capable man, but I rather doubt you can deal with Mr Blegg, as you put it."

"We've not exactly got a whole host of choices," Quire muttered.

There was quite a crowd on the pavement outside the Assembly Rooms. Many of them were the drivers of the hackney carriages which, as Quire had predicted, were lined up on the street awaiting the custom of departing guests. The drivers leaned against the pillars of the portico, smoking pipes, quietly trading gossip. There were quite a few casual onlookers too. Those who would never be invited to such a gathering, and were curious at the light and music drifting out on to the street, and hoping to get a look at some of the elaborate costumes.

Quire and Dunbar moved their companion briskly away from the throng, keen to get a bit more space around them. They went from one pool of gaslight to the next along the street, the gentle whine of each lamp growing louder as they approached it and fading away behind them as they passed beyond it. It was late, and the fine shops were closed, most of the great houses quiet.

They turned down on to the sharp slope of Frederick Street and Quire looked back as they moved around the corner. A single figure was separating itself from the shadows beneath the portico of the Assembly Rooms, moving smartly after them.

He pushed Durand into a trot as they descended towards Princes Street.

"Is there going to be trouble?" Dunbar asked as he jogged along at Quire's side.

He was entirely serious now, any notion of the evening's events as some kind of game discarded. The soldier in him came to the fore less easily than did Quire's, but it was there nonetheless.

"Maybe," Quire said. "I don't know. Should've brought a pistol."

"They'd hardly let you carry such a thing into the Assembly Rooms. You'd have had trouble hiding it in that clown's outfit, anyway."

Quire glanced down at his motley dress, and was struck by what an absurd, and obvious, figure he cut, hurrying along the New Town streets like a fugitive from some wandering theatre troupe. He had vaguely thought he would have the chance to shed the disguise before leaving, but that, in hindsight, had never been likely.

They emerged on to the broad expanse of Princes Street with the soaring dark mass of the castle before them, like a vast umbrageous thundercloud detached from the night sky and settled down to rest atop the crags. It was dotted, though, with points of light: the windows of its huge barracks, and lanterns burning here and there along its meandering walls.

There were no buildings along the south side of Princes Street – none save the Royal Institution, a short way further east – just a long run of black, spiked railings and beyond them the sweeping gardens that plunged down and across to the base of the castle's huge rock. Those gardens were a black, blank void, obscured by the glare of the tall gaslights lining the street.

Quire looked back. Blegg – he was almost certain it was him, though he could not make out his features at this distance – was coming down after them, walking quickly.

"We need to shake him off," Quire muttered.

Directly ahead of them, opposite the foot of Frederick Street, a gate broke the line of the iron railings. It would be locked – the gardens were a private pleasure for the residents and shopkeepers of Princes Street – and was, like the railings themselves, head high. But it had no spikes atop it.

"Into the gardens," Quire said promptly. "No light there. We can lose him, or spring a little trap of our own."

"Right," Dunbar said.

He did not sound entirely convinced, but responded without hesitation to the taut urgency in Quire's voice.

Dunbar darted forward, set his strong hands on the top of the gate and swung his legs up and over with a great heave of his shoulders. Quire put his hands to Durand's waist even as they drew near the gate, and lifted him from his feet. Dunbar reached over and hauled the Frenchman into the gardens. The two of them fell in a heap, crunching down on to the gravel path.

Quire did not need to look around to know what Blegg was doing. He could hear running feet, pounding closer. He flung himself at the gate, hitting it hip high, folding himself over the top of it, landing on his back on the path beyond. He rolled and scrambled to his feet, glimpsing Blegg's dark form rushing down the last of Frederick Street's slope, coming into the pools of light cast by the chain of streetlights. The man was fast; unnervingly so.

Quire ran after Dunbar and Durand, already disappearing into the profound darkness of the gardens. He could hear them clearly enough, though, for the gravel path was not made for silence.

"Get off the path," he called softly, and followed them as they veered off over the manicured lawns.

They crouched into one of the big thickets of ornamental shrubs. Most of the bushes were foreigners; evergreens with thick, heavy concealing leaves. Durand was gasping for breath.

"Be quiet," Quire whispered.

Blegg appeared, up there at the railings. Peering down into the gardens. Seeing, Quire hoped, not much more than they had: just the inky, lightless nothing. Blegg moved slightly to one side. His head was framed by the glowing lantern head of one of the gaslights, like a radiant halo.

"There's three of us," Dunbar murmured. "We could sort him out easy enough, couldn't we?"

"Maybe," said Quire. He was reluctant to trust any assumptions regarding Blegg's capabilities. "In any case, there's only two of us worth the counting, I'd guess."

"Quite true," Durand whispered. "And he would kill both of you, most likely."

"I didn't sign up for getting killed, any more than I did killing," muttered Dunbar.

Blegg carefully, deliberately, set both his hands atop the gate and vaulted it in a single leap, swinging his legs up high and clear. A manoeuvre that Quire could not have matched.

"Shit," Dunbar whispered, evidently reconsidering the advisability of confrontation.

They eased themselves further back amongst the bushes. Quire had never been inside the gardens before, and could remember precious little of any use as far as their layout was concerned, even though he had often enough looked down over the railings and thought it a pleasant view. One thing he did remember, with something approaching certainty: the only other gates were further along to the west of them, down towards St John's and St Cuthbert's, the chapel and church that dominated the far end of Princes Street.

"Right, well I'll draw him off, and you get your little French package here away," Dunbar said suddenly.

"No," hissed Quire.

Dunbar was already shifting his weight, settling himself on the balls of his feet.

"Hush. It'll be easy enough. I'll just take him off into a corner somewhere and slip out over the railings. Once he sees it's just me, he'll leave off pretty sharp. It's you two he's after, you poor buggers."

"No, you don't ... " Quire said desperately, but he was saying it to Dunbar's heels.

Dunbar went crashing away, thrashing through the shrubs with abandon, and pounding his feet on the turf as he plunged into the darkness.

"Christ," groaned Quire.

They heard Blegg ghosting past over the grass; a much lighter tread. Quire's heart hammered away, and his legs trembled with the desire to throw himself out and after Blegg. He struggled with the instinct, and stifled it.

Dunbar was quick on his feet, and nobody's fool. He could take care of himself if he had to. That was all Quire could hope as he dragged Durand hurriedly but quietly away in the opposite direction.

XXV

Kites

Durand shook. Not from cold, that was certain; which left fear or fever. Quire suspected it was both.

The Frenchman had a sheen of sweat across his brow, and his eyes were red-rimmed, looking sore. Sick, then. It had come on quickly and without warning, within an hour or two of his arrival in Agnes McLaine's house. Now, as the morning advanced, it had a firm grip of him. The fear had preceded it, and persisted still. Durand might be reconciled to his change of allegiance, but he was still quite clearly most fearful of its consequences. Neither the sickness nor his terror had yet silenced him, though.

"When I went into exile from my homeland," he said, "I was forced to abandon most of my private collections. Too heavy, you see. Too difficult to transport. What I did bring with me to your country was only the best, the most significant.

"Clay tablets, in particular. Ancient texts. Magical texts, from Babylonia, Ur, Akkad. Mesopotamia. The oldest of old times, you understand, when Man lived in a wholly magical world?"

He looked questioningly from Quire to Agnes. Quire offered no response. He was standing by the window, holding the blanket just far enough away from the glass to give him a view out on to the narrow, crowded street. He was listening intently to what Durand said, but his eyes were mostly on the good people of Leith. He absently scratched at the cuff of the overly tight shirt he wore. Agnes had found him some clothes to replace the harlequin costume, but they did not fit him well.

Agnes, though, smiled and nodded encouragingly to the Frenchman. He sat on the bed, cocooned in her blankets, hugging them to him as if desperate for protection against the iciest of blasts.

"Tablets that were gathered together in Egypt," Durand continued, "long before the days of Alexander, long before the rise of Rome. Two thousand years they lay buried in the dust of empire, until it was my privilege to uncover them, following in the wake of Napoleon's armies. To become their ... I do not know the word. Keeper? No, not quite. Custodian, perhaps. I took them from Egypt to France, and from France, when the time came, to England, and then here."

"Are you following all this?" Quire asked Agnes, without looking away from the bustling scene outside the window.

"Close enough," she said.

Her pipe had been lit for several minutes now, and had filled the room with floating strata of fine smoke, undulating slowly.

"I fell in with John Ruthven," Durand said, suppressing a cough and pulling his blankets tighter about him. "By chance, or by fate. He was the magister. The chief of our quartet: me, Ruthven, Carlyle, Blegg."

Quire turned aside from the window then, irresistibly summoned by those names, which between them held all the answers he so desired. Durand, Ruthven, Carlyle, Blegg. There was the skein in need of untangling.

"Carlyle made the equipment," Durand said. "The electrical

equipment. I did not entirely understand it, then or now, but there is galvanic stimulation of nerves. The heart is made to beat once more, do you see?"

Durand's bleary eyes were weeping, though whether it was from sickness, or sorrow, or fear, Quire did not know. Agnes gestured with her pipe for Durand to continue, and he obediently did so. He was a husk of a man, much reduced in stature and will. Resigned, Quire suspected, to death. Or worse.

"Others in Italy and Germany, and my own homeland, showed it long ago: the movement of a corpse when electrical force is passed through it. Ruthven found a way to harness it, though. To make use of it. That was the greatest of his insights.

"So. Carlyle to make the equipment. Ruthven to apply it. They began with dogs, before ever I became a party to their enterprise. Ruthven had crude magics, then. He was … fumbling, you would say; fumbling in the dark. But he is a Prometheus, make no mistake. He found light, out there in that dark, and brought it forth. He learned to do things that surpass the wildest dreams of the ancients, and the most unlikely hopes of the present."

Quire returned his attention to the street. The life of Leith continued outside, oblivious and indifferent to the madness being described in the little room. He was envious of the mundane concerns he knew ran through the men and women going up and down the narrow street: the simple desires and hungers, the vague hopes and small sadnesses. He would much rather have himself filled up with such things than with the memories and the furies and the fears that occupied him now.

"A great man," Durand was saying, "but one who succumbed to temptation. He had to reach further, deeper. He began to work upon human corpses. He wanted to restore life. No; more than that. He wanted to restore souls. It was a noble ambition. So I thought, when I became privy to it. But he had not succeeded.

His experiments ... well, let us say no more than that they did not succeed. Except Blegg. Blegg is different."

"What about Blegg?" Quire asked sharply.

"A moment, please." Durand coughed, a loose rattle in his chest. "I will come to the matter of Blegg in a moment. I allied myself with Ruthven, and I brought my own secrets. Recipes for preservative elixirs, something for the hearts that Carlyle's machines revived to pump around the body. Invocations and bindings, recorded on tablets older even than Egypt; transcribed on to the hands of the corpses, they bind an animating force to the flesh."

"Not a soul, though," Agnes said quietly, and Durand hung his head. Shivered.

"No, not a soul. Never a soul. In that, we all fell short of our ambitions. Formless, mindless things that we brought forth and incarnated in the dead. Animating force, nothing more. Fierce. Savage, without the dominating will of a mind to guide it. And never lasting. Always, the bindings failed in time; the body failed. Then it was burned, and the next was begun."

"You dug up graves to get the bodies," Quire said.

"*Oui*. Blegg did. The invention of that foul habit at least is not amongst our sins. You had body snatchers aplenty before ever the dead began to flow through Ruthven's door."

"Aye."

"It became too much for Carlyle. He took to drinking, then tried to remove himself from the affair entirely. The dogs did it for him. Anyway, after your exploits at Duddingston, the grave robbing stopped. Of late they have been buying bodies, letting others do the digging – or the killing, I know not which – on their behalf. They've abandoned the farm, brought the apparatus to Ruthven's house, in the cellar. Blegg pays a man called Hare, and the corpses ... well, they appear in Melville Street."

"You say Blegg is something different, though?" rasped Quire, his impatience rising like bile. "Not like these other . . . creatures Ruthven has made?"

"Blegg. *Oui.* He is something different, something very old. I think the madness that is in that house – it came with him, I think. The worst of it.

"You understand: it is not Blegg, not his mind or his spirit, that occupies his form. Whoever Blegg was, he died before I ever met him. I never knew quite how, though I always had the feeling that he was somehow the first real victim in all of this. Anyway, Ruthven, in his careless explorations, woke something else in Blegg's corpse. Invited something in. Something that is much more than the dull animal spirits of the others."

"Do you believe all of this?" Quire asked Agnes softly.

She had sat quite still all through Durand's speech, save for the flex in her cheeks and lips as she drew smoke down into her chest and let it leak out again. She blinked, very slowly, very heavily, and looked up.

"Maybe," she said.

She pointed at the morose Frenchman with the stem of her pipe.

"Look at him. Sick to the very root of him, and it's no natural sickness, I can tell you that."

"No," Durand grunted. "It is Blegg, telling me to come home. Like a man calling out for his straying dog. He and Ruthven think – wrongly, as it happens, but no matter – they think there are further secrets I can yet uncover for them. If I do not heed his call, I will be dead long before I could offer testimony at any trial of your foes, Monsieur Quire. They are not careless in such matters."

"Not that any'd give much credence to such testimony in these times, eh?" Agnes said to Quire. "Not talk of dead men rising, and spells dug up out of deserts."

"No. There'll be no trial, I think."

He absently let the blanket fall back across the window.

"I have to go," he muttered. "I have to find Dunbar. You're sure you're willing to watch over Durand?"

"Aye." Agnes nodded. "They'll not find him here, and it might be I can do something for his fever."

"They will mean to kill you, assuredly," Durand said in a matter-of-fact tone to Quire.

"They will try, I know. Perhaps I will kill them."

The Frenchman grunted, and wiped a weary hand across his damp brow.

"You will not find it easy to kill what is in Blegg. Not easy at all. Still the heart, remove the binding spells from the skin of his hands. Destroy the body, utterly, to its last scrap. And even then ..."

Durand shrugged, which made him cough and tremble once more. It took a moment or two for him to recover, before he could speak again.

"He is an old thing. Not like we poor mortals. It takes no more than a fever to put an end to us." He smiled bitterly. "Should you see Mr Blegg in your travels, perhaps you could enquire whether he has some little figure of me – made of clay or wood, most likely – about his person.

"He is a great one for making such things. Each of the dead we have raised had one of its own, as part of the binding of flesh and spirit. He hides them away somewhere up on that great hill of yours – Arthur's Seat. It is a place of old power, evidently. One might be used just as well, I suspect, in the right hands, to separate flesh and spirit. It would need some part of me – hair, perhaps – but he might easily have obtained such a thing while I slept."

"I'll bear it in mind," Quire said.

"Thank you. He will not part with it, of course, but you could ask. This is not how I would choose to die. Ha. How many of us choose how we die, though?"

A flock of kites swept and swirled across the wind. Half a dozen of them, each tethered to the earth, to the hand of a child, by a long, taut string. Each straining against that tether, trying to tear itself free and escape into the sky's embrace; go dancing off with the wind into the distance.

They floated close by Holyrood Palace, rising up from the fields just to the east of it. There was little by way of flat ground in the King's Park, and what there was drew families. The parents brought their children, and the children brought paper kites, painted with faces and trailing sinuous tails of ribbon bows. The grass was grazed low by sheep and cattle, and for the younger children in particular it must have felt like a limitless, soft expanse, fit for running and falling and tumbling.

Quire knew, for his friend had told him often enough, that Wilson Dunbar's was one of those families to be found here, on any Sunday suited to the flying of kites. He walked across the turf towards them with a feeling of sick dread in the pit of his stomach.

He could hear the kite strings thrumming in the wind, and the crack and snap of their long tails. If he had closed his eyes, it could have been the rigging on a fleet of little boats, stirring. The laughter of children fluttered around and through it, light and joyous. Dunbar should be here, a part of it. This, Quire thought miserably, was what he had taken the man away from.

Ellen Dunbar was standing with her back to him, watching her sons happily wrestle with the straining kites, dragging them across the breezes, shouting encouragement up to them. Quire did not know the boys well, for he had never intruded much upon the privacy of Dunbar's familial life, but he knew how precious that life was. He envied it, though the envy had never troubled their friendship.

"Hello, Ellen," he said as he drew near.

She half-turned to him, not wanting to lose sight of the boys. The wind that buoyed the kites above them lifted her hair.

"Adam," she said quietly. "Where is my husband?"

"I thought perhaps he might be here."

"And I thought he might still be with you, sleeping off drink on a floor somewhere."

She kept her voice calm and subdued, but Quire could hear the cords of anger, of worry, tight within it. She hid it well. When the boys glanced back from their games with the sky, they saw only their mother in easy conversation with the man they knew as a friend of their father's.

"So not here, not with you," Ellen said. "Where is he, then? I don't know what games the two of you were playing last night, Adam, but I'll be needing my husband back."

"I will find him," Quire said, his guilt souring in his gut. "I promise you that."

"Be sure you do. Be sure you do."

Quire stood there, at her shoulder, watching the kites. His gaze drifted up towards the rough, rising swell of Arthur's Seat. Jackdaws and ravens were cavorting on the boisterous air, up above the high ground, like scrappy black kites launched by the great hill itself. But not tethered, those wilder flags; riding the wind freely, ever on the border between being its master and being mastered by it. Revelling in their nature.

"Get along, please, Adam," Ellen said. "I don't want the boys thinking something's wrong. I don't want them talking to you."

*

Quire approached the Holy Land cautiously, discreetly, in expectation of trouble. It had already proved itself a less anonymous hiding place than he had – perhaps foolishly – hoped. He might not have gone there at all, but for his desire to arm himself. His one remaining pistol and his French sabre resided there, under Cath's bed.

He found nothing untoward as he turned into Leith Wynd. All was quiet, as only a Sunday could make the Old Town quiet. Those out on the streets were, most of them, in their best church attire, and though some of the shops were open and some stalls doing a sluggish trade, it was not a day for toil.

Quire would not permit himself to relax into the general mood of calm, though. He climbed the stair of the Holy Land quietly, alert to any hint of danger. There was nothing but the usual stale stink of the place, and the light breezes ebbing and flowing through the window apertures.

For all his caution, he was taken entirely unawares by what awaited him within the room he shared with Cath. Isabel Ruthven was seated on the bed.

Cath was kneeling at the fire grate, blowing to put some life into the embers there. She looked up as Quire entered, and smiled broadly at him.

"Ah, Mr Quire," Isabel said, before either he or Cath could speak. "I was assured you would appear here sooner or later, and I'm glad it was not too much later. There's just starting to be a little chill on the air, don't you think?"

She wore a short, light coat, the bell of her skirts blooming out from under it. Her hands, neatly folded in her lap, were clad in very soft, tan-coloured gloves.

"Here I am," he said flatly. "Cath, could you leave us alone for a bit?"

Cath's expression faltered. She caught the leaden tone in Quire's voice.

"Leave the fire be," he said, and she rose to her feet, and brushed her hands off on her skirt.

"I'll see if Emma's about," she said, moving carefully past Quire towards the door.

She paused at his shoulder, and whispered to him.

"Did I not do right, letting her in, Adam? Only she said she knew you, and needed to see you quite urgent."

"It's all right," Quire said.

He had not taken his eyes from Isabel Ruthven since entering the room, and did not do so now, as the door scraped shut behind Cath and he edged backwards to set his heel firmly against the base of it. He did not want anyone bursting in behind him.

"What are you doing here?" he asked.

"Oh, dear. I hoped we might attempt, at least, a little civility."

"That would depend on why you're here, wouldn't it?"

"I suppose it might. I fear I am about to disappoint you, then. I have a message for you, Mr Quire."

Quire curled his lip in distaste. It had not occurred to him to count Isabel Ruthven amongst the ranks of his enemies. But little about that household had been as it seemed, so he supposed he should not be entirely surprised.

"Ruthven's got you running foul little errands for him now, has he? Like some scullery maid?"

"Oh, don't be so wearisome. I'd not run errands for John if my life depended upon it. He's been no husband to me for years."

"Blegg, then?"

"Blegg, as you so rudely put it. An entirely different proposition. Really rather intoxicating, when one develops a taste for men possessed of real power. Do you think me dreadful?"

She tossed the question out on to the air like a diaphanous handkerchief, without the slightest interest in what he truly thought. He told her anyway.

"Dreadful. Aye, that might be one word for it."

She smiled once more, wholly unperturbed by his rasping hostility. She tugged at her delicate calfskin gloves, tightening them over her hands.

"It is rather sad, to see a man such as yourself so overmatched. So out of his depth."

"Might want to wait a wee while yet, before coming to that opinion."

"How exciting," she said drily. "You really don't understand, do you, you poor man? Still you do not grasp who you are dealing with. My husband is quite untouchable, Mr Quire. Quite untouchable. He counts as a friend everyone whose influence can help to keep him safe. I should know, for I've watched every penny we once had to our name flow out through the door in the service of that very aim."

"Best give me your message, before I run short on patience."

"Ah. Very well. I'm told that your friend is at my husband's farm, and if you would be so good as to bring Mathieu Durand there, an exchange of some sort will be transacted."

"Cold Burn Farm."

"Indeed. Do you know it?"

Quire could not tell if her placid innocence was feigned or genuine, and did not greatly care. She was no fool, and could not be unaware how crude and cruel was the business she transacted.

"In any case," Isabel said, "you have until nightfall tomorrow, I understand, to complete the rendezvous. That's what Durand's people would call it, I think? I'm told he is probably gravely ill by now, and will likely expire if you delay beyond that, which would be unfortunate for all concerned. I know I would regret it, myself; I always rather liked the man, for all his somewhat feeble, miserable manner. I do hope it won't come to that."

Quire regarded her coldly for a moment or two, staring into

her bright eyes, wondering at the poison beneath that fair exterior. Slowly, deliberately, he hawked up a gobbet of spittle into his mouth and spat at her feet.

She looked down at the unsightly, muculent smear on the floorboards, then at Quire. She arched her eyebrows, and rose from the bed.

"And what if I made a prisoner out of you?" Quire said. "Would that not put your menfolk at something of a disadvantage?"

She laughed.

"Oh, I'm not nearly so precious to either of them as Mathieu is. My husband would be inconvenienced by my disappearance only until he concocted some explanation for it that satisfied the gossips of the New Town. And as for Mr Blegg . . . I am not so foolish as to think it would trouble him overmuch either."

Quire moved aside from the door and pulled it open. Isabel Ruthven gave him a buoyant nod as she drifted past him and out on to the stair. He slammed the door behind her, hard enough to shake its feeble hinges.

XXVI

Cold Burn Farm II

Merry Andrew's cart was a rackety old contraption, too shabby and brittle for carrying much in the way of anything. The last time Quire had been aboard it, he had been the cargo, bouncing along over the Water of Leith bridge with Merry Andrew's grave-robbing tools for company; now, he drove it. It had been a fair few years since he was called upon to steer a horse in harness, but he had done it often enough as a child on his father's farm, and sometimes when he had been at war, for no army moved much of anywhere without a mighty train of wagons in its wake.

Nor did Quire, this time, ride alongside spade and crowbar and sacks for the bagging of bodies. His one French pistol rested on the seat beside him, rocking gently as the wagon progressed up the lumpy track. It was loaded and primed. The hammer could be cocked in a moment. Quire found it difficult to imagine any outcome that would not involve its firing. It was a day waiting for the shedding of blood. Whose it would be – that he would learn soon enough.

Beyond the pistol, hunched down under an oversized cloak – entirely buried by it, in fact, the better to obscure his features –

was Spune. Flat on the bed of the cart, beneath a light canvas, lay Merry Andrew and the third of his grave-robbing triumvirate: Mowdiewarp. Which was a nickname Quire might have thought funny, had he not been entirely preoccupied with other concerns. Mowdiewarp was an old country name for a mole. A digger.

Merry Andrew was complaining, rather indistinctly due to the concealing canvas, as he had been for a considerable length of time.

"Have you never driven a wagon before?" he hissed. "I've got a bruise on every bone, the way you keep finding out the ruts, you daft fuck."

Quire ignored him. He could imagine that Merrilees' elongated, bony form made for a hard ride over these rough tracks, but it could not be helped. Merry Andrew could never have passed for Durand, no matter how bundled up in cloak or cape. The two were far too dissimilar in form and carriage. It was not possible to make a heron look like a grouse, whatever the size of the bag you put over its head. So Merry Andrew stayed hidden in the back, and Spune – the only one of them, in fact, of even passingly similar stature to the Frenchman – sat glumly up front, pretending to be sick and keeping his face well hidden.

Arrowheads of geese were ploughing the sky, honking as they went. A buzzard was mewing, off over the slopes of the Pentlands, quartering the heather and grassland with lazy glides. The wagon pitched and yawed and grumbled. And through it all, Quire could still hear Merry Andrew's whining complaints.

"I'll have your guts for fiddle strings if this doesn't play out right after all this bloody misery, you police bastard."

Quire had made a neat little confection of lies and truth for Merry Andrew and his boys; close enough to the latter to let him say it with an air of conviction, enough of the former to make his proposal tempting to them.

It had taken him longer to find them than he would have liked. A few hours of rummaging around in Edinburgh's darker corners, and the distribution of coins he could not really afford to part with, not if he was ever to eat again. From the distillery where Spune was – occasionally – employed, he had been sent to an inn in the basement of a half-ruinous tenement near the canal basin at Port Hopetoun. The place was bursting with bargees and canal workers, for all that it was early in the morning, and the air so thick with tobacco he could have chewed it. He had, though, missed both Spune and Merry Andrew by an hour or more. Look for him at the Flesh Market, Quire was told, once he paid over a thrupenny piece.

The Flesh Market was down on the low ground between Old Town and New, in the shadow of the North Bridge. It was a mazy place packed with barrows and stalls and little shops. It was a stinking place too, and a raucous one, with meat traders and butchers and provisioners all competing to get themselves heard one above the other.

Quire found the butcher he had been sent to and was told that Merry Andrew had been there but minutes before, settling a debt. After that, an ironmonger's shop in Blair Street, run by a man who was an uncle to the city's thieves, and plied a secret trade in a great deal more than ironwork. But Merrilees was not to be found there either, and the ironmonger was at first unwilling to offer any alternative suggestion. He read some fell and fixed determination in Quire's face, though, and the passage of a few more coins was enough to loosen his tongue.

Finally, wearily, Quire found Merry Andrew getting himself shaved at a barber's beside the Royal Exchange. He waited outside, watching the razor sweep its way back and forth over the soapy skin. Andrew Merrilees looked to be entirely at his ease, his lanky frame stretched out in the barber's chair, his head tilted back. Anyone not knowing him might have thought him a man of some means, a righteous member of the city's merchant class, perhaps, tidying himself up in anticipation of a meeting to discuss business proposals with fellow traders.

Quire approached Merry Andrew when he emerged, fresh-faced and neat. The man seemed hungry for what Quire disingenuously offered: the chance to settle accounts with those rivals who had caused him such trouble last winter, and broken up one of his cronies; to rid himself of competitors in advance of the next body-snatching season.

"I know where they are," Quire had murmured, "and I'm not meaning to arrest them, not now. There's only one or two of them, and none at all after I'm done. That's my plan. Anything you can find on them or about them is yours. I'm not caring about the law these days."

And Merry Andrew had smiled, in his brutish, gawky way.

So the four of them rode the cart up the track towards Cold Burn Farm. Spune, it turned out, was even more enthusiastic about the enterprise than Merry Andrew, for it was his cousin had been beaten half to death when they met Blegg in the grounds of Greyfriars Kirk. The boy was still half-crippled, Spune told Quire bitterly, and would never walk right again.

They were not the kind of allies Quire would once have chosen for himself, but he lived by different rules now, and for the work at hand he could think of few better. He had made the mistake once of coming to Cold Burn Farm alone; it was only fools who failed to learn the lesson of their follies.

Quire was equipped for savagery if – when – it came to that. Not just the pistols, but the sabre sheathed at his waist. Though he had never been much of a swordsman, he knew the rudiments of its use. Gently curved, with a broad, single-edged blade and a simple but solid bar for a hand guard, it was very much a thing of purpose, not decoration.

Merry Andrew had a pocket pistol, Quire knew; a tiny little snub-nosed thing, but it would be damaging if he was close to his target. He had seen Spune and Mowdiewarp loading their pockets and belts with knives and – in Spune's case – a short iron truncheon that looked brutally heavy. It was a fearsome enough armament, though whether it would meet the needs of the day, Quire was not certain. It would probably depend, as such things usually did, not on the weapons themselves, but on the conviction of the men who wielded them. All three of his companions seemed to Quire to be pleasingly set upon doing violence.

Though fire was a thing Quire loathed, and feared, he had come ready for that, too, as Durand had recommended it. There were lit lanterns in the bed of the cart, beside Merrilees and Mowdiewarp, and bottles of lamp oil. He had done what he could to prepare himself, and now wanted only to get done what needed doing.

The gate partway up the track stood open. It was impossible to say whether it was invitation or negligence. Quire let the horse take its own pace through the gate and on towards the copse of trees, which he remembered all too well from his encounter with Davey Muir. It was agonising, to now grind slowly along with the dense thickets on either side, expecting at any moment to be suddenly assailed. But they came safely through, and trundled up towards the farm steading.

"Get yourselves ready, lads," Quire said under his breath. "Not until I tell you, though, right?"

A discontented grunt from Merry Andrew was the only response.

Quire could see at once that things had changed at the farm. The barns and house looked just as dilapidated and neglected as before, but the low cowshed at the far end of the yard, where Quire had inadvertently disturbed Davey, was now in considerably worse condition. It had, from the look of it, been gutted by fire. Part of its roof was fallen in, and there were ugly black streaks over some of its stonework, where smoke had leaked out through cracks and crevices. The doors were hanging from their hinges, one of them blackened and much reduced by flames.

Quire shot a glance up to the chimney of the farmhouse. No smoke. There would be someone here somewhere, though. He was sure of that. If it was Blegg or Ruthven, all he needed was to draw them close enough with the temptation of the false Durand at his side, and he would put a ball in their head. There would be no petty talk, no hesitation. If Dunbar was even still alive, Quire was all but he certain he would not have long remained so – none of them would – had the real Durand been handed over. This way, at least there was a chance. But only if he got the first kill in.

The cart creaked to a halt in the centre of the farmyard. A flock of pigeons that had been roosting on the roof of the barn burst into the air at the sound, clattering their way into the cloudy sky with flailing wings. They carried Quire's gaze with them for a moment. He watched them coalesce into a flock and go sweeping down behind the building. And because he did that, he did not see the hounds straight away.

"God damn, Quire," Spune said with feeling. "You never said anything about dogs."

Quire snapped his head back. They were loping across the yard from the open door of the cowshed. Two of them, closing quickly. As filthy as he remembered, and with those same dead and lightless eyes.

"What's happening?" Merry Andrew shouted, stirring beneath the canvas.

The horse reared in alarm, violently enough to shake the front end of the cart, but its harness dragged it back down. The leading dog came bounding up and sprang at the horse's head. It seized hold of the animal's nose and lips with its teeth, and tore away a strip of skin and flesh as the horse screamed and twisted and tried to raise its head.

"Jesus Christ," Spune said, rising to his feet, sloughing the great cloak from his shoulders and whipping out his iron cudgel.

Quire dropped the reins and reached for the pistol to prevent it from sliding away as the cart slewed round, dragged by the distraught horse. The first dog was under the horse's neck, snapping at it, tearing at it. The second lunged up at the side of the cart, close by Spune, trying to get a hold on his ankle. Spune leaned down and hit it hard on the side of the head with his truncheon. The beast fell back, rolled, and recovered its feet in an instant, coming bounding back towards the cart.

Quire had his pistol in hand now. He cocked the hammer. He might have tried a shot at one or other of the dogs, but the horse succumbed entirely to its terror then, and bolted. It pounded its attacker beneath its hoofs and swept the cart over the fallen hound, crashing off in directionless panic, trailing streamers of blood and mucus and spit from its mangled muzzle.

Merry Andrew and Mowdiewarp, flailing around in the back, trying to free themselves of the smothering canvas, were screaming abuse at the horse, at Quire, and the world in general.

The sudden, violent movement pitched Spune off the cart altogether, and flung Quire against the back of his seat. He tried to steady himself as best he could, one-handed, but would likely have been thrown clear had the horse not found itself under renewed assault. The very dog it had trampled just moments before came racing up to its rear leg, passing dangerously close to the spinning front wheel of the cart, and unhesitatingly leaped up and fixed its teeth into the horse's hamstring. That was enough to slow it dramatically, and it limped desperately along on three legs as the hound put the whole weight of its body into a violent shaking, intended to tear out a mouthful of muscle.

Quire leaned forward and down from his seat and shot the dog in the head. The flare and roar of the gun startled the horse all over again, and it staggered sideways, but it was lapsing into that state of numb shock Quire had seen in its kind before when they were seriously injured. The pistol spat its ball into the dog's skull just behind the eye, and blew a hole the size of a half-crown coin in the far side of the animal's head, sending a portion of its skull and ear spinning away across the yard. The impact was enough to knock loose its grip upon the horse's hindquarters, though it left deep gouges behind it, and thick rivulets of blood coursing down the horse's leg.

Quire jumped to the ground, landing on the balls of his feet and dropping into a crouch. He could hear Spune screaming, and began to turn to look for him, but the dog he had shot came at him, its head horribly open and misshapen now.

It leaped at Quire's face, and he barely got the discharged pistol up in time to block its jaws. A vile, musty stench of dead flesh and rotting fur washed over him. The hound bit down on the gun, and shook it with such terrible strength that it tore it from Quire's grasp and pushed him on to his backside. The silence of the attack was uncanny and horrible. Quire could hear the faltering snorts of the horse, Merry Andrew shouting something, Spune wailing; but not a sound from the dog that was remorselessly trying to kill him.

Quire made to draw the sabre from its scabbard, trying to rise as he did so. The dog let the pistol fall from its mouth and came at him again. He fell on to his back, letting his own weight take him down, and got his foot into the creature's chest as it lunged once more for his face.

He folded his knee, taking the hound's weight and speed into his leg, then kicked out with all his strength. He meant to send it back the way it had come, but his boot slid off its slick, half-rotted fur and it went twisting and tumbling sideways instead. Again, it was quickly on to its feet, but he was ready for it now. He met its charge with the tip of the sabre's blade, angled in along the line of its throat, punching through the skin of its barrel chest and bursting through the ribcage deep down into the chest cavity.

It was no way to use a sabre, but it had the desired effect. Durand had told him to aim for the heart, and he had been right. The hound fell on to its side. Its legs still shook, and its jaw still worked open and shut, but it could not rise. Quire left the sword buried in the beast and turned towards the farmhouse.

Spune was on the ground, no longer screaming; limp, as the second great dog shook him. Mowdiewarp was bent over the creature, stabbing it again and again in the back and flank with a butcher's knife. Merry Andrew stood, feet firmly planted in a wide stance, back straight, right arm extended perfectly level, pointing his tiny pistol at the door of the farmhouse. Where Blegg stood, looking directly at Quire.

Quire heard the horse slumping down to the ground behind him.

"Aim for the heart," he cried out to Merry Andrew, though he doubted the man could aim at much of anything with such a trinket of a gun.

Merrilees was not listening anyway.

"There's the bastard I want," he shouted, and fired.

Blegg's shoulder twitched. That was the only way to tell that the shot had hit him. A tremor went through his face, perhaps; that contemptuous smile faltered for a second, before reasserting itself.

Merry Andrew howled in frustration, and fumbled for his

powder pouch. Blegg took a single long step backwards and disappeared into the farmhouse.

Quire set his foot on the still twitching dog he had impaled, and pulled the sabre out. It came grudgingly, rasping against bone. He hurried over to where the other beast was blindly, mindlessly savaging Spune and pushed Mowdiewarp roughly aside. He took a moment or two to steady himself, and choose his spot, then drove the blade in between two ribs and skewered the heart.

"Bastard," Merry Andrew was saying over and over again. "Bastard. Bastard."

Quire did not know if it was meant for him, or Blegg, or God for that matter. He glanced down at Spune, who was pale and moaning. One arm of his jacket was entirely soaked through with blood, and he had an ugly wound to his cheek.

Merry Andrew started towards the farmhouse door.

"Wait, Merrilees," Quire snapped. "You'll need more than that wee gun if you're going in there."

When Merry Andrew glared at him, he nodded towards the cart.

"Bring the lanterns, if they're still alight, and the oil. We'll burn the place down."

Quire retrieved his pistol, and hurried to reload it. If he was to have any chance of finding Wilson Dunbar alive, it would be now, in the next few moments. Nothing mattered but that.

He kicked in the door of the kitchen, and found it bare and damp and cold.

"Dunbar," he shouted, feeling despair winding itself about his heart. "Blegg!"

There was no answer, but he heard the creak of floorboards above his head. He looked at the ceiling. The sound came again. He ran out into the hall, almost colliding with Merry Andrew as he came loping into the house. In each hand he carried a burning lantern and a bottle of thin oil, tied together with fine rope. Quire hurriedly sheathed his sabre and took one of the cumbersome bundles from Merrilees.

"Up there," he said to the grave robber, and led the way up the stairs.

When Quire was halfway up, Blegg heaved a linen chest over the railing of the landing above. His timing was off, but only by a fraction. The massive wooden box plummeted down just behind Quire, struck Merry Andrew a glancing blow on the shoulder, shattered the banisters into splinters and cracked the stair upon which it landed. Quire heard the sharp click of Merry Andrew's collarbone breaking an instant before the man's yelp of startled pain; and an instant before the sound of glass shattering and the soft whump of flame erupting through the spray of spilled oil.

A surge of fear rushed through Quire, and he scrambled further up the staircase, out of reach of the blooming flames. He twisted, raised his gun and fired just as Blegg darted back out of view. Quire looked back down towards the hall. Merry Andrew was kneeling on the floor down there, head bowed in pain, one hand clamped to his shoulder. Flames were leaping between the two of them, crackling away as they took hold of the staircase. Quire shied away from the memories that sight brought forth.

He stowed his pistol and drew the sabre once more. He climbed the stair with sword in one hand, improvised fire grenade in the other. The doorway through which he thought Blegg had likely retreated was open. He approached it cautiously, trying to shut out the sound of the fire hungrily consuming the old, dry stairs. He could tell just from the roar of it that it was spreading quickly. Already, smoke was thickening all about him, stinging his eyes and his throat.

He looked into the room, and saw Blegg leaning over Dunbar, who was lying quite motionless on a wide bed. Blegg had his hands over Dunbar's mouth and nose. Quire shouted and rushed at him, sword raised, but Blegg was a good deal too fast for him. He straightened and turned quickly, and caught Quire's descending arm by the wrist. With his other hand he punched Quire once, solidly, in the chest. Pain lanced through Quire. It felt as though his whole chest was cramping.

Blegg pushed him backwards, towards the open doorway and the landing and the rising flames beyond it, and Quire could not help but go, for the man was terribly strong. His wrist was crushed and bent in Blegg's grip.

With all his strength, he hit Blegg on the side of the head with the lantern in his left hand. It did not break, but Blegg paused in his determined advance, and looked down at Quire's hand, and reached to block it with his own. Quire swung again, and this time the oil flask cracked and spilled some of its contents across the lantern with a little flash of flame, and that little flash became a cloud, blinding Quire even as he twisted away, billowing over Blegg's face and head and shoulders.

The two of them parted, Quire staggering along the landing, dropping what remained of the lantern and his sword, pulling frantically at the collar of his coat to drag it off over his head. The left sleeve and breast of it were burning, and he could feel the awful heat of the flames already in his skin, and with it the panic that he knew would master him completely if he could not free himself of the coat.

He did manage to tear it off, and cast it into a corner. He blinked through the churning smoke as he felt for his sabre. Blegg was a bright, awful beacon of flame, reeling about at the far end of the landing, close by the top of the stairs and the window there. His hair was alight, and his shirt. The stink of burning flesh, which he knew all too well, made Quire gag, and he clamped his hand over his nose and mouth to keep both it and the acrid smoke out as best he could.

Flames were licking up around the railings on the landing. Quire shrank away from them. His hand found the hilt of the sabre and he took a firm grip of it. Blegg was still upright, still pawing at his burning scalp as if impotently trying to pat the flames out. It was difficult to be sure through the obscuring, shifting veils of smoke, but Quire thought Blegg's face was blackening. Charring.

He moved closer, and hacked at Blegg with the sabre, desperate to put an end to this. The heat coming from the burning man was too much for him to get a great deal of force behind his blows, but they were enough to topple Blegg backwards, and he broke through the window behind him. The sudden gust of wind sucked a great roaring sheet of flame up the staircase and across Blegg's body. He hung there for a moment, half in and half out of the window, then his legs came up and he tumbled backwards out of the house.

Quire went to Dunbar, who was battered and bruised and pale. But still breathing; not strongly or deeply, but still breathing. Quire called to him, and lifted him from the bed, but Dunbar did not stir.

The room overlooked the farmyard. Merry Andrew was sitting cross-legged by the cart, clutching his shoulder. Mowdiewarp was kneeling beside the unmoving Spune. Quire kicked out the window, and shouted, again and again, at Mowdiewarp until the sheer noise of it penetrated the man's fug of bewildered disbelief and persuaded him to leave Spune's side. Quire lowered Dunbar down to him. He lowered himself from the window after, and dropped the last half-dozen feet. He turned his ankle as he landed, and for a moment thought he had broken it, so sharp was the pain. But the bone held.

He hobbled around to the back of the farmhouse, coughing at the smoke that had settled into his lungs, watching great clouds of the stuff spilling out from the building.

Blegg was gone, leaving only a filthy, black, oily smear on the ground where he had fallen.

XXVII

All Hallows' and All Saints'

All Hallows' Eve was a night of rude celebration in Edinburgh's Old Town. The poor and unwashed folk of the city fashioned from that fell night, when the lore of their forefathers told them that the Devil and his spirits stalked the darkness, an excuse for light and merriment and drinking.

In every tenement, no matter how squalid, how impoverished, there would somewhere be dancing and noise late into the night, as if by that commotion the evils lurking without might be held at bay. The Old Town seldom slept deeply, or for long, but on this night more than any other it shrugged off the darkness and busied itself deep into the wee small hours. The whisky shops, strewn in dense profusion along almost every street and wynd, stayed open late, lighting their windows with lamps and drawing in a constant stream of drunken customers, seeking to replenish their dwindling supplies. They brought empty bottles, and the whisky sellers filled them up from tapped barrels and sent them on their way; then, an hour or two later, the same folk would stagger in off the street, with the same bottle, empty once more, to be filled.

There were scuffles in the street, the whisky-fed frustrations and rivalries of the Old Town boiling up. It was in the nature of the place that with the release of celebration came too the release of its darker side, for the one could not be set free without the other. Small violences were done amidst the songs and the jigs; hard words said amidst the laughter. Everywhere, voices were loud, whether in argument or frenzied pleasure.

Some there were who tried to sleep amidst the tumult. They could not escape it, though, not in this layered, crowded place where folk lived as dense as bees in their hives.

Mrs Conway, in her room in the West Port, tossed and turned uncomfortably in her bed. Her husband slumbered deeply, leadenly, at her side, as he always did. She, whose need for sleep was the more acute, since she must be up at four to make him his breakfast and it was already close on midnight, was kept from it by the Old Town's restless convulsions. The witching hour drew near, and could be nothing other than restless on All Hallows' Eve.

With every passing sleepless moment, Mrs Conway grew more anxious and bitterly resentful of those drunken celebrants robbing her of her rest. Rough sounds added themselves to the mix, grating upon her weary senses. Scuffling, shouting, angry curses. Coming from the Burke house just next door. That was no great strangeness in itself, for it was a turbulent and drunken house on any night, let alone this wild one, but there was a harsh extremity to the clatter and thumps and voices leaking through the wall. Mrs Conway could hear William Burke's voice chief amongst those raised in anger, and the noise of it seemed to go on and on. Until at last it faded, and a quiet settled. Mrs Conway whispered a small thanks to God, and slowly, slowly drifted off to sleep.

Hugh Alston had a grocer's shop on the West Port, and lived

with his wife in the flat above it. The two of them made their way, only a little the worse for drink, towards their stair as the witching hour turned. It had been a long day. They were tired but happy, for trade had been good of late.

The racket that greeted them was out of tune with their contentment. There were men shouting indistinctly at one another, a violent quarrel. Tables or chairs being overturned.

"It's coming from Burke's house," Mrs Alston said, as they stood together on the street, listening in dismay to the cacophony.

Then, sharp, cutting through the male voices, quite clear, a woman crying out: "For God's sake, get the police. There's murder here."

The Alstons looked at one another in consternation.

"Get yourself upstairs," Hugh said to his wife, "and lock the door behind you."

Once sure his wife was safely climbing the stair to their apartment, he ran up the West Port to the watch-house there, and beat upon its door. But the nightwatchmen of the Old Town had many calls upon their attention that night, of all nights, and there was no answer. Its windows were dark, its lock secure.

Troubled, Alston went cautiously back down to his shop and home. All was silence now. Not a whisper escaped the house of William Burke. He sighed, and shook his head, and followed after his wife.

They slept uneasily through what remained of the night. And as they slept, that night turned and the city's frenzy spent itself, and All Hallows' Eve became All Saints' Day.

The morning came in bleak and cold and cloudy. Sergeant John Fisher was on duty in the entrance of the police house at Old Stamp Office Close, and looked out through the open doors upon a High Street rousing itself more sluggishly into life than was its wont. The excesses of the night before weighed heavily upon the Old Town, and it had woken with bleary eyes and sore limbs and aching heads.

A man – agitated, fidgety – came in off the street.

"I've seen a body in a house on the West Port," he said without preamble or introduction. "A poor woman, murdered."

Fisher went with the man – Gray, his name turned out to be – up along the quiet High Street, and down the arc of West Bow on to the Grassmarket. Bottles and rubbish were strewn about there. They walked its length to the West Port, and Gray showed Fisher the house of William Burke.

A dark passage led back into a tenement. At its end, a narrow stair descended into gloom. Gray let Fisher precede him down the stair, and thus it was Fisher who came face to face with another man, climbing up.

"That's him," Gray said in alarm. "That's Burke."

"Would you let me into your house please, Mr Burke," said Fisher, ignoring the ferocious glare Burke was fixing upon Gray.

The room to which Gray guided them was a picture of wretched squalor. Rags and straw were scattered all over the bare floor, and every corner was piled high with disordered heaps of tattered and half-made shoes, and with the tools of the cobbler's trade. A pot of boiled potatoes stood by the cold ashes of last night's fire. There was not a single piece of furniture save a crude, low bed stretched out against one wall. It was the humblest of things, a few planks and sticks roughly nailed together. There was no mattress on it save a tightly packed mat of straw and old cloths. A faded, striped nightgown lay on the bed.

"There's no body here," Sergeant Fisher observed.

"A body you're after, is it?" Burke muttered, his Irish brogue made harsh by his anger and contempt. "You'll not find one here, whatever you've been told."

"It was there, on the bed," Gray insisted. The fear was plain in his voice.

"He's saying it from spite," Burke scoffed. "I turned him and his wife out last night, since I needed the bed for someone else."

Fisher raised his eyebrows and looked questioningly at Gray, who did not deny it, but rather nodded.

"That's right, that's right. Mary Docherty, her name was. He turned us out to give her the room, but we came back this morning since we'd lost our boy's stockings and thought them left here. And she were there, in the straw. Dead."

Fisher went closer to the bed. He was reluctant to reach into it, or lift the nightgown, for fear of bugs or lice. But he needed to do no more than lean down and look closely to see the bloodstains smeared on its frame and dried on the stalks of straw.

He turned about and regarded William Burke thoughtfully.

XXVIII

A Witch at His Bedside

The ward to which Wilson Dunbar was consigned in the Royal Infirmary was long, and high, and flooded with light from the tall fretted windows that lined it. It had the faintly echoing, marmoreal quiet of a church, to Quire's ear. Even the nurses, in their uniforms and aprons, walking on soft feet between the rows of beds, put him in mind of nuns. There was something faintly reverent in their considered, careful movement.

It was not a restful place, though, as a church might be. Too many connotations of suffering, and of loss. The scent on the still air was not of incense or candles, but soap and sickness. And if the residents or visitors offered any prayers, they would be only for the abatement of suffering, the abeyance of death.

Quire hated it, though he knew better than most how much worse it could have been. It was, if nothing else, clean. It was ordered, and bright. Not like the madness of the vast crowds of wounded that had been crammed into makeshift hospitals in Brussels after Waterloo. Hundreds of soldiers, broken in service of their country, wailing and dying on pallets and stretchers as the surgeons rushed from one to another, hunting out those they might yet save by swift application of their amputation knives and saws. Dirt everywhere, and blood, for there had been neither time nor space for the niceties of cleaning.

Quire had lain there for days, fevered, agonised by the burns upon his arm, thinking himself, in his darker moments at least, on the verge of death. Knox had dug out from his flesh all that did not belong there, but no one could do anything for the pain. There was not enough laudanum to spare it for any save those sent near mad with their suffering.

That was what Dunbar's ward made Quire think of. He walked, still limping heavily from his sprained ankle, with his head down, averting his eyes from those filling the beds.

Agnes McLaine was already there, sitting at the bedside on a stool, her hand resting upon Dunbar's chest. She could have been an attentive mother, just one amongst the many come to this place to stand watch over their afflicted kin. But Quire knew better. He saw the charm clasped to her breast, smelled the herbal scent soaking out from the little bag that was beneath her palm on Dunbar's chest. He saw that her lips moved, shaping tiny, near silent invocations, even as she looked up and nodded to acknowledge his arrival.

"He's no better, then," Quire murmured.

Sound carried far and clear in this chamber of high ceilings and bare, hard walls. Each stirring of protest or mew of discomfort went rippling along from bed to bed, making itself known, revealing itself. Quire did not want any secrets of his own doing the same.

"No better, no worse," whispered Agnes, gently folding both her hands into her lap. "That's no bad thing. Means he's got strength in him still."

Dunbar made for a dismaying sight, stretched out there beneath the starched white sheets. A motley congregation of bruises about his jaw and cheeks. A gash in his brow. Much of his body was the same, Quire knew. Battered and beaten and wounded. No one wound in itself that could threaten his life, but in their accumulation, a cruel assault. Not enough to explain his deathly slumber, the doctors had said, puzzlement etched upon their faces. Quire cared little for the opinions of the medical profession now. He had learned there were other ways of reading whatever signs the world saw fit to offer its observer.

Dunbar had likely been given a noxious draught of some sort, Agnes had said when first she set eyes upon him. Perhaps laid under a malevolent charm. He would wake, in time, or he would not. That was the sum of her predictions. But she willingly came here, at Quire's request, and offered the oblivious victim of Blegg's abuse whatever small help she might be able.

"You've become a nurse to ailing men," Quire said. "I never meant to make you such, but I did."

Agnes smiled.

"Durand, you mean? Aye, he's still safely locked away, abed. Abed when I'm not there, at least; sleeps on the floor when I'm needing the bed myself. He's not dying fast, if he's dying at all. The totem used against him, or the man who was using it – one or other's been destroyed, I'd say."

"The place was burned out, top to bottom. Everything in the house went to ash or smoke. As for Blegg – I don't know. Maybe he crawled away and died in a ditch or out on the hills. I couldn't easily go looking for him" – he gave his injured leg a careful shake by way of demonstration – "and there was none of those with me in a state, or of a mind, to do it either. I was lucky enough they didn't kill me."

He had thought they might, for a time, in their anguish and shock and fury, with Spune dying there in the farmyard and the conflagration of the farmhouse roaring at them. But they were in the grip of dread, Merry Andrew and Mowdiewarp, and bewildered by what they had seen. Their confusion had saved him, Quire suspected, for they wanted nothing but to get away from that place, and forget its horrors. There had been a clear message at their parting, though, that Merrilees would be inclined to slip a knife under Quire's ribs should they meet again, just on the general principle of stilling those who brought down such infernal misfortune upon others.

In service of that same principle, they had refused him a seat on their cart, and left him there. Alone and half-hobbled, it had taken him a cruelly long time to reach the road, and to find a conveyance back to Edinburgh.

"I can't pay you for any of this," Quire said quietly to Agnes. "Not for Durand, not for Wilson. I've hardly two pennies left to rub together."

"I ken that well enough, son," Agnes grunted. "It's writ plain and clear all over you."

She looked Quire up and down meaningfully. He made for a sorry figure, he knew. Unshaven, barely washed for days now, and standing in clothes he had been wearing for just as long. He had not dared to return to his home, for fear of what might await him there, and so lodged still with Cath in the Holy Land.

"The police came by to have a look at him," said Agnes, nodding down at Dunbar. "So the nurses said. Wanting to know how a man might get himself in such a state. His wife couldn't help them with that, I don't suppose."

He might have been undone, had Ellen Dunbar told the police that Adam Quire was the man to speak to if they wanted to know what had happened to her husband. But she had not done so, and he thought it more likely to be out of loyalty to Dunbar's friendship with him than any affection of her own.

"No, I don't suppose she could," he murmured.

"And you'll not be telling them, or her?"

Quire shook his head.

"Not yet. I'm not done yet. When I am, then maybe a wee bit of the truth'll come out, but the police aren't what's needed to mend all this. Ruthven'd shake them off, or slip away and disappear soon as they came sniffing round. Either way, they'll not get him to answer to anything."

"But you will?"

"I'm the one lifted up this rock, and set the worms to seething. I'm the one put Wilson in this bed. I'm the one'll end it, once my leg's fit to take my weight again." He smiled grimly. "I've nothing else to do with myself these days."

Quire's ankle twinged. The burns on his hand and arms stung. They were not bad, those burns, but they were far worse, to his way of thinking, than any turned ankle. He dreamed of nothing but fire now, every night. If he closed his eyes while awake, even, he could see flames.

"I only stopped in to check on him," he said.

He began to turn away, but paused when he saw the gas fittings up on the wall. They were there high above every bed: copper pipes and embrasures and nozzles. Silent and lifeless now, on a bright winter's morning.

"He's no great liker of gaslights, is Dunbar," he said sadly.

"He'll like them fine, when he wakes to see them," Agnes told him.

Quire was bound up with his own thoughts as he limped along the tiled corridor of the hospital, so much so that he almost collided with a man hurrying in the other direction, equally distracted.

Quire held up an apologetic hand, staggering slightly as he tried to adjust his balance. It took him a moment to recognise the man he faced.

"Sergeant Quire," Robert Christison said. "Ah, except it's no longer Sergeant, is it? Forgive me. Force of habit."

"Professor," Quire nodded, wincing a little at the throbbing of his ankle.

He lifted his foot a fraction from the floor, to take the weight off the aching joint. Christison glanced down, his expert eyes narrowing.

"Are you injured? Getting treatment, perhaps?"

"It's just a turned ankle, sir. Taking its time about healing, but it's on the mend. I'm sorry to have got in your way there, but the ankle makes me a bit less nimble than I was."

"Oh, don't worry, don't worry. I was paying less attention than I should myself. Rather distracted, I confess."

The professor gave a sharp, sad shake of his head.

"A dreadful business, Quire. You'll not have heard, I suppose, being no longer ... well, anyway, word has not yet started to spread, though I fear it surely will."

He glanced about suddenly, apparently to ensure there was no one else within earshot.

"I've a woman awaiting me on a slab downstairs, found in the cellar of Robert Knox's theatre. Another day or two and she would have been under his knife, for the edification of his students

"The police went looking for her there because they've got two Irishmen in custody and it seems – hard to credit, but evidently there's some sort of confession already – it seems they've been supplying his cadavers by way of murder. Burke and Hare. Unthinkable."

"Hare, you say?" said Quire.

"Indeed. William Hare. And Burke's a William too, come to that. It's incredible, quite incredible. That men should murder for profit, and not just this once, by any means. If the rumour's true, it's a dozen or more. Can you believe it?"

"William Hare," murmured Quire.

"As I said. I'm to interview Knox myself, at the request of the Lord Advocate. By God, Quire, if this gets out, if it's proved he had knowledge of how these cadavers were being procured, the scandal will be extraordinary."

"I never had the impression you were too close a friend of Knox's, sir."

"I can't stand him," Christison admitted without hesitation. "He's an insufferable prig, and oafishly arrogant. Takes the most unseemly pleasure in slandering the entire medical staff of the university, in the main because the Town Council did not see fit to appoint him to the chair he wanted. But the consequences if he is shown to have knowingly paid over money for the victims of murder ... "

Christison shook his head once more, dismayed by the implications of his own words.

"Well, the entire undertaking of medical education in this city could be profoundly damaged. Irreparably."

Quire could not summon up the vigour to pretend any great concern over the reputation of the medical establishment. Nor was he greatly engaged by the question of Knox's complicity or otherwise in whatever crimes had been committed. What did capture his interest, though, and leave him wondering about it all the way back to the Holy Land, was that name: William Hare.

XXIX

Melville Street

John Ruthven stalked the empty, cold corridors and rooms of his great house like a caged, waning beast in some vastly inhospitable menagerie. It was a ruin, in many ways; all ways that mattered, save its fabric. Or a graveyard. That, perhaps, was the more apt description. So much had turned to dust within these walls. The fortune come down to him, dwindled now to a meagre rump. His marriage, though that had never been a thing of great consequence to him, for he had seen the cracks running through it before the ardours of the wedding bed had even run their course. The dreams and possibilities that had seemed close enough to touch as he delved ever deeper into the secret truths none before him had uncovered.

He went from darkened room to darkened room on the uppermost floor of the house. He carried no light, for the darkness suited him. He stared at the empty walls, the innumerable absences.

In the room Durand had until recently occupied he kicked half-heartedly at the box of unread, and now unreadable, clay tablets. What secrets might they hold that could have moved him on, taken him further? He would never know, without the Frenchman to stand as intermediary between him and the ancient priests and magicians whose explorations they recorded.

He left Durand's room and stood at the top of stairs, staring up at the stars that glimmered through the wide skylight. A thousand eyes, watching him. Waiting for him to uncover the truth of the fires that lit them, and all things.

A tremor of sound, from deep down in the house beneath him. Ruthven held his breath, tilted his head a fraction. It did not come again, but he was sure his ears had not deceived him. Glass breaking perhaps, or something brittle falling. He stood there, prey now to irritation and trepidation. It was not Isabel returning home, of that he was sure. It had not been that kind of brash sound. Shy, rather. Unmeant.

He could not tell where the sound had come from, but the inspirited corpse that remained locked in the cellar had become restive these last few days. Since Blegg's disappearance, in fact. It might be that the bonds between the meat and the force it carried were weakening, as they always did over time; or it might be that without Blegg, whose incantations played their part in calling the corpses into movement, something was going awry. In either case, it made Ruthven uneasy. He was unsure of his ability to calm or control the thing, should the need arise.

It was foolish even to keep it in the house, of course, but without aid – ideally from Blegg – he was not at all certain that he could destroy it. And there was Wallace's corpse down there too, preserved in a barrel. Intended for the next experiment, which now might never take place. Blegg had killed the man, once they had abandoned Cold Burn Farm. It was distasteful, but the soundest course; they had no further need of his services, and he had seen far too much to be left to his own devices.

Ruthven went to the room he slept in. There was no bed, just a mattress laid on the floor, with heavy woollen blankets rumpled carelessly across it. A wardrobe, though, one of the last elegant reminders of how the whole house had once been furnished, and a few fine clothes within it. And a single tall mirror, standing on shapely carved legs.

In that glass, illuminated by cold moonlight, Ruthven glimpsed his own form and face; saw, in the sag of his shoulders and the limp brow, an unfamiliar despondency. The eyes looking back at him carried a doubt, the hint of folly grudgingly recognised, that made him turn away from the reflected visage.

He reached into the wardrobe and withdrew his cane-sword. An innocent thing, to all appearances, a walking stick made of Malacca wood with a plain but neatly formed metal grip at its head. It concealed a narrow, straight blade.

An oil lamp stood on the floorboards at the side of the mattress, its brass base and handle surmounted by a curving glass shade. Its flame guttered low, shedding almost no light. He turned the little wheel that would bring the lamp to life, and it chased the shadows from the room. Standing, he drew the sword slowly from its cane sheath. It had not been exposed to the air for years, and he had thought it might be stiff or stuck, but it came smoothly out and the lamplight laid soft yellow gleams out along its blade.

There was no further sound from below, but that silence did nothing to still his racing heart. He could think of no cause for the earlier disturbance that would be welcome. Isabel was almost never here now, keeping her own strange hours and telling him nothing of what she did. Treating him, in fact, with the contempt that had been for so long understood but not often so crudely expressed between them. He would have turned her out long ago, but for the need to preserve appearances. She, no doubt, would happily have gone of her own accord, once their funds were all but exhausted, save for Blegg. The perverse desire for him that had grown in her. Or been inflicted upon her by that presence inside Blegg. Ruthven did not know, or care, precisely how their corrupt union had come about.

Sword in one hand, lamp in the other, he went down the stairs. He trod as lightly as he could, but there was no carpeting on these upper flights, and the boards creaked beneath his feet no matter how much care he took.

He paused on the middle landing, peering over the banisters. There was nothing but darkness down there. His lamp set weaving, faltering patterns of soft light flowing over the walls. It merely accentuated the gloom in those parts it did not reach, and made the lurking shadows seem all the more impenetrable. Ruthven flexed his fingers about the hilt of the sword and resumed his cautious descent.

Every one of those he had relied upon in his enterprise had betrayed him. If he was guilty of folly, it was surely in that reliance as much as anything. They had come so close, after all; breathed life into the dead, performed an alchemy of souls. Yet he had become not the conqueror of death but its transmuter, giving it movement and vigour, but not sentience. He had not returned the departed to their bodily shells, but instead replaced them with raw, formless spirits whose nature he did not understand.

Except Blegg, of course. What Ruthven had instilled in Blegg's corpse was of different substance. It was a soul, indisputably. An old, immutable presence that brought with it appetites and insights and whispered memories and promises. Now, though, Ruthven began to doubt whether he had even called forth what resided in Blegg's form in the first place. It may be that it had come of its own accord.

He had killed Blegg with his own hands. Strangled him. His submissive, obedient thrall, aghast at the wonders Carlyle's machines and Ruthven's magical knowledge performed upon the corpses of dogs, had discovered an unwonted courage. Threatened all manner of scandal. And thus became the first human subject for Ruthven's experiments. It had seemed a triumph of sorts at the time. Perhaps that had been illusion, Ruthven dully thought.

Down to the entrance hallway he went. Still there was no further sound other than that which he made himself. The ornate mirror standing on the side table caught the light of his lamp. Shadows spun around the walls as he turned. Perhaps it was imagination, but he thought he felt the slightest drift of cold air, easing its way through from the rear of the house. He made to go that way, back towards the kitchen, but stopped. He heard a single, muted scrape, the movement of one thing against another. Brief, almost inaudible.

He went to the top of the dark stairway that led down into the cellars. It had come from down there, that whisper. The door to the store room in which all his secrets were stowed was locked. The walking corpse within should not have been able to escape it; yet they were strong, those things, and unpredictable.

Heart sinking at what he might find, Ruthven went down. The darkness fled before him, swirling away into the corners and edges. He stepped out from the stair, and found himself looking down the muzzle of the pistol Adam Quire was pointing at his chest.

Three weeks, Quire had waited, until his ankle was strong again. All of it under Cath's attentive care.

He had come to loathe the Holy Land: the stink of it, and the noise, and the secret delinquencies practised behind its every door. But he had few choices, and Cath was there. Emma Slight had grown ever less happy at her extended eviction to make room, and peace, for Quire, but the Widow made sure her frustrations went no further than bitter looks, should she and Quire happen to pass on the stair. Mary Coulter gave Quire her protection, and that did not sit well with him, but he needed it and took it. She found it amusing, he suspected, to have him there, dependent upon her goodwill.

He and Cath had barely a penny between them, for he had no wage and she, to his unbounded relief, would not work while he was sharing her rooms. They ate sparsely, and drank hardly at all, which was for neither of them an entirely easy abstinence.

Yet it was a strangely happy time. Quire found a certain contentment within him, that was invulnerable to the vicissitudes of each day. It was a still, quiet thing settled into his breast founded upon the sense that he could not choose how this fragment of his life would end, and thus simply let it carry him along and took from it what comfort it offered. He was upon an island, having come out of the stormy sea, and would shortly descend once more into the chaos of rough waters, but for now he was ashore, and not alone.

He could have brought in a decent bit of funds by selling his French pistol and sabre, but those he would not part with, for he knew he would likely have a use for them yet.

"I've not treated you well," Quire murmured, laying a soft kiss on Cath's brow one night in the bed. "You'd no need to take me in here. I've not earned it."

"No, but I'm a saint," Cath whispered.

She stroked his neck.

"You're a rare breed, then," Quire smiled.

"We all are, aren't we? There's not a one of us so alike to another to be called the same. Not when you look proper close."

"Maybe that's true."

Quire rolled, and stretched out an arm to snuff the candle by the bed. The flame vanished between his blunt fingertips, and he felt only the faintest sting of its heat as it departed. The room fell into darkness, so that he could not see her eyes or her hair any more, only feel her skin against his.

"One more thing I've got to do," he said quietly, "and then, with luck, I'm a free man."

"You're a free man now."

"Not quite. I've not settled with all those need the settling, not yet. And I'll have no peace until that's done. Not from them, not from myself. Once a thing like this is begun, you have to see it through to the finish, or someone else will, and that's when a man dies. When he lets someone else do the finishing."

"Hush," Cath whispered. "Hush."

And she dispelled the future with just that word, and made it unreal. She chose the present, for both of them, and tied him into it. She closed his lips with a kiss.

So Quire went to Melville Street, to finish it. He had come without knowing precisely what would happen, and that did not trouble him greatly. War had taught him that the world, and whatever fates governed it, did not treat lightly those who thought they knew what was to come. He went because he knew that if he did not, someone would come for him, or no one would; and that latter chance was little better than the first, for if nothing changed he would live for ever in the company of fearful expectation.

He went in through the back of the house, from the dingy lane there. He had looked down the length of Melville Street first, and seen no light in the windows of Ruthven's house. There were works on the pavements, holes dug for the setting up of gas lamps down the whole length of the street. Some of them stood there already, an abbreviated row of black iron columns, not yet ready to throw out their fierce illumination, but waiting patiently for the new age they were inheriting and fostering to call them into life. The workers had gone home, or gone to their drinking dens. A solitary watchman remained, sitting far down the road on a pile of lifted paving stones. The columns of gas lamps lay in the roadway beside him, like felled trees, roped off and watched over by this one guardian. He wore a thick coat, its collar turned up against the cold night, and had his hat pulled down hard over his head. His lantern put a yellowish tinge over him.

There was little other activity on the street. One or two couples going quietly home. A single drunken gentleman, veering this way and that in his intermittent progress down the pavement, his top hat tilted at an unpromising angle on his head, his walking cane tucked under his arm. Little activity, but still entirely too much for what Quire had in mind, so he went down the dark lane on stealthy feet, and stood listening at the door to Ruthven's kitchens.

Not a sound. The whole house, rising up above him in its skin of great sandstone blocks, was quite still and silent. Quire knocked in a pane of glass in the nearest window, doing it as gently as he could with the handle of his pistol wrapped in a scarf. It still sounded loud, the thud of the blow and the brittle shatter and spill of glass splinters, but he waited a while longer in the shadows, and no answer came from within. He reached through the broken pane, turned the latch on the window and pushed up its lower half. He pulled himself through, and down on to the stone floor of the kitchen. Glass that had fallen there cut his hand, but he paid it no heed.

The cellar, Durand had said. That was where the truth lay Perhaps, if he still lived, it was where Blegg lay. Quire went quickly, on the balls of his feet through into the main hallway. The stretch of carpet running down its centre muffled his footsteps. He passed the drawing room where he had first met Ruthven and the others. A hint of light fell from the skylight far above, just a pale blush of the moon. Quire was interested in the narrow stairs leading down into darkness, not the broad, noble flights that rose towards the stars.

The silence of the house, though welcome, was unnerving. It felt heavy, cavernous, as if the place had stood empty and unloved for years. The building had a cold indifference to it. Quire went down into its underbelly with a tightening unease in his breast.

There was only the barest thread of light there, following him down the stairway. He stood still, letting his eyes educate themselves in the gloom, and saw the curve of the ceiling, the rough brickwork of the walls. The emptiness, for there was nothing here. He went cautiously along a narrow, low passageway, looking into one bare room after another, each darker than the last, until he could see almost nothing, and tell only by the still, cold air and the sound of his own breathing that the place was abandoned. Until he came to a heavy door, locked.

Before he could test it, he heard footsteps, coming down to him out of the body of the house. Light was suddenly spilling out of the stairwell. He took a couple of quick paces closer, and levelled his pistol just in time to aim it at the breast of John Ruthven as he emerged into the basement.

Ruthven stared at him, mouth open and eyes wide with surprise.

"I've come to kill you," Quire said. "Or bring you away with me to give full confession of your crimes."

Ruthven held a long rapier of a blade in one hand, a flickering oil lamp in the other. He stared back at Quire dumbly.

"My inclination is to kill you," Quire said honestly, "but I might find a reason not to. I'll surely do it, though, if you don't put that wee knife down."

Ruthven looked down at the blade, hefted it in his hand.

"You don't think much of my cane-sword, then, Mr Quire? I

paid a hefty price for it, long ago. Never had cause to use the thing."

He dropped it, and it rang upon the hard floor.

"Is Blegg here?" Quire asked. "Anyone else?"

Ruthven shook his head.

"I don't know where Mr Blegg is. I'm rather glad to find you don't either, mind you."

"What's his real name? The name of whatever it is walking around in his skin."

"Ha. You have come a long way in your understanding, Mr Quire, but even I cannot tell you that. He is what he is, and it has no name that I know of. A force of Nature, or of Hell, or of the human soul. I don't know. He exists, that is all; perhaps he was always done so, wearing one form or another."

"Weir's amongst them."

"Very good. Yes, Major Weir's amongst them. Until they burned him out."

"Come away from the stairs," Quire said, giving the muzzle of his pistol a twitch.

Ruthven complied, but there was nothing meek in his manner. He seemed to Quire undismayed by being under the gun's shadow.

"I want to see what's behind this door back here," Quire said.

"Do you?" said Ruthven with raised, almost mocking, eyebrows. "The key's on a hook beside you."

Quire dared a glance, and sure enough a heavy iron key hung on a rusty hook in the wall within his reach, revealed now by the light of Ruthven's lamp.

"Open it for me," Quire said.

"I am thinking of leaving Edinburgh, you know," Ruthven said as he pushed the key into the lock. "Perhaps travel for a while, and put all this behind me."

He twisted the key, seeming to struggle, as if the mechanism was stubbornly resisting him.

"Would that not suffice to rid me of you, Mr Quire? I would dearly like to be rid of you."

"And I you," Quire grunted, "but no, it won't suffice. Not for what happened to Wilson Dunbar. Not for all that you've done."

"Ah, well," sighed Ruthven, and the key turned in his hand and he pushed the door open.

He stepped back, holding the lamp up high, and extended his arm to invite Quire in.

"After you," Quire said.

Ruthven did as he was told, and Quire followed him into the room. He had only a moment to take in the extraordinary display that greeted him. Shelves of stoppered jars and vases; a table laden with curving, bulbed glass vials with tubes extending from them like a beetle's legs, and with bowls and tumblers and burners; another shelf holding a row of skulls. Boxes everywhere. Two huge barrels, covered over with a sheet. On a narrow bench against the wall, three tall stacks of metal discs laid one atop the other, with burnished copper rods attached to them.

All of that was glimpsed in the barest instant, for the only thing Quire truly saw was the tall man standing naked in the corner, his skin puckered and loose, his big hands entirely covered in illegible inscriptions, a horizontal slit in his chest as if a knife had been put in there. And dead eyes, falling upon Quire as the loathsome figure turned to look at him.

"Tell it to stand still," Quire shouted.

He kept the pistol on Ruthven, though he yearned to turn it upon this naked monstrosity.

"Tell it to stand still," he shouted again.

"Be still," Ruthven said, and for the first time, Quire caught the quaver of nervousness in his voice.

The dead man took a step forward, lifting its long arms. Making fists of its hands, great cudgels of skin and bone and slack flesh.

"Be still," Ruthven said more urgently, edging closer to Quire.

The naked figure rushed suddenly forwards. Quire snapped the pistol round and fired into its chest. The shot was deafening, shaking the air of that confined space. Quire's target was so close that the pistol sprayed hot powder across the pallid skin, and he saw the black, burned hole the ball made in it. The monster staggered slightly sideways, but did not fall, and made of its imbalance a smooth, reaching movement. It seized the rim of one of those barrels with both hands and swung it up and around. It shattered one of the shelves as it came, scattering a thousand broken pieces of jar, and a multicoloured mist and rain of their contents.

Ruthven struggled to get past Quire to the doorway, trying to barge him aside. Quire fell backwards, out into the passage, Ruthven on top of him. The barrel came down and broke against the frame of the door, erupting into its constituent parts and releasing a great gush of stinking liquid and the corpse it contained.

Ruthven flailed atop Quire. The lamp went from his hand and burst against the wall of the passage, its oil taking light and burning over the bricks.

Quire cried out and threw Ruthven off him. The naked man was flinging aside the sundered staves of the barrel, dragging at the corpse that had fallen from it, all to clear a path out and into the passageway.

Ruthven rolled and ran for the stairs. Quire went after him, a stride or two behind, his useless pistol still clutched in his right hand. The dancing light of the burning oil picked out the blade of Ruthven's discarded cane-sword, lying on the ground at the foot of the stairs. Quire snatched it up, and paused, just for a moment, to look back. The creature came out into the passage-way, stepping over the outstretched leg of the corpse. As it did so, the vile slick of fluid that had vomited out of the barrel reached the patch of flame-crowned oil.

Quire threw his arm across his face as blinding light and a great fiery howl burst forth. A shooting sheet of flame raced back into the room, flooded around the naked man. Who ignored it entirely and ran at Quire.

Quire sprinted up the stairs into the hallway. He could hear Ruthven pounding up the main stairs.

"Ruthven," he shouted, but his voice was all but drowned out by a booming explosion down in the cellar that shook the floor and almost made him lose his footing. A blast of hot air and flaming embers blew out of the mouth of the stairwell, and he backed away.

The hulking form of his pursuer came reeling out into the hall, patches of thick, burning ooze adhering to its back. It crashed into the opposite wall. It was between Quire and the kitchens. He might have been able to reach the massive front door of the house, but if it was locked, or if he was slow in getting it open, he would be pinned there. He followed Ruthven, up into the heights.

To the very top of the stairs, beneath the glass ceiling of the skylight and the starry sky beyond it. Ruthven threw himself at Quire, rushing from a room off to one side, pinning his sword arm against him, scrabbling for a hold around his neck. Trying, Quire realised at once, to throw or tumble him back down the steps into the path of the creature he could hear thundering up behind him.

It was a desperate last hope on Ruthven's part, for strong as he was, he was no match to Quire's solid bulk and breadth. Quire cracked his pistol against the side of Ruthven's head, opening up a messy gash across his temple. He raked a heel down the man's shin and as he wailed, Quire shrugged, lifted and turned him about. He hit him again in the head, and Ruthven's hands came loose. Quire threw him off, and back into the arms of the naked brute that came rushing up to catch him.

Quire backed up, sword at the ready, thinking for a moment that he would now face the two of them, and no doubt die. But the dead man was not saving Ruthven. It seized him by his upper arms, and held him up high as it advanced, and shook him. Terribly, like a furious child punishing a rag doll. Ruthven's head flailed about. He screamed. He was swung against the wall, once, twice.

The naked monster, its back still afire here and there, the stink of its skin and flesh burning filling the air, looked at Quire and advanced on him. It still held Ruthven with one hand, holding him up as easily as if he were weightless. Ruthven hung limp and unmoving in that grip, his feet dragging over the floorboards. But his eyes were open, and alive, and Quire saw the horror and terror in them.

Quire edged himself backwards along the landing. He had never in his life used a rapier, such as that he now held, but he had seen others wave them around in practice or show. Never in anger. The thing came quickly at him, hauling Ruthven along, reaching out for Quire with its free hand. He lunged forward and planted the tip of the sword into the breast, right beside the hole the pistol had already put there. Something in the way he did it was clumsy, for his weight did not pass through the blade as he had hoped; but it hardly mattered, for the movement and mass of the body into which it sank did the work for him.

The dead man shuddered, and swayed, and stumbled to one side. Quire whipped the sword back out of its flesh. He might have hit the heart, he thought; he was not sure. Ruthven was whimpering, or moaning; blood bubbled at his lips.

Quire heard the wooden railings along the landing groan as the huge figure fell against them. Its torso bent back for a moment, over the balustrade. Quire darted in again and stabbed the long blade upwards, into the exposed chin. It went up through the jaw and mouth and lodged somewhere in the bone of the skull. The creature spasmed, and it arched over the handrail into the deep space of the stairwell. The handrail cracked and split, the balusters splayed apart, and the creature fell backwards, pulling the sword from Quire's hand and taking it down, jutting from its chin. Quire had one last glimpse of Ruthven's rolling, anguished eyes, and then the man was snatched away and went plunging after his creation, his arm still locked in its iron grip.

By the time Quire reached the foot of the stairs, flames were already licking around the bodies. The hall carpet was alight, and the wallpaper on the walls nearest the cellar stairs was burning, coming away in black cindery sheets that swirled about and rose to be consumed in the roiling fire spreading itself across the ceiling.

The heat was too ferocious for Quire to get near the two twisted corpses, but he was not minded to do so anyway. Neither looked likely to rise again.

He ran to the front door and hauled it open, and rushed out into Melville Street, and away into the quiet Edinburgh night.

XXX

Nobody Sees William Hare

Mathieu Durand looked to Quire to be on the very brink of death. Both the Frenchman himself and Agnes McLaine insisted otherwise. Durand's version was that he was indeed fatally ill, but that his final decline was further off than he had expected; Agnes' was that Durand was a morose, fatalistic fool whose mortal dread of Blegg was doing as much to drag him down as any magics that might have been laid upon him, and if he could but shake himself free of it, he might well recover. Despite their differences, they seemed to Quire to have developed a certain rough affection – or respect, at least – for one another during their enforced cohabitation.

For all Quire knew, Durand deserved to die; perhaps that he had broken with Ruthven and Blegg did not excuse his earlier part in their transgressions. Quire chose not to judge that.

"What man would not prefer to die with the soil of his homeland under his feet?" Durand said as the three of them worked their slow way along the Leith seafront.

Quire had his hand under Durand's arm to give him some support, and Agnes had found him a dusty, battered old walking stick from somewhere that he leaned heavily on. He was much reduced, even from the comparatively delicate figure he had cut when Quire first saw him, what felt an age ago in the drawing room of Ruthven's house.

"Do you know," Quire said, "the first time I met you, I guessed you might be quiet because you could not speak more than a word or two of English. Couldn't have been much more wrong about that, could I?"

There was a broad expanse of dark, muddy sand laid out before them. The tide had retreated so far that the little breakers were mere flecks of white. Almost in those waves, at the very border between land and sea, a horse went pounding along the beach in full gallop. Its rider was crouched over its neck, tiny. The great horse stretched its long legs, and its mane and tail streamed out on the wind. The sand made fountains at its heels.

Quire and Durand and Agnes all stopped to watch it. For Quire at least there was something uplifting in the sight of that powerful creature running through the edge of the ocean, making for the horizon, putting its every effort into the simple act of the gallop.

The truth of it was rather more mundane, and mercenary, he knew. Every summer, a goodly portion of Edinburgh's entire population could be found down here, on the Leith sands and all along the seafront at the back of them, for the day of the races. Whole squadrons of horses swept up and down the sands on that day, and whole fortunes swept back and forth through the hands of the bookmakers and the touts and the thieves. Some of the horse trainers liked to run their charges on the beach all year round, for the sake of familiarity and the endless flat softness of the place.

"Perhaps that is my boat, is it?" Durand said quietly.

Quire looked beyond the horse, and the beach, out across the restless sea lying between them and the shores of Fife. A steamer was there, looking frail and delicate at this distance, laying behind it a long trail of smoke that paled and frayed as it fell behind the vessel's stacks, dissipating on the wind.

"It could be," Quire said.

"Driving a boat with fire," Agnes McLaine mused. "It's an age of miracles we live in, right enough."

It was Durand's intent, within the hour, to take ship down the east coast, to England, and thence across the Channel back to France. To die there, as he would have it, and be buried. Quire could understand that. Even an exile might want, at the end, to go back into the earth of the land that birthed him. Better than dying, and staying, on foreign fields, as so many of the men he had known had done.

If Durand died at all, of course. Quire did not know whether the Frenchman or Agnes was right in judging his fate. Agnes thought the cruel spirit that had animated Blegg's form was likely gone, unhomed and thinned, and thus unable to exert any malign influence upon the Frenchman; Durand could not bring himself to believe that, as far as Quire could tell.

"It was Hare you said was the name of the man bringing bodies to Blegg, wasn't it?" Quire asked Durand absently.

The Frenchman nodded, and shrugged his cloak more tightly about him. It was a bright day, but the wind coming in off the Forth had sharpness to it.

"Same one they've used to try this man Burke?"

"I do not know," Durand said. "But how many men of one name would you have in your city who sell the dead?"

Quire grunted. Burke's trial was a grisly sensation. Its substance had overspilled the bounds of the court, too awful and ghoulish to be contained. It filled every newssheet, and was the talk of every tavern and coffee shop; it had roused the folk of the Old Town to a state of fevered outrage and fury unlike anything seen in years. Not a little of their anger was directed upwards, towards Edinburgh's lofty masters, for the outcome of the prosecution was not what the instincts of the mob demanded.

Sixteen murders, by most reckoning. Sixteen innocent men and women cruelly slain, all smothered and consigned to the dissecting table of Dr Robert Knox. And from out of all that horror, there was but one man set to answer for it. William Burke would hang. Knox was spared any legal assault at all, and Hare – Hare it was who sent Burke to the hangman, for he had turned King's evidence. The lawyers had bought his testimony with the promise of freedom. And that, the people of Edinburgh had clearly concluded, was obscene travesty.

"He's to go free, they say," Agnes said. "Hare."

"He is." Quire nodded. "He's under the King's protection now, still locked up, but he'll be turned loose soon enough. And then he'll be back to Ireland, I should say, since he'd be torn to pieces if he's recognised around here. And anything he knows about Blegg or Ruthven'll go across the sea with him. The papers have said nothing about that. Only the business him and Burke did with Knox. There's no mention of any corpses going Ruthven's way."

"You should leave it be," Agnes said quickly.

"I don't know if I can," Quire said, watching the steamboat plough its way through the waves, closing on the harbour.

"They decided it was a gas explosion," Quire told Wilson Dunbar. "I read it in the *Evening Courant*, a few days after. Tragic loss of one of Melville Street's finest houses, and the three poor dead souls found inside. Burned beyond recognition. The gas works was having none of it, of course, but what else would they say?"

"Christ." Dunbar puffed out his cheeks. "You're a lucky

bastard, I'll give you that. It was me they called Impervious, but the name's not fitting me any more, so I'm thinking you'd best have it."

Dunbar indeed seemed anything but impervious now. He had been reduced, for a time at least, by his suffering. He was thinner than Quire had ever known him, and his shoulders stooped a little. He walked with the aid of a stick.

He would surely have died, there in the hospital, but for the water the nurses and his wife had trickled into his mouth, and the food paste they fed him as if tending to a babe. Perhaps he would have died but for the ministrations of Agnes McLaine. Quire did not know. All he knew was that Dunbar lived, and grew stronger every day, and for that he was intensely, unquestioningly grateful.

They walked on the flat ground by the palace, where children flew kites in the shadow of Arthur's Seat. Flat ground was the kind Dunbar liked best, for the moment, since he tired quickly. There was low cloud down, hiding the top of the hill in mists, and a fine drizzle on the air.

"Is it done, then?" Dunbar asked. "The whole business, I mean. You've burned the man's house down, and he's cooked to a cinder. Not much more to concern yourself with, at a guess."

Quire regarded his feet as they trudged along through the damp grass. He had shared nothing more than the barest outline of all that had happened, for he knew that was all Dunbar really wanted. He remembered nothing of the night in the Princes Street gardens beyond rushing away from Quire and Durand, and hearing Blegg coming up behind him. Quire had seen in his eyes, when he talked of it, the haunted look, quickly dismissed but there, quite plain. He would do nothing to add to the man's burdens.

"It's done," he said, as lightly as he could. "Let's leave it to rest, should we?"

"Aye, if you like."

Quire was walking slowly, to match his pace to Dunbar's. The subtle rain was soaking into his coat and his hair.

"I know you're liking your fresh air these days," he said, "but maybe we'd best be getting back. It's a bit dreich out here."

Dunbar grunted and looked up at the cloud-cloaked heights of Arthur's Seat, as if noticing for the first time the inclemency of the day.

"If you like. Ellen'll have porridge she wants to get down my neck, anyway. She's of the belief that there's no better fodder for the healing body. Spoons it down me every hour of the day or night."

"Can she speak of me yet without cursing?" Quire asked.

"Let's just say she'd as soon not be seeing you."

"Can't fault her for that. If I was her, I'd probably come after me with a kitchen knife."

"Aye, well, the thought maybe crossed her mind, but I dissuaded her, so that's one more thing you owe me."

"Fair enough."

They walked in silence for a little way, then Dunbar gave a chuckle as if at some funny thought.

"How's your own woman?" he asked Quire.

"Cath? She's fine. There's a discussion to be had whether she's to come out of the Holy Land and take up lodgings with me, but for now, it's fine."

Quire had removed himself from the Holy Land, with a whole medley of conflicting feelings about doing so, and taken up residence once again in his own quarters. He did not feel entirely safe or restful there, and might never again, but nor was the Holy Land a place he would ever be inclined to call home. Cath would follow after him, he thought, if he asked; he had not done so, but was thinking it might be the wisest thing to do. Perhaps the wisest thing he had ever done.

"And work? What about that?"

"Oh, I've not thought of it. Had other things on my mind of late."

"You're well out of the police business, maybe," grunted Dunbar. "This affair with Knox and the Irish boys is a bloody thing, isn't it?"

Quire could not quite agree with the first part of that, but the second gave him no great difficulty.

"A bloody thing for sure," he said as they came to the foot of the Canongate.

The factories were in full clamorous flow, sending out their plumes of smoke to melt into the low roof of cloud. The drizzle was damping things down a bit – the stinks and the smoke and the folk all alike – but still the place was awash with carts and barrows and men hurrying this way and that.

"If you ever doubted me when I've said blame don't follow as close in the footsteps of guilt as it should, you'll know better now," Dunbar opined. "Look at Knox, buying the bodies and not a charge against him. And Hare. They saw he was the worse of the two of them, and he's to be free, just because he told them what they needed to send his friend to the gallows."

Quire smiled to hear the bubbles of anger pushing up into Dunbar's voice. It was a very fine thing, to hear the man getting back into his vituperative, argumentative flow.

"There's a fair few folk baying for Knox's blood," Quire said. "He may not come out of this so pretty. But Hare – aye, that's not right."

Dunbar shook his head, despairing at the iniquities of the world and those who held its reins. An ease came over him, as if he were comforted by the reliable, familiar availability of targets for his critical appraisal. It told him, Quire hoped, that nothing of consequence had changed; that he would be hale and healthy and strong again soon, and back flying kites with his sons, forgetting what had happened.

"It's barbarous times we're living in, wouldn't you say?" Dunbar said quietly. Not melancholy; just reflective.

"I would. Aye, I would."

Calton Hill, which rose at the east end of Princes Street and looked out over the whole of Old and New Towns alike, held three prisons. The Debtors' Jail, the Bridewell where the indigents and prostitutes and petty troublemakers found themselves, and the new Calton Jail, little more than ten years open, where the hard men went: the killers and the wounders, the blackmailers and the inveterate thieves. The jails stood side by side on the hill's southern flank, lined up along the top of low cliffs and staring grimly out like a threefold threat and reminder for the city's inhabitants of the consequences of transgression.

The Calton Jail presented by far the grandest and most fearsome countenance of the three. It was vast, like an amalgamation of castle and stately manor. Magnificent on the outside, in its austere way, as befitted such a prominent player in the architectural pageant of Edinburgh's heart. On the inside, vile, malodorous and dangerous. Quire had been within its walls on several occasions, and every time had emerged from it eager for the cleansing airs and lights of an open sky. It was not an experience he was eager to repeat, but he went there in any case.

Nowhere was the jail more like a fortress than in its approaches. Its gatehouse stood on Regent Road, a wide boulevard that curved around Calton Hill's southern slopes. It was a prodigious structure, with two towers flanking the huge gates. Walls thrice the height of a man stretched away on either side, enclosing the prison yard and the enormous building that stood at the heart of it.

Once, Quire might have talked his way through the watch at

the gatehouse without any difficulty, for a sergeant of police could come and go as he pleased; but he was no longer such a thing, and he found himself instead taken into one the offices built into the gatehouse, to face David Maclellan, a captain of the prison guard he knew of old. Not well, but at least he did know him.

"Of course I can't let you in," Maclellan said, pained at both the suggestion and the need for him to explain its impossibility.

"I thought maybe, since you've known me long enough, I might just get an hour. No more than that."

Maclellan set his elbow on the desk, and rested his chin upon the upturned palm of his hand, staring meaningfully at Quire.

"You're not making much sense, Adam. I ken you fine, but I ken you're no policeman too, not any more. You're just a man, and that's not the kind of folk who get in to see William Hare."

Quire gazed out of the office's barred window in disappointment. It faced on to the main prison, and he could very faintly hear hand bells being rung in there. Feeding time. He had been there, once, when the inmates got their food, and it had been the worst slop he had ever seen, in or out of the army. Hardly fit for pigs.

"There's been some got in to see him before," Quire complained. "Reporters and the like; so they claim in the newssheets, anyway. I thought I'd have a chance at getting a word with him."

"There's no man here had more visitors than he did before the trial," Maclellan grunted. "Lawyers and priests and all sorts. Aye, and maybe a reporter or two. But nobody sees William Hare now. Not unless they're police, or have their permission and escort. That Jack Rutherford was the last, bringing the Ruthven woman. You must know him well enough. Ask him to bring you along, and maybe we'll see about getting you in."

Quire did not say anything. He remained quite still, staring out through the thick, speckled glass at the jail.

"It's the best I can do, Adam, you must understand. This Hare ... Jesus, he's not just another prisoner. The city's on the boil over the whole business. Everyone's calling for his head. And he's stopped talking, in any case. Hardly saying a word to anyone."

"Isabel Ruthven, was it?" Quire asked, still not looking at the guard captain.

"Aye, might have been. I don't particularly remember the name."

"What was her business with Hare, do you know?"

Maclellan sat back in his chair and crossed his arms over his chest.

"I've no idea, Quire. Maybe a relative of one of the victims or something. I've no idea."

"Would you do something for me?" Quire leaned across the desk, and put every ounce of sincerity and gravity he possessed into his appeal. "Would you just get a message to me if either of those two come back to see Hare? Rutherford or Isabel Ruthven. Either of them, or both. Send a message to my house – I'll tell you where to find it – to let me know they've been."

"And why would I do such a thing?"

Maclellan sounded more puzzled than affronted by the suggestion.

"Just because it might be very important to me," said Quire, his mind working quickly, trying to tease sense out of the tangle of his thoughts. "It might be nothing, but it might not."

He could see the hesitation in Maclellan's face. So he gambled.

"And because I'll put ten pounds your way if they come and I know of it within the hour."

XXXI

Burke's Last Day

A bloodlust had hold of Edinburgh such as it had not felt in centuries. Perhaps ever. It was in ferment, so bloated with outrage and accusation that it trembled upon the brink of riot. There was but one thing that might stay the mob's fury, for a while at least, and that very thing was about to be delivered unto them.

It had rained prodigiously in the early hours of the morning, cataracts spilling from the countless jostling rooftops of the Old Town. The rainwater had run in a myriad little rivers down the length of the High Street, gushing down the closes, sending even the rats scurrying for shelter and making the scavengers retreat with their barrows to the watch-houses to wait out the storm.

The rain did pass, but it left every eave dripping, every crease and crevice in the cobbled streets a pool. None of which did anything to deter the assembly of the greatest crowd the city had ever seen. They filled the Lawn Market, that highest part of the High Street, at which it approached the last narrow run up to the castle. Thousands upon thousands of them, standing shoulder to shoulder, all waiting; and all manoeuvring, as best they could in such a close-pressed throng, for a better sight of the gallows.

The most fortunate ones were those leaning from every window in every high tenement around the place of execution. They hung dangerously far out over the ledges, jeering at those confined to the street below. Some, unable to force a place at a window, or dissatisfied with the view thence, had taken leave of their senses and climbed up on to the very rooftops themselves. They perched there upon the ridges, or clung to the chimney stacks, slipping and slithering on the wet tiles, promising at any moment to go sliding down and pitch themselves into the heaving, swaying mass of their fellow townsfolk on the street below. Such was the hunger to see William Burke die.

Only St Giles' Cathedral, brooding in all its sombre stateliness just a short way from the gallows, was spared the indignity of having onlookers scattered about amongst its spires and buttresses. It would, in truth, have offered some of the very finest views, but there were none willing to trespass upon its holy territory.

For all the fervent anticipation attendant upon his death, when they brought Burke out from the lock-up in Libberton's Wynd where he had spent his last night it was not only his name the crowd roared, nor only his blood it bayed for.

"Where's Knox?" some cried, and others: "Bring us Hare!"

The guards surrounding the gallows struggled to hold back the enlivened crowd. Such was the tumult that arose as he emerged on to the street that Burke quailed at it, and hesitated, and then seemed overcome with a longing for all of this to be over, and went quickly to the foot of the steps. Some in the mob tried to reach him as he passed them, but the guards pushed them back.

Burke went up the steps on to the platform so hurriedly that he almost stumbled. Abuse teemed around him, coming from every quarter, raining down upon him like a storm of stones.

There was no ceremony to it, little by way of preamble. Burke stood there, staring fixedly ahead, as the executioner prepared him for the moment to come, adjusting his collar, turning his necker-chief, so that the rope would fit about his neck clean and snug.

And the noose was settled over his head. For a breath or two a hush descended, broken only by the distant screech of seagulls circling far overhead. The executioner pulled the lever, the trap-door sprang and Burke dropped down and passed beyond any mortal concerns. His feet gave two sharp, vigorous twitches, and he was gone.

The twenty thousand or more who had come to see it done erupted in fierce joy, so violent their cries that the windows shook and the walls rang and rang with the echoes of them. And many of them did not depart, unwilling to concede that the momentous event was over, merely because its principal player was dead. They waited, and milled about in the High Street. For so long as Burke hung there, they waited.

It was not for another hour that they finally took his body down, and nailed it into a coffin and carried it off. Then began the scramble for pieces of the gallows, and sections of the hang-man's rope. As the workers who had built it moved in to dismantle the lethal contraption, so a host of the most stubborn spectators closed about them, and fought and argued over who might salvage what little scrap by way of memento for this extraordinary day.

Adam Quire and Catherine Heron did not watch William Burke's execution. They climbed up, instead, to the crest of Salisbury Crags, and walked along the top of those long, curving cliffs, looking over the city laid out beneath them.

They walked hand in hand much of the way, and had the hill to themselves. The grass was wet and slippery, the air still damp from the downpour that had come before dawn; half the population of the Old Town was gathered about a single gallows. It all made for a near-deserted hill, and an eerie calm to the place.

They heard, though, when the time came, the great tumult rising from the Old Town, muted a little by distance, but unmistakable. The crying out of thousands of voices, all at once. The collective yearning of a city. They could tell, from the sound, the moment when Burke died.

They were at the highest point of the Crags by then, and stood in silence, holding one another's hand, while the single voice of the city rolled around them.

William Burke might be dead, but he was not yet done as the centre of the city's attention. The sentence passed upon him did not end with his execution.

The day after the hanging, the coffin into which his corpse had been nailed was taken to the University of Edinburgh's huge college, close by the Royal Infirmary and Surgeon's Square. It was the largest building in the city by some way, unless the whole complicated castle was accounted a single structure. It contained within it a broad quadrangle, surrounded by balustraded terraces. The four sides of the huge rectangular edifice that enclosed that quadrangle held, amongst many other riches, the university's Medical School.

It was to there that Burke's body was conveyed; specifically, to the largest of its lecture theatres. In that great bowl of an arena, the lid of the coffin was prised up and Burke's corpse removed. His clothes were taken from him and he was laid out upon the slab at the heart of the amphitheatre. Shortly after noon, Professor Alexander Monro, the incumbent of the university's Chair of Anatomy, applied a saw to the late William Burke's cranium, cutting in a neat ring around the whole circumference of the head.

With a little difficulty, he then removed the entire top of his skull, and in a great gush of thick and foul blood exposed his brain to the huge crowd of students and other curious spectators assembled in the theatre.

It took close to two hours for Monro to complete his dissection of William Burke, for the edification of those who had succeeded in obtaining a ticket for the much-anticipated event. Those who had been unsuccessful rioted in the quadrangle of the college, so aggrieved were they at their exclusion from the drama. They broke windows and tore up paving stones, and fought off the gang of baton-wielding police that was dispatched from Old Stamp Office Close.

The disorder did not end until Professor Christison brokered an agreement with the ringleaders of the mob whereby Burke's corpse, returned to something approaching its natural state, would be put on public display for two days.

So the people of Edinburgh, in their thousands, filed past the corpse of the wretch whose vile deeds had fouled their city and comforted themselves with the knowledge that, upon this one man at least, the most perfect justice had been done.

And with the execution of that justice, the need to hold William Hare a prisoner in Calton Jail came to an end.

XXXII

Two Sergeants

In the dull twilight, a small carriage turned in to the entrance of Calton Jail, and rumbled under the arch of the gatehouse. Lamps burned on either side of the driver's seat. It drew up on the yard, in the shadow of the great prison, where a small group of men awaited it. The governor, Captain Maclellan of the guards, a handful of his officers. And William Hare, in a heavy, high-collared coat that hid much of his face.

The police sergeant who drove the cart dropped down on to the yard's cobblestones. Maclellan came forward to meet him.

"Jack Rutherford," Maclellan said. "It's a miserable duty you've got yourself tonight. Someone at the police house got a grudge against you?"

"Volunteered," Sergeant Rutherford said, and when he saw Maclellan's surprise, he shrugged. "Somebody's got to do it. The man's under the Crown's protection, after all. Got to see him safe out of the city. Let them lynch him somewhere else if they like, just so long as it's outside the city bounds."

Maclellan shook his head in amazement.

"Still. A devil like him, it's a damn shame."

"I don't mind. Nobody else wanted to do it, and like I say, it needs doing."

The governor murmured a few words to Hare, but the Irishman – no longer a prisoner, no longer under any obligation to feign civility or gratitude – paid him no heed, and climbed into the carriage with a sour grin upon his face.

It was done with no more ceremony than that. The worst killer any of the men present had ever encountered – none of them were in any doubt of that – walked free of Calton Jail. Rutherford jumped back up on to the driver's seat, clicked his tongue at the horse, and gave it a touch of the switch to bring it around, and the carriage rolled slowly out through the gatehouse and into Regent Road.

The men drifted off, back to their duties, none happy with the one they had just discharged. Maclellan lingered, though, a moment or two longer than the rest, staring after the disappeared carriage. He came to a decision, and called one of his men back to his side.

"Get me one of the lads can run a message down to the Canongate, would you?" Maclellan said. "Quick as you like."

The carriage made its way slowly down towards Princes Street. It did not travel far, though, for outside the grand theatre on the corner of North Bridge it came to a halt, close in to the pavement so that it should not obstruct the other coaches and hackneys moving along behind it.

Isabel Ruthven walked smartly forward from where she had been waiting beside a street lamp. She reached up and pressed a banknote into Rutherford's hand. He said nothing, but tucked it quickly away into a pocket. Isabel climbed into the carriage and settled in beside Hare. Who leered at her, baring his teeth.

"Wasn't expecting to see you tonight," he said, "but I'll be damned if you're not a sweet sight for a man's been in a jail cell longer than he needed."

"A charming compliment, Mr Hare." Isabel smiled.

The carriage lurched into motion once more. As it eased away from the kerb, the doors of the theatre opened, and the departing audience began to flow out on to the pavement, all abuzz at the splendour of the opera they had witnessed.

"Mr Blegg wanted me to convey his appreciation for your silence on the matter of his dealings with you," Isabel said, looking out at those gorgeous, glittering opera-goers crowding out.

Hare grunted.

"Never much of a worry. The lawyers gave me immunity for everything I done with Burke. Nothing else. They'd have hung me alongside him if the other stuff came out."

He looked sharply at Isabel.

"Still, you said I'd be paid for it, the time you came to see me. Twenty pounds, you said."

"Indeed. We'll get you your money this very night, shall we? But here, I brought you something to toast your freedom with."

She produced a hip flask, bound in worked leather, and offered it to him. Hare sniffed it, and grinned at the smell.

"Whisky," Isabel confirmed. "A very fine variety, I'm told, though I'm no drinker of it myself."

Hare took a long drink from the flask, tipping his head back. The carriage jolted over cobbles, and he spilled a little of the amber fluid across his lips. It ran over his chin as he reached out a hand and laid it on Isabel's knee.

"I could do with some other kind of celebrating," he rasped at her.

She guided his hand away, not roughly, but firmly.

"No, Mr Hare. Not tonight. Not if you want that twenty pounds."

The carriage rolled on, up to the High Street, and there it turned west. Hare leaned across in front of Isabel to peer out into the street.

"I'm supposed to go to the southern mail. Get out of this damned city."

He was slurring his words. They came sluggishly off his clumsy tongue.

"Don't you worry," Isabel said, pushing him back into his seat.

By the time the carriage was rattling down West Bow, and slowing to a halt at the foot of it, Hare was quite asleep. Rutherford dismounted and looked in.

"You'll have to help me with him," Isabel said casually. "Just to get him inside, then you can wait with the carriage. Hold on to this for me, would you?" She handed him the whisky flask that she had lifted from Hare's limp hand. "Don't drink from it, though. We'll be needing you awake."

The two of them worked Hare out of the carriage, and held him up between them, each getting themselves under one of his arms. It was not the kind of scene entirely unfamiliar to the inhabitants of West Bow or Grassmarket, and not many folk paid them much heed.

"Give me one of those lights," Isabel said.

Rutherford unhooked one of the oil lamps hanging from the end of the driver's seat and handed it her.

"In here," Isabel told him.

They went through a low, dark passageway into the foul-smelling, rubbish-strewn courtyard beyond. Isabel showed the way with the light of the lamp, and the two of them bore Hare into Major Weir's house.

The dreadful oppression of the place made Rutherford ever more agitated as they moved through its ruins. He started at every flicker of flame light across the crumbling, slumping walls.

"All right," Isabel said. "This will do."

Rutherford let Hare fall.

"You can go back to the carriage," Isabel told him.

"Thank you," Rutherford breathed with heartfelt relief, and made to retrace their steps through the grime and debris.

"Wait a moment."

The voice came from the impenetrable darkness of the back room. It was an ugly sound, uneven and rattling. Thick.

"Just listen," the voice came again. "We'll send Hare out to you shortly. When he comes, you take him on where he needs to go. We'll not be joining you."

"Aye, all right," Rutherford said. "You're paying, so whatever you say."

He went quickly away. Isabel looked into the darkness.

"I don't understand," she said. "Are we not to leave together?"

"I'll explain, but let's get done what needs doing first. It's not easy for me to talk. I need Hare."

Isabel set the lamp down on a rotting length of timber, and went to the corner. She lifted a rag and began to bring out the items it had concealed. As she worked, Blegg crawled yard by effortful yard out into the lamp's light.

His skin was crusted and blackened, burned back to the bone where it had been thinnest, over his scalp. His eyelids were gone, and the great white orbs of his eyeballs shone in the light. Much of his lips was gone too, scorched away. Across the whole upper half of his torso, scraps of charred clothing were merged into what remained of his flesh. Both hands were hooked into stiff, raw claws, the fingers bent inwards and flayed by heat.

Isabel laid a pair of gloves side by side on the floor. Next a shallow wooden bowl, into which she poured black ink from a small bottle. Last a stylus made of reed.

"I can lie across him," Blegg said, "but my hands aren't up to the rest of it. Just close up his mouth and nose. That's all."

Blegg hauled himself across Hare's chest and lay there, a dead weight. Isabel knelt down and did as she had been told, pressing one hand over Hare's mouth, pinching shut his nose with the other.

"He won't wake," Blegg hissed.

And he was right. William Hare died in his sleep. Suffocated.

Afterwards Blegg had Isabel wedge the stylus into his crippled hand, for he could not pick it up himself. He dipped it into the ink she had stolen from her husband's stores, and began to write over the back of Hare's hands.

"One thing I learned from Ruthven and that French bastard," he grunted. "This does help with keeping a hold on the body."

After that, he said nothing more that Isabel could understand for quite a time. He coughed out streams of Latin phrases from his ravaged form as he worked, his voice faltering and dwindling all the time. His body shook, collapsing beneath the strain of its exertions. Isabel sat close by the lamp, her hands folded in her lap, waiting quietly. It did not take all that long for Blegg to sink down, slumping incrementally on to Hare's corpse, and for his rasping voice to fade away to nothing. He lay there, perfectly still. Perfectly empty.

It remained thus for a time. The woman sitting silently, staring at the two corpses lying amongst the detritus of decades. The lamp's glow fluttering around the walls. A steady, slow drip, somewhere out in the shadows, of rainwater that had leached its way down through the seams of the vast building above and fell now into this ruinous hollow at its base.

And at last, Hare shuddered. Isabel rose, her hands clasped, watching with gleaming eyes. Hare stirred, and shook, and rolled his head. He heaved, and pushed Blegg's ghastly charred corpse off him and away. He did not even look at it as he rose to his feet, and stood there swaying and blinking.

"Is it you?" Isabel asked, hope and fear and anticipation all layered in the words.

Hare looked at her.

"Always me," he said with a wolfish grin. "Always me."

He held up his hands and splayed them, examining the inscriptions straggling across the back of them.

"It will have to do," he said. "Needed more time, more tools to really make it hold and work, but this will do, for a while. Give me those gloves."

Isabel brought them to him and he pulled them over his hands.

"I hardly dared to believe," she said, almost breathless with excitement.

"You should have," Hare scolded her lightly. "I told you I was not done yet. You should have believed me. Just needed the right place to do it – a place that remembered me well – and the right kind of man to host me, the right blackness of heart to open up the way as he departed. I knew Hare would be what we needed. I like to think I played my small part in making him what he was, so it seems only fair I should be repaid with the use of him."

She embraced him, and he held her for a moment or two before easing her away.

"What now?" she asked. "You won't leave me here, surely, whatever you said to Rutherford? I came to find you, didn't I? Out at the farm. You couldn't ask more of me than that."

Hare ignored her.

"Is there any sign?" he asked, turning his face this way and that to show her his cheeks. "Any bruising, or scarring?"

"No, no." She shook her head. "But listen, what comes now?"

"Turn that lamp down. No point taking even the smallest risk of discovery, now that the hard part's done."

She groaned in frustration, but bent down to quench the flame and return Weir's house to its natural state of gloom. She straightened, and turned, and found Hare right in front of her, very close. He put his gloved hands about her throat, and pushed her roughly back against the wall.

"All good things come to an end, Isabel," he whispered as his fingers tightened. "This city's done for me now. I've known that for a long time now, even if your husband could never see it. So I'm away, I don't know where. But I do know I'll be going alone, and I'll not be leaving behind anyone who knows what face I'm wearing."

He held her there for long minutes, squeezing ever more tightly, until she breathed no more, and hung limp in his grip.

Hare strode out on to the West Bow with a confident gait, tugging the black gloves tight on his hands. Rutherford, taken somewhat unawares by his abrupt reappearance, hurriedly tapped out the pipe he had been smoking on the heel of his boot. He frowned at Hare.

"Did they not give you the lamp to bring back?" he asked irritably. "It's police property, this carriage. I'll have to answer if it doesn't go back just as it came out."

"You got paid, didn't you?" Hare snapped.

"Indeed I did, Mr Hare. Just like you did, I'd imagine, so have a care with that tongue of yours."

"Don't call me Hare. That's a dangerous name these days."

"Oh, aye? What would you have me call you?"

"It doesn't much matter to me. Why not Mr Black? That's simple enough for you to remember, I should think."

Rutherford curled his lip in loathing. He might have pursued the discussion, and pushed on into argument perhaps, but Hare brushed past him and clambered into the carriage, sinking back into its concealing shadows.

"The southern mail coach, isn't it?" he said from inside there. "We'll need to make good time now, if we're not to miss it."

Rutherford vaulted up to his station at the front of the carriage, muttering invective under his breath. He fell silent, though, as they moved off and the horse broke into a trot under the encouragement of the whip. A puzzled frown etched itself upon his face. Hare, he was thinking, no longer seemed to talk with quite the same strong Irish accent he had before.

They caught the mail coach by only a matter of minutes. There was but a single space remaining, on the high seat on the back of it, when they found it waiting by the roadside in Newington, south of the Old Town.

Hare climbed up there nimbly enough and settled himself in. He had the collar of his coat pulled high, and his soft cap tugged down over his brow, as if a man dreadfully troubled by the cold. Rutherford looked up at him. It seemed fitting, and prudent, to say something innocent of the sort that might pass between two men parting.

"Goodbye, Mr Black," he said. "I wish you well home."

Hare glanced down at him, and Rutherford caught the momentary contemptuous sneer, if no one else did. He stalked back to the carriage, reflecting bitterly upon the ingratitude of murderers.

Rutherford lived with his wife and daughter in a flat at the back of a court along Nicolson Street. It was a good place to live. Edinburgh had not expanded southwards with the same grand visionary rigour that had been applied to the northward growth of the New Town. Its advance here had been, instead, incremental, one new building or development outside the city wall following another as inclination and opportunity arose. Nor had it matched the stately grandeur of the New Town's long terraces and garden squares, but there were corners of elegance and a general mood of prosperity. For a police sergeant, spending his days scouring the streets and closes of the Old Town, it was a pleasing release to return there each night.

Rutherford walked down Nicolson Street with a weary tread. It had been about as long a day as he had suffered in months. By the time he had left Hare on the mail coach, and got the carriage back to the police stables, and endured the inevitable barrage of questions from his fellow officers in the police house, it was closing on midnight. He would have left without answering a single one of those eager enquiries if he thought he could manage it without causing indignant offence and disappointment, but instead he dutifully recited the tale of how William Hare had left Edinburgh. He made no mention of Isabel Ruthven, or of the delay in the West Bow.

He wondered absently about those things as he trudged homeward through the emptying streets, though. He did not know, nor want to know, what grubby transaction had been enacted while he waited and smoked his pipe with the carriage. With luck, his connection with the Ruthven family was entirely at an end now, and he would never have to spare another moment's fretting over it all. The money had been good, of course – there was never enough of that, no matter how a man scrimped and saved – but it was not, Rutherford had come to feel, worth the worries that attended upon it.

He nodded to one or two people he knew as he drew near to his home. Were he less tired, he would have stopped to talk with them. It paid a man to keep in good standing with his neighbours. But his exhaustion was heavy upon him, and he walked on and turned empty-handed into the court where his family and, more importantly he felt, his bed awaited.

"Jack Rutherford."

Rutherford turned, startled. Adam Quire stepped out from the darkness beneath the arch of a stairwell's entrance. Rutherford hung his head and gave a nervous laugh.

"You gave me a turn there, Adam," he said, knowing by his gut and by some indefinable quality in the way Quire held himself that here was a problem, and perhaps a grave one.

His weariness fell from him in an instant, dispelled by the shiver of alarm that went up his spine.

"Are you keeping well, Adam?" he asked, with a broad smile.

"That's a good question," Quire said. "You know, it took me a while to find out where you lived. I didn't remember us ever talking of it, when we shared the same employment, so I suppose we can never have been great friends."

"Friends?" Rutherford repeated, feigning bewilderment at the course of the conversation, and taking a step closer to his own stair, at the far end of the court. "I'd like to think so, aye."

"How much did Ruthven pay you to break that bond?"

Rutherford frowned, shrugged.

"I'm not understanding you, Adam."

The smallest tightening around Quire's eyes told him that his acting skills had failed him. Quire had always been good at reading men. Good at breaking them, too. Rutherford began to grow seriously afraid then.

"That your stair over there, is it?" Quire asked, tipping his chin up to indicate the dark opening in the furthest tenement.

"Aye," Rutherford said, looking that way, "that's . . ."

Quire's hand was over his mouth, his arm about his chest, dragging him violently backwards. Rutherford kicked and scrabbled to get his feet back under him, but Quire was the bigger and stronger of them by some distance. He hauled Rutherford into the nearest stair, and threw him down on to the first few steps. Rutherford turned on to his back, but did not rise.

Quire loomed over him, blocking out what little light there was in the courtyard. He held a pistol in his upraised hand, brandishing it like a cudgel.

"I'll beat your head in if you give me the reason," Quire hissed.

Rutherford lifted his hands, set them between him and Quire as if to fend him off.

"You've gone mad," he said, as loudly as he dared.

Quire gave the pistol a warning shake.

"You keep your voice down, or that'll be the reason for breaking your head," he said quietly.

"All right, all right."

The only thing Rutherford could think to do was delay matters, stretch them out, until some passer-by should disturb them and save him from Quire's wrath. Quire, unfortunately, had always been a man inclined to hurry right to the meat of any talk.

"You're the one told them I was going to the Assembly Rooms. You tricked it out of the boy bringing the message, somehow. If you lie, I'll know it."

Rutherford believed that to be true, so he chose to say nothing at all, merely giving out a faint whimper that he hoped would sound at least as piteous and frightened as he felt.

"Told Baird, too, that I'd been talking to Cath, maybe? Lost me my wage and my calling, in that case. Were you watching me, Rutherford? Spying on me for Ruthven and Blegg? Baird, too?"

Rutherford snorted.

"Baird's a prancing prig."

Quire suddenly hit him in the face with his free hand, looping it around outside the shield Rutherford had made of his arms. The blow broke open the corner of his lip, and punched his head back against the sharp edge of one of the stone steps. He moaned, and blinked in surprise and pain.

"For God's sake, man," he gasped.

"Hold your tongue."

Rutherford had never heard quite such steady contempt and threat in a man's voice. Quire had always carried a rather intimidating presence about him, but this was something different. This was cold, purposeful determination undiluted by any pretence at fellow feeling or human concern.

"Just tell me this, and I'll leave you be," Quire said. "It's not you I'm after, Rutherford. You're just the rat running around the edges. But tell me this: you've taken Ruthven money, and you told them I was going to the Assembly Rooms."

Rutherford tasted blood in his mouth. He licked at the wound with his tongue, buying a fragment of time in which to think. This was not entirely the Quire he had known; he did not know precisely by what rules he now worked.

"Listen," Rutherford murmured, making his choice and praying for a bit of good fortune. "You're not wrong. I've a family, and I needed the money. Nothing more to it than that, Quire. You know how it is. It was nothing much they wanted of me, just a word now and again of what got talked about in the police house. Letting them know if any name they might be interested in ever came up, their own most of all.

"But that business with you getting turned off the force, and then the Assembly Rooms . . . aye, I might have played a wee part in all of that, but I broke with them after, Quire. I swear to you, I wanted nothing more to do with them after that. It was all getting too rich for my blood, and I never thought it would come to such a pitch. Taking a man's profession and living away from him, that's not right, not right at all."

He waited with held breath to see the effect of his confession upon Quire. The result was not precisely what he had hoped for.

"Except you didn't, did you? Break with them. You've been

taking Isabel Ruthven to see William Hare in the Calton Jail, haven't you?"

Quire made to bring that cruel-looking pistol down, and Rutherford flung up his arms to protect himself against what proved to be a feint. Instead, Quire bent down and punched him hard in the stomach. Rutherford coughed, and curled himself over, clutching his midriff.

"You were there tonight," Quire said, calm and level. "I know it, so don't deny it. All you need to do is tell me what she wants with Hare, and what you've been up to tonight. Tell me that, and we're done."

Rutherford recounted to him in great detail the events of the evening. He could see nothing in the business with Hare that could outrage Quire any more than the injuries that had been directed against his own person, so there seemed only gain to be had from trying to keep the brute happy.

"In the West Bow," Quire said with unusual precision and clarity. "Through a short arched passage into a yard that looks like it's not had a scavenger go through it in years. An empty apartment, at the back of the yard, foul and falling down. You're sure of all that?"

Rutherford nodded.

"And someone waiting in there, for you and her to bring Hare?"

"Aye. Never saw who it was, and it was only Hare came out, like I said. He was acting a wee bit odd, right enough, but he's not exactly what you'd call an ordinary man, is he? Can't be, to have done the things he done. Look, can you let me up off these steps, Adam? It's a damned uncomfortable bed you've got me lying on."

"How do you mean, odd?" Quire asked. "What was odd about Hare?"

"I don't know," muttered Rutherford, almost as much irritated as afraid, now that the ardour of Quire's violent passion seemed to have cooled somewhat, to be supplanted by a thoughtful intensity. "He was fiddling about with strange gloves he'd got from somewhere. Talking a bit different. Still a cocky bastard, mind. He just sounded different, like he'd changed his accent or something. All right?"

Quire at last tucked that pistol into his belt, and Rutherford felt a wave of relief washing through him. If he got out of this with a split lip and a bruise on his belly, he would count himself blessed.

"And you put him on the coach," Quire said.

It did not sound like a question, but Rutherford chose to make it such, eager to display his compliance.

"Dumfries, that's right. He's gone to Dumfries, on the mail. I put him on the coach, in Newington."

And then suddenly Quire's fists were darting in again, both of them one after the other, battering Rutherford on either side of the jaw. Quire took hold of his hair, and lifted his head by it, pulling so hard that Rutherford feared a handful of it would be torn from his scalp.

"The thing of it is," Quire murmured with chill contempt, "you've cost me more than I can easily pardon, Sergeant Rutherford. My employment's bad enough, but it's not the worst of it. You told them I was going to the Assembly Rooms, and by that telling you put a good friend of mine in a great trouble of deal. Trouble that's still got him walking about with a stick. I don't hold much with forgiveness, Rutherford. Not these days."

Rutherford heard what was coming in Quire's tone, and kicked out at his crotch. Quire was too alert for that, and turned to take the blow on his hip, then batted Rutherford's leg aside and closed down upon him in a flurry of blows.

XXXIII

The Annan Road

There was rioting in Dumfries when Quire staggered out, aching and stiff and weary, from the black coach that had brought him south. It had done so at remarkable speed. Remarkable, and punishing for any passengers, of which Quire had been the only one. His conveyance was the well-appointed funereal coach of the Widow, Mary Coulter, and it was as comfortable as any of its kind might be, but the road was rough and long, and no coach could make that a pleasant experience. He did not feel himself ready to confront the raw vigour of a mob run wild, but that was what he found.

Dumfries was not a large town, nor one with a reputation for much in the way of trouble. Despite that, Quire guessed there were well in excess of five thousand people besieging the jailhouse when he stepped down on to the main street. They were waving sticks and flinging stones at the windows and the gaslights. As Quire watched, a stone went through the hood of one of the lights, and it shattered and went out with a snap. Half the windows of the courthouse and its jail were already put in.

Quire pulled the big, heavy bundle off the seat of the coach. It was wrapped in many layers of sacking, and was cumbersome enough to test even Quire's considerable strength.

"You'd best wait for me back at that coach inn," Quire said to the driver who had brought him south in such haste.

Fleck, the Widow had told Quire his name was, and the very sole of discretion. So much so that he had hardly uttered a word to Quire in all the journey, and his expression never varied from one of sour repose. But he knew his way about a coach and horse, Quire had to concede that.

Fleck now turned the black coach about in the road and went trundling off. Quire gave his attention to the great mass of irate townsfolk that blocked off a long stretch of the high street. It was as febrile a mob as he had seen in a long time, and a big one for a town the size of Dumfries. Whatever had brought so many furious folk here, it had brought them from far afield.

A hundred or more local militiamen were arrayed across the front of the judicial building, armed with canes and staves and batons. They watched the surging crowd with uneasy, tense expressions, many of them turning their weapons in their hands, or tapping them upon the ground. Quire had an idea of how these things worked. If men were sent out with guns, as often as not they were for show, meant to cow the mob into order; if men were sent out with batons, as often as not they were meant to be used, and they usually were. The chaotic scene before him had the clear feel, in his estimation, of impending violence.

He needed to find out what was happening before that storm broke. Shouldering his ungainly bundle, balancing it there with one arm, he managed to separate a man, more composed than most of his fellows, from the fringes of the throng. He was composed, true enough, but he had paving cobbles in his hands that he had torn up from the street. Quire ignored that, and played the ignorant visitor.

"What's the cause of all this?"

"They've got Hare in there," the man said, a little breathless, a little ruddy-cheeked. It was an invigorating business, riot. "The Edinburgh murderer," he continued. "The one who killed all they folk and got away with it."

"You sure it's him?" Quire asked, looking towards the jail-house.

Those militiamen were pushing back against the encroaching, bellowing mob. They laid about them with their sticks, and there were yelps of pain mixed in with the shapeless rumble of anger the crowd gave out.

"Aye, sure." The man was watching events at the front of the crowd as closely as Quire, as if anxious not to miss out on anything. "He was recognised on the mail coach. One of the other passengers knew him, from the trial. A lawyer. There's some ill luck for the evil bastard, eh? Getting put on a coach with a man who chanced to know his face."

"Nobody ever did deserve more in the way of ill luck."

He was not sure what he himself had done to deserve such good luck, either, but he would gladly take it.

"Right," the Dumfries man said. "That's right. So the coach arrives, word gets about, and folk start thinking maybe we should hang the bastard ourselves, since the Crown didn't see fit to do it. We almost got him, at the King's Arms, but the police snuck him out a back window. Now he's in there."

As he spoke, the line of militiamen suddenly plunged into the front edge of the crowd, their batons rising and falling with an entirely more vicious and emphatic speed than they had previously done. Panic sped through the mob like a thought in a mind, communicating itself to the furthest reaches in mere moments. People began to run. Others began to turn their missiles upon the militiamen, rather than the buildings behind them.

Quire moved smartly away, already knowing the outcome. He kept himself well out of sight, down a narrow lane, as the great crowd was first beaten back, then muted, then routed and dispersed. He watched them fleeing into the night, scattering in all directions, their righteous fury abruptly forgotten in their haste to get out of the reach of the militiamen.

By the time midnight was past, Dumfries high street was deserted. It was littered with stones and broken glass and abandoned clubs. The militiamen were gone, their brutal duty discharged with rare efficiency. The rioters were gone, to nurse their bruises and their sore heads, and no doubt spin happy tales of the day's excitement. Only Quire remained, sitting at the foot of a wall, just a little way down that lane, far enough from the light of the street lamps to keep himself safely hidden in shadow. He could see the jailhouse from there, and waited with the most profound, perfect patience for it to reveal its secrets to him.

He had not killed Jack Rutherford. The temptation had been there, certainly, but Quire had no wish to become any more of an executioner and a widow-maker than he already was. Than he needed to be. So he settled for knocking out a few teeth, and putting a mortal fear into the man.

He had not slept since then. There had been too much to do. He had gone to Major Weir's house. Alone, almost overcome by fear, but finding there only the dead. Lying close by one another in a derelict room: Isabel Ruthven and what remained of Blegg. Quire had covered his mouth against the stench of rot and charred flesh that wafted from Blegg's horribly disfigured corpse. The rats were already at work upon the flesh. They scattered from the body as Quire brought unwanted light into their dismal domain, flowing like brown shadows across the ground and vanishing into their tunnels.

He had formed himself a plan quickly after that, but it had taken much of the night to turn it from thought into deed. He had traded his French pistol to a disreputable dealer in curios and oddities who kept a dingy little shop on St Mary's Wynd. The man had been furious to be roused from his sleep for no better reason than a trade, but he was somewhat mollified when he saw what Quire proposed: a fine French flintlock, complete with case, in exchange for an old Brown Bess and a score of prepared cartridges. It was a transaction so imbalanced in the dealer's favour that he could hardly demur. Quire regretted the loss of that pistol, but there was nothing to be done about it. For hunting, a man needed a long gun.

Thence, Quire went to find the Widow, and he made himself her debtor. He needed ten pounds from her to pay for Maclellan's message from the prison. He needed a carriage to carry him along the road taken by the southern mail. Mary Coulter had smiled, and Quire had foreseen in that smile all manner of difficulties and regrets in his future, but she asked nothing of him now, and gladly gave him money and the loan of her own black coach.

Last, a kiss to Cath's sleeping forehead – she stirring at the touch of his lips but not waking, which was as he wished it – and he was away.

So he found himself sitting in an alleyway in Dumfries, in the bitter cold early hours of the morning, when the police brought William Hare out from the jailhouse. They did it cautiously, surreptitiously. They had a jacket hung over his head, but that made no odds to Quire. He would not have recognised the face in any case. The anonymous figure the police escorted down the steps of the jailhouse to the waiting carriage wore black gloves, though, and that was enough to make Quire sure he had the right of it.

He waited until he saw which road the carriage was taking out of town, and then ran for the King's Arms. It was a big, ramshackle coaching inn of the old-fashioned sort, built around a wide yard, with stables and plenty of bedrooms and even a little smithy and wheelwright's workshop. All quiet now. All still.

Fleck was dozing, stretched out on the seat inside the coach, with his legs crossed and his tall black hat settled over his face like an upturned pot. Quire shook his boot to rouse him, and the man sprang instantly, almost unnaturally, to full wakefulness.

"They've gone out on the Annan road," Quire said.

Fleck made no complaint at being woken at such an ungodly hour. He had spent the whole day, and much of the night, sitting high up there as the coach bounded along. Quire was coming to a certain admiration for the man's dour resilience. He rode up there with him now, not wanting to be shut away in the body of the coach where he would see, or hear, nothing.

They followed the little police carriage out along the road running south-east towards Annan village. That was close by the border with England, and to ports where a man might find a boat to take him to Ireland. Hare – whatever he now was, whatever now resided behind his eyes – might be intent upon either of those paths.

They followed not by sight, for the darkness was still deep, barely touched, out on the far eastern horizon, by the first premonition of dawn. Instead they kept their distance, and paused now and again to listen for the rattle of the other carriage over ruts. If they heard nothing, they pressed on a little faster, but never so close as to risk being seen. There were in any case no turnings from this road down which a carriage was likely to go until well past Annan, as best Quire could think.

The sky slowly lightened, inching its way towards what looked likely to be a bright and cloudless daybreak. That would be some time yet, though. The moors that flanked the road were only grudgingly released from the concealing darkness. They made a great, wild land through which to ride. Not a tree in sight, for as far as Quire could see in the gradually retreating gloom. Just mile after mile of heather moorland, rising in a series of long, low waves, each crest growing fainter and losing its brown and green patterning in stages to a flat grey.

He had grown up amidst land like this, and found it familiar and comfortable then, but he had been gone from it long enough that it seemed to him to have something of the wilderness about it now. He had travelled a long distance from the boy he had been then. He did not know, as he swayed across the moors atop the Widow's coach, whether the journey had been well done, or quite what its conclusion would be.

They crested a low rise in the road, and Fleck hauled unceremoniously at the reins, bringing the weary black horse to an abrupt halt. Quire shook his head and rubbed at his eye. He had been drifting, half-lost in a dull stupor of exhaustion. That cleared quickly enough when he saw that the police carriage was stopped, perhaps a quarter-mile ahead. There was not a cottage or a farm or a track to be seen in any direction, just the featureless heath. Quire jumped down on to the road. It hurt his stiff and tired legs.

"If you keep back out of sight, I'll just wait here a bit and see what happens," he said to Fleck who, as ever, silently did as he was told.

Quire was concerned that the big black coach would not get behind the skyline quickly enough, and would be seen, but there was no sign of life at all from the carriage up ahead. He laid himself down in the heather at the side of the road, and watched.

It did not take long. A single figure stepped out of the little carriage, and walked away from it, straight out into the heather, without a backward glance. The carriage slowly, inelegantly,

turned about in the road and began to come back up towards
Quire. He was not interested in it any more, though. He had eyes
only for that lone figure, loping away from the road into the
wilderness.

Quire ran back to the Widow's coach, and threw open its door.
Fleck watched him with mild curiosity; the most expansive emo-
tion Quire had seen him display thus far.

"You'd best get back to Dumfries, I'd say," Quire called to him
as he worked. "Wait there for me till noon tomorrow. Or the
morning after if you're feeling generous. If you don't see me by
then, get yourself back to Edinburgh."

He unrolled the sacking bundle. It had been thickly wrapped,
the better to conceal its contents. He took the musket out first,
and slung it over his shoulder. Then pouches of cartridges that he
set upon his belt, and the French sabre that he threaded on there
too. Last a backpack, heavy, that he hung on his other shoulder.

"Police are coming," Fleck observed, startling Quire with his
sudden loquacity.

He looked up, and saw and heard the police carriage make its
shaking approach along the track towards them. Quire darted
around to the far side of the coach, hiding himself from their
view. He watched Fleck doff his hat and call a greeting as they
trundled past, but neither of the two police officers in the carriage
responded. They looked, from the glimpse of their faces Quire
caught through the windows of the coach, thoroughly dejected.
As would he be, he supposed, if his official duties involved saving
men such as Hare from the justified wrath of the common folk,
and escorting them safely on their way.

Once the police carriage was out of sight, Quire went to the
front of the coach and reached up to offer Fleck his hand. The
coachman regarded it blankly for a moment or two, then took it
in his own and gently shook it.

"I'm grateful for your help," Quire said in the dawn's gathering light.

Fleck just nodded.

"I'll hope to see you in a day or two," Quire said.

And with that they parted, Fleck to Dumfries, Quire to the moors. Before he went, he loaded the musket. The movements were more familiar now than they had been for years. He had made Fleck stop, on a wild stretch of road somewhere a couple of hours south of Edinburgh, and spared a few precious minutes from the pursuit to get a feel for the gun and his handling of it. Standing there, on the edge of bleak, empty fields, he loaded, and fired, four or five times over, the shots booming out over the barren land. Each time he had been a little faster, a little surer. As he would have to be, he suspected.

He ran out into the heather. He did not try for too much pace. He was tired enough already, and had no wish to bring himself to his knees any sooner than he had to. And he remembered, from his youth, just how treacherous these places could be to a man who attempted to cover too much ground too quickly, hiding all manner of pits and hollows and tripping roots beneath the endless, featureless carpet of heather.

Hare was out of sight, swallowed up by the vast landscape, but Quire did not concern himself with that. He had marked the man's course, and angled his own to meet it, out there in the trackless waste. If he could not see his quarry for now, it would only be some hollow in the land, or the tiny dip of a valley cut by a little burn, that was hiding it from him.

Grouse burst from his feet and went churring away low over the heather, like winged balls shot from the mouth of a cannon. The first time it happened he almost fell, so alarming and unexpected was the noise and blur of movement; after that, he was not so easily startled. Watchful, though. Always watchful.

There came a time when he slowed, first to a trot, and then a walk. And, at last, to a halt. He stood, knee-deep in the brittle heather, and looked out across the undulating ground before him. Slowly, he unshipped the Brown Bess from his shoulder and pulled back the hammer until it locked into place. He fixed his gaze upon one patch of heath, a hundred yards or more away. There was a hue mixed in there, a patch of it, that did not quite belong. Quire stared at it, and waited.

Hare rose to his feet. Quire could see the feral glee in the man's smile, even at that distance.

"You're a plague, Quire," Hare shouted out across the heather. "A revenant, sent to haunt me again and again, is that it? Do you not know I'm under the King's protection?"

It was the first time Quire had heard the voice of his enemy. While it resided in Blegg, it had never once spoken to him. It did so now in a soft Irish brogue. Whether mimicry or memory or pure invention, Quire did not know. It did not matter. He did not mean to listen to much of what the thing might have to say.

Hare began to run towards him. Quire dipped his left shoulder to let the backpack slip from it. The pack's fall was cushioned by the mat of springy heather. He dropped on to his right knee, and breathed slowly in and out. He rested his left elbow on his left leg and set the musket's butt to his shoulder. He looked out along the line of the barrel, across the moor, to the figure running towards him.

He willed his weaker left arm to hold steady, willed his heart to slow, his eyes to clear. The fear was in him, but he pushed it away, far enough that it did not cloud him.

He could hear the heather thrashing against Hare's legs. Could see the wild hatred in the man's eyes. A tremor went through him, but he tensed himself to still it, and then let his muscles go slack once more. Closer and closer he let Hare come, knowing that if his first shot missed, he might not live long enough for a second. He had been a fine shot once, and needed to be again. Closer, until he could see little glints of the risen sun on the buttons of Hare's waistcoat, until he could bear it no more.

He held his breath, and squeezed the trigger, and the Bess roared in his hands. He shot Hare in the knee. It spun the man about and sent him crashing down into the heather, tall and straggly enough there to swallow him up completely.

Quire did not wait for him to rise, as he knew he would. He leaped to his feet, and began the ritual of reloading. His fingers shook, just slightly, as he fumbled the next cartridge out of his belt pouch. He heard movement, out there in the heather. He bit out the top of the paper packet, tapped just enough of the grey, grainy powder into the pan to prime it. He heard Hare rising. Held the gun erect, tipped powder down the barrel.

"Quire, you bastard," he heard Hare cry at him.

Turned the cartridge about in his fingers, still less steady than he would have liked. Hare was running at him. He saw the dark shape, coming unsteadily now, hampered by his ruined knee. Got the ball into the gun's mouth, pulled the ramrod up and out from its home. Punched it down Bess' gullet. He looked up. Twenty yards, no more. Hare's lips were pulled back in a snarl. Quire kept hold of the ramrod, shouldered the musket, shot Hare in the other leg.

They were so close that the smoke plumed out over Hare, and he fell forwards through it.

"You're a hard man to kill, someone told me a while ago," Quire said as he stepped back, out of reach of the hands clawing for him, "so I've given it a bit of thought, on the road down here."

Hare was not done yet, though. Quire had misjudged the ferocious will and power of what was inside the man. Hare surged up once more, and part-staggered, part-rushed forward, throwing himself at Quire, who sprang away. Quire's heel caught on a gnarled heather stem, and he fell back. He tried to roll at once, but the dense heather hampered him, and in less than a heartbeat's span, there were hands like stone wrapped around his left ankle, pulling at him. The scabbard of the sabre caught about a half-buried stone as Hare dragged him nearer, and he used that to lever himself up so that he could hammer with the butt of the musket at the arms that held him.

He hit his own leg as much as any limb of Hare's, and the pain was excruciating, but the hands did come away from his ankle, once a few of the fingers were battered and broken. Quire scrambled away, and got rather gingerly to his feet. He put more ground between him and Hare as the latter rose again, swaying and rocking on legs too crippled to do much more than hold him there. He managed to move them, even so, and though he fell, and had to struggle back on to his feet, he came stubbornly on at Quire.

Who reloaded the Brown Bess again. He was strangely at peace, now that there was nothing to do, nothing to think about, save the immediate and obvious necessity. That calmness lent a speed to his hands. The musket was ready to fire again in no more than twenty seconds, and he brought it smoothly up and had the luxury of another second or two to measure his breathing and take good aim. That second shot had missed the knee at which it was aimed by some little way. The third did not, blasting out the joint in an eruption of shredded cloth and meat and bone splinters. Hare fell, and this time Quire did not think he would be rising soon.

"What are you?" Quire asked as he began to work his way through the movements needed to make the musket ready once more. It was mechanical now; the instinctive memory of it reawakened in him by repetition. He barely needed to watch what he was doing, and could keep his eyes upon Hare.

Hare was still trying to get to his feet, but his legs buckled beneath him and he went down. He lifted himself up on his hands and leered at Quire.

"What does that matter?" the beast laughed. "I'm here. I'll always be here."

"Maybe, maybe not." Quire grunted. "Future's full of surprises, I've found. Best not to concern yourself overmuch with it. Concentrate on the present."

He looked at his right hand. There was a fine layer of gunpowder dusted across it now. He wiped it clean on his trousers.

"Are you not the Devil, then?" he asked.

Hare laughed.

"No, Mr Quire, I'm not your Devil. But think of me that way, if it makes you happy. I'll not mind. Just stop with all your questions. You'd as well ask what the wind is, or the water, or the earth, as what I am."

"They'll have answers to all that, likely as not, the way the scientists and the philosophers and such are getting so busy these days," Quire said as he raised the musket to his shoulder.

"Never to me," Hare shouted, "never to me."

To Quire's amazement, he hauled himself to his feet yet again, bone crackling in his knees as he did so, his legs twisting and bending unnaturally. He took a long, sinking pace towards Quire, his face contorted into a mask of such pure hatred that it rendered it almost inhuman. More beast than man.

"Never to you," Quire muttered, "Aye, you might be right about that."

And he shot Hare for the fourth and last time, in the heart, and knocked him down with the force of it.

Quire set the Brown Bess aside then, leaving it safely out of reach of the still writhing figure in the heather. He drew his sabre as a flock of ravens went croaking overhead, rolling about. He glanced up at them, and saw for the first time that the sky was blue now; a pristine field of azure, from horizon to horizon.

He looked at Hare. He was lying face down. The violence of his movements was diminishing. Quire trod on one of the man's outstretched arms and pinned it down. He hacked at the wrist with the sabre. It took a few blows to separate hand from arm, and it came away without much in the way of blood or gore. The spirit inhabiting Hare did not seem to notice.

Quire peeled the glove off the hand, and looked impassively at the crude writing and symbols scrawled across the skin. None of it he could understand; there was no meaning to it for him. But Durand had said to clear the writing from the hand, and Quire thought that taking the hand from the body should serve just as well.

He cut the other hand away more easily. He rolled Hare on to his back. There was no movement in the limbs now, but the eyes still darted from side to side. They found Quire's face, and held on to his gaze. The lips trembled, trying to recall the shape of a sneer.

Quire trotted over to his backpack and tipped it out. He gathered up the flasks of lamp oil and carried them to Hare's corpse. He poured most of the oil over the body, and then set about the business of gathering as much dry, old heather as he could, slashing at it with the sword. It would dull the blade, but he hoped to have no further use for the thing. He heaped the loose, leggy clumps of heather over Hare's prostrate form.

He meant, as well, to have no further use for the cartridges in his belt pouches, so he tore them all open and made a little mound of the powder close by the pyre. He soaked some more heather in the last of the oil, and laid that over the pyramid of gunpowder. And then, at last, he knelt, and held the musket low down, and sent sparks from the flintlock scattering out into the powder and the oil-soaked heather.

He sat on a low rock, perhaps thirty yards away, and watched Hare burn. Great yellow flames licked up into the sky, and thick, stinking black smoke that made coils of itself as it rose.

Quire felt a good deal more calm and content than he had expected to. There was, he realised as the flames consumed the corpse, a remarkable lightness about his life now. It contained almost nothing, had almost no weight to it. Blegg, and Ruthven, and everything that went with them were gone; so was his place on the city police. No wage, none of that purpose that his work had put into his life. Nothing left to him of it. All burned away, just as Hare was now, out on the moors.

There was Cath, though. He thought of her as he sat, looking out over the vast silver expanse of the Solway Firth that the bright day had discovered, far to the south, and freed from the shackles of darkness. The sun sent a thousand rippling, glittering shards of light racing over the surface of the sea.

Quire reached down and plucked a sprig of heather from beside his hard seat. He would take that back to Cath, he thought. For luck.

extras

www.orbitbooks.net

about the author

Brian Ruckley was born and brought up in Scotland. After studying at Edinburgh and Stirling Universities, he worked for a series of organisations dealing with environmental, nature conservation and youth development issues. Having had short stories published in *Interzone* and *The Third Alternative* in the 1990s, Brian started working as a freelance consultant on environmental projects in 2003 in order to concentrate seriously on his writing, which now takes up almost all of his time. He lives in Edinburgh. His website and blog can be found at www.brianruckley.com

Find out more about Brian Ruckley and other Orbit authors by registering for the free monthly newsletter at www.orbitbooks.net

interview

Have you always known that you wanted to be a writer?

From a very young age, writing fiction felt like a reasonable and natural thing to be doing. Crucially, nobody ever disabused me of that notion, so although I had plenty of other interests that I was quite happy to pursue professionally, writing was always there, in my head, as an option.

Did the idea for *The Edinburgh Dead* come to you fully realised or did you have one particular starting point from which it grew?

I had one very specific, pretty simple starting point. I was thinking about Burke and Hare, two of Edinburgh's most famous historical inhabitants, naughty chaps who murdered lots of innocents in order to supply the city's anatomy schools with corpses. A straightforward question occurred to me: what if the teachers of anatomy weren't the only people who wanted to get their hands on some corpses back then? The whole book flowed from that one thought.

What is it about Edinburgh that made you want to set your book there?

Two things: familiarity – since I was born and brought up here, and know the place and its history far better than anywhere else in the world – and the richness and strangeness of that history. For a relatively brief period in the late eighteenth and early nineteenth century, Edinburgh was at the very forefront of global scientific and philosophical thought, and at the same time there were some seriously dark and dodgy things going on here. It's just a very tempting mixture to go and play around with.

Did you have to carry out extensive historical research before you began writing?

I already had some idea about Edinburgh's history, but did a lot of reading to fill in the details, on things like the police force and the medical establishment. That was the most fun bit of writing the book, to be honest: any excuse to spend hours digging into the contents of a good library. Much more enjoyable than actually trying to turn words into sentences and paragraphs.

Do you have any particular favourite authors who have influenced your work?

It can be difficult to trace specific influences, but my sense of what speculative fiction is and can be has certainly been shaped by any number of writers I admire (or should that be envy?) greatly. People like Guy Gavriel Kay, Dan Simmons, George R. R. Martin.

What advantages and disadvantages do you see in using fantasy as the vehicle for your stories?

That's a big question. One advantage is that it comes naturally to me: I'm a long-time reader of fantastic fiction, and the alternative – of writing mainstream, "realistic" stories – just doesn't feel as instinctive. And, of course, fantasy allows the author to play around with themes and subjects in a vivid, exciting context that plugs right into the reader's imagination. Disadvantages . . . well, it deters some readers, but then it potentially attracts rather a large number, too.

Do you have a set writing routine and, if so, what is it?

In a lot of ways I wish I had more of a routine than I do, really. In general terms, I actually write best (and fastest) in evenings and at night, but sadly the demands of real life don't conform to my selfish preferences, so I end up doing most of my writing in the morning.

Some authors talk of their characters "surprising" them by their actions; is this something that has happened to you?

Not much. I like to think I'm the boss, on the whole. What does sometimes happen, though, is that I will change my ideas about what a character should do, or what fate should befall them, as I write a book. It's not so much a case of me being surprised, as that I just have second thoughts about some particular plan. Once or twice, I've liked characters more than I expected to, and ended up saving them from nasty fates I originally had in mind for them, because I thought they deserved a rather happier outcome. Does that make me soft?

Do you chat about your books with other authors as you're writing them, or do you prefer to keep them in your own head until the first draft is complete?

I talk to almost no one – author or otherwise – about what I'm writing until it's basically complete, at least in draft form. Any conversations about the story are only in the vaguest and briefest of outline form until I've got enough text to be reasonably sure there's something worth talking about there. Even then, I'm absolutely lousy at talking about my own work. Can hardly ever think of anything much to say.

If you have to live for one month as a character in a novel, which novel and which character would you choose?

Too many possible answers to this, so I'll just pick one of the dozens that leap to mind: Dr Watson, in pretty much any of the Sherlock Holmes stories, just to explore that world, and get to watch Holmes doing his thing. (And no, I wouldn't really want to be Holmes himself – too manic depressive for my taste.)

If *The Edinburgh Dead* was ever filmed, who would you like to see directing and starring in the movie?

Directing would probably be Christopher Nolan, since I can't remember any film he's touched being less than interesting and distinctive. Starring ... that's harder. How about Daniel Craig? He'd be a pretty good fit for my lead character, Adam Quire, I think.

What would you do if you weren't a writer?

I would no doubt be doing what I was before the writing thing took off: working in the environmental or nature conservation field, probably in the charity sector. I enjoyed that work and, much as I like writing, I miss my day-to-day involvement in it, so it'd be no hardship to be living that life again.

if you enjoyed

THE EDINBURGH DEAD

look out for

THE DEVIL YOU KNOW

by

Mike Carey

1

Normally I wear a Tsarist army greatcoat — the kind that some-times gets called a paletot — with pockets sewn in for my tin whistle, my notebook, a dagger and a chalice. Today I'd gone for a green tuxedo with a fake wilting flower in the buttonhole, pink patent-leather shoes and a painted-on moustache in the style of Groucho Marx. From Bunhill Fields in the east I rode out across London — the place of my strength. I have to admit, though, that 'strong' wasn't exactly how I was feeling: when you look like a pistachio-ice-cream sundae, it's no easy thing to hang tough.

The economic geography of London has changed a lot in the last few years, but Hampstead is always Hampstead. And on this cold November afternoon, atoning for sins I couldn't even count and probably looking about as cheerful as a *tricoteuse* being told that the day's executions have been cancelled due to bad weather, Hampstead was where I was headed.

Number 17, Grosvenor Terrace, to be more precise: an unassuming little early-Victorian masterpiece knocked off by Sir Charles Barry in his lunch hours while he was doing the Reform Club. It's in the books, like it or not: the great man would moonlight for a grand in hand and borrow his materials from whatever else he was doing at the time. You can find his illegitimate architectural progeny everywhere from Ladbroke Grove to Highgate, and they always give you that same uneasy feeling of déjà vu, like seeing the milkman's nose on your own first-born.

I parked the car far enough away from the door to avoid any potential embarrassment to the household I was here to visit, and managed the last hundred yards or so burdened with four suitcases full of highly specialised equipment. The doorbell made a severe, functional buzzing sound like a dentist's drill sliding off recalcitrant enamel. While I waited for a response I checked out the rowan twig nailed up to the right of the porch. Black and white and red strings had been tied to it in the prescribed order, but still . . . a rowan twig in November wouldn't have much juice left in it. I concluded that this must be a quiet neighbourhood.

The man who opened the door to me was presumably James Dodson, the birthday boy's father. I took a strong dislike to him right then to save time and effort later. He was a solid-looking man, not big but hard-packed: grey eyes like two ball-bearings, salt-and-pepper hair adding its own echoes to the grey. In his forties, but probably as fit and trim now as he had been two decades ago: clearly, this was a man who recognised the importance of good diet, regular exercise and unremitting moral superiority. Pen had said he was a cop: chief constable in waiting, working out of Agar Street as one of the midwives to the government's new Serious and

Organised Crime Agency. I think I would have guessed either a cop or a priest, and most priests gratefully let themselves go long before they hit forty: that's one of the perks of having a higher calling.

'You're the entertainer,' Dodson said, as you might say, 'You're a motherless piece of scum and you raped my dog.' He didn't make a move to help me with the cases, which I was carrying two in each hand.

'Felix Castor,' I agreed, my face set in an unentertaining dead-pan. 'I roll the blues away.'

He nodded non-committally and opened the door wider to let me in. 'The living room,' he said, pointing. 'There'll be rather more children than we originally said. I hope that's okay.'

'The more the merrier,' I answered over my shoulder, walking on through. I sized the living room up with what I hoped looked like a professional eye, but it was just a room to me. 'This is fine. Everything I need. Great.'

'We were going to send Sebastian over to his father's, but the bloody man had some sort of work crisis on,' Dodson explained from behind me. 'Which makes one more. And a few extra friends . . .'

'Sebastian?' I inquired. Throwing out questions like that is a reflex with me, whether I want answers or not: it comes from the work I do. I mean, the work I used to do. Sometimes do. Can live *without* doing.

'Peter's stepbrother. He's from Barbara's previous marriage, just as Peter is from mine. They get along very well.'

'Of course.' I nodded solemnly, as if checking out the soundness of the familial support network was something I always did before I started in on the magic tricks and the wacky slapstick. Peter was the birthday boy: just turned fourteen. Too old, probably, for clowns and conjurors and parties of the cake-and-ice-cream variety. But then, that wasn't my call to make. They also serve who only pull endless strings of coloured ribbon out of a baked-bean tin.

'I'll leave you to set up, then,' Dodson said, sounding dubious.

'Please don't move any of the furniture without checking with me or Barbara first. And if you're setting up anything on the parquet that might scratch, ask us for pads.'

'Thanks,' I said. 'And mine's a beer whenever you're having one yourself. The term "beer" should not be taken to include the subset "lager".'

He was already heading for the door when I threw this out, and he kept right on going. I was about as likely to get a drink out of him as I was to get a French kiss.

So I got down to unpacking, a task which was made harder by the fact that these cases hadn't moved out of Pen's garage in the last ten years. There were all sorts of things in among the stage-magic gear that gave me a moment's – or more than a moment's – pause. A Swiss Army penknife (it had belonged to my old friend Rafi) with the main blade broken off short an inch from the tip; a home-made fetish rigged up out of the mummified body of a frog and three rusty nails; a feathered snood, looking a bit threadbare now but still carrying a faint whiff of perfume; and the camera.

Shit. The camera.

I turned it over in my hands, instantly submerged in a brief but powerful reverie. It was a Brownie Autographic No. 3, and all folded up as it was it looked more like a kid's lunchbox than anything else. But once I flipped the catches I could see that the red-leather bellows was still in place, the frosted viewfinder was intact, and (wonder of wonders) the hand-wheeled stops that extended the lens into its operating position still seemed to work. I'd found the thing in a flea market in Munich when I was back-packing through Europe: it was nearly a hundred years old, and I'd paid about a quid for it, which was the whole of the asking price because the lens was cracked right the way across. That didn't matter to me – not for what I principally had in mind at the time – so it counted as a bargain.

I had to put it to one side, though, because at that moment the first of the party guests were shepherded in by a very busty, very blonde, very beautiful woman who was obviously much too good for the likes of James Dodson. Or the likes of me, to be fair. She was wearing a white bloused top and a khaki skirt with an asymmetric hang which probably had a designer name attached to it somewhere and cost more than I earned in six months. For all that, though, she looked a touch worn and tired. Living with James Super-cop would do that to you, I speculated: or, possibly, living with Peter, assuming that Peter was the sullen streak of curdled sunlight hovering at her elbow. He had his father's air of blocky, aggressive solidity, with an adolescent's wary stubbornness grafted onto it: it made for a very unattractive combination, somehow.

The lady introduced herself as Barbara, in a voice that had enough natural warmth in it to make electric blankets irrelevant. She introduced Peter, too, and I offered him a smile and a nod. I tried to shake hands with him, out of some atavistic impulse probably brought on by being in Hampstead, but he'd already stomped away in the direction of a new arrival, with a loud bellow of greeting. Barbara watched him go with an unreadable, Zen-like smile which suggested prescription medication, but her gaze as she turned back to me was sharp and clear enough.

'So,' she said. 'Are you ready?'

For anything, I almost said – but I opted for a simple yes. All the same, I probably held the glance a half-moment too long. At any rate, Barbara suddenly remembered a bottle of mineral water that she was holding in her hand, and handed it to me with a slight blush and an apologetic grimace. 'You can have a beer in the kitchen with us afterwards,' she promised. 'If I give you one now, the kids will demand equal rights.'

I raised the bottle in a salute.

'So . . .' she said again. 'An hour's performance, then an hour off while we serve the food – and you come on again for half an hour at the end. Is that okay?'

'It's a valid strategy,' I allowed. 'Napoleon used it at Quatre Bras.'

This got a laugh, feeble as it was. 'We won't be able to stay for the show,' Barbara said, with a good facsimile of regret. 'There's quite a lot still to do behind the scenes – some of Peter's friends are staying over. But we might be able to sneak back in to catch the finale. If not, see you in the interval.' With a conspiratorial grin she beat her retreat and left me with my audience.

I let my gaze wander around the room, taking the measure of them. There was an in-group, clustered around Peter and engaged in a shouted conversation which colonised the entire room. There was an out-group, consisting of four or five temporary knots spread around the edges of the room, which periodically tried to attach themselves to the in-group in a sort of reversal of cellular fission. And then there was stepbrother Sebastian.

It wasn't hard to spot him: I'd made a firm identification while I was still unfolding my trestle table and laying out my opening trick. He had the matrilineal blond hair, but his paler skin and watery blue eyes made him look as if someone had sketched him in pastels and then tried to erase him. He looked to be a lot smaller and slighter than Peter, too. Because he was the younger of the two? It was hard to tell, because his infolded, self-effaced posture probably took an inch or so off his height. He was the one on the fringes of the boisterous rabble, barely tolerated by the birthday boy and contemptuously ignored by the birthday boy's friends. He was the one left out of all the in-jokes, looking like he didn't belong and would rather be almost anywhere else: even with his real dad, perhaps, on a day when there was a work crisis on.

When I clapped my hands and shouted a two-minute warning, Sebastian filed up with the last of the reguard and took up a position immediately behind Peter – a dead zone which nobody else seemed to want to lay claim to.

Then the show was on, and I had troubles of my own to attend to.

I'm not a bad stage-magician. It was how I paid my way through college, and when I'm in practice I'd go so far as to say I'm pretty sharp. Right then I was as rusty as hell, but I was still able to pull off some reasonably classy stuff – my own scaled-down versions of the great illusions I'd studied during my ill-spent youth. I made some kid's wristwatch disappear from a bag that he was holding, and turn up inside a box in someone else's pocket. I levitated the same kid's mobile phone around the room while Peter and the front-row elite stood up and waved their arms in the vain hope of tangling the wires they thought I was using. I even cut a deck of cards into pieces with garden shears and reconstituted them again, with a card that Peter had previously chosen and signed at the top of the deck.

But whatever the hell I did, I was dying on my feet. Peter sat stolidly at front and centre, arms folded in his lap, and glared at me all the while with paint-blistering contempt. He'd clearly reached his verdict, which was that being impressed by kids'-party magic could lose you a lot of status with your peers. And if the risk was there even for him, it was clearly unacceptable for his chosen guests. They watched him and took their cue from him, forming a block vote that I couldn't shift.

Sebastian seemed to be the only one who was actually interested in the show for its own sake – or perhaps the only one who had so little to lose that he could afford just to let himself get drawn in, without watching his back. It got him into trouble, though. When I finished the card trick and showed Peter his pristine eight of diamonds, Sebastian broke into a thin patter of applause, carried away for a moment by the excitement of the final reveal.

He stopped as soon as he realised that nobody else was joining in, but he'd already broken cover – forgetting what seemed otherwise to be very well-developed habits of camouflage and self-preservation. Annoyed, Peter stabbed backwards with his elbow, and I heard a *whoof* of air from Sebastian as he leaned suddenly forward, clutching his midriff. His head stayed bowed for a few moments, and when he came up he came up slowly. 'Fuckwit,' Peter snarled, *sotto voce*. 'He just used two decks. That's not even clever.'

I read a lot into this little exchange: a whole chronicle of casual cruelty and emotional oppression. You may think that's stretching an elbow in the ribs a touch too far – but I'm a younger brother myself, so the drill's not unfamiliar to me. And besides that, I knew one more thing about birthday boy than anybody else here knew.

I took a mental audit. Yes. I was letting myself get a little irritated, and that wasn't a good thing. I still had twenty minutes to run before the break and the cold beer in the kitchen. And I had one sure-fire winner, which I'd been meaning to save for the finale, but what the hell. You only live once, as people continue to say in the teeth of all the evidence.

I threw out my arms, squared my shoulders, tugged my cuffs – a pantomime display of preparation intended mainly to get Sebastian off the hook. It worked, as far as that went: all eyes turned to me. 'Watch very carefully,' I said, taking a new prop out of one of the cases and putting it on the table in front of me. 'An ordinary cereal box. Any of you eat this stuff? No, me neither. I tried them once, but I was mauled by a cartoon tiger.' Not a glimmer: not a sign of mercy in any of the forty or so eyes that were watching me.

'Nothing special about the box. No trapdoors. No false bottoms.' I rotated it through three dimensions, flicked it with a thumbnail to get a hollow *thwack* out of it, and held the open end up to Peter's face for him to take a look inside. He rolled his eyes as if he couldn't believe he was being asked to go along with this stuff, then gave me a wave that said he was as satisfied of the box's emptiness as he was ever going to be.

'Yeah, whatever,' he said, with a derisive snort. His friends laughed too: he was popular enough to get a choric echo whenever he spoke or snickered or made farting noises in his cheek. He had the touch, all right. Give him four, maybe five years and he was going to grow up into a right bastard.

Unless he took a walk down the Damascus Road one morning, and met something big and fast coming the other way.

'O-o-okay,' I said, sweeping the box around in a wide arc so that everyone else could see it. 'So it's an empty box. So who needs it, right? Boxes like this, they're just landfill waiting to happen.' I stood it on the ground, open end downwards, and trod it flat.

That got at least a widened eye and a shift of posture here and there around the room – kids leaning forward to watch, if only to check out how complete and convincing the damage was. I was thorough. You have to be. Like a dominatrix, you find that there's a direct relationship between the intensity of the stamping and trampling and the scale of the final effect.

When the box was comprehensively flattened, I picked it up and allowed it to dangle flaccidly from my left hand.

'But before you throw this stuff away,' I said, sweeping the cluster of stolid faces with a stern, schoolteacherly gaze, 'you've got to check for biohazards. Anyone up for that? Anyone want to be an environmental health inspector when they grow up?'

There was an awkward silence, but I let it lengthen. It was Peter's dime: I only had to entertain him, not pimp for him.

Finally, one of the front-row cronies shrugged and stood up. I stepped a little aside to welcome him into my performance space – broadly speaking, the area between the leather recliner and the running buffet.

'Give a big hand to the volunteer,' I suggested. They razzed him cordially instead: you find out who your friends are.

I straightened the box with a few well-practised tugs and tucks. This was the crucial part, so of course I kept my face as bland as school custard. The volunteer held his hand out for the box: instead, I caught his hand in my own and turned it palm up. 'And the other one,' I said. 'Make a cup. *Verstehen Sie* "cup"? Like this. Right. Excellent. Good luck, because you never know . . .'

I upended the box over his hands, and a large brown rat smacked right down into the makeshift basket of his fingers. He gurgled like a punctured water bed and jumped back, his hands flying convulsively apart, but I was ready and I caught the rat neatly before she could fall.

Then, because I knew her well, I added a small grace note to the trick by stroking her nipples with the ball of my thumb. This made her arch her back and gape her mouth wide open, so that when I brandished her in the faces of the other kids I got a suitable set of jolts and starts. Of course, it wasn't a threat display – it was 'More, big boy, give me more' – but they couldn't be expected to know that look at their tender age. Any more than they knew that I'd dropped Rhona into the box when I pretended to straighten it after the trampling.

And bow. And acknowledge the applause. Which would have been fine if there'd been any. But Peter still sat like Patience on a monument, as the volunteer trudged back to his seat with his machismo at half-mast.

Peter's face said I'd have to do a damn sight more than that to impress him.

So I thought about the Damascus Road again. And, like the bastard I am, I reached for the camera.

This isn't my idea of how a grown man should go about keeping the wolf from the door, I'd like you to know: it was Pen who put me up to it. Pamela Elisa Bruckner: why that shortens to Pen rather than Pam I've never been sure, but she's an old friend of mine, and incidentally the rightful owner of Rhona the rat. She's also my landlady, for the moment at least, and since I wouldn't wish that fate on a rabid dog I count myself lucky that it's fallen to someone who's genuinely fond of me. It lets me get away with a hell of a lot.

I should also tell you that I do have a job – a real job, which pays the bills at least occasionally. But at the time currently under discussion, I was taking an extended holiday: not entirely voluntary, and not without its own attendant problems relating to cash flow, professional credibility and personal self-esteem. In any case, it left Pen with a vested interest in putting alternative work my way. Since she was still a good Catholic girl (when she wasn't being a Wicca priestess), she went to Mass every Sunday, lit a candle to the Blessed Virgin and prayed to this tune: 'Please, Madonna, in your wisdom and mercy, intercede for my mother though she died with many carnal sins weighing on her soul; let the troubled nations of Earth find a road to peace and freedom; and make Castor solvent, amen.'

But usually she left it at that, which was a situation we could both live with. So it was an unpleasant surprise to me when she stopped counting on divine intervention and told me about the kids' party agency she was setting up with her crazy friend Leona – and the slimy sod of a street magician who'd given her an eleventh-hour stab in the back.

'But you could do this so *easily*, Fix,' she coaxed, over coffee laced with cognac in her subterranean sitting room. The smell was making me dizzy: not the smell of the brandy, but the smell of rats and earth and leaf mulch and droppings and Mrs Amelia Underwood roses, of things growing and things decaying. One of her two ravens – Arthur, I think – was clacking his beak against the top shelf of the bookcase, making it hard for me to stick to a train of thought. This was her den, her centre of gravity: the inverted penthouse underneath the three-storey monstrosity where her grandmother had lived and died in the days when mammoths still roamed the Earth. She had me at a disadvantage here, which was why she'd asked me in to start with.

'You can do real magic,' Pen pointed out sweetly, 'so fake magic ought to be a doddle.'

I blinked a couple of times to clear my eyes, blinded by candles, fuddled by incense. In a lot of ways, the way Pen lives is sort of reminiscent of Miss Havisham in *Great Expectations*: she only uses the basement, which means that the rest of the house apart from my bedsitter up in the roof space is frozen in the 1950s, never vis-ited, never revised. Pen herself froze a fair bit later than that, but like Miss Havisham she wears her heart on her mantelpiece. I try not to look at it.

On this particular occasion I took refuge in righteous indig-nation. 'I can't do real magic, Pen, because there's no such animal. Not the way you mean it, anyway. What do I look like, eh? Just because I can talk to the dead – and whistle up a tune for them – that doesn't make me Gandalf the bastard Grey. And it doesn't mean that there are fairies at the bottom of the sodding garden.'

The crude language was a ploy, intended to derail the conversation. It didn't work, though. I got the impression that Pen had worked out her script in advance for this one.

'"What is now proved was once only imagined",' she said, primly – because she knows that Blake is my main man and I can't argue with him. 'Okay,' she went on, topping up my cup with about a half-pint of Janneau XO (it was going to be dirty pool on both sides, then), 'but you did all that stage-magic stuff when we were in college, didn't you? You were *wonderful* back then. I bet you could still do it. I bet you wouldn't even have to practise. And it's two hundred quid for a day's work, so you could pay me a bit off last month's chunk of what you owe me . . .'

It took a lot more persuasion, and a fair bit more brandy – so much brandy, in fact, that I made a pass at her on my unsteady way out of the door. She slapped off my right hand, steered my left onto the door handle and kissed me goodnight on the cheek without breaking stride.

I was profoundly grateful for that, when I woke up in the morning with my tongue stuck to my soft palette and my head full of unusable fuzz. Sexy, sweet, uninhibited nineteen-year-old Pen, with her autumn bonfire of hair, her pistachio eyes and her probably illegal smile, would have been one thing: thirty-something Earth Mother Pen in her Sibyl's cave, tended by rats and ravens and Christ only knew what other familiar spirits, and still waiting for her prince to come even though she knew exactly where he was and what he'd turned into . . . There was too much blood under the bridge, now. Leave it at that.

Then I remembered that I'd agreed to do the party, just before I made the pass, and I cursed like a longshoreman. Game, set and match to Pen and Monsieur Janneau. I hadn't even known we were playing doubles.

*

So there was a reason, anyway, even if it wasn't good or sufficient, why I now found myself facing down these arrogant little shits and prostituting my God-given talents for the paltry sum of two hundred quid. There was a reason why I'd put myself in the way of temptation. And there was a reason why I fell.

'Now,' I said, with a smile as wide as a Hallowe'en pumpkin, 'for my last and most ambitious trick before you all go off and feed your faces – I need another volunteer from the audience.' I pointed at Sebastian. 'You, sir, in the second row. Would you be so good?' Sebastian looked hangdog, intensely reluctant: stepping into the spotlight meant certain humiliation and possibly much worse. But the older boys were whistling and catcalling, and Peter was telling him to get the hell up there and do it. So he stood up and worked his way along the row, tripping a couple of times over the out-stretched feet that were planted in his path.

This was going to be cruel, but not to stepbrother Sebastian: no, my un-birthday gift to him was a loaded gun, which he could use in any way he wanted to. And for Peter ... well, sometimes cruelty is kindness in disguise. Sometimes pain is the best teacher. Sometimes it does you no harm to realise that there's a limit to what you can get away with.

Sebastian had made his way around to my side of the trestle table now, and he was standing awkwardly next to me. I picked up the Autographic and slipped the hooks on either side, wheeling the bellows out fully into its working position. With its red leather and dark wood it looked like a pretty impressive piece of kit: when I gave it to Sebastian to hold, he took it gingerly.

'Please examine the camera,' I told him. 'Make sure it's okay. Fully functional, fully intact.' He glanced at it cursorily, without enthusiasm, nodded and tried to hand it back to me.

I didn't take it. 'Sorry,' I said, 'you're my cameraman now. You have to do the job properly because I'm relying on you.'

He looked again, and this time he noticed what was staring him in the face.

'Well – there's black tape,' he said. 'Over the lens.'

I affected to be surprised, and took a look for myself. 'Gentle-men,' I said to the room at large. 'Ladies.' A five-second pause for howls of mocking laughter, nudges and pointing fingers. 'My assis-tant has just brought something very alarming to my attention. This camera has black masking tape over the lens, and it can't therefore take photographs –' I let the pause lengthen '– in the normal way. We're going to have to try to take a *spirit* photo.'

Peter and Peter's friends looked pained and scornful at this sug-gestion: it sounded to them like a pretty lame finale.

'Spirit photographs are among the most difficult feats for the magician to encompass,' I told them gravely, paying no attention to the sounds of derision. 'Think of an escapologist freeing him-self from a mailbag suspended upside down from a hook in a cage which has been dumped out of a jet plane flying about two miles up. Well, this trick is a little like that. Less visually spectacular, but just as flamboyantly pointless.'

I gestured to the birthday boy. 'We're going to take your pic-ture, Peter,' I told him. 'So why don't you go and stand over there, by the wall. A plain background works best for this.'

Peter obeyed with a great show of heavy resignation.

'You have another brother?' I asked Sebastian, quietly.

He glanced up at me, startled. 'No,' he said.

'Or a cousin or something – someone your own age, who used to live here with you?'

He shook his head.

'You know how to use a camera?'

Sebastian was on firmer ground here, and he looked relieved. 'Yeah. I've got one upstairs. But it's just point and shoot, it doesn't have any . . . focus thing, or . . . '

I dismissed these objections with a shake of the head, giving him a reassuring half-smile. 'Doesn't matter,' I said. 'This one focuses manually, but we're not going to bother with that anyway. Because we're not using either the lens or ordinary light to form the image. But the thing you're going to be clicking is this.' I gave him the air bulb – sitting at the end of a coil of rubber tubing, it was the only part of the camera that I'd had to replace. 'You squeeze it hard and it opens the shutter. When I say, okay?'

I hadn't loaded the Autographic for more than a decade, but all the stuff I needed was right there in the box and my hands knew what to do. I lined up a new plate, peeled away one corner of the waxed cover sheet, then slammed it into place and tore the cover free in one smooth movement. It wasn't what a professional would have done: partly because there was bound to be some seepage of light if you loaded the camera like that in an ordinarily lit room – but mostly because I was loading print paper rather than negative film. We were cutting out one stage of the normal photographic process. Again, it didn't matter, but I noticed as I was tightening the screws up again that James and Barbara Dodson had wandered in and were standing at the back of the room. That was going to mean a louder eruption, but by this stage I didn't really give a monkey's chuff: Peter had gotten quite seriously under my skin.

I got Sebastian into position, steering him with my hand on his shoulders. Peter was getting bored and restive, but we were almost done. I could have ratcheted up the tension a bit more, but since the outcome was still in doubt I thought I might as well just suck it and see. Either it would work or it wouldn't. 'Okay, on my mark. Peter – smile. Nice try, but no. Kids in the front row, show Peter what a smile is. Sebastian – three, two, one, now!'

Sebastian pressed the bulb, and the shutter made a slow, arthritic *whuck-chunk* sound. Good. I'd been half-afraid that nothing would happen at all.

'Now, we don't have any fixative,' I announced, as my memory started to kick in again, piecemeal. 'So the image won't last for long. But we can make it clearer with a stop bath. Lemon juice will do, or vinegar, if you—?' I looked hopefully at the two grown-ups, and Barbara slipped out of the room again.

'What about developing fluid?' James asked, looking at me with vague but definite mistrust.

I shook my head. 'We're not using light,' I said again. 'We're photographing the spirit world, not the visible one, so the film doesn't have to develop: it has to translate.'

James's face showed very clearly what he thought of this explanation. There was an awkward silence, broken by Barbara as she came back in with a bottle of white-wine vinegar, a plastic bowl and an apologetic smile. 'This is going to stink,' she warned me as she retreated again to the back of the room.

She was right. The sweet-sour tang of the vinegar hit and held as I poured out about two-thirds of the bottle, which covered the bowl to half an inch or so deep. Then, with Sebastian still standing next to me, I slipped the plate out of the camera, very deliberately blocking with my body the audience's line of sight. 'Sebastian,' I said, 'you're still the cameraman here. That means you're the medium through which the spirits are working. Please, dip the print paper in the vinegar and slosh it around so that it's completely soaked. An image should form on the paper as you do this. Do you see an image, Sebastian?'

Peter hadn't even bothered to move from his place over by the wall: in fact, he was leaning against it now, looking more sullen and bored than ever. Sebastian stared first in consternation and then in amazement at the paper as he sluiced it round and round in the bowl.

'Do you see an image?' I repeated, knowing damn well that he did.

'Yeah!' he blurted. Everyone in the room was picking up on his tension and astonishment now: I didn't need to go for any verbal build-up.

'And what *is* that image?'

'A boy. It's – I think it's—!'

'Of course you can see a boy,' I interrupted. 'We just took a photo of your brother, Peter. Is that who you can see, Sebastian?'

He shook his head, his wide eyes still staring down at the muddy photograph. 'No. Well, I mean, yeah but – there's somebody else, too. It's—'

I cut across him again. Everything in its place. 'Somebody you recognise?'

Sebastian nodded emphatically. 'Yeah.'

I like to see what I was doing here as siding with the underdog: but if there had been no element of sadism in it, I wouldn't have been looking at Peter as I said the next few words. 'And does he have a name, this other boy? What dark wonders from the spirit world have we captured and pinned to the wall, Sebastian? Tell us his name.'

Sebastian swallowed hard. It was genuine nerves rather than showmanship, but the strained pause was better than anything I could have choreographed myself.

'Davey Simmons,' Sebastian said, his voice a little too high.

The effect on Peter was electrifying. He yelled in what sounded like honest, naked terror, coming away from the wall with a jerk and then lurching across to the bowl in three staccato strides. But I was too quick for him. 'Thank you, Sebastian,' I said, whipping the print out of the bowl and waving it in the air as though to dry it – and as though keeping it out of Peter's reach was only accidental.

It had come out pretty well. In black and white, of course, and darkened around the edges where the light had got in at the paper, but nice and clear where it needed to be. It showed Peter as a sort of grainy blur, only recognisable by his posture and by the darker splodge of his hair. By contrast, the figure that stood at his elbow was very distinct indeed: sad, washed out, beaten down by time and loneliness and the fact of his own death, but not to be mistaken for marsh gas, cardboard cut-out or misapplied imagination.

'Davey Simmons,' I mused. 'Did you know him well, Peter?'

'I never fucking heard of him!' Peter yelled, throwing himself at me with desperate fury. 'Give me that!' I'm not hefty by any means, but for all his solidity Peter was just a kid: holding him off while I showed the print to his friends wasn't hard at all. They were all staring at it with expressions that ran the gamut from sick horror to bowel-loosening panic.

'And yet,' I mused, 'he stands beside you as you eat, and work, and sleep. In his death he watches you living, night into day into night. Why do you suppose that is?'

'I don't know,' Peter squealed, 'I don't know! Give it to me!'

Most of the audience were on their feet now, some surging forward to look at the print but most pulling back as if they wanted to get some distance from it. James Dodson waded through them like a battleship through shrimp boats, and it was he who took the print out of my hands. Peter immediately turned his attentions to his father, and tried again to snatch the photo, but James pushed him back roughly. He stared down at the print in perplexity, shaking his head slowly from side to side. Then, with his face flushing deep red, he tore it up, very deliberately, into two pieces, then four, then eight. Peter gave a whimper, caught somewhere between misery and the illusion of relief: but from where I was standing it looked like he'd be living with this for a while to come.

Dodson was working on thirty-two pieces when I turned to Sebastian and solemnly shook his hand.

'You've got a gift,' I said. He met my gaze, and understanding passed between us. What he had was a lever. Peter wasn't going to be as free in future with his elbows, or his fists, or his feet: not now that everyone had seen his guilt, and his weakness. There wasn't any extra charge for this: I work on a fixed rate.

I'd noticed the miserable little ghost hovering around Peter as soon as he'd come into the room. They're harder to spot in daylight, but I've got a lot of experience on top of a lot of natural sensitivity, and I know what to expect in a house where they don't keep their rowan sprigs up to date. I didn't know what the connection was, but unless Davey Simmons had no family at all there had to be a damn good reason why he was haunting this house rather than his own. He couldn't get away from Peter: his soul was tangled up in him like a bird in a briar patch. You could read that in any number of ways, but Peter's violent reaction had ruled out some of them, changed the odds on others.

Anyway, things got a bit confused after that. Dodson was yelling at me to pack up my things and get out, and spitting and spluttering about a lawsuit to follow. Peter had fled from the room, pursued by Barbara, and barricaded himself in somewhere upstairs to judge by the bangs and yells that I could hear. The party guests milled around like a decapitated squid: lots of appendages, no brain, faintly suspect smell. And Sebastian stood watching me with big, solemn eyes, and never said another word as long as I was there.

When I asked Dodson for the money he owed me for the performance, he punched me in the mouth. I took that in my stride: no teeth loosened, only a symbolic amount of bloodshed. I probably had that coming. He went for the camera next, though, and I went for it too: me and that Brownie went back a long way, and I didn't want to have to go looking for another machine with such sympathetic vibes. We tussled inconclusively for a few moments for control of it, then he seemed to remember where he was: in his own living room, watched by a gaggle of his son's best friends, whose fathers he also no doubt knew well in work or club circles.

'Get out,' he told me, his eyes still wild. 'Get out of my house, you irresponsible bastard, before I throw you out on your ear.'

I gave up on the money. It wouldn't be easy for me to argue that traumatising the birthday boy was within my remit. I packed everything up laboriously into the four cases, under James's glaring eyes and stertorous breathing. He was suffering a kind of anaphylactic reaction to me now, and if I didn't get out soon he might crash and burn as his immune system tore itself apart in its desire to remove the irritation.

Out into the hall, and I caught sight of Barbara on the upstairs landing. Her face was pale and tense, but I swear she threw me a nod. With four suitcases worth of heavy freight I was in no position to wave back – and it might have been tactless in any case.

It was about half past six by this time, with the November dark already settled in. Pen would be waiting for me back in her basement, eager for hard news and harder currency. Under the circumstances, I couldn't really give her either.

The moon was three days from the dark: like most people these days, I kept my eye on the almanac when I was planning to be out after nightfall. The dead didn't follow the phases of the moon, of course, but there were lots of nastier things that did – and the dead I can deal with in any case.

So I drove around to Craven Park Road. It was somewhere to go, and I have to stop by the office once every couple of months if only to throw out the mail: otherwise the slowly accumulating weight of unpaid bills would threaten the structural integrity of the building.

Harlesden isn't the best place in the world to put up your shingle. You have to park your car out on the main road if you want to have an even chance of it being there when you get back to it. The Yardie boys tout coke out on the street and stare you down hard if you accidentally make eye contact. And the beggars who sit exhausted in the doorways, their hollow-eyed stares spearing you like the Ancient Mariner's as you walk by, are mostly the risen-again. Not ghosts, I mean, but those who've come back in the body: zombies, for want of a less melodramatic word. They're a sad bunch, on the whole, but that doesn't stop your flesh from crawling slightly as you walk by.

But tonight everything was pretty quiet: even the sign over my door was holding up pretty well. Sometimes the kids from the Stonehouse Estate come by with their airbrushes and turn the sign into something whimsical and baroque, obliterating in the process the simple, dignified face I present to the world. But tonight the words F. CASTOR ERADICATIONS stood out in all their austere clarity.

Grambas, the proprietor of the kebab house next door, was leaning in his doorway enjoying a roll-up cigarette whose heavy smoke hung around him like a shroud. He grinned at me as I unlocked the street door, and I shot him a wink. We've got an understanding: he's promised me that he won't lay ghosts or bind demons so long as I don't serve greasy fried food and over-matured salads.

My office is actually above the kebab house. Once inside the door, there's a narrow flight of awkwardly high stairs that leads up, with a sharp, right-angled bend, to my first-floor premises. Pen says the stairs are high because the conversion was a weird one, swapping between three storeys and four depending on which of the original residents sold out and which ones stayed. I reckon the builders were working on margin: twenty high steps are quicker to throw up than thirty normal-sized ones.

I scooped up a thick handful of mail and headed on up. Even if you're fit, you get to the top of those steps a little breathless. I'm not fit. I kicked open the office door, breathing like a dirty phone call, and flicked on the light.

It's not much of an office, even by Harlesden standards. Being over a kebab shop – while it has its advantages in terms of daily sustenance – tends to lend a greasy miasma to the walls, the furniture and the air you breathe. And Pen had never made good on her promise to get me some decent furniture (although her offer still stood if I ever got even on the rent), so all I had was a formica-topped self-assembly desk and two tubular steel chairs from IKEA. The filing cabinet was a two-drawer midget which also served as a table to hold the kettle and tea things. By way of decoration I had six framed illustrations from *Little Nemo in Slumberland* which I'd got from IKEA on the same expedition that brought me the chairs. They made clients feel relaxed and receptive. Also they weighed in at less than four quid each.

Yes. It was pathetic. But it was mine.

Or, at least, it had been.

I sat down in one of the chairs, put my feet up on the filing cabinet and started to flick through the post. For each piece of real mail there were two curry-house fliers and a great investment opportunity, which made progress fairly fast: not many envelopes actually needed to be opened before making the fall of shame into the already overflowing wastepaper basket. An electricity bill, black, and a phone bill, red ... These colours change with the seasons and are a gentle reminder of time's passing.

I stopped short. The next envelope in the stack was pale grey, and bore a return address that I recognised. The Charles Stanger Care Facility, Muswell Hill. My name was written on the front of the envelope in a pained, cramped hand in which curved lines were approximated by collections of short, angular jags. It was fractal handwriting: looking at it, you imagined that under a microscope every stroke of the pen would open up into a thousand angled flecks of tortured ink.

Rafi. Nobody else wrote like that. Nobody sane *could* write like that.

I opened the envelope carefully, peeling back the gummed flap rather than just tearing off one end and running my finger along. Rafi had caught me with a razor blade once, taped into the corner of the envelope: I'd almost lost the top joint of my thumb. This time, though, there was nothing except a single sheet of paper, torn from a notepad. On it, in very different handwriting from that which had addressed the envelope (but still Rafi's hand – he had several), there was a message that, if nothing else, was admirable in its brevity.

> YOURE GOING TO MAKE A MISTAKE YOU
> NEED TO TALK TO ME BEFORE YOU MAKE
> A MISTAKE YOU NEED TO TALK TO ME NOW

I was still staring at the letter, unsure whether to put it into my pocket or to let it fall into the basket, when the phone rang. Picking it up was a reflex action: if I'd thought about it I would have let it lie, because it was bound to get me into a conversation that I didn't want or need.

'Mister Castor?'

It was a male voice: dry and harsh, with an overtone of stern disapproval. It conjured up an image of a preacher with a bible in his hand and his finger pointing at your heart.

'Yes?'

'The exorcist?'

I considered lying, but since I'd confessed to my name there wasn't any point. Anyway, it was entirely my own fault. Nobody had made me pick up the frigging phone: I'd done it of my own free will, as a consenting adult.

And now I had a customer.